ONE
OF
THOSE
FACES

ONE OF

A NOVEL

OF

THOSE

FACES

ELLE GRAWL

THOMAS & MERCER

Published by Thomas & Mercer, Seattle

www.apub.com

Amazon, the Amazon logo, and Thomas & Mercer are trademarks of Amazon.com, Inc., or its affiliates.

ISBN-13: 9781662500862
ISBN-10: 1662500866

Cover design by Olga Grlic

Printed in the United States of America

For my husband, the love of my life

SUMMER

CHAPTER ONE

Her face is just like mine. But cold and gray. Unmoving.

I remember holding myself back from reaching in and shaking her. As if she would wake up. But she wasn't asleep. She didn't look real, her skin like polished alabaster.

The open casket was a terrible idea. Everyone realized it too late. They all wanted to see their favorite one more time, no matter the cost.

It's that same face staring back at me in my nightmares. She ages with me. Now, I see a twenty-five-year-old version of myself lying in that coffin, and I stare down into the gray, bloated face that mirrors my own.

I lean in closer in every dream and bend down as if she would whisper something.

Her eyes rip open, broken seams dangling between her eyelashes, and a hand made of ice around my throat.

———

I opened my eyes in the darkness. My throat and arms were stiff, cold logs anchoring me to the bed. My comforter was below my waist and tangled around my legs, the light from the TV flashing onto the blades of the ceiling fan as it spun above at full speed.

I craned my neck to the right side toward the window. Woodstock sat purring on the sill, licking his bright-orange fur.

I picked my phone up from the nightstand and nearly dropped it. It felt like trying to pull a bowling ball onto the bed with my hand, still tingling back to life.

5:20 p.m.

I hoisted myself up with a groan, the evening news song chiming behind me as I stretched my hands overhead.

"We have an update today about a murder that has set the Logan Square community on edge. Police have now identified the victim as mother and—"

I grabbed the remote control and switched the TV off before the anchor could finish her sentence.

Crime. That was the news. Always.

I pulled my hair up from my shoulders and wrapped it with the elastic band from my wrist before ambling into the bathroom and turning on the light. I kept my eyes down, focused only on the counter in front of me, but caught a glimpse in the mirror as I reached for the medicine cabinet.

I jolted at the eerie countenance staring back at me. I was almost as gray and pale as the specter in my dream. Before I could look away, I'd already caught sight of the scar along my neck down to my collarbone. It was red and angry from hours of my tossing and turning. I arranged my hair over my ear and in front of my neck, covering the scar.

I dug my fingers into the side of the counter, averting my eyes again from the mirror.

Breathe.

Some days it was harder than others to wake up. To remember.

By the time I left the bathroom, Woodstock had relocated to my drafting table and was licking his front paws. I walked over and tugged at the drawing underneath him until he jumped down. My self-imposed isolation of the past few days hadn't been nearly as productive as

I'd hoped. I was still far behind on my latest illustration job. I brushed away the cat fur from the pen-and-ink drawing of a mouse in trousers and a billowing white shirt. His eyes were too far apart and his fur essentially artless scribbles, clearly the product of working at three o'clock in the morning after staying awake for thirty-six hours straight. I sighed and crumpled the paper and dropped it to the floor, barely missing the garbage can.

I couldn't handle any more time here alone with myself. Or with Issi.

"Sarah? Hi!"

I looked up from the picture book in my hands at the frazzled woman clasping the wrists of two small boys desperately trying to wriggle free. "Sorry," I muttered. "I'm not Sarah."

The woman released the boys and appraised me, her gaze lingering on my bulky black sweater before drifting back to my face. Wearing winter clothes in the middle of summer tended to attract attention. Curiosity. "We met last week," she insisted. "At the museum? You had your daughter with you. Kimmy introduced us."

I let her finish. Partially because I was too tired to stop her but mostly because this was already the longest conversation I'd had this week since ordering a late-night hot dog three days ago. "Yeah, I'm sorry, that wasn't me."

She blinked several times, the fringe from her A-line bob beginning to edge toward her uneven eyebrows. "I'm sorry. I could've sworn it was you." She turned and walked toward her kids, who were now playing with the model train track between the aisles of bookshelves.

I opened the picture book again and browsed the watercolors of a mouse and fox on a spunky adventure. Perusing the children's book section was always my last and most desperate attempt to draw inspiration for projects. It had been a while since I'd been commissioned to do any watercolor illustrations of nonhuman subjects. I glanced up and noticed the woman staring at me over her kids' ginger heads.

I closed the book and replaced it on the shelf before sliding out of the children's section. This wasn't the only time I'd been mistaken for someone else, but this was perhaps the first time someone had been so insistent.

I popped into the bookstore coffee shop. I was hot under my sweater, but I ordered a regular coffee before settling at a table near the counter.

As I took the initial sips of my black, steaming coffee, I scanned the rest of the shop. The bored mother in the seat in front of me scrolled Instagram on her phone while her daughter furiously scribbled on a coloring book page. The petite blonde barista all too cheerily whipped up a latte for the muscular college student across the counter. The muscular college student adjusted his baseball cap.

An elderly man sat across the café, sporting an enormous handlebar mustache and dressed in a bolo tie.

Perfect.

I set down my cup and pulled my sketchbook from my bag. I briskly scribbled the shape of his rough and square face and dotted the page where his features were. I wanted to make sure I got that mustache down before he left.

My pencil drew over the paper in a familiar movement, filling in the man's mustache with quick strokes. I looked up regularly to catch him in between bites of a muffin, after which his mustache wriggled like a wild woolly caterpillar. Someone crossed into my line of sight and took a seat in front of Mustache, but my view was still mostly unobstructed. A couple of times I looked up and accidentally locked eyes with the man sitting in front of my subject. I didn't focus too much on his face in those quick moments, but his eyes were alert and bright, his jawline carved and rigid.

But I had already begun a project. I couldn't shift focus to a new subject now. The next time I looked up, the man with the granite jawline was gone.

I added some shading under Mustache's eyes, right around the swollen, dark rings underlining them.

"I couldn't help but notice you staring."

The depth of the voice made me jump. I flipped over my sketch pad, which was already barricaded from view by my bag, before looking up at the man standing on the other side of my table. It was the jawline who had been partially blocking my view of Mustache. The edges of his lips were slightly curved into a curious smile.

"What?"

A flash of nervousness flickered across his face for the briefest moment before that crooked smile reappeared. "I was just saying, I noticed you staring from across the café."

"Oh, um, I was just sketching someone else," I said in a lowered voice, worried that Mustache might overhear. "You were sitting right in front of him."

Jawline's smile remained, but his cheeks became tinged with red. He laughed. "Really?"

My hands began to shake a little as I turned the sketch faceup. "Yeah, he has a really killer mustache," I said. I gestured with my head toward Mustache at the other end of the shop.

Jawline shifted slightly to look over my shoulder at the drawing and looked up toward Mustache. "You really captured his essence." He scratched behind his ear and took a step backward. "Sorry, I assum—"

"Thanks, it's not easy to spot facial hair like that in the wild," I remarked. It wasn't unusual to have strangers walk up to me while I was drawing. Sketching in public tended to raise questions.

Jawline pulled out the chair across from me and sat. "Do you do this a lot?" He gestured toward the drawing.

"Yes, occupational hazard."

His eyes got a little bigger. "So you're an artist, not just a random voyeur?"

I grinned. "They're one and the same, right?"

"You may have a point."

To fill the pause that came next, I asked, "What do you do?" and took a sip of my coffee. My tongue burned from the hot steam, but I needed to keep my hands and mouth busy.

"I study and *kind of* teach psychology." He leaned back in his chair slightly.

Of course. I flinched. "You look a little young to be a professor."

His lips curled. "I never claimed to be a professor. I'm getting my master's in psychology, and I have to teach a couple of classes in the meantime."

So maybe he wasn't too far gone yet. I shuffled my sketchbook and pencils around nervously.

He met my gaze. "I have to get back to campus now, but I'd love to buy you a cup of coffee sometime. Maybe see some of your work?"

I didn't make a habit of giving my number or name out to just anyone, no matter how good they looked. "I come here a lot, so maybe I'll see you around."

His eyes drifted to my name written in the barista's hasty and slanted cursive on my coffee cup, the *r*'s in *Harper* looking more similar to the swirl of an *s*. Well, so much for privacy. "Maybe next time *I'll* have a mustache worth drawing."

I laughed at that. "We'll see, I guess."

I watched as he took his coffee cup and left, grinning at me over his shoulder as he pushed through the door onto Milwaukee Avenue.

"Shit!" I glanced at the time on my phone. Yep, I already had two texts from Erin asking me where I was. Technically I wasn't even late yet, but Erin's overbearing tendencies as a friend poured over into her role as boss.

I hiked the strap of my messenger bag over one shoulder and took the steps out the door to the street two at a time. I was willing to bet even if I made it to the studio right at six o'clock, Erin would still say I was late.

I turned the corner at the end of the block, nearly bumping into a man with a goatee and beanie in my hurry to the studio door.

"You're late. I knew it," Erin called over her shoulder as she placed wine bottles on the table in the center of the room.

By one minute. I walked past her on the way to the back, then tossed my bag in the corner of the room and pulled my painting apron from a hook.

"Is everything okay? You don't look so good." Erin shook a mason jar of paintbrushes at me. "And your apron's inside out, by the way."

I instinctively raised a hand to the dark circles under my eyes. "Oh." I tugged my apron over my head and flipped it so the Tipsy Paintbrush logo—a cutesy image of a paintbrush dipped into a glass of red wine—was facing out. "Yeah, I'm fine. Just tired." I set empty wineglasses along the counter at the front of the shop. Soon they would be full and in the hands of novice artists who were almost always more interested in the wine than the actual painting class.

Erin resumed setting up the painting supplies around the room. "Coffee can only do so much, you know. Sleep is what you need."

"I know." It had been almost a week since I'd slept more than two hours per night. The fear of nightmares usually kept me up until morning. "I'll be able to sleep better once I finish the illustrations for that book."

"You're still working on that?" Erin lifted some folded easels and handed one to me.

It had only been a couple of months. Sometimes that type of work could take six months or more with the back-and-forth changes between author and artist. "Yes," I muttered. Of course she didn't know that. Why bother explaining?

"I never see you," she whined, leaning across the counter toward me.

"I saw you on Saturday."

"Yeah, but you were teaching here, and then you went straight home after." She rolled her eyes. "When was the last time you went out . . . in public?"

"I actually went to the bookstore today. And I even spoke to a person," I said with a bite of sarcasm.

"The barista?" She snorted. "That doesn't count."

To me, it did. I remembered Jawline. "Not just the barista. Some guy came up to me." I looked up as I unfolded the legs of the easel.

Erin's mouth was open and her eyes at full attention. "And? Was he cute? What did he say?"

I shrugged. "He was kind of . . ." Annoying? No. He was just . . . unexpected?

"What's his name?"

"I didn't ask, because I'm not interested."

Erin's face dropped. "Why not?"

"Eh," I sighed.

She leaned forward again. "Come on, why *not*?"

You shouldn't have said anything. You know how she is.

"I don't know," I groaned. *Yes, you do.* "I mean, it's weird. Who goes up to a stranger like that?"

She frowned and pushed away from the counter. "He's outgoing. That's how you meet people!" She grabbed a paintbrush and set it by one of the ten easels around the room. "It's either that or Tinder."

I ignored her and unwrapped my paintbrushes, slowly removing each one from the canvas cloth.

She watched me through narrowed eyes. "What's the real reason? Did he have a full-face tattoo or something?"

"Let it go," I said, twisting the hairband on my wrist between my fingers until it snapped in half. To Erin, friendship was like a game of tug-of-war. Once she latched on to something, she just couldn't leave it alone. She relished the moments when she could pry away more information about my past, boys, or random details about my day.

She turned her back to unlock the front glass door. "Well, I think—"

The desk phone rang. I was halfway across the room, but I bounded for it, grateful for the distraction. I picked up on the second ring. "Tipsy

Paintbrush," I panted. My voice didn't hit quite the chipper high pitch that Erin reached effortlessly when she answered or greeted customers.

"Hi," a man's voice said on the line. "I, uh, registered for the class tonight, but I won't be able to make it. Can I get a refund?"

His voice was calm and deep. Mellow and smooth.

"We don't give refunds," I said.

Erin flapped her hands wildly and mouthed something as she approached.

I didn't bother trying to read her lips.

"Oh, okay. Is there a way to reschedule then?" the man asked.

I fumbled for the clipboard with the registration information. "What's your name?"

"Iann."

I scanned the page. Iann Park. Spelled it with two *n*'s. That was a first. "Okay, I see you on the list," I said, cradling the phone on my shoulder and marking a line through his name. "I can sign you up for a different class this week if that's what you want."

He hesitated. "Okay. What about Friday?"

I turned away from Erin. "I wouldn't sign up for that one if I were you," I said in a hushed voice. "It's a garden gnome painting."

There was a long pause. "Did you say garden gnome?"

I smiled. I had told her that was a stupid theme, but she claimed she was aiming for a "new demographic," whatever that meant. "Yep. I would suggest coming to tomorrow night's class if you can. It's paint-your-pet night."

"Okay, I'll come in tomorrow night then. And 'paint your pet' means you put paint on your pet, or do I need to bring a picture or something?"

I stifled a laugh. "No, leave your pet at home, but bring a picture."

"Yeah." He exhaled softly. "That was a bad joke. I'll be there tomorrow. Thanks."

I lingered on the line for a moment before hanging up.

Erin grabbed two bottles of wine from the counter as the first group of women drifted in. "You could've been a little more polite," she said.

I bit my lower lip, trying to refrain from rolling my eyes.

"You're going to finish cleaning those glasses on the counter, right?"

I picked up the dish towel and lightly ran it over one of the glasses as Erin greeted the women.

She fancied herself a real entrepreneur because she'd gotten me the job and was working on getting her business degree. The reality was that she'd flunked her first quarter of general studies so badly that her parents insisted she take a few months off to "find her why."

Erin's dad had lucked into the trend of painting classes with complimentary wine at the right time and had opened the Tipsy Paintbrush in a storefront in Wicker Park. He'd interviewed me just to save my pride, or at least that's what I'd assumed. I had felt his reticence at the end of the interview. My portfolio was considerable from having random art jobs on and off for several years by that time, and I'd somehow managed to make money through selling my work online, but my attitude didn't inspire much confidence. I imagined he'd only relented because, first, it paid minimum wage, and second, he didn't want Erin's motivation in business to take any hits, no matter how minor. She'd probably begged that he give her dropout, slacker friend some kind of a job to report to so I didn't fall off the face of the earth. And with the purpose of holding it over my head.

I watched the last couple of stragglers filter into the shop. "Hello," I greeted everyone once they were in their positions. I turned back to my own canvas at the front of the room and lined up my paintbrushes on my palette for what must've been the fifth time. Each time I blinked, my eyelids grew heavier. I could never quench that sweet ache of closing them and completely losing myself in sleep, a dreamless sleep without Issi. Without her icy grip on my throat.

CHAPTER TWO

If we were all being honest, I probably wasn't charismatic enough to teach any level of art class. But I had some artistic ability, and the students had wine. That's what had gotten me through this position over the past couple of years.

Once the wine and brushes began flowing, my thoughts kept drifting to the guy from the café. As much as I had been annoyed at the interruption, chills rose along my skin as I remembered his eyes. I remembered the flickers of hesitation when he spoke. Those moments of uncertainty made him the most appealing.

The words "check him out" made it to my ears among the other chatter in the room.

The gaggle of girls closest to me were not moving their paintbrushes at all but instead were surveying the guys in the room. I had often heard students say that our studio was the only one that had guys. Well, *unattached* guys. It was all women everywhere else. This was why Erin sat in the corner of every class the entire time, trying to look busy doing the bookkeeping. She called it "shopping."

I glanced over to her now, and she was staring at the same guy the girls in front of me had fixated on.

He was tall and bronze with platinum-blond hair, happily painting and laughing with his group of friends. The other guys he was with were also really good looking, but he appeared to be the only uncoupled one.

Erin's eyes had been trained on him for some time although she was absently flipping through the binder on the counter. She shot up from her perch when she noticed his wineglass was half-empty. "Excuse me, can I get you some more wine?" she asked, appearing by his side.

The man raised his eyebrows when he saw Erin. She was exactly the girl you would picture with a guy like him, beautiful and trendy. And she was fun enough that you could almost forgive her volatility.

She pointed at his painting, leaning in as she gestured to the canvas, commenting. He smirked and angled his body toward her.

When class ended, everyone started packing up their creations, and Erin nodded to me from the back as she pulled a bottle of leftover wine from the counter and slipped behind the employees-only door. I waited until the last woman said thank you a little too loudly while tumbling over the threshold, and then I rushed over and locked it and turned off the front light. I watched the last car roll out of our tiny parking lot and walked to the back.

Erin already had the wine bottle uncorked and was well into her first glass. It had become our routine after a class to snag one of the leftover bottles and finish it up. Since it had already been budgeted for the class, her father wouldn't notice it was missing. Although I suspected that even if he did, he wouldn't have cared.

"I'm not sure I feel up to drinking tonight." Since I taught four days a week, that ended up being four nights I staggered home buzzing on cheap red wine.

Erin tapped the table across from her. "Come on, let's at least finish the bottle. That guy asked for my number, by the way," she said. They always did.

I complied and sat across from her at the tall break-room table. In the back of the studio was a small kitchen and then a bunch of shelves with wine and painting supplies. Mostly wine.

Erin pushed the bottle and a clean glass toward me. "I'll clean up the front tonight. Are you walking home after this?"

"Yeah." After pouring a little less than half a glass, I tried to put the bottle back down.

"Nice try," she slurred, tipping the bottom of the bottle while it was still in my hands. "I can't finish this on my own." She didn't let go until the wine almost spilled over the brim of my glass. "You should be careful. Did you see the story about that girl that got murdered a couple of weeks ago?" she asked.

The first mouthful of wine coated my tongue and throat with a bitter, chalky aftertaste. "Kind of. I heard the news mention it. In Logan Square, right?"

Erin poured the rest of the bottle into her glass. "Yeah. They still haven't caught the person who killed her."

This didn't alarm me much. It was Chicago, after all. "I'm not too worried about it. I mean, my place is just fifteen minutes from here."

"It doesn't take long to get murdered."

I choked on my next sip of wine. "Maybe I'll take an Uber, then."

Erin smiled darkly. "What if the murderer is an Uber driver?"

"What are you talking about?"

She laughed. "I have no idea." Her lips were growing darker from the stain of wine. "Full disclosure, I pregamed with a few glasses while you were teaching."

I rolled my eyes.

"I heard she was strangled." As a true-crime aficionado, Erin lived in the gory details. "It sounds like it was really brutal."

Of all the horrible ways to die, I had always imagined suffocating or drowning to be the worst. Maybe it was because I always remembered Issi's swollen neck and her face contorted in pain. I saw her eyes as I blinked, cold and gazing at me in quiet terror. "I really need to head out. I'm exhausted." I stood up so quickly that the chair almost fell behind me.

Erin sighed. "Okay. Well, I drank too much, so I'm going to have to clean up in the morning." She shrugged and rose to her feet. "Do you need a ride?" She laughed as she patted her pockets for her keys.

My cheeks burned, and my head started to rush a little. "How much did you drink? I'm not getting in a car with you. Come on, let's walk together." She lived only a few blocks south of my place.

Erin nodded and tossed the wine bottles into the recycling bin with a crash as I grabbed my bag and swung it over my shoulder.

We stepped out into the alley, and I reached in past the door to turn off the lights. Erin fumbled with the keys to lock up. I looked into the darkness behind the building. It was quiet overall, but I could hear the sounds of crowds laughing and a jumble of drums and horns in the background. There was usually some kind of street performance going on. The sound of dogs barking nearby cut through the music.

My body tensed as something moved in the dark near the entrance to the street.

"Okay," Erin exclaimed. "All locked up—let's go!" She seemed to be getting tipsier by the minute. "Do you want to stop by the Bearded Monk on the way home?"

"No, I just want to get into bed and pass out," I said, turning back toward the street as we started walking.

"It's only ten o'clock!"

Something dark shuffled again by the street. It fluttered on the ground by the dumpster. "Did you see that?" I pointed to the end of the alley as we continued toward it.

Erin's eyes got big. "The murderer . . . ," she said in a low, mocking voice.

I pushed past her to the street, the dark fluttering continuing on the sidewalk. I bent over and squinted. It was a red scarf with one end pinned under the dumpster, the rest of it blowing violently in the wind. "No murderer," I called back at Erin. "Let's go."

She scurried over to me, and we stepped out of the dark alley and joined the lively throngs congregating on Damen Avenue. Once we were in front of the buildings, I could hear the saxophone and drummer playing Beatles covers on the corner.

"I love these guys!" Erin exclaimed and ran ahead of me in the crosswalk, shaking her hands above her head and cheering, startling the saxophone player. He glanced over his shoulder and raised his eyebrows, his lips curling into a smile over the reed.

"Wow." I grabbed her shoulders and steered her away down the sidewalk. "That wine really went to your head. Maybe we should get you some food?"

She laughed. "No, I know them! I'm fine."

The jazz followed us, the breeze drifting the notes through the humidity. The cool air wove through my knit sweater, bringing me some relief in my thick garb.

"So, what else happened with that guy tonight?" I asked once we were safely past the group tapping their feet on the corner and tossing dollars into the sax case.

Erin smirked. "We're going out tomorrow after the last class."

"He's taking another class?" I asked, dodging a passing couple on the sidewalk.

"No, he's swinging by afterward."

"He's exactly your type."

She nodded. "I know. His name's Jeremy." She looked at me and raised her eyebrows meaningfully. "He has a motorcycle."

I remembered the call from Iann earlier and his calming voice. "Have you wondered why so many guys come to the studio?"

"You mean so many *hot* guys?" she emphasized. "I don't know. Wicker Park's known for art stuff. I guess there are more painter guys in this area? Or . . ." She glanced at me sidelong. "Maybe it's because our studio has a gorgeous, mysterious teacher."

"You mean Hannah?" I asked. Hannah was one of the alternate teachers who came in on the nights I didn't or when I was sick. She was a retired art professor pushing eighty and somehow an even less enthusiastic teacher than I was. She'd mastered a disinterested scowl to a degree I could only aspire to.

Erin burst out laughing. "Yes," she said when she could breathe again. "Hannah's the stud magnet."

Erin's building loomed directly ahead of us, a group of dark figures smoking on the narrow stoop. "Okay, I'll see you tomorrow night unless you want to come up and help me choose a date outfit?"

She definitely didn't care about my opinion, so it would just turn into a self-indulgent fashion show and then possibly an intervention about my own style. "No, I'm going to head home. I'll see what you choose tomorrow at work."

"Okay, good night!" She hugged my shoulder and climbed the stoop. The guys smoking grew quiet and all looked up from their phones to watch her stagger inside the building.

I noticed for the first time how chilly it was as the wine started to wear off. I zipped up my jacket and continued down the sidewalk, past the smokers. Several streetlights were out along the way. I glanced across the street and realized that the whole opposite side was out. It grew quieter the farther I walked. Of course, I lived in a considerably worse part of the neighborhood than Erin. My apartment was one level of a rickety, unloved wooden two-story house, a relic of Wicker Park's darker period. My building was one of the last holdouts on a street full of restored Victorian homes.

Erin's dad helped out with her rent, so she lived in one of the newest sleek apartment buildings not far from the hub of bohemian bars and artisan cafés. Although she didn't need roommates, she wanted them. I couldn't imagine her spending days at a time in silence like I did. She had tried to get me to room with her initially, but I couldn't afford to ever leave my current place.

I had stayed in a downtown youth hostel when I first ran away from home. I had figured I could stay there indefinitely until I decided to look for a place where I could actually sleep rather than staying curled up the entire night, listening for drunk and drugged travelers seeking out a vulnerable kid like me. I had lost a lot of trust in humanity during that time and a lot of my scant savings.

I'd been lucky that Erin's lead on an affordable place hadn't been merely a ruse to mug me. Her friend Mo had been getting ready to move out and introduced me to his landlord, Bug. His real name was Todd, but his bright, bald head was always glistening like a beetle, even in winter, and his quick footsteps made a sound similar to a cockroach scuttling across the floor.

I passed the Gothic houses with windows all like terrified eyes, stretching high and wide, the gables tapering sharply as they scraped the trees above. Most of the windows were dark inside, but as I passed by, I could see a couple watching TV and a dog looking out, its mouth suddenly dropping open right before a loud bark.

I whipped my head to look across the street as a loud metallic crash erupted through the silence. I couldn't see anything in the darkness. I quickened my pace, my boots beginning to chafe the skin between my ankles and the fabric of my jeans. I saw my building, the only one without outside lighting and hidden behind a large dead tree.

I glanced over my shoulder toward the sound of continuous rustling but saw nothing. Then there was the sound. Like the distant wailing of the L but weaker and fading.

Screech.

I jogged down the street until I reached the stairs to my apartment. I bounded up the steps to the second floor and swung my bag onto the wooden landing. I always walked with my keys in hand, but in the rush to leave the studio, I had forgotten. As I unzipped the outside pocket of my messenger bag, I gazed into the dark alley once again. The scraping continued, now accompanied by the rasping of the wind.

Screech.

My hands trembled as I unlocked the door, then dropped the keys when I heard a faint rustle down the steps behind me. I tossed my bag and kicked the keys over the threshold as I scampered inside, catching a glimpse of a figure as the door slammed behind me.

CHAPTER THREE

I hadn't even realized I'd drifted to sleep on my desk until my eyes opened in the darkness.

My ears strained for the sound of a movement or a breath in the dark. Something that would reveal I wasn't alone. But it never came.

I fumbled for my phone, switched on the phone light, and flashed it around the room. No one.

Keeping the light on, I checked the screen.

3:00 a.m.

I groaned and glanced toward the front door, for the first time noticing something dark outlined on the floor right beside it.

I squinted but couldn't make it out. I sat up with a heavy sigh and flicked on the light. As I walked toward the door, the light-gray object took shape.

It was a rabbit's foot. I bent over, steadying myself with one hand on the door. It was one of those tacky key chains sold at gas stations. I hesitantly picked it up. It was soft, but the fur had stiffened quite a bit, as if a liquid had been spilled and then dried. I dropped it after a moment's speculation on what liquid it could be.

Woodstock suddenly appeared between my legs, inquisitively batting one feline paw at the foot.

Where did he get this? I had never owned a rabbit's foot charm.

As a tingle traced along my spine, I glanced around the entire room. The light reached only to the edge of the wall as it led to the bathroom and my closet.

Woodstock rubbed against my leg, and I locked eyes with him. This hadn't been the first time he'd brought something weird to my attention. The first time I'd let him in, he had dug up a dead rat from the moving boxes in my closet.

I swayed sleepily to the kitchen and grabbed a paper towel. As I walked to the front door, Woodstock sat and whipped the rabbit's foot around between his two front paws, playfully. "Thanks for the gift, buddy, but I'm not interested," I muttered, scooping it up with the napkin.

His yellow eyes narrowed at me. I glanced at the pile of his untouched toys in the corner of the room. Like all cat owners, I had gone through phases of saving up and buying really nice toys for Woodstock, and he'd never played with any of them.

I examined the foot. I could convince myself that the stickiness was Woodstock's drool, which wasn't ideal but better than whatever else it could be. I let it fall back to the floor, and he immediately accepted it into grateful paws before kicking it under the bed and disappearing.

I rubbed my eyes and crouched by the window, carefully lifting the shades up. The street was empty, the lone wail of a single siren trilling to the west. I stared at that dark alley. The only light nearby came from the floodlight of the detached garage on one side, but it was turned the opposite way, shooting directly into the street. I let the blinds fall back into place.

It was nothing. Surely if something had happened last night, I wouldn't have been the only one of my neighbors to hear it.

After approaching my drafting table nestled in the corner, I sank into the rolling chair. The latest project I was working on was for a children's book about a mouse and his family trying to escape the clutches of an evil cat. It wasn't a very original idea for a book, but it was a job.

I grabbed the remote control and directed it over my shoulder to turn on the TV. The familiar piano theme from *The Office* blared throughout the room. The late-night talk shows had wrapped up hours ago. It was the rerun phase of night. I had learned to measure time by the late-night television schedule. The infomercials would be on next.

I fanned out the drawings I had finished so far for the book. The evil cat, Harold, was modeled after Woodstock. A lazy choice, maybe, but he did look like the type of cat that a Bond villain might have. He had been a stray when I'd found him and even had a mysterious scar running above one eye, so it seemed fitting.

I chose the most incomplete painting from the middle and stacked the others back against the wall. If I couldn't sleep, I could at least get some work done. I pulled a broad, fat paintbrush from the mason jar with the others and wet it.

———

I awoke to constant electronic pinging and my hand dangling over the water jar. I blinked my eyes and realized I was facedown on my painting, staring at the illustrated cat. The paper was still wet. I jerked my head up and winced at the crick in my neck.

My phone pinged again two, three times in a row. I picked it up. *8:50 a.m.*

The texts from Erin kept coming in.

Erin (8:01 a.m.): Oh my god!

Erin (8:12 a.m.): Are you okay?

Erin (8:21 a.m.): Why aren't you answering?

Erin (8:23 a.m.): Call me ASAP!

Erin (8:25 a.m.): you're freaking me out.

Erin (8:45 a.m.): just let me know you're okay!

And then five missed calls.

I pressed the missed-call notification and dialed.

"Oh, thank god! Are you okay? Where have you been?" Erin demanded, each syllable growing shriller.

I cleared my throat, massaging my neck back into place. "I was sleeping. What's going on?" I rasped. I put the phone on speaker and carried it with me to the kitchen. My eyes still half-closed, I fumbled for my coffee mug on the counter.

"A girl was murdered right across the street from your place last night!" Her screech filled the apartment. "It was on the news when I got up! When you didn't answer, I-I freaked out!"

Leaving my phone on the counter, I stumbled over to the window by the front door and lifted the blinds. Across the street, several officers were at work in the alley, nosy passersby glancing over their shoulders as they walked.

"I'm already on my way over!" Erin continued, the hysteria in her voice dying down a little. "Since you're not dead, let's go get coffee."

Some of the officers were bent over and looking at the toppled garbage cans lying askew on the asphalt between the two garages. Two others were talking with the owner of the house next to the alley.

"No, I can't," I croaked. "I have to work. I'll see you at the studio."

"Jesus," Erin breathed after taking a pause. "I seriously almost had a heart attack! I can't believe I let you walk alone last night. That could've been you!"

"I have to go. See you tonight," I said, squinting through the smudges on the window. The police were gathered around one partic-ular trash can lid.

I hung up and pulled a black hoodie over my faded Charlie Brown T-shirt and tugged it down until it covered the waistband of my yoga pants. I tossed my phone onto the table and slid into the sandals by the door, keeping one eye out the window at the gathering crowd.

Heads turned as I clattered down the staircase and across the street to join the fray, the bottoms of my shoes slapping loudly against my feet. Too short to see over almost everyone, I shifted my weight to glance over a couple of shoulders and into the alley. There wasn't a body, at least not anymore. But there were a couple of gloved cops.

The metallic echo of last night reverberated through my mind.

You could have helped her.

CHAPTER FOUR

Erin's paranoia had mostly dissipated by the time I entered the studio for my next class.

"How are you not more freaked out by this?" she asked as we set the last supplies out on the tables. She had finally finished recounting the full story about the murder after I'd told her I hadn't watched the news.

I shrugged and set another bottle of wine on the counter. "I mean, it's not unheard of. A girl from your building went missing."

"Yeah, but they found her later. She wasn't murdered by some psycho."

I actually *was* bothered by the proximity of the murder. And the timing. I thought about that metallic scratching emitting from the alley. I remembered the cops hovering around the garbage can and shook my head.

The first few people drifted into the studio. Erin approached and escorted them to their painting stations.

As I looked up, the door closed again, and I noticed a man glancing around the studio before making his way to Erin at the front. I froze.

It was Jawline from the bookstore.

"Are you with a group?" Erin asked, leaning over the counter toward him.

"No, just me," he said, briefly surveying and then dismissing her with his deep brown eyes.

Erin showed him to the only empty easel in the back. She then fixed her eyes on me across the room. "Harper, do you want to come and explain how this works?" she called. Jawline didn't look up; he flipped through his phone and placed it on the table in front of him.

I shook my head, and she smiled bigger and nodded. I relented and walked to the back.

"This is Harper, our instructor," Erin said, gesturing toward me and then leaving us.

He lifted his head finally, and recognition lit up his eyes. "Hi," he said, his lips slowly parting into a smile. "So you *really* are an artist."

I tugged my hair over my shoulder, hoping it covered the scar. "Are you here alone?" I asked.

"Yeah." His cheeks flushed a light pink under his golden cheekbones. "I was supposed to come yesterday with some friends, but apparently they don't give refunds here?"

I now realized why I had recognized the voice on the phone the other night. "You're Iann? I was the one on the phone last night rescheduling your class," I said.

"Oh, yeah. Well, you really sold the paint-your-pet night."

"Do you have a pet?"

"A dog," he said, picking up his phone. He turned it toward me, showing off a picture of a large scruffy golden retriever with kind brown eyes not unlike his. I always found it uncanny how almost everyone's pet resembled the owner in one way or another. "His name's Leo."

"He's cute," I commented. "More importantly, he's easy to paint."

"Thank god," Iann sighed.

I returned to the front of the group once it looked like every person was accounted for.

"Do you know him?" Erin asked, raising her eyebrows.

"He's the coffee shop guy," I muttered, turning my back to the class and taking up my brush. As I directed the class and began painting on my canvas, I could feel his eyes on my back. I felt a heat and nervousness that I usually didn't anymore when I taught a studio crowd. Almost like I was performing.

As the night went on, I found myself stealing glances at Iann in between my walks around the room, giving tips when requested.

I made sure to stop by Iann's station on my last survey of the room. He was leaning away from his canvas, glaring at it. I stepped around the easel and surveyed his work. "It actually looks like a dog," he said in mock disbelief.

I smiled and returned to the front to describe the final steps. My subject for painting was a generic fluffy brown dog since that was the pet that most people came to paint. "Thank you for coming," I said, facing the room. "Everyone's paintings turned out great."

Erin suddenly appeared beside me. "Our artist will be sticking around for a little bit if you have any questions." She looked at me and tilted her head toward Iann before clapping her hands softly together and addressing the packing painters. "Please check out our event calendar by the door or online and join us for another class!"

The door opened, and Erin's date slipped into the studio. Iann turned and smiled at the guy, exchanging words.

Erin grabbed her purse and jacket from underneath my easel. "Okay, I'm heading out with, uh . . ." She furrowed her brow. "Jeremy," she declared, triumphantly. "Good luck with the bookstore guy."

Both Jeremy and Iann walked toward us.

"Okay, I'll lock up," I said to Erin.

"Hi, Jeremy," she purred, touching his shoulder lightly. "This is Harper, our resident artist."

"Ah," he said, extending his hand out toward me and giving me a once-over. "I enjoyed the class last night."

Probably not as much as he would enjoy tonight. I shook his hand, resisting the urge to recoil from his limp and cold grip. "Thank you." I withdrew my hand. I wanted to wipe it on my apron, but he was staring right at me. "Have fun." I turned to Erin. "Text me when you get back tonight," I said in a low voice.

She rolled her eyes. "Yeah, okay."

"See you later, man," Jeremy said to Iann as he ushered Erin toward the door, his arm already around her waist. Other painters quickly followed behind them, gingerly cradling their canvases.

Iann remained beside me.

"Do you know each other?" I asked.

"Jeremy? Yeah, he's in the Psychology Department with me."

So that was the group Iann was originally going to come with? "His painting turned out okay."

He raised his eyebrows. "So you have to close up alone tonight?"

I nodded past him to the last two students as they drifted out. "Yeah, since Erin ditched me."

"Do you want to go for a drink after you finish?" He had that slightly nervous smile on his face, mirroring the one he'd worn in the bookstore earlier. "I can wait."

My heart clenched. It was an innocuous enough invitation, but I didn't love the idea of walking through dark streets with a man who knew I was on my own tonight. "I still have to work after this. Maybe some other time." I turned and walked toward my easel and began gathering my brushes.

He didn't follow me. I glanced over my shoulder, and he was back at his station grabbing his painting.

My whole body stiffened. *You're blowing it.* "Your painting looks great."

He looked up, canvas in hand. "Thanks. This was fun, actually. Have a good night." He grinned over his shoulder before walking out the door, the chime dinging as it closed behind him.

I stood there with my brushes clenched into my palms and watched him leave. His wineglass was beside his easel, untouched. As I walked to the front door to lock it, I saw his Jeep pulling out of the parking lot.

Starting with Iann's station, I picked up all the used brushes and worked my way around the room, gathering the dirty wineglasses. I dumped his leftover wine into the sink last, wondering if he hadn't drunk because he was lost in his painting. Every time I had peeked at him, his eyes had been narrowed and determined. Calculating, almost.

I flicked off the front studio lights and ducked into the back room. Normally I would have walked home after closing up, but the memory of the haunting sound made my hands tremble at the thought.

I sank onto one of the stools next to the shelf of wine and pulled the break-room table closer toward my waist. I reached into my bag and fished out the completed illustrations I had for the children's book so far. I liked to keep my entire project with me until it was complete so everything turned out in the same style and somewhat cohesive.

I laid out the drawings to the side and tore a fresh page from my sketchbook. I dug out my page full of thumbnail drawings and placed it at the very top of the table. Instead of starting on the next illustration, I flipped over the page of thumbnails and began sketching two sideways ovals, which soon became eyes on the page. Iann's eyes.

I opened my worn leather bag and surveyed the color choices before extracting four pencils from within. Black cherry. Burnt ochre. Bronze. Gold.

I hastily layered the colors, the gold flecks dancing among the richer brown of the iris. I took my charcoal pencil and filled in the pupils, careful not to smudge.

I leaned away from the paper and peered at the disembodied eyes before turning over the page again. If he had missed his friends coming the previous night, why did he want to come alone rather than reschedule with others? And what were the chances in this enormous city of him coming to my work after our chance encounter?

Stranger things have happened.

Without examining the next thumbnail in my storyboard, I doodled the hero mouse from the story, Arnie. I sketched a quick outline of the cat, Harold, standing behind him menacingly.

When Erin and I had first met, she had been surprised to see my artwork. She had described it as "playful" and "innocent." From my demeanor, she had expected the disturbed art of a tortured soul. In interactions, I didn't come across like most imagined a children's book illustrator would, between my dark, baggy clothes and my reluctance to smile or make eye contact with most people. The events in my life that had made me this way were exactly what drew me to illustrations. My imagination was the only thing that had helped me survive my father's sharp cuffs across my face, the broken bones. All those years I had felt the other, truer part inside, screaming to get out. I'd hidden what art supplies I could scavenge in small corners of my room, playing piano to appease my father and stealing moments to draw when I could.

I had always preferred drawing to playing music, even before Issi's death. But especially after, I came to view the piano as the silent accomplice to my abuse. Well, maybe not so silent. I still dreamed in the notes of the piano from songs I'd played over and over during that time.

My strokes had become darker and harsher as I got lost in thought. I eased up on the pencil and moved on to outlining the next drawing on a new page. Throughout my childhood, my art had been the only way to keep those I had loved and lost close to me and to create new realities to escape mine.

———

Identical blue eyes pierce through the water into mine.

I stare back, motionless, suspended under the weight of the water above. Her eyes cut through the green-and-brown murk between us.

She drifts toward me, moving right through the moss and leaves in the water.

As she comes closer, pieces of the flesh on her face disintegrate and float into the water as she moves.

Her arms stretch out toward my neck.

I open my mouth to scream, a violent torrent of bubbles erupting into the water in front of me.

———

My face was frozen on the marble tabletop in the break room.

My eyelashes fluttered against the hard surface. I lifted my head and heard a sharp crack. My jaw was still clenched.

Only when I heard the buzzing of the fluorescents above did I realize I was still in the studio.

I looked down at the paper I'd fallen asleep on. All my illustrations were ripped into quarters on the table, some pieces littered on the floor. The page directly under me was not of my mouse and cat characters but of two young girls with their backs to me, the paper covered in bright-red blood, still wet.

Chills rose all along my arms, and I felt a sharp pang in my palm. I looked down at the two broken halves of red pencil embedded in a jagged cut in my clenched hand. I opened my palm, and one of the broken halves fell to the table. The other, smaller half was splintered into the cut, dried blood trailing down my palm and wrist.

I took a shaky breath and pulled the pencil out. I gasped as the sharp pain intensified, and a new, fresh stream of blood poured out over the two girls on the paper.

I ran to the sink and washed the splinters out. The dripping continued, so I wrapped two paper towels around my hand and stumbled back to the table. I tapped my phone.

5:02 a.m. There was a message from Erin hours ago.

Erin (2:06 a.m.): I'm home! Lots to tell!

Without looking over my destroyed illustrations again, I swept them into my open bag along with my colored pencils.

I stared down at the primitive drawing of the two girls holding hands. I realized they were standing in water. The blood was seeping through the paper and onto the table. I recognized the dresses the girls wore. Of all the sudden realizations upon waking up, that was the most troubling.

They were the green dresses with blue flowers that Mom had made us wear that last day we all went to the beach as a family. Issi had liked the dress, but I had hated the flowers. I'd hated the way it flared up when I ran.

Clutching the paper towel closer to my palm until the wound stung, I took the new drawing and ripped it up and tossed it into the trash can by the door.

I swung my messenger bag over one shoulder and unlocked the dead bolt on the back door. It was still dark out, but the sky was the faint blue color that accompanied dawn. I let the door slam closed behind me and grabbed the studio keys from my bag. As I locked the door, with the morning chill rustling through my thin jacket, I still thought about that drawing. Not that my illustrations were destroyed. Not that I had impaled myself with a pencil. But those two girls.

My body was heavy as I dragged my feet along the pavement, determined to get home. The throbbing in my palm gave way to the numbness overtaking my entire hand. I wondered how long it had bled while I continued to sleep.

It was early Friday morning, so the street was quiet, still hours before the city would roar to life.

A couple of shadowy figures exited the apartment buildings ahead. I passed the alley across from my window, shuddering at the memory of the grating sound that rattled through my mind, my search for my keys becoming more frantic. A rush of relief flowed through me as my fingers closed around them. I jammed them into the lock and swung the door open.

Woodstock was exiting his litter box in the corner at the exact moment I entered.

He surveyed me and gave a disapproving meow. If I had been home, he would have been well into his second hour of yowling for breakfast while I slept.

I walked past him to the kitchen and unwrapped the paper towel around my hand. The blood had dried, but I could still see some splinters from the pencil in the cut.

As I poured some food into Woodstock's bowl, I started to consider my damaged illustrations. I had one more week until the deadline for the author. I could probably get an extension, but that cheapskate would try to negotiate down the other half he owed me. I was already close to not making rent for the month.

Woodstock buried his head into his food, and I collapsed onto my unmade bed, stomach down. I fished for the TV remote in the covers, then flipped through a couple of channels of static before landing on the local news. I couldn't close my eyes. Instead, I rolled over on my back and fixated on a space on my empty white ceiling, that haunting picture of the girls projected before me.

"The young victim of a suspected homicide has been identified by law enforcement." The voice of the news anchor snapped me out of my reverie. My heart pounded as I sat up, watching the replay of footage of the crime scene. "The body of a young woman was found in Wicker Park on August seventh and has recently been publicly identified as twenty-seven-year-old Holly Elizabeth Bascom, an Iowa native. Holly was a junior associate at Blue Rivers Investment Firm and a recent MBA graduate from DePaul University. Police have yet to release any details about the condition her body was found in, but they have stated they're investigating her death as a possible homicide."

The screen switched to a photo, and I was suddenly looking into a mirror. Her eyes were bluer than mine, which verged on gray. Her nose was slightly longer, her hair smooth and straight, but otherwise the same shade of dark auburn as mine. It was a graduation portrait, and she was wearing bold, dark-framed glasses.

The anchor's voice broke through my daze, and I took a breath for the first time in almost a minute. "At this time, the police have not named any suspects or persons of interest. If you have any information about this case, please contact the Chicago Police Department at the number on the screen."

As she moved on to the next story, I let my shaking hand lean against my forehead. I was dizzy. Was I really that tired? Had I imagined that the victim was the adult Issi from my nightmares?

I reached over Woodstock's curled-up body and grabbed my phone. On Google, the same images of Holly popped up. She was my double. No, she was better than my double. She was what Issi would've grown into. She looked gorgeous. Intelligent. Ambitious. If it was possible for a person to convey all that with their appearance, that certainly wasn't what I looked like. I was the Mr. Hyde version of her. A little rougher and scarier than the hero of the story.

I clicked on the first article and skimmed it. While police remained silent, the person who had called in her body had told a reporter that Holly's body had dark, thin bruises around her neck and that the tips of her fingers on one hand were bloodied and the nails broken. There were fingernail marks on a garbage can lid where she had clawed at it in her final moments.

My heart lodged in my throat as I moved from the articles to her Instagram page. Photo after photo of Holly among coworkers in pencil skirts and blazers and selfies of her on her morning jogs. Halfway down her feed, one picture caught my eye. Holly was photographed from the passenger seat in front of the steering wheel of a BMW, her key ring dangling from the ignition. Beside the key was a rabbit's foot charm.

It couldn't be.

I leaped to my feet and stumbled to Woodstock's usual hidey-hole in the closet. The charm was nowhere to be seen among the small collection of cat fur and dirty clothes. I shuffled the blankets on my bed, seeing if anything rolled out.

I lost track of how long I combed through the apartment until my phone rang. Sunlight was now obnoxiously streaming through my blinds.

It was Erin.

"Hello?"

"Hey, did you forget something last night?" Erin snapped.

I knew that tone. My stomach dropped. "What?" Had I remembered to throw that drawing away or only imagined doing it?

"You didn't lock the front door!" she screeched through the speaker.

I kneeled beside the bed, leaning onto my shoulder and placing my cheek against the floor to peer underneath. I definitely had. "I locked it right after the last person left," I said weakly. I considered the drawing, the blood, the torn illustrations. "Did someone break in?" Goose bumps erupted all along my neck. Had someone been in the studio with me while I slept?

"No, everything is still here. Nothing is missing."

I sighed, squinting into the darkness under the bed. "I'm so sorry. I could've sworn I locked that door. Really." There it was—a tiny shadow. I could probably reach it if I stretched.

She was silent for a moment. "Did you leave through the front?"

"No, I left through the back."

"Well, whatever. It's just disappointing."

I stopped caring as the last word left her mouth. "How was your date?" I didn't care about that either, but I saw a way out of the current conversation. I stifled a grunt as I outstretched my fingers and closed them around the rabbit's foot.

"It was amazing," she gushed after a long pause. "We went to this great restaurant. I can't wait to tell you the other stuff." Her voice lowered. "But Dad's here this morning, so we'll have to do brunch on Saturday or something."

"I can't," I said, relieved to have an excuse other than that I was short on money. My idea of brunch was a two-dollar breakfast taco, but Erin's included Bloody Mary bars and lobster Benedict. "The illustrations for that cat-mouse project got destroyed, so I have to start the entire thing from scratch."

"Ugh!" she scoffed. "So I can't see you all weekend?"

"Yeah, but I'll see you in the studio next week when I come in."

"Okay, well I covered for you with Dad and told him I came in a little earlier and forgot to lock the front door, in case he mentions it to you."

He and I hadn't spoken other than my ten-minute interview years ago. She knew that. She wanted me to feel like I owed her something.

I swallowed. The charm in my hand was identical to the one in Holly's photo.

But how?

What did you do?

"Okay," I said through clenched teeth. After we hung up, I replayed the previous night in my mind. My eyes had met briefly with Iann's through the glass door as he climbed into his Jeep. *I locked that door.*

CHAPTER FIVE

The next days were a blur of frantic drawing and buckets of coffee, divided only by three hours of sleep at a time. I ignored the calls and texts from Erin. I didn't even respond to the author's vaguely threatening emails about the upcoming deadline.

Woodstock insisted on being let out on my landing intermittently throughout the day and basking. Those few seconds when I opened the door for him were the only times I saw the sun in days. With the added pressure of the nearing deadline, I had made good time and was almost caught up to where I'd been before that bizarre incident at the studio. I laid out the illustrations sequentially along the table. They were slightly worse than the previous iterations that I had sent for approval, but they would have to do. I leaned back in my seat and tugged at the blinds, letting the light come in. It was overcast outside, with the sun peeking out only through small cracks in the clouds occasionally.

I opened my laptop. The article about Holly was still on the screen. I hadn't been able to resist looking at that photo when I'd taken a lunch break earlier. I observed it again now, recalling the contents of the article. She had bloodied her fingers trying to get someone's attention while she lay there dying. I had kept walking because I was scared. I stroked the rabbit's foot in my palm. I couldn't explain why, but after I'd found it again under the bed, I'd washed it, mentally weighing the dangers of holding on to it or calling the police. What good would it do? It wasn't like they could pull DNA from it—at least not any nonfeline DNA.

I powered the laptop down quickly. Where Holly's picture had been was now my face reflected in the black mirror of the blank screen.

You walked away from her. And now she's dead. You could have helped her.

You could've helped me.

I hummed aloud suddenly, breaking through the child's voice in my head. Startled, Woodstock glowered at me from his perch on my lap. I petted him on the head and coaxed him onto the table.

If I had stopped to investigate the sound the night of Holly's murder, I probably would be dead too.

You know that's not true. You were scared.

I stood up and dragged my feet across the floor toward the bathroom, my humming growing louder. Without turning on the light, I opened the bottom cupboard, my fingers clumsily fumbling over the grainy wood until they wrapped around a folded piece of toilet paper. I pulled it out and quickly unfurled it to reveal the small pile of the remaining white pills.

Sleep was what I needed. Only for a few hours and I could quiet that voice. If I took two, I could probably forget about Holly and Issi altogether until tomorrow. If I took more I could forget everything forever.

I shook two pills into my hand, then counted those that remained before dropping them back into the paper. Erin had to have nonaddictive sleeping pills for a long time after she left rehab, which weren't an ideal substitute. But she hadn't refilled her prescription for those in nearly a year. She slept just fine these days. I had to stretch out these last pills or else snag the remaining few from her old hiding spot, which she was bound to notice eventually. I rerolled the pills and pushed them to the back of the cupboard and slammed the door. I didn't leave the bathroom quickly enough, catching a glimpse of my reflection in the unlit mirror as I turned.

I grabbed clothes from the pile of clean laundry in my closet, throwing on the first shirt and pair of jeans I laid hands on. The walls were crushing me. The weight on my body threatened to choke the air from my lungs.

I considered the rabbit's foot beside my laptop once again, staring at the matted fur before gripping it and twisting the attached metallic ring onto my own key fob.

I dropped it into my bag and bolted out the door, the wind instantly defying my escape and lashing my skin as I locked the door, tangling and twisting my hair against my scalp.

As I stepped onto the sidewalk, the same heaviness from before pulled me down the street and into my familiar bookstore. I walked through the front row of shelves, with my eyes trained on the coffee shop on the other end of the store. My mouth was dry and salty from drinking my own brewed coffee over the past few days. I always let the coffee grounds sit and brew for too long.

Once I reached the empty counter and peered around the café to catch a barista, I noticed a familiar face. Iann was sitting at a table in the corner, where the café led into the shelving of the bookstore.

"What can I get for you?" The barista had suddenly materialized behind the counter.

I turned back to face him. "Black coffee, please."

"What size?"

"The largest cup you can find."

The college kid laughed, and I handed him the crumpled five-dollar bill I had crushed into my fist. As I turned around, Iann was looking down at his table, furiously scribbling on a stack of papers.

The barista handed me my change. I glanced over my shoulder to see Iann shaking his head and marking the page in front of him with a red pen several times.

I picked up the coffee the barista had silently placed on the counter behind me and walked to Iann's table. I stood behind him, watching as he marked harsh red lines through double-spaced typed pages. I tapped his shoulder, and he jumped.

"Oh, hi," he said when he finally looked at me. "How long were you standing there?"

I took a sip of coffee. "Not long. You're very focused on whatever that is." I knew what it was. My father had reveled in paper grading. With each red mark, he would laugh and explain to anyone standing close enough to hear why his student was wrong.

Iann shoved two large textbooks into the chair directly beside him and moved the stack of papers to the edge of the table. "Do you want to sit here?" His eyes seemed slightly glazed over. He hadn't had much sleep either.

I settled across from him into the wooden chair.

"What brings you here today?" he asked, leaning back and stretching his arms behind him.

"I needed some fresh air." I cradled my mug between both hands and took a sip. The bite of the coffee reinvigorated me in a way the fresh air hadn't. "I've been working at home for the past couple of days."

He nodded and rubbed the edge of his jaw. He was somewhere else entirely in his thoughts. He hadn't shaved in several days. There was scruff darkening his cheekbones and chin.

"What are you working on?" I asked.

He finally met my eyes. "Oh, I'm grading final papers." He patted the stack in front of him. "I also needed some fresh air."

I grasped my cup more tightly and took another swig. The steam rising from the coffee burned my nose slightly. "How's Leo?"

He stared at me for several seconds before answering. He was somewhere else again. "He's part of the reason I had to get out of my apartment. If I work at home, he keeps trying to get me to play with him."

He also took a sip of his drink, and we looked at each other awkwardly. "Uh, did you hear anything about your friend's date with Jeremy?"

"No. I've been avoiding her so I can get my work done. She's similar to a golden retriever."

He finally smiled. "Well, the date went fine, I guess. I ran into them near campus this weekend."

I wasn't shocked. Erin usually played around with one guy for at least a month before moving on. She reminded me of Woodstock with that rabbit's foot the other night. Maybe she was more like a cat than a retriever. "That's good, right?"

Iann looked down for a second. "Yeah. Jeremy's . . . fine." He shrugged.

"It doesn't matter," I offered. I had already figured as much. Jeremy seemed like a meathead. "They'll both be sick of each other by next weekend, I'm sure."

"You're pretty cynical, aren't you?"

Yes, and tired. I merely responded with a nod.

His eyes continued to survey me. "What kind of work have you been doing from home?" he asked.

"I've been working on an illustration project for a children's book."

His eyes got bigger. "When do I get to finally see some of your work?" It was definitely *maybe* genuine interest.

"You already saw my mustache guy and my painting from the class."

He laughed, one of those full chest laughs that requires your head to tilt back so it can properly erupt. "That's right, the mustache guy. Do you still have that?"

"Yeah, it's lying around somewhere."

He was still grinning and looked across the table at me. "I could use a *real* break from all this work," he said, gesturing to the pile of papers. "Do you want to grab some dinner?"

My feet stiffened, ready to bolt. "I'm really behind on that project. I should get back." I eyed the door and clutched my coffee cup.

He looked down at the table. "Okay, well, it was nice to see you. Good luck with your project." Without gazing up again, he reopened his book and spread out his papers on the table in front of him.

"Thanks," I mumbled, getting to my feet. "Bye."

Once I had my hand on the door, I turned around to look at Iann's profile as he flipped through his book. What was I so eager to get back to? There was definitely no hope for a restful night with this seventh cup of coffee. I couldn't go back to the apartment alone with my thoughts. Not now.

I paused, ready to push out to the street before turning on my heel, a strange determination in my step.

"You know what?" I said once I was back by Iann's side, my heart racing. "Dinner sounds great."

CHAPTER SIX

"What changed your mind?" Iann asked. The train was packed, so we both stood facing each other and grasping the overhead handles. We'd decided on a Korean barbecue place near Logan Square that Iann knew about. Wary of getting into a car with a stranger, I'd suggested we take the train.

"What?"

He glanced down at his feet and shuffled away from the person beside him before meeting my eyes. "Well, you shot me down so many times already." He laughed. "What changed your mind?"

"I don't know."

Once we got off at our stop and started down the sidewalk, I had an answer. It wasn't the real answer. But it was true and it was *an* answer. "I was just hungry, I guess. I've been mostly living off of coffee alone the past few days."

Our shoulders touched as we made way for a couple passing on the sidewalk.

He nodded. "You seem like you take your work really seriously."

Work is all there is. There's nothing else. No one else. "Doesn't everyone?"

Iann shrugged, not catching my biting tone. "No, I mean I take my work seriously, too, but it must be hard for you to balance your work since you have to manage everything yourself."

My hackles eased back down.

"Especially if it's something where you bring your work home all the time, like you and me," he continued. "Do you have any hobbies?"

"I guess drawing *is* my hobby," I answered after a moment. The smell of grilled meat and sesame reached me, and my stomach rumbled. We were getting close.

"See, but it's also your work," he said. "You should try to find something that's totally different from your work to take your mind off everything."

"Okay, so what's your hobby?"

"I like to go running." I must've made a face, because he laughed and continued, "I'm not good at it, but I enjoy it." I appreciated this attempt at humility.

"So, you're a health nut?" I asked.

"No." He grinned. "I eat terribly, and then I run. It's very cathartic."

We crossed the street and walked into the restaurant. There wasn't a long line like at most of the trendy restaurants in the area, so we were seated right away. It was a little early for a Friday-night dinner. Once in our booth, I looked at the list of all-you-can-grill meats.

"Is there anything in particular you want?" Iann asked, flagging down a waiter.

I shrugged. "I'm up for anything."

He ordered in Korean without looking at the list once, and the waiter nodded before walking away.

"Do you come here a lot?" I asked.

"Oh yeah, this is where I eat a ton of meat before I go running," he joked. "So, where are you from?"

And with that, the tennis match of first-date questions began. "I'm from Evanston, originally," I said. This was the tamest background question that I didn't mind responding to. "What about you?" I batted back.

"Oh, so you're a local," he said, grabbing one of the waters the waiter had placed in front of us before disappearing again. "I'm from Washington."

"DC or state?" I asked.

He smiled. "State."

I saw the next question coming.

"Do you have any siblings?"

"No," I said quickly. *Not anymore.*

He waited for more.

"What about you?"

He nodded. "Two sisters. One of them, Rose, has two adorable girls, and they're amazing. I'm kind of the helpless pushover in the family when it comes to my nieces."

The smile on his face when he said it filled me with a strange jealousy. What must it be like to grow up with a loving family? To have a father whose first impulse wasn't violence?

"Are your parents still in Evanston?"

My skin went cold. "My father still lives there." *And Mom is buried there.*

He looked at me, waiting for more of an explanation.

Thankfully, the meat arrived, saving me from blurting out the last part. "Thank you," he said to the waiter.

I pulled my hair back into a bun low on my neck in preparation for the messy food. The longer my hair grew, the more often I found it accidentally in my mouth while eating.

Iann stared at my neck and then looked away when I caught his gaze.

I tapped the scar where it began below my ear. I traced it to the point it stopped, just above my collarbone. "My hair usually covers this, but it's pretty hard to ignore, I guess," I said.

He shook his head and looked down. "No."

I weighed the cost of telling a small truth. "I was in a car accident when I was a kid," I began. It was hard to make this sound light hearted, but I tried. "I was lucky to get out with only this." Nothing scared people off like telling a story about confronting your own mortality as a child.

"I'm sorry," he said, looking me in the eye again.

I wasn't used to people making eye contact like that. I didn't mind, though. Who wouldn't want to look at those eyes a little longer?

"It was a long time ago." It still felt like yesterday. The scar on the outside was nothing compared to the gruesome wounds inside our family that lingered. There was no moving on from that accident. But people liked to hear about personal tragedies dismissed and overcome.

Iann grabbed the tongs handed to him and loaded up the tabletop grill with all the meat. "What does your dad do?" he asked.

I took a deep breath. "He's a music professor."

"Really? At Northwestern?"

I nodded, watching as the meat sizzled and darkened on the grill.

"So, I bet you went to school there too?"

"I actually dropped out after a year." I chose a fleck of pepper on my plate and locked my eyes on it.

Iann had started chewing a piece of beef. He moved on smoothly once he swallowed. "What were you studying?"

"Music."

"What instrument do you play?"

I sighed. Clarinet was my first love, but I had poured everything I had into piano. Not by choice. "I studied piano, mostly."

"How did you get into visual art?"

I had always been passionate about painting. It was challenging, and I enjoyed being able to see my creations, not just hear them. I loved music, too, but I didn't feel it in me at every moment of every day like Issi had. Music had become a weight around my neck near the end. I hated it now. "It's more tangible, I guess."

"Sounds like you knew what you wanted to do and you didn't need school for it. I'm sure your dad is really proud that you're making it on your own in Chicago."

I shook my head. "Not so much." I had followed his plan for Issi perfectly as long as I could. I'd graduated early from high school but had only lasted one year at university. Fleeing Evanston and moving alone to Chicago with no money at sixteen wasn't his idea of success.

He looked at my face and furrowed his brow. "You're not close with him?"

"Is this a psych evaluation?" I asked, fiddling with some pork between my chopsticks.

He shook his head. "No, I-I'll stop asking about your family."

The tightness in my chest lifted. "Yeah, let's talk about yours. Do they come to visit you here?"

Iann turned over a piece of meat on the grill. "Occasionally, maybe twice a year. And I go back home for the holidays usually."

"How did you end up in Chicago?"

He paused, a frown briefly flashing across his face. That expression surprised me. Maybe he was holding back as well.

"I wanted to get out of my hometown," he said. "I knew from the beginning that I wanted to study psychology, so I applied for the undergraduate program here, and I never left."

"Why psychology?"

He looked up. "I don't know. Maybe I just like to figure out what makes people tick."

We carried on for a few more moments in silence. "Why did you come to the studio the other night?" I asked abruptly. It was a question I had been holding on to since that night.

Iann was still chewing, his eyebrows raised. "The place you work?" He swallowed. "I told you, I was supposed to go with my friends, but I couldn't make it."

"So why did you reschedule and come by yourself?"

He took a sip of the water in front of him. "You told me that the Tipsy Turtle—" He looked at me for affirmation.

"Tipsy Paintbrush," I corrected.

"Right, so you told me the Tipsy Paintbrush doesn't offer refunds. Is that weird?"

I shrugged. "It's a little awkward going to that kind of place alone, isn't it?"

"Well, it turns out I knew you . . . I mean, kind of." He laughed.

"Yeah, but what are the chances that we met a day before you came to the studio?" I asked.

"Fate, I guess."

I didn't believe in fate. On the night I'd found out that Jawline was the Iann who had called to reschedule, I had briefly weighed the probability of it being a coincidence. What cosmic glitch had to occur for us to meet again so quickly after that first interaction? What had to occur for him to even approach me at all in the bookstore that day? I shrugged. "It's a little weird for a man of science to cite fate as a legitimate reason."

He smirked. "Well, psychology is a *social* science. And I think there are some things you can't explain." With his chopsticks, he wrapped a leaf of kimchi around a piece of pork on his plate. "For instance, why did you suddenly agree to go out with me? If that's not a freak occurrence, I don't know what is."

I stabbed at a mushroom on the edge of my plate. "Have you always lived in Wicker Park?" I asked.

"No, I live in the graduate housing downtown."

"If you live downtown, why are you in Wicker Park so much?"

He shrugged. "I bartend part time at the Robey, so I end up on this side of town most of the week." The Robey was the swankiest old hotel in our part of town, with a rooftop bar. I'd heard Erin talk about it. It was where she brought her parents when they came to visit from out of town to check on the business.

"You bartend?"

He laughed. "I mean, I'm a grad student in Chicago. Of course I have to work two jobs. That's the bare minimum to feed myself," he said.

Once we were completely stuffed full of grilled meat, we waddled to the front counter, and Iann insisted on paying.

It had been such a long time since I'd been out with someone, and it felt wrong to accept a free dinner. "I'll buy coffee, then," I said as he handed his card to the cashier.

The cashier deliberately turned to me and said, "Hey, why didn't you tell me you were here!"

I was taken aback and silent for a beat. Iann looked at me expectantly. "I, uh, I'm sorry, but do I know you?" I asked.

The cashier squinted at me, and then his eyes suddenly widened. "I'm so sorry! You look like my wife's little sister." He shook his head, his cheeks bright red, and ran Iann's card. "Your name isn't Jenny, right?" He chuckled nervously.

Still startled, I shook my head.

He handed Iann the card and receipt. "Sorry about that," he continued. "I—the resemblance is uncanny. Have a good night!"

"That was weird," Iann muttered as we stepped out the door and onto the sidewalk.

"That's never happened to you before?" Now that we were in the open air, I could tell that we both smelled like smoke.

"Definitely not. I guess you just have one of those faces. I'm too weird looking."

Not weird. But certainly distinguished. His deep-brown eyes were framed by black lashes. His nose and jaw were sharp and strong, like they'd been carved with a chisel into granite.

"Honestly, I've had it happen a few times over the years, and I've come to the conclusion that apparently nobody actually can tell the difference between pale dark-haired women."

He snickered.

Usually I could write off the claims that I "looked familiar" relatively easily. The people who made the claims typically couldn't put a name to who I looked like, just that they felt they'd come across a similar face at some point.

The recent rash of incidents was unsettling. These doubles had names. Sarah. Holly. It felt like my darkest nightmares come to life. Like there was another me walking around, still alive. Like Issi was back and I was disappearing. Like how it used to be.

———

When we arrived at my building, my heart raced. I hadn't invited a man up in over a year. For a while, each guy had been a nice distraction followed by a good night's sleep. But the morning after wasn't worth it.

"Thanks for finally saying yes."

I didn't turn to Iann as he spoke. I stared ahead at the stairs. The stairs back to where I wouldn't be able to sleep. Where Issi was waiting for me.

"So, you're back to working on that project, I guess?" he asked.

I shuddered as the memory of the screeching sound from nights before played through my mind. I weighed the risk of inviting him in against my fear of being alone tonight. "Do you want to come up?" I blurted out.

He hesitated.

"For a quick drink," I added. He was a good guy. Or at least he thought he was. I'd found that good guys didn't want transparency. They were too careful. They didn't want an "easy" girl. Or they didn't want it to seem like that's what they wanted. But I wasn't looking for that tonight anyway. I just couldn't go back in alone.

Both of Iann's hands were in the pockets of his jacket. "Are you sure? You have a lot of work to do, right?"

If I was really going to do more work, I definitely couldn't do it sober. "Screw it." I waved my hand. "Do you want a drink or not?"

He laughed. "I could go for coffee. I think I still have to power through tonight."

I shrugged and took the first step toward my door. The heaviness remained but was somewhat lighter. I pulled out my keys and turned the lock. Glancing over my shoulder, I noticed Iann standing two steps below me. When I flicked on the light, Woodstock meowed loudly at me from his perch on my drafting table. Without bothering to make sure the door didn't slam in Iann's face, I lunged for the table and shooed Woodstock from my illustrations. Luckily, no smudges. I couldn't afford another delay.

Iann caught the door and stepped in, then let it go behind him. "Cute cat," he said, reaching down for Woodstock before the fur ball scurried under my bed and out of reach.

"He is, but is it worth the fur?" I asked myself aloud as I brushed the leftover orange tufts from my table.

Iann observed my apartment. There wasn't much to see. Erin called it "an artist's loft," but it was really a crappy studio efficiency at best. His eyes lingered on the portrait half-hidden below my drafting table. "Can I look at this?" His hand was already on the edge of the dog-eared paper.

My objection never left my mouth.

"Wow, did you make this?" He leaned in closer to the black-and-white portrait of young Issi. I had only been able to afford charcoal and cheap paper in my first days on my own. The portrait had flowed out of me one afternoon when my apartment didn't even have any furniture other than this table. There were still black smudges on the floorboards where I had gone a little wild with the charcoal and never bothered to clean. I had crammed it behind the leg of the table almost immediately after finishing it. Her long dark hair wasn't in its usual braid but freely flowing behind her. But her spirit wasn't in that portrait. It was her dark, angry shell brought to life on paper. She had never been angry like that. "Who is she?" he asked.

No one, not even Erin, had seen this, so I hadn't needed to generate an explanation before. My mind stalled.

"She looks like you," he said before I could answer.

I grabbed the paper and slid it back behind the table. "It was an old project." I started for the kitchen. "Do you want something to drink? I think I have rum."

He followed behind and leaned against the bar counter, peering into my tiny kitchen. "Do you have coffee?"

"Come on, you're a bartender, right?" I leaned onto my tiptoes to open the cabinet. There was a full bottle of rum from the last time Erin had come over. She never came to hang out without hard liquor of some sort.

He watched as I shook the bottle and set it onto the counter. "Yeah, but I'm a grad student tonight," he said, eyeing the bottle. "Okay, maybe one wouldn't hurt."

CHAPTER SEVEN

"To be honest, I'm surprised you asked me up," he said, his cheeks a little flushed. One drink had turned into eight.

I swallowed the last of the copper-colored liquor pooled in the bottom of my chipped coffee cup and poured another halfway. "Why?"

"I don't know." He took a quick sip from his cup. "You seemed a little . . . standoffish."

"What do you mean?" I played dumb.

"I mean, I got the impression you really didn't want to tell me very much about yourself. Did it bother you when I asked about your family?"

I frowned. "Do you want to add some Coke?"

He tilted his head. "What?"

Without waiting for an answer, I got to my feet, grasping the edge of the table for support. I grabbed a couple of cans and brought them to the kitchen table. "It sounds like your family is really close knit and mine is—" *Broken. Fractured. Disturbed. Nonexistent. Dead. Well, mostly dead.* "Don't take it personally. I don't talk about that with anyone."

He opened one of the cans and poured it into my glass. "Oh . . . I get it. Sorry."

I poured him another glass of the cheap rum. My head started dipping forward and my arms felt limp as I held my glass up to my mouth and sipped. The words bubbled at the base of my throat. "Don't be. I mean, there really isn't any family to speak of anymore."

He looked at me expectantly.

"My mom died when I was little, and my sister died in that car accident I told you about."

His eyes saddened. "I'm so sorry."

My hand started shaking as I took another sip. "It was a long time ago." I swallowed and continued, "When I was ten."

"I can't imagine. What about your dad?"

It was a reasonable question. The answer was less so. "He kind of lost it after the accident, and we don't talk anymore." I glanced up from the table and realized Iann was firmly clutching his glass.

Maybe the rum was making us both braver, because he ventured a question further. "Why don't you talk with him anymore?"

He thought the wrong one died. Issi was the future of our family, and everyone saw it. She was the embodiment of Mom and my father's dreams born long before we existed. She was what kept hope alive for my father after Mom was gone. I shook my head. "You're really pushing it." I finished the last of my drink.

He laughed and raised his hands in surrender. "You can't blame me for trying." His questions along with the alcohol were dredging up exactly what I'd left the apartment to avoid.

I recalled the panic when I'd walked into my room a couple of weeks after the accident to find all my clothes were gone. My father had explained back then that he'd made a mistake but that I would have to wear Issi's clothes for the time being. Deep down, I knew there had not been a misunderstanding. Issi's closet had been full of bright dresses and skirts, and mine was all shirts and shorts and jeans. Mom had stopped dressing us alike almost immediately after our third birthdays when our personal fashion choices diverged. I had to wear only my dead twin's clothes for the next couple of years until I grew out of them. That was about the time I stopped looking in mirrors. My reflection was no longer my own.

Even though my stomach was still swollen from dinner, I took another drink of my rum and Coke. My eyes hazily trained on Iann's flushed cheeks. He was well on his way to drinking too much as well. His eyes were getting duller. I was relieved. Nothing was more embarrassing than being the only drunk one.

More words suddenly clawed their way out. "A couple of nights ago, a girl was murdered right over there." I lazily nodded past my bed to the door.

"In your apartment?" he asked.

I shook my head. "Across the street. In the alley." My throat was tight. *She looked exactly like me.* "I think I heard it happen." I dropped my head down toward the table. I hadn't actually acknowledged that out loud to anyone else. It felt worse to say it.

"What?" Iann asked, his hand warm as it covered mine.

I looked over at him and tried to focus on his face. "Never mind."

I could read Iann's thoughts in that moment. He was thinking I was a mess.

He's right, you are.

I shakily got to my feet, clutching the table. "I'll be right back."

Iann stood a little easier. "Are you okay—do you need help?" He held out his hand to me.

I shook my head and stumbled to the bathroom. I threw the door shut behind me and knelt over the toilet, immediately purging. It wasn't the alcohol. It was the truth making me sick.

My heart raced, the beat thudding in my ears as I grabbed the counter and got to my feet. I immediately regretted inviting Iann up. I regretted telling him anything about myself, especially after I had tried to forget.

I quietly gargled with mouthwash and surveyed my counter. I knelt down and opened the cabinet under the sink, then reached for that folded toilet paper again. I shook out one of the white pills and threw it into my mouth. I shut the door and swallowed it before grabbing a handful of water from underneath the faucet to help it down.

Gripping the edge of the counter, I looked into the mirror. The dark crescents under my half-shut eyes were more pronounced than before.

I opened the door and staggered back to the kitchen. Iann was standing over my drafting table with his back to me, and my heart sank. What was he looking at now?

He heard me behind him and turned around. "How do you feel?" he asked.

I made it to where he was standing and looked at the table. My sketchbook was laid open to the Mustache drawing. I laughed. "Why are you looking at this?"

He smiled. "I wanted to see how it turned out. He looks great."

I leaned forward into Iann and kissed him. I was suddenly conscious of the fact that I had vomited just moments earlier and pulled away. But he tugged me closer, pressing his warm lips harder against mine and putting his hand behind my ear.

He broke away after a moment. My heart fell through my body and dropped to the floor as he said, "I think you need to rest."

I blinked sleepily. Maybe I had imagined him kissing me back. The regret renewed itself in the pit of my stomach.

He placed his arm around my shoulder and escorted me over to the edge of the bed. "Are you feeling okay?" he asked.

I lay curled up on my side and closed my eyes. I reopened them as I heard the shuffle of fabric. Iann was putting his jacket back on. "Don't leave," I called.

He turned around. "It's okay. I'll let myself out." His cheeks were still flushed from the rum, and his eyes were drooping.

"I don't want to be alone." I closed my eyes again as the room began to shift.

Another rustling of fabric. He removed his jacket. The bed sank beside me as he sat down.

Still lying on my side, I looked up at him. "Is your dog going to be okay?" I asked.

He smiled. "Yeah, my roommate will take him out. I texted him earlier."

I patted the bed next to me. "Lie down," I slurred.

He lay on his side facing me, his hand supporting the side of his head.

"I'm sorry," I said. I felt the heat of tears sting the backs of my eyes. This was why I only got drunk at home alone.

"Sorry for what?"

Sorry I'm like this.

———

Her back is to me. She's wearing the green dress with the blue flowers, but her body isn't that of a ten-year-old. She's tall and slender, auburn hair spilling past her shoulders.

I take a step toward her as my eyes adjust to focus on her in the dark room. She stands in front of a mirror, but my reflection doesn't appear as I approach from behind. I reach out to grab her shoulder. My fingers meet the mirror instead.

I stare into the glass. I'm wearing the dress. My face is my own but prettier, the skin smoother and the eyes blue instead of steel gray. The nose is straighter, the lips fuller.

I press a hand onto the cold mirror.

My fist rears back and strikes the mirror, long cracks branching from the impact. I pull my head back and smash it forward, pieces of glass falling all around me. Blood drips into the cracks. I touch a hand to the bloody veins etched into the glass and drive my forehead into the mirror.

———

My eyes snapped open. I lay still on the bed, my hands shaking. I jolted up when I saw the blood dripping from my palm onto my white blanket.

Unfurling my hand, I saw the cut from the broken pencil had reopened. I looked over at Iann sprawled out facing away from me and slowly rose from the bed. Once I escaped the bed with only a slight creak, I rushed to the kitchen sink and ran the water over my bleeding hand.

Woodstock rubbed against my leg as I turned off the faucet and wrapped a paper towel around my palm. I winced and hissed through my teeth.

Iann stirred on the bed and blinked. His eyes widened as they focused on me, and he shot up to his feet. "What happened?" His voice was hoarse. He wrapped both his hands around mine and lifted up the bloody paper towel. He looked at me when I didn't answer.

I shrugged and pulled away, then ripped another towel from the roll with my free hand. "I tripped the other day, but it started bleeding again."

He edged closer to me and pressed the towel down on my hand.

I struggled for words. A boy hadn't stayed until morning since . . . well, not since Danny. The fact that we hadn't actually done anything only made it more awkward. "Good morning, I guess," I said.

The corner of his mouth tugged into a smile. "Yeah, good morning."

I tucked the napkin around my hand and under my thumb. "Coffee?"

He ran a hand through his pillow hair, making it even wilder. "Yeah, that sounds good. Go ahead and sit down; I'll make it."

"Really? I can do it," I insisted, reaching for the french press.

He was quicker. "I got it," he said, his fingers grasping the handle.

"The kettle is on the stove." I lingered in the kitchen as he surveyed the counter before making his move.

He grabbed the kettle and brought it to the sink. "I've got this. Go sit down," he said over his shoulder.

I sat on the edge of the bed, absently running my fingers along the scar on my neck. My cheeks grew hot as I recalled the previous night. My head pounded, my hangover more painful since I'd added Xanax to the mix. It ached more when I considered all that I had told him.

He didn't seem bothered by it, though. Iann set the french press on the bar and poked his head around the corner. "Where are your mugs?"

Maybe he had forgotten? Best case, he had been less sober than he'd appeared and completely forgotten everything I'd said.

"Oh, above the sink," I said, snapping out of my thoughts.

He disappeared back into the kitchen. The burnt chocolaty aroma wafted throughout the apartment, the clank of ceramic in the background. He reemerged and poured from the press before handing the Snoopy and Woodstock mug to me. He kept the Charlie Brown mug with a chip on the side for himself. He pulled out a chair from the table and turned it to face me before taking a seat. "So, you're a big Charlie Brown fan, huh?"

I glanced at my mug and nodded.

"Where did you find these? I never see this kind of thing anymore," he asked, then took a sip. While he was trying to act cool, this attempt at small talk betrayed the awkwardness of our situation.

I rested the bottom of my mug against my injured palm, the heat soothing and piercing at the same time. "When I first moved here, there used to be a swap meet over on Damen every Saturday." I gestured to Woodstock, his eyes barely visible underneath the TV. "That's where I found the cat too."

He had found me, actually. When I'd reached for those mugs underneath a folding table, he'd been sitting right behind, tufts of his fur sticking up in weird spots, like raging orange flames. He'd followed me when I went to pay for the mugs and then trailed me as I walked back to my apartment. In the following weeks, he had appeared at my door nearly every time I opened it. I'd started leaving a can of tuna in front of the door until one day he came in.

Iann followed my gaze to Woodstock. "He was a stray?"

In a lot of ways, he still was. Some days when I left, he would follow me out and disappear for the day only to return and scratch on the door at night. I let him come and go as he pleased. After all, he had survived in Chicago on his own long before he chose me as his roommate. "Yeah, he followed the mugs home with me. That's why I call him Woodstock." I tapped my fingernail to the yellow bird on my mug.

"I didn't even put that together." Iann laughed.

I took a swig of the coffee. It was much stronger and richer than my brew typically turned out. I still hadn't quite mastered the water-to-bean ratio.

"Sorry," he said. "I'm not very good at making coffee."

"No, it's perfect."

He drained the remaining coffee from his cup. "Well, I guess I need to get back to it," he said, rising up from his chair.

I stood up, my head reeling with sharp pain as if someone were banging on my skull with a chisel. "Back to grading papers?"

He sighed, placing his mug in the sink. "Yep. Someone has to read all those horribly written essays about Freud. If not me, then who?" He smiled and stepped closer toward me. Close enough to kiss, but I kept my face down. "You're probably going to have a pretty bad hangover. Are you going to be okay?"

It was only going to get worse. "Yeah, I'll be fine." My head pulsed as if to disagree.

He grabbed his jacket from the bed and folded it over his forearm. "What's this?" He bent down and picked up a sheet of paper from the floor.

I caught a glimpse over his shoulder at the drawing and lost my breath. It was identical to the one I had ripped to shreds at the studio. Two girls with green dresses facing water. Blood was smudged on the edges, although not as much as on the previous drawing. I tugged it from his grip. "I don't know," I said breathlessly.

He looked at me. "Did you draw that?"

I stared down at the two girls. They were facing toward the water again like in the last drawing. "I don't know."

"Is that real blood?" His eyes were wide as he stared at the drawing.

"I have a headache. I think I need to lie down." I tossed the drawing onto the bed and put my palm to my temple. "I . . . we drank too much last night."

He continued to look at me as he edged toward the door. "Are you really okay?"

I massaged my forehead. "Yeah, I, uh, let's talk later."

He reluctantly stepped outside. "Okay, see you."

I closed the door, latching it behind him before I sprang back to the drawing. The pencil strokes were furious and had worn through the paper in several places.

My foot stepped into something wet, and I recoiled. There were small dark-red puddles on the floor. I bent down on my knees and wiped up the blood with a paper towel, my palm still aching from the cut. I tore off another sheet and wiped another couple of spots away under the corner of my bed.

I walked to the bathroom, shed my clothes, and staggered into the shower. The shock of cold water lasted two seconds too long, and my headache grew worse for it. Looking down, I watched as a stream of black water swirled down the drain. I lifted one foot as a dark puddle formed around it. Dirt was caked on, along with a few leaves. I grabbed the bar of soap on the ledge and furiously scrubbed away at my foot before moving on to the next one.

I sat on the edge of the tub, water trailing down my body and feet, gathering together in a cakey clump of mud right before it swirled down the drain. Leaving the water running, I opened the shower curtain and wrapped a towel around my body and walked over to the bed. I yanked the comforter away on the side I had slept with it wrapped around me. On the sheets, there were dots of blood from my hand, but at the end of the bed, there were dirt and leaves where my feet had been only minutes before.

I ripped the sheets off the bed and flipped the comforter over. In the shower, I rigorously scrubbed at the dirt on the sheets. Goose bumps rose along my skin as I watched the brown leaves trail down into the basin and clog the drain.

CHAPTER EIGHT

Sitting on the bed, I tried to calm myself by stroking Woodstock. The news was on. Unseasonably warm the next few days until rain on Saturday. It wouldn't matter much to me since I was going back into hibernation until my project was finished.

There was a shuffle outside my door, and a paper appeared through the worn rubber sealing and fell to the floor. I listened for quick, heavy footsteps down the stairs outside before leaving the bed and snatching the paper. It was an overdue-rent notice. Typical Bug. He handwrote all his notices in red ink on slightly yellowed paper he got from god knows where.

I crumpled the notice and tossed it onto my nightstand. Now I had one more reason to finish the damn project. I had missed too many days at the studio to make up the difference this early in the month. I settled into my desk chair and pulled out the thumbnail drawing board. Only two more drawings to finalize. As I picked up my pencil, I refocused on the TV playing behind me.

"A murderer is still at large after a young local woman was found strangled in an alley in Wicker Park."

My hand froze the pencil in the middle of the paper, and I spun around in my chair. A picture of Holly was on the screen as the broadcaster continued. Seeing her again was just as jarring.

"Police are asking for anyone with information about this case to come forward. You can call the number at the bottom of the screen."

My fingers pressed down on the pencil. It snapped in half. I threw the remaining fragment onto the table and pushed away. If I was going to pull an all-nighter to make my rent money in time, I would need coffee. The good kind. And lots of it. A small allowance of fresh air probably wouldn't hurt either.

I grabbed my bag and jacket and bounded out the door.

"Who was that guy?" The grating voice arose behind me as I reached the bottom step.

My heart clenched. I turned around to see Bug standing halfway outside his door behind the staircase, cigarette in hand. "What?"

He puffed a big mouthful of smoke and grinned. His teeth were stained terribly. "That boy," he said deliberately. "I saw him last night. He didn't leave until this morning, huh?"

I couldn't fight the sneer that curled my upper lip. I backed away from the steps and shoved my hands deep into my jacket pockets. I turned toward the street, but I heard the rapid scuttle behind me.

"Wait, you owe me," he shouted, tugging at my shoulder.

I pulled out of his grasp. "I know. I'm working on it."

He looked me up and down. "Working on it, how? With your little art projects?" He laughed. "Why don't you get a real job? It's been seven years, and you haven't been able to pay me once on time."

It had been closer to nine, actually. I zipped up my jacket. "Thanks for the career advice, but I have managed to pay you every month," I retorted. "Does it really matter if it's been on time or not?"

He crammed his cigarette between his front teeth and waved me away before returning to his cave. I retreated quickly down the sidewalk, glancing over my shoulder to make sure he was gone.

Turning the corner, I joined the bustle of patrons browsing through a street sale in front of the bookstore. I took a breath and thumbed through the volumes on the cart. I wasn't actually in the position to buy coffee, much less a book, but I couldn't resist looking through them.

"Sarah!" The shout came from down the sidewalk. "Sarah!" The voice and hurried footsteps grew closer and more urgent.

A forceful tug on my shoulder spun me around to face a hysterical middle-aged woman, her eyes puffy and full of fresh tears. "Sarah?" she shouted shakily in my face.

Stunned, I only shook my head, leaning away from her. Her grip tightened around my shoulders. "No," I said.

The woman's pupils darted back and forth, searching for something in my eyes.

A man around my age suddenly ran up to us. "Are you okay?" he asked the woman, taking her hands into his.

She quietly said "Sarah" again and burst into sobs.

The man looked over at me and winced. "I'm so sorry," he said, holding my gaze a second too long. The woman clung to him, her legs wobbling. "Let's go sit down," he said to her and led her away.

Still shaking from the sudden encounter, I looked around and noticed several people outside the bookstore staring at me and the woman hobbling away to a nearby bench.

I hugged my jacket tighter around my waist and ducked into the store. Once I was at the café counter, I glanced out the large window.

The barista followed my gaze. "What was that all about?" he asked, tying his apron around his waist as he walked from the espresso machine to the cash register.

I opened my mouth to try to form an answer, but the man from the sidewalk was suddenly at my side. "Can I get a cup of water real quick?" he asked. The barista nodded and went to grab it for him.

The man looked at me and shook his head. "I'm so sorry about that," he said. He looked at me deeply again with the same expression as the woman. "You look a lot like her daughter and she just—she passed away." He looked very near tears as well.

"Sorry." I couldn't form any other words. I was still shaking from the woman's grasp.

He took the plastic cup of water from the barista and left to rejoin the woman outside.

The barista looked at me again. "What did he say?"

"Medium coffee, please, no room," I said, pulling out my thinning fold of cash.

His expression fell as he printed my receipt.

"Actually, make it a large, please." I unwrapped one more bill.

I grabbed my bag and waited at the bar until he handed me my coffee, reliving the encounter with the woman. I walked to the window in the shop and saw her sitting hunched over on the bench. Her head was in her hands, the man sitting slouched beside her.

They stood up and walked down the street. There were still a few people peering at them from other storefronts after witnessing the odd scene earlier. Once I realized they were going the path opposite of my way home, I left the bookstore.

Was it possible to resemble someone so closely that her own mother could make that mistake?

I readied my keys and floated through the door in a haze, absently stroking the rabbit's foot key chain. Although I didn't see him, Woodstock meowed at me from nearby. I sat at my drafting table and switched on my laptop. I got as far as the blank Google search before I realized I had nothing to search. I tried anyway.

Sarah.

Chicago.

Obituary.

The first page only had a series of pictures of graying and white-haired women of all races. Right. Sarah was a common name across the board. Also, there were two ways to spell Sarah.

Sara.

Chicago.

Obituary.

Same types of results.

Sitting back in my desk chair, I looked through the window to the alleyway across the street. I traced the scar from my ear down to my collarbone. My eyes trained on the slab of dirty concrete between the brick buildings. I could still hear that grating sound.

I scrolled to the search bar and typed something new.

Holly Bascom murder.

Her picture flooded my browser. It was one I hadn't seen before, a professional headshot. She had a smile in it that made me second-guess the resemblance. Had I ever been that happy? I clicked on the first link.

Each article ended with the same call to action. The cops wanted to speak to anyone in the community who had seen anything suspicious the night of Holly's murder. She lived nearby, and it was believed she had called an Uber and was on her way home. They were speaking to her driver, but he was not considered a person of interest.

I wondered if she lived in the building she was killed outside of. Was she only moments from getting home and being safe in bed? If I had been on the street just a few seconds before her, would I be dead? My eyes grazed over the suggested links in the corner of the site and locked onto one word in a headline: *Sarah.*

I clicked without reading the full title, and immediately a photo loaded. Almost identical to Holly. Almost identical to *me.* In the picture Sarah Jenkins was outdoors with her hands on her hips, standing on a rock in front of a waterfall. She was fit and young, her hair highlighted several shades lighter than mine. I recalled the woman who had accosted me in front of the bookstore. With my pallor and darker hair, she'd probably thought I was a ghost of her daughter. There wasn't a chance I truly was mistakable for this healthy, vibrant woman.

Like Holly, she looked like how I expected Issi would have.

Sarah lived in Logan Square with her fiancé and daughter. Back in July, she had called her fiancé on the walk home and never showed up. The next morning, she was reported missing, but her body wasn't found until a week later, underneath the train line that went over West Schiller Street, less than a block from the studio. The police didn't have any leads on this one, either, or at least not any public leads. She had been strangled, and there were signs of sexual assault.

My stomach turned.

The police estimated she'd been murdered the night she was walking home, and her body lay there the entire time she was missing. Her family said she wouldn't have traveled through alleyways or by the train at night because it was dangerous. They believed someone brought her there and then killed her.

I turned off the screen and put both my elbows on the desk, cradling the sides of my head. What were the chances? There had already been two people with my exact face, me and Issi. But two *other* girls with a striking resemblance in the same city?

A shadow appeared from the corner of my eye outside the window, and a booming knock sounded on the door. I jumped, my feet raising slightly off the carpet. I couldn't get a clear look at the person in the corner of the window, but I saw a shoulder. I crept quietly to the front door and raised my eye to the peephole.

A man wearing a crumpled slate-gray suit stood in front of my door, looking directly into the peephole. I instinctively ducked down, and he knocked again. Door-to-door salesman? Unkempt Jehovah's Witness? He looked worn out, his forehead creased in three harsh lines.

"Police!" he announced in a monotone voice, the door rattling under my hands as he knocked. "I just have a few questions." He reached for a wallet from inside his suit.

Without opening the door, I called out, "Do you have a badge?"

He turned back to the door when he heard my voice and opened his wallet, holding a badge up to the peephole. Chicago PD.

It was probably a real badge. They sold souvenir badges to tourists downtown, but this was *most* likely real.

I opened the door and peered out. "How can I help you?"

The man straightened up. "I'm Detective Wilder. We're currently investigating a suspected homicide in the area," he recited, his tone growing flatter with each syllable.

Suspected homicide? What else could it be?

"A few days ago the body of a young woman was discovered in the alley just across the street from you. I've been interviewing people in the neighborhood to see if anyone saw or heard anything. I stopped by your place before, but you were out, I guess." He glanced over the top of my head into my apartment.

I narrowed the gap between my body and the door. "Homicide?" I asked. I didn't know why I was acting coy. Half the neighborhood had huddled around when Holly's body was recovered.

He stared at me for a second. "Yes, a body was found just a few days ago. Have you been out of town?"

"No, I've just been busy."

He observed me for a long moment. "Do you have a minute to answer a few questions?"

I nodded, the alcohol from the night before burning the edge of my throat, threatening to come up. "Absolutely."

He glanced behind me at the door half-open. "Is there a reason I can't come in?"

I stepped out and let the door completely shut behind me. "I have a cat. He might get out," I said.

He pulled out one of those tiny notepads as if we were on *Law & Order* and jotted something down. Something about my cat, I guessed. He looked back up at me. "What's your full name?"

I hesitated. Where would this information appear if I told him? If I told him about that night, would a reporter show up next and cite me as a witness? *You're not a kid anymore. He can't do anything to you.* Still, I couldn't bear the thought that he might find me here. "Isabella Mallen," I lied.

His pen halted its crawl across the notepad. He took a moment to review his paper before glancing at me through narrowed eyes. "Isabella?"

I nodded.

"Where were you on August seventh around midnight?"

That grating metal sound echoed through my mind. "I was walking home from work around that time."

"Where do you work?"

"The Tipsy Paintbrush. It's one of those wine and painting places," I elaborated.

He gestured behind him to the alleyway across the street. "So you would have been passing right by that alley around that time?"

I sighed. "Yeah, I guess so."

He looked at me sidelong. "Did you hear or see anything?"

My stomach flipped again. That sound could have been anything. *You know what it was.* "I *may* have seen a shadow . . . and I heard a, uh . . ." I paused. "A metallic scratching sound around there." I nodded over to the alley.

"And?" He stopped writing and looked at me.

I glanced away. "That's it."

"You didn't check to see where that sound was coming from?" he prodded.

You could have saved her. "It could've just been the L," I said. The image of the darkness in the alley as I looked over my shoulder flashed before me.

"How long have you lived here?"

"A few years," I answered.

"So after a few years, you don't know what the L sounds like?" He narrowed his eyes and looked me up and down.

My muscles tensed. "I didn't think the sound was that strange. It could've been anything."

"Okay. Do you know Holly Bascom? Did you ever meet her?" He handed a photo to me. It was the same one from the news. "Do you recognize her?"

I swallowed and gave it back to him. "No."

He returned it to his coat pocket. "Have we met before?"

I put my hand behind my back and rested it on the doorknob. "No, I don't think so."

"You look really familiar," he continued.

"I get that a lot," I muttered. "Is that all, Detective?"

"Yes, but if you remember anything else later or if you hear something, please let me know." He flipped through his wallet and handed a business card over to me.

I took it and nodded. "Okay."

He turned to walk back down the stairs. "Really, if you think of *anything*, let me know." He started down the first step.

"Should I be concerned?" I called after him.

He looked over his shoulder and then pivoted back to me. "I mean, you should always be alert and stay cautious at night," he said.

"Yeah, but, is this connected with that other murder? By Logan Square?"

He held my gaze, his eyebrows raised. "You mean the woman found by the train?" His surprise wasn't encouraging. Was this the first time he'd considered a connection?

"Yes, Sarah Jenkins."

He pursed his lips. "We're investigating both murders separately, for now." He turned to walk away again.

"That sound I heard," I started, and he stopped where he was. "That wasn't . . . that doesn't have anything to do with the case, right?"

He stepped back over to me again, his brow creased. "I really can't say," he said through his teeth. "We're not releasing any details about the crime scene to the public at this time." It was a canned response. Something they had to say to the media and nosy neighbors.

As he walked away, I turned the doorknob behind me, almost tripping over Woodstock as I backed in through the door.

Wilder was either a bad detective or I didn't resemble Holly as much as I'd originally believed.

———

I open my eyes against the pressure of water weighing my lids down.

In the cold water, Issi's face is before mine. Instead of swimming, I reach out and touch her face. As my hand touches her cheek, her eyes flash open.

She wraps a red cloth around my neck and pulls. Her eyes unflinching, her face withered and pruney.

My arms dangle out in front of me in the water, motionless as I gulp and choke. My throat seals shut.

———

I gagged and coughed, expelling the imaginary water from my lungs. My eyes fluttered open as my phone chimed. There was a text from Erin.

Erin (10:11 p.m.): Look who I found!

Attached to Erin's text was a dimly lit picture of her and Jeremy with Iann in the background behind a bar counter. His eyelids were heavy. I could only assume they were at the Robey. There were several other blurrier pictures of her cocktail and the rooftop sent all within a thirty-minute period.

The most recent message was from Iann.

Iann (12:01 a.m.): Are you awake?

I groaned and lifted my head up just long enough to prop my elbow and hand underneath. I typed out my response with one hand.

Yeah.

I rubbed my eyes while my phone buzzed beside me.

Iann (12:13 a.m.): Your friend is really wasted. Can you come pick her up?

Of course she was. I pulled up Erin's number and dialed. The ringing disappeared into the sound of her excited scream over a background of jazz music. "Harp—er!" she yelled.

I yanked the phone away from my ear. I was definitely awake now. "Are you drunk?"

She laughed. "Oh, yeah!"

"Okay, stay there. I'm coming over."

She continued yelling right before she hung up on me.

I stood up and glanced down at my black leggings and oversize blue sweater, the knit fabric stretched out from me folding my legs underneath it when I sat at my desk. I pulled my longest coat out from behind the desk and zipped it up before tugging my boots on. As I opened the door, the wind whipped my hair across my neck. I paused at the top of the stairs and texted Iann back.

On my way.

CHAPTER NINE

I hadn't ever been inside the Robey Hotel although it had often made an appearance in my sketches. The hotel was the tallest landmark in Wicker Park and the earliest skyscraper constructed outside of downtown. It had survived the neighborhood's darker days and was the revitalized art deco icon that beckoned the trendy bohemian crowd through its doors. Now it was best known for its rooftop bars on each tower, the highest and better-known bar being the Up Room.

The Up Room was classier than the other places Erin usually dragged me to. When we first met, she'd managed to smuggle me into many downtown bars when I was nineteen, before she left for rehab. While she didn't party quite like she used to, she couldn't let the alcohol go.

The sound of Erin's chatter reached me as soon as the elevator doors opened on the top floor. Vibey indie music played from overhead speakers, and the lights were low and ambient, particularly where Iann stood beside Erin in the back corner. He set a glass of water on the table in front of her, then pushed up the rolled sleeves of his black button-up shirt. He looked up as I approached, and smiled. "Hey—"

"Harper!" Erin interrupted, reaching up from her chair to hug me, her eyes half-closed.

I waved her arms away. "What's going on?" I turned to Iann.

He tugged on his tousled hair, making it even more disheveled. He pushed the water closer toward Erin, but she knocked it over onto the wood table. He didn't even flinch. "I don't know, she came here with Jeremy and stayed after he left and just kept drinking."

"Why did you keep giving her drinks?" I accused, setting the glass back upright.

He ruffled his hair again. "She seemed fine until a little while ago," he said. "And she got more drinks from Mike whenever I stepped out." He gestured to the bar, where a man with a shaved head and bold-framed glasses stood, wiping down the counter.

I believed him on both accounts. Erin could down a lot of alcohol before she started acting like a lunatic. And she became surprisingly crafty whenever people tried to cut her off.

"Sorry," he continued. "We're about to close, and I didn't know who else to contact. I tried to call her a car, but she's refusing to leave at all."

I sat in the seat across from Erin. She was slumped back in her chair, her skirt precariously edging up her thigh. "Erin," I said, my voice still hoarse from sleep.

Her eyes widened suddenly. "Harper!" She grabbed for my hand.

"You've got to get up. I'm taking you home."

Iann shifted beside me. "I brought my car, so if you can wait with her until I get off in a few, I'll give you both a ride."

I didn't relish the idea of fighting and dragging her all the way to her apartment on my own. "Okay, we'll be here."

He dashed back to the bar as the last few customers walked to the elevators, casting curious looks over their shoulders at Erin. Mike glanced at us and nodded before Iann reached over the bar and grabbed his jacket.

Erin slipped back into her seat and closed her eyes. I shook her shoulder, and one eye popped open.

"Okay, he's going to finish everything on his own, so I can give you a ride now," Iann said, pulling his jacket on. "Is she asleep?"

I stood and shook her more vigorously. "Erin, come on."

She straightened in her seat long enough for me to wrap my arm around her before she slumped over.

"Do you need help with—"

I shook my head. "No, I've got her. Let's go."

We got to the elevator, and she slouched in a corner as we rode down.

"Is she normally like this?" Iann asked, fishing his keys from his pocket. "It doesn't seem like you're surprised."

I shrugged. "Sometimes." But usually not without reason. "Did she and Jeremy fight or something?"

"I have no idea. We were really busy around the time they came in. They seemed fine."

I put my arm back around Erin as the elevator opened, and we walked out, Iann holding the door behind us.

"Why don't you wait here, and I'll pull my car up front?"

I nodded, and Iann sprang out the back door.

The doorman nodded at Iann as he passed before quickly walking over to us. "Here, I'll get the door for you," he said. He swung the heavy wood door open to the street, eyeing Erin.

"Thanks," I muttered, straining to walk over the threshold. She was falling asleep again, and her legs weren't moving. I shook her shoulder once we were on the sidewalk, and she snorted, her eyes flying open. "Are you okay?"

She turned her head and rested it on my shoulder. "Thank you," she slurred.

Iann's Jeep turned the corner, and he pulled up to us before getting out.

"For what?" I asked her.

"For coming."

Iann opened the door and helped me lay Erin onto the back seat. She immediately fell down across the vinyl.

"I'll ride up front," I said.

"Where do you want me to take you?" Iann asked, buckling his seat belt.

I glanced back at Erin. Her roommates were the worst, and they would just leave her passed out in her room without a second thought. "Can you take us to my place?" I turned to the front and leaned back against the headrest as he started down the street. "I'm glad you texted me. About Erin, I mean."

He smiled. "I'm glad you came. I had no idea what to do with her. She tried to start a fight with a waitress."

I laughed. "What?"

He rubbed his eyes. "Yeah, she started yelling at one of the waitresses and threw a drink at her. Mike wanted to call the police, but I convinced them not to, and we told the waitress to go home a little early."

"Was she like that when Jeremy was there?"

He shook his head. "No, she seemed really normal and quiet until, like, an hour after he left. I have no idea what happened." He slowed down, peering out his window. "This is your place, right?"

The unlit, slouched, unpainted wood shack? "Yes, that's the one."

We both got out once he parked, and he met me at the back. "How should we get her out?" he asked as we looked at her.

I grabbed her shoulder. "Erin, wake up."

She pulled on my arm to hoist herself up. "Where are we?"

I slid my arm around her waist and guided her to the edge of the car seat. "You're staying with me tonight, okay?"

She limply placed both feet on the sidewalk. "Okay."

Iann put his arm around her other shoulder, and we slowly started up the stairs, the sound of Erin's heels dragging across the wood.

In front of my door, a rock dropped into the pit of my stomach. The door was ajar, and the lights were off.

"What's wrong?" Iann asked before turning to the door.

I took a step back. "My door's open."

Iann released Erin's arm and pushed the door wide open. "Are you sure you locked it?"

I couldn't remember, but I nodded. "And the lights were all on when I left."

"Go back downstairs. We should call the police." He pulled his cell phone from his pocket.

I shifted under Erin's weight, remembering that detective from before. Surely, if there was a burglary in this neighborhood, he would find out about it and start asking more questions. Questions about who I was. And questions about how I had a key chain that looked an awful lot like Holly's. "No. I'm sure it's fine. Maybe I just don't remember." I had left in a hurry, but I knew for a fact the lights and TV had been on.

"Stay here—I'll check it out." He reached his arm in and flicked on the overhead light, then disappeared inside.

I strained my ears for any sound. "Is everything okay?" I called.

Erin lifted her head suddenly. "Yeah, it's fine," she said.

I rolled my eyes. "Not you," I muttered. "Iann?"

I stepped over the threshold and set Erin on the bed.

Iann emerged from the bathroom. "I think everything's fine. But don't you think we should call the police just in case?"

I glanced around the room. Woodstock was perched on my drafting table, looking at Iann with his ears pressed back against his head. "It doesn't look like anyone has been in here." Still, my hands were shaking. Why couldn't I remember if I'd locked the door?

He looked at Erin on the bed, her head against my pillow. "Okay, well, I'll get out of here if you're really all right." He stepped toward the door.

"I'll walk you out," I said, closing the door behind us.

We lingered at the top of the stairs. "Are you sure you left the lights on?" he asked again.

I massaged my temple, my head still aching from the night before. "Maybe not. I haven't really been sleeping well," I confessed. "I'm sorry. You can't catch a break."

He cocked his head to the side. "What do you mean?"

I nodded back inside. "Dealing with drunk girls two days in a row."

He laughed and looked down at his feet. "Yeah, well, at least you're a friendly drunk."

I narrowed my eyes. "Am I?"

"Well, definitely more friendly than when you're sober," he said with a smile. "Plus, it gave me a chance to see you again."

It felt unnatural to have someone speak so earnestly like that. "Yeah," I said in a weak effort to reciprocate. "Thanks again for looking out for her. She can be kind of a mess sometimes."

"No problem." He turned and started down the steps.

I wanted to keep him longer, but there was nothing more to say. "Good night."

He reached the last step and looked back, raising his hand and waving before getting into his car. I watched his car disappear down the street and walked back into my apartment.

Erin was exactly in the position I'd left her in, her arms outstretched by her sides. I took her heels off and threw them to the floor before turning off the light and crawling onto the comforter beside her and collapsing.

Maybe I had turned off the lights before leaving.

CHAPTER TEN

"Harper!"

The strangled scream startled me awake. My eyes opened, and I was staring down at my hands pressing against Erin's shoulders, her eyes wide.

She pushed against me, and I fell down on the bed. "What the fuck?" she screamed. She sat up and rubbed her arms. "What are you doing, you psycho!"

I rolled to my side. "I—what happened?"

She inched away from me on the bed. "Were you asleep?"

I raised a hand to my forehead.

"I woke up and you were on top of me! You almost choked me!" Her voice was piercing.

I propped myself up on my elbow. It was light outside. "Sorry, I—" My wrists ached. "I don't know what happened."

"I told you what happened. God, what's wrong with you?"

I ran a hand over my face. My thoughts were hazy, like I was still asleep. "I'm sorry."

She glared at me, resting her head against the wall. "Why am I here anyway?" She glanced around the apartment, her upper lip slightly raised when she saw the growing tower of dishes in the sink.

"You got drunk at the Up Room, and I came to get you."

Her anger subsided. "Oh." She frowned. "Iann called you?"

I nodded, massaging my searing wrists. "Yeah. What happened last night?"

She shook her head and crossed her arms over her chest. "You remember Jeremy? Well, he's an asshole."

I waited for more, but she just closed her eyes. "What did he do?" *Do you really care?*

She took a long, deep breath before turning to me. "Do you think I'm shallow?" She looked close to tears.

Yes. "No," I said in a hurry. "Why? Did he say that to you?"

"Yeah, he made it clear last night that he thinks I'm a shallow idiot." She pushed her hair away from her eyes, smudging her day-old mascara around the edges. "Anyway, it doesn't matter." Her eyes suddenly widened. "So, how did Iann have your phone number?" she asked with a grin.

Dammit. I looked away.

"Oh my god! Are you seeing him?"

"No." I groaned. She was so loud. Maybe she was still a little drunk. "We ran into each other the other day. Nothing more than that."

She raised her eyebrows. "Okay, sure. He's a cool guy, though."

"How would you know? You just met him too."

She glanced down quickly, and her smile weakened. "Yeah, but I can tell."

I fiddled with the edge of the blanket in my hands. "I don't know why he's even interested in me."

She stared at me, tugging at a strand of stray hair on my shoulder. "You're a mess, Harper," she said. "Guys like girls like you."

"Like me?"

She nodded. "Yeah, beautiful and damaged. They want to try to fix you. And when that doesn't work, they move on." Her matter-of-fact tone pissed me off. "Hell, that's probably the only reason I still hang out with you. Trying to help you makes me feel better about all the crazy shit I do."

My fists hurt from gripping the blanket so tightly.

"I'm going to take a shower." She poised herself on the edge of the bed, casting a wary look at Woodstock hunched on the kitchen counter facing her.

"Towels are by the toilet," I said, sinking back into the sheets.

She stood up, bracing her arm against the wall as she staggered to the bathroom.

I turned on my side, toward the window and door. My eyes drifted to the floor, and I shot up to my feet. There were faint shoe prints leading to and from the door and around the edge of the bed. They were big, bigger than mine, and clearly not made by Erin's high heels. I followed them around the corner of the bed, where they stopped. I looked at the door again. It was locked.

They must've been from Iann when he came inside last night, right? I stared down at the shoe prints until Erin emerged from the bathroom nearly thirty minutes later. She walked to the kitchen and opened the fridge. "Do you want to grab some breakfast? I'm starving," she said, closing it with a slam. She was wearing the same short dress from the night before, her wet cropped hair hovering just above the neckline.

I crossed my toe over one of the shoe prints, smudging it along the warped wood floor. "No, I really need to start working." My phone buzzed on the nightstand, and I reached to grab it. It was from a blocked number. My heart started racing.

You don't know that it's him.

I rejected it, and it immediately started buzzing again.

"Okay," Erin said with a shrug. She grabbed her heels from the floor and walked past me to the door.

I followed behind her. "Are you going to be okay—about Jeremy?"

"Oh yeah, screw that guy." She unlocked the door and turned the knob.

"But you seemed really upset about it," I said quietly.

She hesitated but didn't turn around. "It's fine. I'm over it." She glanced at me, now with a smile. "Thanks for coming to get me."

I nodded. I watched her stumble down the first couple of steps and then closed the door. I faced the tracks of mud again. My foot was small beside them. I stepped over the dirt and unlocked my phone. There were no messages. Why was I disappointed? Shit, what if Erin was right? Maybe I did want Iann to text me. But maybe he'd already realized I was a lost cause and given up.

My stomach rumbled. I should've taken Erin up on her offer for breakfast. Surely she would've paid. Well, maybe not after how she woke up. I rubbed my wrists, still throbbing from the grip I'd held on her shoulders. I stood and grabbed my sweater from the floor and pulled it over my T-shirt. There was still time to catch the Sunday taco truck before it moved on to Bucktown. I picked up my bag from the floor and crammed a five-dollar bill into my back pocket before opening the door and jogging down the steps. I halted at the last step when I heard a car door slam.

Detective Wilder was walking around his car parked at the curb, heading toward me.

I resumed walking until he intercepted my path.

"Good morning," he said. "I have some more questions for you."

"I'm headed somewhere," I said absently.

"This'll just take a second."

I gripped the handle of my bag harder. "I'm not sure I'll be of much help but okay."

"Great," he said, leaning closer. "Let's start with your real name."

Goose bumps rose along my arms. "What?"

He positioned himself between me and the sidewalk. "Isabella Mallen died fifteen years ago."

I swallowed. Why had I even bothered lying? I guessed I'd been hoping he wouldn't care enough to check.

"Do you know it's a criminal offense to lie about your identity to a police officer?"

I heard a shuffle behind me and turned. Bug was standing outside his door, watching us with big eyes, one hand on the knob.

"Do you know him?" Wilder asked, nodding to Bug.

"He's my landlord," I said, my heart still racing. "Can we talk somewhere else about this?"

Still looking at Bug, he nodded. "We can talk at the station."

I froze. "No," I said quickly. "Let's walk." I started toward the sidewalk, hoping he would follow. He did. A little too closely. "Am I in trouble?" I dared to ask once we were down the street. I stopped and turned to him, spotting the taco truck over his shoulder in the distance.

His gaze softened. "It depends. Why did you lie? What's your real name?"

"Harper Mallen," I breathed. "I-I didn't want to get caught up in all of this."

He wasn't satisfied with that. "What do you mean 'caught up' in this?"

"I don't want my name in any public record. I don't want my family to know where I am."

He looked down at his shoes. "Why not?"

I quickened my pace. "You couldn't figure that out, but you could find out that Isabella was dead?"

"I want to hear it from you," he said.

"I ran away from home when I was a kid."

He nodded. "You can understand why you lying to me like this is concerning, right? Especially in a murder investigation."

Yes. But I started to feel more with each step that he couldn't really do anything to me about it. "Will you excuse me for a minute?" I continued past him up to the window at the truck. "Two carne asada and egg tacos, please."

Wilder appeared by my side as I fished the money from my back pocket and handed it to the sweaty man inside.

"What do you want from me?" I asked in a low voice, stepping back from the window to wait.

He ran a hand along the back of his neck. "Look," he began. "I'm going to level with you. I didn't think last week's murder was related to the Jenkins murder. Until you mentioned it."

I could feel the heat rising to my cheeks. *Why did you say anything?*

"When I looked into it, you were right: there are a lot of similarities." He paused. "And now I realized where I'd seen you before, or why I thought I had." He pulled two photos from his pocket and held them out in front of him, close to my face. He nodded and lowered them. "Why do you think these murders are connected?"

Be honest or lie? "I saw Holly and Sarah on the news, and I thought there was a resemblance. That's it." I chose honesty. There wasn't a reason to lie anymore. He knew everything.

Wilder nodded. "You're right. Why didn't you say anything last time we spoke?"

"I *did* say something," I snapped. "That's why you're here right now."

He leaned back and shifted his weight, frowning.

The man reemerged at the taco truck window and nodded to me, extending two rolls of foil.

"Thanks," I said, walking over to grab them and then returning to the sidewalk, where Wilder was standing with his arms crossed now. "I would have thought the connection would be obvious to the police," I continued once I was back in earshot.

"Is there anything else you want to tell me?" He stepped beside me. "Is there anyone that may be targeting you?"

I paused, letting my hand with the tacos fall to my side. "What?"

"Surely it must've occurred to you that you may be the true target of all this?"

I turned to look at him. "I—what do you mean?"

"Do you think it's just a weird coincidence that two girls who look remarkably like you turn up dead in your neighborhood?" I could tell from his cocky smile that he felt vindicated after my insults.

"I—"

"I mean, this last one was just right across the street from you. So, again, is there anyone that would be trying to target you?"

I shrugged. "No."

He uncrossed his arms. "I'm not trying to scare you or anything," he said.

Could've fooled me. I held his gaze. "You didn't."

He chuckled. "Good. Keep an eye out, then, and let me know if you remember anything." He pulled out a business card.

"I already have one," I muttered.

He flicked the edge of the card with his index finger before returning it to his pocket. "Right. Well, be careful." He pointed to my hand. "And enjoy your tacos, I guess."

I thought about the blocked calls, about Holly, as I watched him go back down my street. There was a nagging response in my mind to Wilder's question about whether anyone would target me specifically.

He might.

CHAPTER ELEVEN

I rubbed at my heavy eyes all throughout teaching the class how to paint an obnoxiously neon boom box for the '80s-themed night. This particular class was made up of mostly middle-aged women having a night out along with a smattering of college kids who definitely weren't alive in the '80s.

Erin appeared at my side as I made the rounds. I couldn't even try to smile at everyone as I talked. "Are you okay?" she whispered. "You look like shit."

"Thanks." I scowled.

"Couldn't sleep again?" She followed me back up to the front of the classroom. "Because of that book thingy?"

I was waiting on feedback on the latest illustrations. "No."

I turned to the class, attempting to drown out their booming voices. "Spray the finishing coat on your paintings, and you're all ready to go. I've enjoyed having you. Come find me if you have any questions." I looked at Erin. "I'm fine," I told her as everyone started gathering their items. "Just stressed out."

"Well, to be perfectly honest," she started with a scandalous grin, "I haven't been getting much sleep either. Jeremy and I have been seeing a lot of each other."

"Oh, I didn't realize that was still going on. What about—"

Her smile flickered. "That was a misunderstanding. We worked it out. I mean, we're not exclusive or anything, but we're going out again."

I gritted my teeth to refrain from rolling my eyes. There were heavier things on my mind other than Erin's love life. "Hey, have you seen that story in the news about the girl who got killed on my street?"

She cast a glance at a couple of women leaving. "Not since it first broke, why?"

I shook my head. "No reason." I reached for my paintbrushes, but Erin snatched them away from me.

"It's okay," she said, waving a hand at me. "I'll clean everything up. You should go get some sleep."

I slung my bag over my shoulder. "Okay, thanks." Without another word to her, I pushed past the lingering women and went into the parking lot.

"Hey!"

I jumped, turning toward the voice. Iann closed his car door and strode over to me.

"What are you doing here?" I asked.

He stood beside me, hands in his pockets. Did I make him uncomfortable? I wanted to bother him, to make him feel something when he saw me.

He glanced toward the studio. "Jeremy left his painting behind last time, and I happened to be in the area, so I came to pick it up for him," he said, gesturing to the shop.

"She's about to close up," I said as another few people left through the front door. "Can you give me a ride home?"

His eyes widened, and he nodded. "Yeah, of course. Do you want to just wait in the car while I get the painting?"

"Yeah." I opened the passenger door and watched through the glass window as he walked up to Erin. Was I imagining the familiarity between them? Iann reached into his coat pocket and handed something to Erin, although I couldn't make out what from that distance.

She smiled and put a hand on his shoulder before giving him the painting over the counter. I wished it had been a lie, a ruse to see me after work. Then again, why wouldn't Jeremy want to pick it up himself? Maybe Iann *did* want to see me.

My phone buzzed in my hand.

Unknown caller.

I closed my eyes and felt the pressure on my lungs, the same sensation from my nightmares. The crushing water filled my mouth, and I could taste the icy pulp of lake scum again.

I rejected the call and leaned my head back against the seat.

The car door opened, and Iann climbed into the seat beside me. "Okay, all set." He buckled his seat belt after a second of observing me in the dark. "Are you all right?"

My phone buzzed again. This time with a voice mail notification. I deleted it right away. "Yeah, I'm fine," I said through gritted teeth. "So why were you in this part of town?"

He turned the key, and the engine roared to life. "I worked at the bar this afternoon. I just got off." I could see his black button-up under his jacket, the collar flipped up on one side.

I stared into my reflection in the window, the streetlights passing orbs across my image. I didn't see me. I saw Sarah. And Holly. And, of course, Issi.

Iann pulled the car over on the street in front of my building. "Are you sure you're okay? You seem really quiet tonight."

I held my eyes steady on my reflection. "Come in with me." I didn't have the patience for pretense tonight.

Seeing Wilder again had rattled me. Not because of the investigation but because he'd confirmed what I'd feared. I was just a copy. The lesser half of a whole.

Once Iann followed me inside, I pressed my lips against his, our mouths open and hot. I edged us both toward the bed and broke away to pull at the buttons on his shirt. I ran my hands over his collarbone and slid his shirt off as I traced over his bare shoulders. I caught a glimpse of a tattoo on his tricep.

He tugged off my jacket, but I gently pushed him onto the bed before he could reach my shirt. My hands and cheeks burned more with each kiss as I joined him on the bed. We looked at each other, and still silent, he brushed my hair away from my shoulders.

His eyebrows wrinkled for a moment, and he traced the scar on my neck. I took his hand in mine and leaned into his chest. I wasn't like Holly or Sarah or even Issi. I was alive. And I was with Iann, his hands cool against the burning flesh on my back, making my hair stand on end.

———

My pillow smelled of coffee and cologne. I rolled over and looked at the cruel light peeking through the blinds of the living room window.

Iann had woken up a few hours before dawn, saying that he had to teach a class in a couple of hours. I had tried to believe him and woke up long enough to see him out the door as he muttered the promise of breakfast some other time.

Then I had crawled back under my down comforter, hoping to capture any remaining hours on the most solid night of sleep I'd had in months.

A few hours later when I officially woke up, I heard meowing. The bed sank as Woodstock jumped up. He slinked over to my pillow and licked my chin. He often performed this morning ritual, but he usually licked my closed eyelids.

It was chilly inside. The coolness of the sheets soothed my aching legs.

I scratched the top of Woodstock's head and sat up. His fur also felt a little cold. I picked him up and carried him across the room to the kitchen counter.

I set him down in front of his food and water bowls. That's when I realized that the window by the front door was cracked open to about a Woodstock-height gap. I rushed over to the window and shut it. I didn't remember opening the window the night before. I didn't leave the window open for Woodstock—I only opened the door whenever he yowled outside. I looked down at the cluster of twigs and weeds on the floor in front of the door.

I blinked sleepily at the debris and went back to the kitchen. Coffee first, then cleaning. I set the kettle on the stove top, making a mental note to do the dishes later.

After turning on the heater and throwing on my knit blanket, I pulled up the news on my phone. There weren't any updates on Holly's or Sarah's cases.

I had spiraled last night because of all this and thrown myself at Iann. Maybe I was focusing on something that wasn't really there. I clicked on the photo of Holly again. No, it was undeniable.

I set my phone down, glancing over the counter to my keys on the drafting table. Even from that distance, something seemed different. I shuffled the sketch pads and loose paper on the table, lifting up and shaking each item.

The rabbit's foot was missing. How?

CHAPTER TWELVE

I took a deep breath and walked into the restaurant. Iann's dinner invitation had been a nice surprise after last night. It was fancy but with booths and stools like a diner. Iann was setting down a white coffee mug after taking a sip. He looked up, standing as I walked over to the table.

"Hi," he said with a relieved smile.

I sat across from him. "Hey," I said in return. It had been years since I'd had this tingling, antsy sensation in my gut. Too many years ago.

"Thanks for coming."

I scanned the half-empty bar beside us. All the possible outcomes of this conversation were flashing before my eyes, my stomach churning. When I dared to look up, Iann was gazing at me. That look made me more nervous. I was so much more broken now than a few years ago, and I hadn't even been able to make a relationship work back then. "What?" I asked.

He shook his head. "I'm glad you showed up. I didn't think you would."

He already seemed to know a lot about me. I almost hadn't shown up. I had paced in front of the record store at the corner, turning on my heel in the opposite direction several times before taking a big breath and charging into the restaurant. "Why wouldn't I?"

He shrugged and set his menu facedown on the table. "I don't know—I had a feeling you wouldn't."

"So, what are we doing here?"

He glanced around the restaurant. "We're . . . eating dinner?" He laughed.

"You didn't have to do this because of last night."

He gagged on his sip of coffee before setting the mug down with a clink. "I'm not. Is it *that* unbelievable that I want to spend time with you?"

Yes. I leaned back in my chair. "Not unbelievable but a little odd. I mean, we don't even know each other, really. Why do you want to spend time with me?"

"I think we know each other pretty well now."

Despite his attempts at invasive questions, we'd only really scratched the surface about my family or life. But pointing this out would only lead to more questions.

"And from what I know, I like," he continued.

I wasn't sure exactly what I felt about him yet. I hadn't *liked* anyone in years, not since Danny.

"I lied to you, you know," he said, smugly taking another drink. "I didn't come by the studio only to pick up Jeremy's shitty art last night."

I smirked. "Yeah, I figured." Although I was pretty sure he got more than he was expecting.

He glanced around the restaurant. "This place is a little louder than I thought it'd be. Do you want to get out of here? I can make something for us back at my place."

Something in his voice melted away the remainder of my defenses. Those barriers had taken years to build and all it took to level them to the ground was a handsome man showing interest. "Are we talking real food or PB&Js?"

He laughed. "Believe it or not, I can actually cook."

Another reason to lean into whatever this was between him and me. "Okay. You have my interest."

"Well, now I feel like I may have oversold my skills." He grabbed his wallet, fished out a few dollars, and placed them by his empty coffee cup.

A waiter lazily slouched by the bar glanced at us as we stood up from the table.

As we approached the door, a girl walked past the window. Seeing her face sent a chill through me. *My* face. I rushed out ahead of Iann to the sidewalk in a trance. I took a few steps toward her as she walked away. I opened my mouth to call out to her.

"Hey! Is everything okay?" Iann asked, appearing by my side.

My eyes snapped away from the girl's bouncing brunette ponytail, and I turned to face him. "Nothing, I—thought I saw someone . . . I know."

———

By the time we arrived at Iann's apartment, I'd nearly forgotten about the girl. I felt so light, walking through downtown with his hand in mine.

Leo was another welcome distraction. He pawed at my lap as I sat at the bar, and then he dug at the hem of my pants where most of Woodstock's fur had gathered. Iann's place was much bigger and cleaner than mine but smaller than Erin's. There were absolutely no decorations, just a TV, sofa, and wood kitchen table with mismatched chairs.

"Nice place," I said. "How long have you lived here?"

"A little over a year now."

I gestured to the empty eggshell-white walls. "Why is everything so . . . bland?"

He laughed. "I guess it is. I don't know, I usually only sleep here and take the dog out, so I guess this is good enough for me. And every other semester, I get a new roommate, so there's really no point in putting my stuff all around." He walked around the counter. "Do you want coffee?"

"Do you have beer?"

"Always." He opened the fridge and pulled out a dark bottle and slid it to me across the counter. He closed the fridge and walked toward me with his own bottle.

I took a swig of the beer before setting it back on the granite. "So, what are we eating?"

Iann placed his bottle next to mine. "What are your thoughts on pasta?"

"Edible. Delicious."

He smiled. "Fantastic. The bar is pretty low if we're just shooting for 'edible.'" He opened the pantry and pulled out a box of angel-hair pasta and walked to the fridge, extracting a small carton of heavy cream and bacon.

"I hope you have a plan . . ."

He grabbed two pots from under the oven and placed them on the front burner. "Don't worry. I make this all the time."

For who? Surely he didn't make rich pasta dishes for himself all the time.

I stood beside him as he emptied the heavy cream into one of the pots and filled the other with water before replacing it on the burner.

As the cream began to simmer, he opened a cabinet and pulled out a handful of spice containers, then sprinkled each into the pot and stirred.

"Is that cayenne pepper?" I asked as the small red dots disappeared into the sauce.

He nodded, filling the spoon in his hands with the cream and then bringing it to his lips. His eyes lit up. "This is amazing. Do you want to try?"

"Uh, sure."

He extended the spoon toward me.

It *was* amazing. The salt and spice blended perfectly with the creamy texture.

"Well?" Iann set the spoon on the counter.

This was all straying away from casual and right into romantic territory. But I didn't want it to stop. Instead of answering, I leaned forward, and my lips met his. I could taste the hint of ground black pepper on his tongue.

I gripped his shoulders, the heat of his mouth warming my entire body. His muscles tightened under my fingers as he lifted me onto the counter, my legs wrapping around his waist instinctively.

I opened my eyes for a moment, and my body tensed. My mirror image was reflected back at me through the glass cabinet door beside us. I had managed to put the image of that girl I saw outside the restaurant from my mind.

Iann pulled away after a moment, sensing my sudden rigidity. "Is everything okay?"

I quickly looked away from my reflection. "Yeah, I'm sorry. I just . . . I think I'm hungrier than I realized."

He laughed. "Right. I owe you an edible dinner. If we keep going like this, everything's going to burn." He helped me down from the counter and quickly attended to the boiling pot of water.

I glanced at my reflection again, thinking back to the way the girl's sleek ponytail had bobbed up and down when she walked away from us.

Who is she?

CHAPTER THIRTEEN

"Are you okay?"

I blinked in the darkness, my eyes focusing on the light of the clock. 3:12 a.m.

Iann stood beside me, his hand on my shoulder. "What are you doing?"

I shivered in my borrowed shorts and oversize T-shirt, my feet trembling on the tile.

He stepped in front of me, bending down to look into my eyes when I didn't respond. "Harper, are you okay?"

I nodded and blinked again. "What's going on?" My voice croaked as it wrenched from my lips.

He slid his hand in mine and led me to a chair. I sank into it, shaking. "I don't know," he said. "You left the bed a while ago, and when I came to check on you, you were just standing here."

I looked around. I was in the kitchen. Leo was staring up at me and panting.

"What were you doing?" he asked slowly.

"I don't know." I didn't remember even getting out of bed. I didn't remember falling asleep in the first place. "Can I get some water?" I rasped.

He left my side, and I could hear the clattering of glasses.

I opened my clenched right hand, and something fell out onto my leg. I brought it up close to my face in the darkness. It was a thick, smooth leaf. The hand I'd held it in was covered in dirt. I let the leaf fall to the floor and glanced at the front door. The dead bolt was locked. I took a deep breath and patted Leo on his soft yellow head.

Iann handed me a glass of water, and I gratefully sipped. "Thank you."

He sat down on the chair next to me, running his hand through my hair from my temple and down my back.

"How long was I gone?" I set the glass on the countertop.

His finger lightly traced a line along my neck. "I don't know. I woke up when you walked out of the room but then fell back asleep." He put his arm around my shoulder. "Were you sleepwalking?"

I shivered and relaxed into his arm. He was so warm. "I don't know."

"Let's go back to bed." He stood up and offered his hand to me.

I rubbed my gritty palm with my thumb. "I'll meet you there. Just give me a second."

He retracted his hand and ruffled his hair until it stuck out from both sides. "Are you sure you're okay?" He yawned.

I stood up. "Yeah, I'm good. I'll be there in a minute." I watched him stagger back into his room, then glanced down at Leo. He was still staring at me, but he had stopped panting. I felt my way through the kitchen to the bathroom and flicked the light on. My right hand was covered in wet brown dirt. I turned on the faucet and rubbed it away. The water seeped into the cut on my palm and stung.

Leo followed me in, leaving tracks of dirt dropping from his feet and chest. I sighed in relief. "Come here." I called him in, and he sat in front of the sink as I wet a paper towel and wiped his fur. *He* must have dragged in the dirt. Hadn't he?

———

I opened my eyes and lay frozen, staring at the white ceiling, the fan squeaking slightly as it rotated. The bedroom door opened, and Iann came in with his phone in hand. "Oh," he said, closing the door behind him before sitting on the bed beside me. "When did you get up?"

My eyes were dry and aching, as if I hadn't slept at all. I pulled his T-shirt farther down past my knees under the covers. "Just now."

He got under the blankets next to me.

I stretched my arms above my head. "What time is it?"

"Seven o'clock." He turned on his side toward me and brushed my hair away from my neck, his eyes darting over the jagged scar. He reached his arm around my shoulder, his shirtsleeve rolling up and exposing the bottom half of his tattoo. It was a compass with coordinates scrawled underneath.

"A bartender with a tattoo?" I lightly tapped the ink. "Isn't that a little cliché?"

I expected a laugh, but instead I was met with silence. "Well, I got it before I started bartending," he said after the pause, pulling his arm away from my shoulders.

"What does it mean?" I traced the coordinates with my fingers.

He stared across the room, his arm tensing under my touch.

"What's wrong?" I settled back onto my side.

He sat up and looked down at his hands. "Nothing," he said. "It's, um, kind of a memorial kind of thing."

My face grew hot. "I'm so sorry, I didn't know."

"Yeah, uh." He ran a hand through his hair and down the back of his neck. "There's no way you would know." His voice lowered. "It's hard for me to talk about."

My mouth dried as words caught in my throat, stopping just before my lips. I was dying to ask a thousand questions.

His eyes seemed to be following a replay of the events in the air in front of him.

I sat up next to him, but he didn't glance my way.

He finally looked at me, his brow furrowed. "Sorry," he said. "It was a long time ago, but I still . . . I don't know."

My truth bubbled in my throat, rising hot toward my lips. But I swallowed quickly before the words could come out. It was too long and awful to speak. Almost impossible to explain. I gripped his hand tighter as the words burned and then died in my chest.

His body softened. His warm breath rustled through my hair as he kissed the top of my head, pulling me closer into his arms. "I have to stop by my professor's office before work," he said after a moment. "What are you doing for the rest of today?" His lips pressed gently against my neck, and chills ran down my skin.

"I have to work on some commissions," I answered, breathlessly, angling my body deeper into his.

"Why don't you come to the bar tonight?" he said. "You can work there, and I can send you free drinks."

I laughed. "Is that allowed?"

He shrugged. "It's a Tuesday. It probably won't get that busy. And as long as there's a drink on the table, no one will bother you. When I get off, we can go grab dinner."

I fought the urge to lock up immediately. This was new territory for me. "Okay," I said simply, before leaning away from him, my feet touching the frigid tile. "I'll try to make it." I lifted my jeans from the floor with my toes and grabbed them, then slid them up my thighs, hoping he hadn't seen too much. The bed squeaked slightly as he got up. I turned around, but he was already grabbing a shirt from his desk against the wall and buttoning it. "I'm going to head out."

His expression was unreadable. "See you tonight," he said. He sounded uncertain. He followed behind me into the living room toward the front door.

I rubbed my hand along the top of Leo's head as he appeared by my side. I opened the door but lingered at the threshold, my eyes drifting to the faint footprints on the floor. They trailed down the hallway to the stairwell.

Iann sensed my hesitation and stayed a few feet behind me. "Harper," he started softly. He was silent for a couple of seconds, and then he smiled weakly. "Can you get home okay?"

It was a stupid question, but it was something. I leaned backward, one foot in the hallway. "Yeah. Bye." I turned and started toward the stairwell, hearing the door close behind me. I gripped the stairwell door as my shoe slipped. The muddy footprints were still wet but drying around the edges. Pushing the door open, I saw that the trail continued down the steps. My knees trembled as I shuffled to the next set of footprints, then slid my sneaker beside the muddy outline. It was the same size. I swiped my shoe across the print, causing the imprint to smudge into a mess. My steps quickened with each flight as my chest grew tighter. I opened the door onto the street and gulped at the warm air, the taste of rain sour on my tongue.

Something crunched under my shoe just as the door closed behind me. I couldn't hear anything else as my heartbeat grew louder in my ears. I leaned back on my heel and lifted the top of my shoe from the sidewalk, revealing a small wooden pendant caked with dirt, lying beside a few freshly discarded cigarette butts. There was a heart etched into the dark wood grain, a carefully layered, delicate Celtic knot at the center of the heart. I glanced over my shoulder. It was quiet on the street, only a couple of people walking away several yards ahead of me. I bent over and grasped the pendant in trembling hands.

I studied the sidewalk nearby and noticed that behind me where the footprints stopped, a pair of wide boot prints picked up, leading away from the apartment and to the curb.

My stomach churned the entire train ride home. I couldn't tell if I was excited . . . or scared. Right before the train pulled into Damen Station, I dared to glance at my phone for the first time since the previous afternoon. There were three new calls—all from a blocked number. I deleted them immediately.

I stared at the tops of my sneakers as my feet hit the sidewalk and passed the park. I ran my fingers over the etched wood in my pocket. *Why did you take that?* The answer to that question was like a memory on the edge of my thoughts but just out of reach.

AUTUMN

CHAPTER FOURTEEN

Fall came pouring into Chicago with more rain than I'd seen in a while after a particularly hot summer. The time had passed so quietly and suddenly, three months gone without an update on Holly's or Sarah's cases. No matter how frequently I refreshed the page, no new articles appeared.

I flipped through the same old articles as I waited at the crosswalk. When the signal changed, I walked deeper into downtown, looking for the Blue Line entrance on Washington Avenue. I had strayed from the path a bit after parting ways with Iann at the coffee shop. I'd insisted on taking the train since I had a few errands to run once I got to Damen.

As my foot struck the curb, I looked up and froze, one foot still dangling behind me over the asphalt. My reflection was staggered behind hers in the storefront window as she adjusted her long brown hair over her shoulders and ran her finger over the lipstick on her mouth. The eyes. The nose. Those lips.

A shoulder jostled me, and I caught myself from falling onto the concrete. I glanced up, but she was gone from the storefront. I scanned the crowd rushing in and out of the train station entrance and spotted her green coat and her shimmering straight hair as she continued down the sidewalk. I froze. I wanted to follow her. But fear gripped my feet, weighing them into the pavement. She was the specter of Issi I had always feared. But alive. And full of color. She disappeared around the corner, and feeling slowly crept back into my legs. I tripped backward toward the entrance before turning and starting down the steps. I touched my throat as if she were the one who had reached for me in my nightmares.

———

I hadn't stopped thinking about the girl I'd seen, even as I sat in the Up Room, glancing up from my drawing every few minutes to see if Iann was there. He was already thirty minutes late for his usual Tuesday-night shift.

"Harper?"

I looked up from my sketchbook. My breath caught in my throat.

He stood there with the biggest grin. "I never thought in a million years I would see you again." He sat in the chair across from me, his face and sandy-colored hair illuminated by the glow of the candles on the table between us.

"Danny," I breathed. "What are . . ." I trailed off, at a loss for words. He looked the same as he had at Northwestern years ago, but he wasn't a lanky eighteen-year-old anymore. His shoulders and arms filled out his dark-blue suit.

"What happened to you? You look like you haven't slept in years. Jesus, I almost didn't recognize you." He laughed and raised a glass to his lips.

I ran a hand through my hair and leaned forward in my seat. "Come on, I looked much worse than this the last time you saw me." It had the cadence of a joke, but his smile flickered. Of course he remembered those cuts and bruises. I glanced around the room. Iann was still missing from the bar. "What are you doing here?"

"Some of my coworkers put together a happy hour thing." He set his glass on the table.

I had accepted a long time ago that I'd never see him again. My head swam with questions. "Are you working in the city?"

He nodded, his bright eyes scanning me from head to toe. "Yeah, I'm at the *Tribune*. Been there four years now and still at the bottom of the food chain."

He had always talked about working for the *New York Times* or going back home to work at the *San Francisco Chronicle*. "Why did you stay in Chicago?" I asked, my heart racing still from the shock. He had never completely left my thoughts. I had often imagined Danny somehow finding me and joining me, away from school and away from my father. That dream had carried me through those first few months.

He shrugged. "I don't know, this place grew on me." He looked out the window at the skyline in the distance. "And there's no better place to be for crime journalism than Chicago."

I shook my head. "I can't believe you're here. What are the chances of us running into each other after all this time?"

His expression darkened. "How are you? Are you good now?"

I peered down at my fingers tightly intertwined on top of the sketchbook. "I'm good," I said quietly. *He would've killed you if you'd stayed.* That was the fear that I had never uttered to anyone, not even Danny. That last morning in Evanston, I had sensed it coming. My father had finally started to realize he could never really control me, that I would never really be like Issi. I had witnessed firsthand what he was capable of when he couldn't get his way. "I'm sorry about—everything just got so messed up back then."

He leaned toward me, and I met his gaze. "I'm glad you got out of there. I mean, it was a little rough after you left. But I'm just relieved that you're okay now." He gauged my silence. "I made the unhappy mistake of going to your house when you didn't come to class that afternoon."

My eyes widened.

"Yeah, exactly," he said with a laugh. "Your dad was not thrilled about that."

"What happened?"

"Well, he tried to ruin my life and get me kicked out of school for a while."

My cheeks burned.

"But, you know me," he continued. "I'm too much of a loudmouth to just go quietly into the night, so he eventually had to let it go."

"I'm so sorry, Danny." I couldn't meet his eyes.

"I'm not." He turned his head slightly as the group by the bar emitted a roar of laughter. "Well, I should probably get back." He looked at me. "So, do you have a phone, or are you truly living that starving-artist life you always talked about?"

I grinned. "Yes, to both."

"Okay. Are you going to give me your number, or do I have to beg for it?"

I glanced behind him at the bar. Iann still wasn't there. "I don't think that's a good idea. I'm seeing someone."

He shrugged. "So what? I have dibs."

I laughed.

He stood up and grabbed his glass from the table. "No, but seriously, we should just reconnect sometime. As friends." He handed me a business card. "And I'd love to meet this supposed boyfriend of yours," he said, wryly.

I turned the card around. Reporter.

"Oh, and if you hear something interesting, let me know." He gestured to the card. "Bonus points if it's before the crime scene is cleared." He winked and walked over to the bombastic group of young men yelling at a table by the entrance.

I tucked my book and Danny's business card into my bag before leaving my seat. "Is Iann coming in today?" I asked Mike as he turned around to hand a woman her drink.

He shook his head. "No, I think he called in a little while ago."

"Did he say why?"

Mike shrugged. "I didn't talk to him." He leaned away from me and toward a girl that walked up to the bar.

I hesitated in front of the elevators. I glanced at Danny, his back among a couple of other men in the corner, the view of the skyline directly in front of them.

My phone buzzed in my hand.

Iann.

"Hi," I answered.

"Hey, I'm sorry," he said, his voice slightly muffled. "I'm not going to make it today."

"Is everything okay?"

He sighed. "Yeah, I, well, there was an . . . incident with one of the patients I saw at the clinic, and uh, he attacked me."

My building anger dissolved. "What? Are you okay?"

"I'm fine," he said slowly. "I'm waiting on stitches right now."

"Oh my god, where are you?" Now the low buzzing and busy background talking on his end of the line made sense.

"The ER but, really, I'm fine. I'm sorry it took me so long to let you know. I called work first, and then I had to fill out all this paperwork as soon as I got to the waiting room."

"I'll head over now. I can wait with you."

He was quiet for a moment. "I don't want you to see me like this," he said in a low voice. "But I'll call you tonight. I'm really sorry."

This rejection stung a bit. "Okay, don't worry about it." *What doesn't he want you to see?*

"I'll call you soon."

"Okay. Bye." After hanging up, I imagined all the possible disfigurements Iann now had. A broken jaw? A missing eye? And if so, how? I remembered that he had required clinic hours for his degree that he somehow managed to squeeze into his schedule three times a week. But he never told me what he did during his time there.

"Hey!"

I jumped at the booming voice behind me and turned to see Danny, his hand pressing the elevator button.

"Are you going down?" he asked.

"Um, not yet."

He took a few steps closer to me. "Well, I'm bailing on those guys. Do you want to go grab a drink somewhere?"

The same guilt from a few moments earlier emerged. "I can't. Not right now."

He smiled. "Okay, well, soon. Just give me a call."

"Yeah, of course." I shifted back on my heels.

"It was great to see you today," he added as the doors began to close.

———

When I returned home, I found myself more restless than I'd been in a while. Between what had happened with Iann and the encounter with Danny, I had managed to channel my energy into a commissioned family watercolor portrait before I realized my brush had stopped painting entirely and I was doodling with my pen in the margins.

Danny was in Chicago. It had been so many years ago that we'd meant anything to each other, and suddenly it was as if we'd never been apart.

Those cold early mornings during winter break together in his apartment had been my favorite. Danny's roommates had fled for the whole period, but he had booked his return to California for Christmas Eve, giving us over a week of alone time. My father had left the day after classes ended for an international conference in Portugal and wouldn't be back until Christmas Day.

Everything had perfectly aligned for once. I could stay over the entire night without rushing home before midnight to avoid the wrath of my father, without Danny visually inspecting me on every meeting, taking a silent inventory of new bruises. That persistent fear and tension was gone during our winter break together. I had dreamed for the past six years of starting college, because I thought I would be free. Although it hadn't worked out the way I'd wanted, being with Danny was the only relief I felt. He was the only choice I'd made that was entirely mine.

I remembered sitting on the sofa in his living room and looking down at the frosty landscape outside, at everything coated in white. "This kind of storm doesn't happen in San Francisco," Danny had said, handing me a mug of coffee.

The Illinois cold was the type of chill that seeped inside you and weakened your bones. "At least it's pretty." I'd set my mug on the coffee table and leaned back against his chest.

His arms had been so warm and heavy around my waist. "I'm glad you don't have to go home today." So was I. "Do you want to go sailing with me?" He'd never given up hope that I'd say yes and finally set foot on his sailboat. And it had been those moments with him that I could actually imagine a future outside of Evanston, away from my father.

"You know the lake is frozen, right?" I'd tried to pass it as a joke.

"I meant later, like in the spring." He'd brushed the hair away from my neck. "You've seen the ocean, right?"

"No."

"I think you'd like San Francisco," he'd said. "There's a huge art scene. And the water's amazing."

In his arms back then, I'd tried to imagine myself on a real beach, tan and kicking at the shallow waves as they reached the shore. Maybe that version of me could have enjoyed the water again. Yes, maybe that version of me could have actually gone sailing with Danny someday.

I dropped the pen and frowned at the tiny sketch of a sailboat, shuffling the painting to the corner of my desk. Something fell with a thud from underneath onto the floor.

I bent down under the table. It was the necklace I'd found outside of Iann's apartment. I leaned forward in my seat and wrapped my fingers around the gritty pendant. I had completely forgotten about it in the excitement of the last few months. Holding it again reminded me of waking suddenly in his apartment. Of the footprints.

CHAPTER FIFTEEN

There's no light in her eyes. Her irises are glassy and gray as she stares into mine, our noses touching. I tug my lips to scream, but they're sealed. My shriek rises and dies in my throat. Cold, withered hands creep along my neck as a tear trails down my cheek. Her mouth rips open, and electronic beeping rattles past her lips, her fingers cutting my skin and crushing my throat with each note.

———

Daylight hit my eyes from the blinds. My fingers were wrapped tightly around the wooden pendant.

The chime of my phone clattered on the nightstand.

My limbs tingled as I stretched and grabbed it, the pendant falling to the table. I ignored Erin's unanswered text notifications and answered the call. "Hello?" I gasped, clutching at my neck, the weight of fingers still pressing against my skin.

"Hey, are you up?" Iann's voice was groggy but back to normal.

I rubbed my eyes and pushed my tangled hair from my face. "Yeah, how are you feeling?"

"Better, actually. I came to take you to breakfast, and it occurred to me just now that you might still be asleep."

I sat up and glanced at the window. "What? You're here?" I jumped to my feet and frantically felt for my jeans with my toes.

"Yeah, I'm sorry—I should've called first," he said, sensing the panic in my voice. "I'll come back later."

I swapped out my pajama bottoms for jeans. "No, it's fine." I tugged a cardigan over my tank top and tripped to the door. I swallowed a small gasp when I swung it open.

Iann stood there with his head slightly lowered, wearing a baseball cap. But I could still clearly see the black eye with a gash trailing from it and the bloody fat lip. "I know," he said when he caught my expression.

I opened the door wider, and he stepped in. "What happened?"

He removed his hat and ruffled his hair. The purple skin was puffy around his left eye. "I was doing a consultation with this man, and he lost it." He winced and touched his lip.

"Here, sit down." I gestured toward the bed.

He sank down on the edge and glanced around the messy room. "I'm so sorry. I'm—" He touched a hand to his temple. "I'm not thinking really clearly on this medicine. I felt bad for bailing on you last night. I wanted to make it up to you."

My eyes scanned all the small bruises under his pallid skin, the cut on the bridge of his nose. "It's not like you did it on purpose," I said, sitting beside him. "It's nothing. Are you okay? Maybe you should lie down."

He shook his head. "No, I'm fine. It's the pain meds. I slept for twelve hours, and when I woke up, I really wanted to see you."

Something moved deep inside me.

"I was already calling you before I realized how early it was," he finished.

"No, I'm glad you came over," I said, sitting on my hand to keep from reaching out and grabbing his. "Let's get breakfast."

He chuckled. "Well, that's the thing. Now that I think about it, I don't know why you would want to be seen in public with me looking like this." He gestured to his battered face.

I surveyed him. "It's not that bad." I laughed. "I mean, you just look like you got your ass kicked at a minor league hockey game. And people go out with hockey players all the time, even when they're missing teeth."

He grinned. "I *do* still have all my teeth."

"Exactly, so you're already better off." I stood up and stepped over Woodstock to grab my coat from the back of my desk chair. "Come on, you look like you could use some coffee."

———

We walked toward the Robey but took a turn past the train station to our favorite diner.

"Two coffees, please," I said once we sat in our seats on the outdoor patio. It looked like rain, but the indoor seating was packed. I zipped my coat up to right below my collarbone. The waitress nodded and walked back inside, casting a glance at Iann over her shoulder.

He looked at the menu, his head tilted down so I couldn't see his face past his cap.

I folded the edge of my menu. "So, what happens now?"

He glanced up at me. "What do you mean?"

"I mean, you can't keep doing that type of work at that clinic, right? It seems really dangerous."

He frowned. "This is the first time something like this has happened. It's an occupational hazard when you deal with people on their worst days."

"Yeah, but can't you work in a different unit at the clinic?"

He held my gaze. "My dissertation is about behavioral and abnormal psych, so no," he snapped.

"I wasn't trying to—" I stopped as the waitress appeared beside us and set the coffee down before eyeing the menus in our hands and vanishing without a word.

Iann rubbed the back of his neck. "Sorry, I hear the same things from my parents all the time." He winced as the coffee mug touched the stitches on his lip and set it back down on the table. "They already think Chicago is dangerous, and I actively go to visit with 'mentally disturbed' people on a regular basis." He shook his head and twisted the mug around on the wooden table. "I'm dreading hearing what they'll say when they see me like this."

"How would they see you?" I avoided the eyes of the waitress as she poked her head out the door behind Iann.

He successfully took a sip from the intact side of his mouth. "Oh, um, they're coming to visit in a few days. I thought I told you."

"Oh." I swallowed a mouthful of coffee. My eyes ached with exhaustion.

"For my birthday," he added.

"Oh," I said again. "I didn't know your birthday is coming up." *How could you? You barely know each other.* That wasn't true.

His face reddened slightly. "Yeah . . . I'd love for you to meet them."

I gagged on my coffee, covering my mouth as I coughed.

"I mean, I'm going to take them to dinner, so you can tag along if you want."

Oh god, he's serious. "It seems a little soon for that," I said, clasping my cup harder.

His eyes widened. "I didn't mean like that," he said in a rush. "I meant as a friend. Some of my friends from school and work are going to come. It'll be a big, *friendly* dinner."

I released the breath I'd been holding. That didn't exactly sound appealing either. "Oh, okay. Yeah, that sounds fun," I lied.

He looked back at the menu before meeting my gaze again. "Although," he said with a smile, "I'd like to point out that we've been together for almost three months now."

I narrowed my eyes and calculated it myself. "Hmm, okay, sure," I conceded with a shrug. But I actually felt . . . pride? I was proud that I could maintain and grow something for once. Maybe there was a small glimmer of hope for me, after all.

———

We lingered in front of my door. I opened it, but he shifted back on his heels, slightly away from me. "Are you going back home?" I asked, trying not to sound disappointed. I wanted to kiss his broken lips and feel his scar.

He shrugged. "I have a shift at the bar later. I need to get ready for that."

"You can't go to work like that." I gaped.

He grinned. "I thought you said it wasn't that bad."

I eyed the tiny stitches along his cheekbone. "No, I said it's no worse than a hockey player," I teased. "Do you think the Robey would allow a battered hockey player to come in and serve drinks?"

He laughed. "You're right. I'll call in sick."

"I think you have to. You need to rest anyway. So . . . can you come in?"

He looked at me for a long time. "You're not repulsed by me?"

I shrugged. "I'm not the Robey. I like your face." *Even like that. Especially like that.*

He smiled again and glanced over his shoulder. "Sure, I could use more coffee."

We didn't have coffee.

No sooner did the door close behind us than I was devouring his coarse lips, resisting the urge to bite harder on his cut. We entangled and rearranged for hours, breaking away only to steal breaths as needed. His fingers rested on my faded scar, and mine pressed against his fresh one until it made him gasp. I kissed each bruise on his chest and arms until we parted and collapsed.

"Are you okay?" I asked, resting my head on his chest.

"Yeah," he panted. "Why?"

"How's your head?" I ran a finger along his jaw, angling to get a better look at the cut around his eye.

"Good." He pulled me closer into him, his breath rustling through my hair.

I was face to face with his tattoo. I stared at the coordinates etched in ink along his skin under the compass. "So how formal is this dinner going to be?" I asked after a moment.

"Hmm?" He was already starting to drift to sleep. "Oh, um, not at all. I'm going to be showing them around all day, so we'll all be exhausted and casual by then."

"Where are you taking them? To eat that night?"

His eyes were closed. "I was thinking Harry Caray's. The one on Kinzie Street."

A steak house. That was formal. "How many sisters do you have again?"

"Two," he said quietly. "But only Rose is coming this time."

"She's the one with the kids?"

He nodded softly. "Yeah, she's bringing them with her."

Eating with kids at a restaurant was a nightmare. Especially a steak house like that. I'd only been once with Erin, and it was a bit too "touristy" for her, so we never went back.

I looked at his tattoo again. Who had earned that memorial on his body?

He hadn't pushed me when I'd evaded certain questions about my family. I wouldn't push him either.

His body relaxed as he sank deeper into his pillow.

I lay awake, my body curved against Iann's as his breathing deepened each second. His body was guarded even in sleep, tensed against some imperceptible antagonist, his brow furrowed. My phone buzzed against the nightstand. I pulled my blanket up to my neck as I reached for it.

Danny (11:01 p.m.): It was good to see you.

I had sent a quick text to the number on his business card with my contact when I'd returned home after seeing him at the Robey. I glanced at Iann as his head rolled onto one side of the pillow, his eyes still shut tightly. Something anchored deep into my stomach.

I had almost forgotten that guilty knot-in-my-stomach feeling from when we'd first met. Seeing him again had sent an unexpected warmth through my body, like homesickness. And regret, so much regret about what could have been and how I'd treated him. It had killed me to leave him, and I hadn't even considered the toll it would take on him.

But here he was, nine years later, happy. He wasn't angry or sad. He was living his dream. Or a variation of his dream. I still couldn't fathom why he chose to stay in Chicago and brave the winters and frozen lake rather than return to San Francisco. Why did he stay?

I held the phone close to my face, and my fingers glided over the keyboard.

(11:03 p.m.): Same here.

I deleted and retyped it three times before my thumb hit the send button, my heart racing. Nine years was a long time. Long enough to forget those cold nights when we'd warmed ourselves with stolen buttered rum and laid against each other on the floor in front of the fireplace watching *Casablanca* when I couldn't fall asleep.

Danny (11:03 p.m.): Goodnight, kid.

I smiled to myself. Maybe it wasn't long enough to forget after all.

I set the phone down on the table, letting it buzz with another response as I nestled against Iann's arm. He turned toward me, still asleep, and I rested my back into his chest. Nine years was a long time to wait for that feeling again.

CHAPTER SIXTEEN

I started carrying the pendant with me. I slipped it on the key ring alongside my apartment key and the backup key for the studio to replace the rabbit's foot. The added weight in my pocket was both unsettling and comforting as I walked around shopping for Iann's birthday gift.

I unlocked my phone and opened my chat with Erin.

(3:23 p.m.): What's a good guy gift?

Erin (3:45 p.m.): For Iann? Idk, DSM-5? lol

Helpful, as always. I sighed and ducked into one of the last stores on the street. I had struck out already at three different places.

What did I even really know about him? I scanned through the CDs near the front of the store. Did people even buy CDs anymore? Most of the shoppers were browsing through the vinyl records. Was vinyl in again? Iann definitely didn't have a record player.

I surveyed the next aisle. My eyes stopped on the man at the counter staring at me. I recognized him.

He glanced away and finished paying the cashier. He had been with Sarah's mother when she ran up to me on the street. His eyes darted over his shoulder at me once more before he pushed through the door.

I dropped the CD I'd been holding and followed after him. "Excuse me," I called after him once I was on the sidewalk.

He turned around and grimaced when he saw me.

I continued to approach him, my hand fidgeting with the keys in my pocket. "I—" Now that I was in front of him, I had no idea what I wanted to say. "You came up to me a while back," I began, "with a woman. She thought I was Sarah."

He sighed, tightening his grip on the plastic bag in his hand. "Yeah," he said. "I remember."

My heart thumped faster, echoing in my ears. *Now what?* "After that, I heard about what happened to Sarah, and I just wanted to say I'm sorry."

His features contorted. "Thank you," he said. His red-rimmed eyes lingered on my face. "Sorry if that was weird for you."

I traced the pendant with my finger. "I know it's none of my business . . ." I took a step toward him. "But have they found who did it?" Detective Wilder had been quiet. A big part of me hoped it was because they'd figured it out.

His lips were curved in a perpetual grimace. "No, they haven't." He was still studying my face. "You really do look so much like her. She was my fiancé."

"Did you hear about—" I hesitated and pushed forward. "About Holly Bascom?"

His brows knit together. "Who?"

My heart raced faster. "Holly—she was killed here in Wicker Park, just a few weeks after Sarah. You should ask the police about it." I immediately regretted it as soon as the words left my mouth.

But he didn't seem upset, just entranced almost. It was always hard to wake up after a tragedy. He snapped out of it and finally looked away from me, reaching into his pocket. "What was that name again?" As he pulled out his phone, the shopping bag fell from his hand onto the sidewalk. A CD and a small colorful paper spilled out between us.

I picked up the illustration. It was of a little girl holding a bundle of balloon strings and floating up. It was one of a few watercolor prints I put into the shops that would let me. I barely got a few dollars off each sale, so I'd stopped after the first round. There was no telling how long this particular one had been on the shelves in the music store. "Did you buy this?" I asked, handing it to him.

He slid the CD back into the bag. "Yeah, it's our daughter's birthday this weekend," he said, brushing the painting off. "She has a few of these."

"That's mine."

He stared at me blankly.

"I mean, I made those," I clarified.

There was a flicker of a smile. "Oh. Well, Anna loves them, especially the one of the girls with the cat. Sarah used to get them for her. I had to look at a couple of different places to find this one."

"Yeah, I made those last year, and I stopped." I flexed my knuckle over the key ring. "I'd be happy to make another one, just for her." *You idiot.*

His expression thawed even more. "Really?"

"Yes," I said, the word squeezing past my lips before I could stop it.

"Uh, thank you. That would be amazing." He tucked the bag under his arm. "I'll give you my number, and I can send you our address."

I pulled out my phone. "Yeah, okay." *What are you doing?* It was strange, on all levels. I typed his number and saved it. My hands felt detached, like they were acting on their own.

"I'm Sam, by the way," he said, unlocking his phone.

"I'm Harper."

His eyes darkened again. "What was the name you mentioned earlier?" His fingers hovered over the screen.

"Holly—Holly Bascom."

CHAPTER SEVENTEEN

I stood in front of the doors to the restaurant, looking around the sidewalk and scuffing my heel on the curb. I glanced down at my phone. I was already fifteen minutes late, but my feet wouldn't move forward. Something burrowed deep into my gut. Dread, maybe?

I inhaled, and my stomach erupted into a growl.

It's a party. It'll be fun.

It was impossible to imagine a fun family "get-together," as Iann had termed it. The last and only time my family had gotten together was to joylessly peer into an open coffin. I blinked, and the image flashed through my mind. I scraped the bottom of my boot over the cement before propelling it toward the door, dragging the second one behind it. My stomach grumbled again as the warm smell of steak and rosemary filled my nose.

"I'm looking for the Parks," I announced breathlessly to the hostess.

She surveyed me dismissively from behind her booth, and I wrapped my coat tighter around my waist. "Who?"

I didn't have the energy to say it again. "The Park family," I wheezed, clutching the small gift box, the cheap fabric scratching my palm.

Her eyes widened. "Oh, yes, they're at the center table in the dining room." She gestured over her shoulder without turning around.

I stopped by the decorative plant right before the entrance to the dining room.

They were talking and laughing, flipping through menus, sampling the wine from their goblets. What kind of restaurant had goblets? Iann was sitting on the edge, only half his face visible from where I stood. The wounds had healed surprisingly quickly, but the older woman sitting beside him kept frowning at the cut along his cheek. She had the same brown eyes and nose as Iann. They had the same smile and wave to their hair, although his was darker and hers a light coppery brown tinged with flecks of gray. The dimples on the sides of their mouths both creased with each smile.

A younger woman with the same brown eyes sat beside two dark-haired toddlers, attending them frequently as they banged silverware against the table. A man with salt-and-pepper hair sat with his back to me.

Watching them saddened me. And scared me. What they had was so fragile, and they didn't even realize it.

What business did I have to intrude on this complete, unbroken family?

Iann's friends spread out across the rest of the table, an air of academia lingering above them. Jeremy was sitting beside Iann's sister and her kids, in a heated debate with a girl in a fedora and wide-rimmed glasses beside him.

I took a step back and hovered there out of sight, shoulders bumping past me on their way in and out. The knot of dread twisted deeper into my stomach, erupting through the rest of my body. I knew I would regret that moment, as I looked on at the smiling faces at the table, at the only empty seat beside Iann's father. It seemed orchestrated. He thought we might get along. That I could get his father's approval somehow.

A hard lump formed in my throat, and I couldn't swallow past it. My own father hated me. How the hell did he believe anyone in his life would think I was good enough? *You aren't.*

I stumbled past the hostess and swung the door open, the cold air lashing my face as I stepped out onto the sidewalk. I'd been fooling myself this entire time, pretending to be someone else with Iann.

It felt like the air had been ripped from my lungs. I glanced back at the restaurant door, loosening my scarf.

I could feel her before I saw her.

The hair rose along my arms as she walked out of the glass door and onto the sidewalk. She passed so close in front of me that I had to take a step back to avoid colliding with her.

My mirror image. The phantom in the green coat from before.

Her hair was longer than mine, straight and flowing down her back in a sleek, dark ponytail sitting high on her head. She wore a clingy red dress that covered only half an inch of her thigh and black stiletto heels.

I had only worn heels once. They had been sturdier than hers, and I had wobbled the entire time. But *she* glided.

I trailed behind her, my heart pounding in sync with the clack of her heels.

I didn't see the streets or the lights. I followed in her footsteps, blind to everything around us.

She disappeared into a building a few yards ahead of me. She had passed the line and the bouncer without intervention. I quickened my steps up to the door and felt the boom of the EDM coming out from the club, watching as she disappeared into the dark.

I glanced at the bouncer reviewing a couple's IDs. I pushed past him through the door.

"Hey!" he yelled, his voice fading against the thud of the music.

A wall of illuminated blue skulls shone down on a stairway to the basement. I ran down the steps toward the music drowning out the sound of the bouncer thundering behind me. In the dark room, light throbbing with the beat of the music, I slipped into the mass huddled around the bar, pushing in between two men. They scowled but just rearranged themselves behind me, letting me cut the line. Thank god for Midwestern chivalry.

I scanned the darkness for her as the crowd shuffled me forward to the bar.

"Drink?"

I turned back to the bar. The bartender tapped his fingers impatiently on the counter.

"Gin and tonic," I said. There she was, dancing in a group of three guys and another girl, her sleek ponytail swaying with her body.

"Do you want to start a tab?" the bartender asked loudly.

I took the drink from the counter and leaned in as if I couldn't hear him.

"Put it on mine," one of the guys behind me said, stepping up beside me a little too closely. Before the guy could even slide his credit card over the bar, I dipped between a nearby couple and walked through the dance floor. I stumbled to a booth at the back of the lounge in the dim lighting. From my seat I could see her, still dancing, a little slower to a different song, now with a large blue drink in one hand.

I took a few sips of mine. Thankfully, it was strong. I sat mesmerized by her. We were made from the same ingredients—same hair color, eyes, nose, and lips—but she was brighter and better somehow. I was the first batch that you burned and tossed down the garbage disposal. I felt a deep longing root in my stomach. She was how I should've been. She had my life if my mother hadn't died. If not for the accident. If I hadn't run away. With one more long sip, my drink was gone.

———

I stood, staring up at her building. I didn't remember the entire walk there, but I had fallen in step behind her, slowed down by the multiple drinks I'd downed over the last three hours. She had entered her key code before I could catch up, and I'd watched through the glass window as she'd disappeared down the apartment hallway.

As a young blond man opened the door, I rushed up behind him and caught it. He smiled at me as he headed to the elevator. "Hey," he said, comfortably.

I nodded and followed him into the elevator. He had already pushed the buttons for the fourth and ninth floors.

"Late night again?" he asked, gesturing to my wild, windblown hair.

From the corner of my eye, I saw him staring at me. I nodded and sighed with relief when he got out on the fourth floor, still looking back at me as the doors closed.

As the doors opened again on the ninth floor, I cautiously stepped out and saw her at the end of the hallway. She was leaning against the wall by her apartment door.

Her heels were haphazardly strewn on the floor beside her as she fumbled with her key ring. She dropped the keys and almost fell over as she stooped to pick them up.

I backed up and stood at the edge of the hall leading to the other apartment doors.

She turned and looked toward the elevator with heavy eyes. Then, she finally succeeded in unlocking her door and tripped inside, leaving her heels behind. There was no click of a lock as she kicked the door closed.

I crept down the hallway to her door and held up one of her heels to my foot. She wore a size seven and a half too. I dropped it back to the floor and stood there, staring at her door and the number printed over the peephole. *906.* I leaned against the wall and fished my wallet out of my bag, digging for Detective Wilder's business card. I held it up and dialed his office number. It rang four agonizing times.

What was I calling to tell him exactly? That I had stalked a girl who looked like the murder victims? And like me? For what reason?

It was weird. Maybe even suspicious.

I was drunk.

And it was 1:41 a.m.

I let the phone and my hand slide out from under my hair and ended the call. Within seconds it was ringing from an incoming call, a blocked ID like before. I sent the call to voice mail and walked back into the elevator.

Once I made it to the first floor, I ran out the glass doors of the apartment and choked on the open air. I bent over, hands on my knees, heaving bile onto the sidewalk. My phone buzzed again but with a text from Iann this time. I dismissed the notification, gripping the brick wall beside me and standing up straight, right as rain droplets hit my face and hair in quick succession. As more rain began to fall, I rallied and observed the streets. I was just north of the river. The sound of the screeching L in the distance drowned out the patter of the rain.

———

The rumbling of the train shook me awake. My eyes adjusted to the fluorescent lights of the train, taking in the empty car. My clothes were soaked through and clinging to my body. I peeled my jacket off and let it fall to the seat. I didn't remember walking down the stairs or standing on the platform.

The motion sent my stomach churning again. I leaned my head back against the side and closed my eyes, the steady clattering almost deafening as we went deeper into the tunnel.

The train screeched to a halt, the eerie metallic wail reverberating in the car. I lost my balance and fell onto the seat beside me, my jacket following and landing with a soft clatter. The conductor's voice boomed through the intercom: "We are currently delayed due to maintenance on the track ahead at the Division Station. Once we're cleared, we'll be moving along once again."

I summoned what little strength I had and patted down my jacket until I felt something hard in the pocket. My fingers dug through the fabric before closing around something smooth and cold. I pulled out a lighter, my heart beating faster. I turned it over in my palms.

J. L.

The letters were etched in cursive script on one side of the frosted pink metal.

The lights flickered off before plunging the car into complete darkness. I clenched my fists and set them on my knee, the lighter scraping the cut on my palm. My body tightened and grew cold. I fumbled for my jacket and slipped it back on, the wet fabric weighing my arms down.

Metallic creaking resounded in the adjacent car. It sounded like the scraping that night in the alley.

It's fine. It must be routine maintenance.

I licked my lips and tried to swallow, but my mouth had dried from the alcohol. The creaks sounded closer now. My whole body tensed.

The lights flickered back on, and I exhaled, unclenching my fists, shoving the lighter back into my pocket. The train still didn't move.

I looked into the next car on my left, and my heart skipped a beat. Through the dirty window on the connecting door, a tall figure stood facing toward me from the back of the other car. The filth on the glass and the distance obscured any features.

I gripped the pole closest to me and got to my feet. The figure stepped closer, and I stumbled backward until I was against the door to the adjoining car. Still staring at the figure approaching from the other side, I turned the handle behind me, and my foot slipped in between the cars. I gasped and reached across to open the other door. Without turning back around, I jumped into the next car as I heard the thunder of footsteps behind me. The door closed, and I sprinted across the car to the next door, the footsteps following distantly. Like heavy boots.

The train jolted back to life as I jumped into the next car and I fell to my knees, one foot dangling above the track. I grabbed my stinging knees and gripped the seat to steady myself as I stood.

"Damen Station," the automated voice announced as we slowed.

I whipped my head to look at the car behind me now. It appeared empty.

The train stopped completely, and the doors opened with a wheeze onto the platform. I stood on the edge and peered outside the doors. The platform was empty. I stepped out of the train, turning to either side, bracing for the footsteps to follow.

The doors closed behind me, and the train blew past. All the cars were empty.

Where's your bag?

I felt the bulk of my keys in my jeans pocket, but my bag was gone. I kicked the concrete with the tip of my shoe, and immediately my knee throbbed. My phone and everything else, gone. I must've left it behind while running away from my imaginary follower. I rubbed my eyes with my fingers.

You're going insane.

CHAPTER EIGHTEEN

She stands in the dark, peering in through my apartment window. Her eyes are black and hollow craters, and her lips are decayed and withering.

My eyes opened and recoiled in the daylight, my limbs still tethered to the bed, crushing pain across my chest. My gaze rolled down to the window. A dark mass stood beyond my blinds. I was still weighed down to the bed, my arms frozen in sleep. The rest of my body was awake, the panic quickening my heart until the sound of its beating in my ears reached a deafening crescendo.

I took a breath and bent one of my fingers, sensation returning to my hand and then to my arms. I sat up, my eyes still trained on my window. The blinds were mostly closed, but it was real. There was a dark mass standing barely out of view, the early-morning sky backlighting the figure. I jolted as a booming knock rattled the door.

The sound reverberated through my head. I glanced over at the clock.

7:15 a.m. I had probably passed out as soon as I'd gotten in from the train.

The train.

That person in the dark. Was it real?

Where's your bag?

I glanced around the room. No bag in sight.

Another violent knock sounded through the apartment as I clutched my temples. I looked back at the door and jumped to my feet. I had left the door unlocked. I tiptoed to the door and gingerly rested my hand on the lock.

There was no way I could lock it without making a noise. I peered through the peephole and sighed.

I turned the knob and swung the door open, my eyes narrowing against the sunlight. "Yes?" I asked, squinting up at the detective. My mouth was like cotton balls.

Wilder had his hand on his back pocket, and his features were scrunched into the center of his face. "You're okay?"

I stared at him, blinking. "What?" My brain was still swimming with the gin from last night.

He relaxed his shoulders and face, but his eyebrows remained furrowed, a large wrinkle crease between them. "I saw you called my office late last night, and then you didn't answer your phone."

He surveyed me, and I was suddenly aware that my wrinkled tank top from the night before was twisted over my torso, exposing one shoulder, and I was still wearing my jeans, but one pant leg was pushed above my ankle. "Can I come in?" he asked, peering behind me.

I probably looked like I'd been attacked. I nodded and opened the door behind me. Surely he'd seen worse than my messy apartment.

He stepped in and immediately took in everything with a sharp gaze, from the pillows and blanket I had thrown to the floor to Woodstock sitting on my drafting table.

I took advantage of that moment to rearrange my shirt. He switched on the light overhead, and I winced. "What is this about, exactly?" I groaned, looking at the floor to avoid the light.

"Why didn't you answer your phone?" he said.

I turned the light switch back off and met his eyes. "I lost my bag last night on the train."

"Why were you calling in the first place?"

The images of that girl and the lighter came flooding back. I shrugged. "I don't remember." The gap between waking up on the train and then in bed was a blur.

"Where did you lose your bag?"

"The Blue Line, um, at Damen."

He ran a hand through his slicked-back ashy hair. "Well, I'm glad you're okay. I thought maybe something happened."

My knees still ached from my fall on the train. Something nearly had happened. Or had it? "Thanks for checking," I said quietly. "Sorry for wasting your time."

His eyes widened as if he'd suddenly remembered something. "You didn't. I was actually planning to stop by anyway." He glanced over my shoulder into the kitchen. "Why have you been talking to Sarah Jenkins's family?"

My body tensed. "What?"

He leaned against the bedpost with one hand. "Yeah, I got a call from Sarah's fiancé this week," he said, his eyes boring into me. "He asked me about the Bascom case. He wanted to know if it was connected somehow."

"I thought you said you were already looking into that."

He glared at me. "I like to keep investigations . . . discreet."

"Why do you think *I* said something to him?" I shifted my weight onto my back leg. "Their pictures were blasted all over the news."

"Are you stalking Sarah's family?"

I glanced at the watercolor illustration on my drafting table. "Of course not," I said, meeting his eyes. "Sarah's mom ran up to me on the street one day, thinking I was her. And I ran into Sam recently. I guess he lives around here."

"I've got to say," he started with a smirk, "for someone who doesn't know anything, you sure are causing me a lot of trouble." He opened the front door, the sunlight stronger behind him now. "What does your bag look like?"

I sat on the edge of my bed, in his shadow to avoid the blinding sunlight. "It's a shoulder bag and, um, olive green."

"You should come to the station. Was your wallet in there?" he asked.

I hung my head. *Dammit.* "Yeah, it was."

He sighed. "Then, yeah, whenever you get your hangover under control, you should come file a report. I'll keep an eye out for it."

"Okay, thanks."

He glanced at me disapprovingly and stepped onto the landing. "And keep this door locked." He walked down the stairs without looking back and got into his unmarked dark-gray car.

I closed the door and immediately turned the lock. As I collapsed on the bed again, a knot formed in my stomach. I wondered if Iann had called. He didn't know why I wasn't responding. I rolled onto my side and succumbed to sleep again.

———

Another knock. I opened my eyes. The light had shifted through the blinds. How long had I been asleep?

This knock was different than before. I pushed against the bed and made sure my clothes were facing all the right directions this time. I stumbled to the door and tossed the hair from my face to look through the peephole.

Iann.

My stomach sank as I swung the door open. "Hi," I said, swallowing the knot in my throat. His eyes were sad, but his mouth was angry.

He leaned forward, one hand against the doorframe, the other in the pocket of his black jacket. "Hi," he returned. He must've been knocking for a long time. "Are you okay?"

He came in and closed the door behind hard enough to shake the floor.

"I'm fine. I'm . . ." *You're sorry, aren't you? You should be.*

He glanced at the bed. "Did you just wake up?"

I nodded. "How was last night?"

He scoffed. "It was good, except I got stood up in front of my whole family."

I reached for his shoulder, but he pulled away. "I didn't stand you up—"

"Are you drunk?"

I could smell it on my breath too. "No, I—"

"Is that what happened? You *planned* to be there but ended up at a bar?"

There wasn't a way out of this.

"What were you doing when I called and texted you last night?"

"I lost my phone. I didn't know you tried to reach me," I lied.

He paused, but his anger wouldn't be assuaged so easily. "That doesn't explain why you didn't show up. You knew where we were supposed to meet."

"I . . ." I threw my hands up to my temple again, my head splitting. "I would've ruined everything, anyway."

He looked away from me. "What are you talking about?"

"I'm screwed up, Iann. And you and your family, it's all too perfect. I would've fucked it up if I was there."

He stepped toward me and firmly gripped my arm before running his hand down my bare skin. He pulled me into his chest. Without saying a word. We stood there, his arms wrapped tighter around my back and his warm breath rustling through my tangled hair. He tugged my waist into his and brushed my hair away behind my ear. "Where did you go last night?" he whispered, bringing his lips to my ear.

Goose bumps rose along my neck. I buried my face into his shoulder. He smelled like rain and fresh linen. "I was at home," I lied again. How could I even begin to tell him everything that had happened last night? It wasn't really me who had followed that girl like a lunatic. It was a momentary lapse in sanity. But everything with my family, that *was* me. It was branded into my every action and reaction.

He slid his hand behind my neck, the pressure drawing my chin up until our lips met. Chills rose over my whole body as he backed me against the wall beside the bed. I ran my fingers along his stubbled jaw and tousled his hair as his warm hands landed under my top and onto my stomach. My skin burned as he caressed the scar along my neck and grazed my chest with his fingers.

I remembered what Erin had said. Did he see me as a project? Every time he saw what was wrong underneath, did he find it irresistible? Did he want to fix me? Would he leave when he realized how broken I truly was?

Maybe he's as screwed up as you.

CHAPTER NINETEEN

Long after Iann had fallen asleep, I lay awake, my shoulder pressed up close against his bare back. It was still only late afternoon, the daylight slowly falling farther away from the window.

I lifted my hand and ran it gently along his skin until he stirred and looked over his shoulder at me. "What's going on?" he asked, blinking through heavy lids and rolling over to face me.

"I need to get ready for work," I said, smoothing his hair down from where it stuck up on one side. I was already neck deep in guilt. What was one more lie?

He stretched his arms over his head. "Okay, I'll get out of here." He yawned.

I kissed his neck. "No, you can stay here if you want. I won't be gone too long."

He lifted his head off the pillow and squinted at the clock on my nightstand. "I should probably get back. I have to get to the bar in a couple of hours, anyway." He sat up and pulled his T-shirt back on. "Do you want me to give you a ride to the studio?"

I looked past him to my drafting table. "That's okay, I'll walk." I also sat up and wrapped the blanket around my shoulders. "What time will you get off tonight?"

"Around midnight," he said, standing up beside the bed.

"Let's plan on you coming over here after your shift?"

He smiled and walked over to my side of the bed before putting his jacket on. "Okay."

That sadness was still in his eyes as he turned to open the front door. He hadn't moved on yet. "Oh, I have something for you." I leaned over the side of the bed, feeling for my jacket. I pulled it into my lap and reached past the mysterious lighter to the box in the pocket. "For your birthday," I said, handing it to him.

He took the small blue box and lowered down beside me. He opened it and smiled. "Perfect."

It wasn't. But it was the best I could do.

He pulled out the bottle opener and looked at his initials etched into the leather handle. "This is amazing. Thank you." He kissed me again. This time a little less sad. But it was still there. "Did you have this made?"

I nodded. "Yeah, there's a shop around the corner that makes them."

He hates it. Hell, he probably hates you now too.

"This is the nicest thing anyone's gotten for me." He was still smiling somehow.

He's a good actor.

"I doubt that," I said with a humorless laugh.

"No, I'm serious. No one's ever given me something custom like this." He tapped my knee and put the opener back into its box. "Okay, I'll leave you to it." He got up from the bed and walked to the door.

"Iann," I called.

He turned around with one hand on the doorknob.

"I'm really sorry about last night."

He nodded, his smile fading only a little. "I know."

After he closed the door, I clutched the blanket around me and dashed to the bathroom. I stepped into the shower and turned the faucet to the hottest setting I could bear, scrubbing away the grime of the previous night at the club and on the train.

I shut off the faucet and perched on the edge of the tub, my back to the shower curtain. I stood up and wrapped a towel around myself before skidding on the tile with damp feet over to the clothing pile nearby.

After I got dressed, I hovered over my desk, staring down at the illustration. Even without Sam's text in front of me, I could still remember the address.

What are you doing?

I carefully took the watercolor and slipped it into a plastic sheet protector.

———

I shuffled my feet as I waited in front of the door, fighting the feeling to bolt.

You promised.

The door to the brownstone opened. Sam winced when he saw me. He eyed the paper in my hand.

"Sorry I didn't text first," I said quickly. "I lost my phone last night. But I wanted to make sure Anna got this." I handed the illustration over to him.

His expression softened when he saw the painting.

I'd asked him to send his favorite picture of Anna for reference. He'd sent a photo of Anna with Sarah, her arm wrapped around the girl's tiny shoulders.

"How much do I owe you?" he asked, reaching into his back pocket.

I shook my head. "Nothing. It's a gift."

He looked again at the drawing. "Thank you. She'll love this." He pushed the door open behind him. "Do you want to come in?"

It was a bold offer unless he was home alone. I could only imagine the horrified look on Anna's face if she saw me. I never again wanted to see the expression that Sarah's mother had made when she'd confronted me on the street. "No, that's okay," I said, taking a step back. "I have to go."

"I looked into Holly," he began before I turned around. "You were right." Something about his gaze unsettled me.

"Oh. I hope they find who did it," I said after a pause.

He sighed. "Thanks again," he said, lifting up the illustration, the sleeve of his shirt rising up to reveal a leather bracelet with a small wooden pendant, the same color and size of the one on my key ring. The bohemian accessory was at odds with his preppy collared shirt and iron-pressed slacks.

I pointed to his wrist. "I like your bracelet."

He glanced at it, and his eyes creased in a grimace, as if I'd injured him. "Sarah used to make these," he said. "She got into woodworking after we had Anna. She used to sell them to that shop that I saw you at in Wicker Park. That's actually how she found your artwork." He twisted the bracelet so he could see the pendant. There was an etched detail in this one as well. It was the same decorative, slanted heart on mine, with a Celtic knot in the center. "She was headed home from there the night she . . ." He shook his head, closing his lips.

So Sarah had a connection to Wicker Park and, on some level, to me. A shiver raised goose bumps along my skin. "Oh." I felt sorry for asking, both for Sam's sake and mine. How had one of Sarah's creations ended up in front of Iann's place and in my hands? "Well, I'll let you get back to it."

He attempted a smile. "Yeah, people will be arriving anytime now. Um, anyway, I appreciate you coming all this way."

"No problem." I lingered for a moment on the top step as he closed the door, before shoving my hands in my pockets, my fingers knocking into the wood pendant and tracing over the heart.

My hands shook the entire way back to my apartment. Instead of racing thoughts, my mind had frozen, unable to conjure even one plausible explanation for how I had ended up with Sarah's pendant. I thought back to that early morning leaving Iann's place for the first time. The muddy footprints, the boot marks that disappeared into the rain. And beside them, Sarah's pendant discarded among crumpled cigarettes.

A car rumbled toward me as I unlocked my front door.

Wilder parked by the curb in his dark-gray sedan. I waited at the top of the stairs as he closed his car door and walked up to me, my bag in his hands. Relief washed over me.

"Where did you find it?" I asked as I grabbed it from him and looked inside. My phone and wallet were at the bottom.

"A Good Samaritan returned it to the station, I guess," he said.

"Thank you," I said, sliding the strap of the bag on my shoulder. "I can't believe everything's still here."

He nodded. "People aren't all bad . . . well, not all the time," he said. "Do you have a minute to talk?"

My hand tightened around the door handle. Had he followed me to Sam's? "Sure."

He trailed behind me to the kitchen and sat at my tiny table between the bar and TV. "Have a seat," he said, motioning across from him.

I resented his attitude but obeyed.

He leaned his elbows on the table in front of him. "Let's talk about Holly."

My back straightened against the squeaky chair. "I told you I don't know anything."

"No," he said deliberately. "You told me you heard a sound. Did you see anything? *Anything?*"

I thought back to that night. "I saw a figure moving, I think. It was really dark. There aren't any lights on that side by the alley."

He settled into his chair. "Have you thought any more about what I asked you before? Is there anyone you think would want to hurt you?"

"Why are you asking me all of this again?" I asked. We'd been here before. Didn't he have anything else to go on?

The answer was all over his face, and it scared me. "Just standard procedure," he said. "Following up with potential witnesses."

I sighed. "I think you're looking at this wrong. There must be something Holly and Sarah had in common." Sarah and I had something in common—something small—although I couldn't tell Wilder how I knew that without risking his wrath. Maybe there was a link between the three of us that I was missing.

He watched me for a moment. "They did have one thing in common that I can tell."

I leaned forward slightly.

"They both looked remarkably similar to you." He tapped a finger on the table. "Describe what the figure you saw looked like."

I rubbed my fingers into my forehead. "Average, maybe? It was so dark. I don't know." I closed my eyes for a moment. "I was looking down from the top of the staircase, so I don't really know how tall he was."

"He?"

I reopened my eyes. "I don't know," I said. "I just assumed . . . I mean, it's a man, right?"

"What makes you say that?" Wilder asked, pulling a pack of gum from his front pocket.

I shrugged. "It just seems like something a man would do."

"Which part?"

"Going around and strangling women."

"What makes you think they were strangled?" he asked.

This wasn't an interrogation, right? Surely police didn't make house calls for those. "I saw an article. The person who found Holly's body said she'd been choked."

He nodded.

"Didn't anyone else see *anything* that night?"

He glanced around the apartment. "Everyone was either asleep or out." He turned back to me before standing up. "I really want to help you if you're in trouble of some kind. But you have to tell me."

I held his gaze. "There's no trouble. Really."

He stared at me for a moment longer. "Okay. Then you're going to keep hearing from me until this is solved."

A promise? A threat?

CHAPTER TWENTY

The next morning when Iann woke beside me, I pretended to be asleep, keeping my eyes closed as he kissed me on the forehead before walking to the bathroom and shutting the door behind him. I opened my eyes and stretched as the door opened, and he walked past me back to his side of the bed.

"Oh, you woke up?" he asked, pulling his wrinkled button-up shirt over his bare shoulders and rubbing his bloodshot eyes.

I glanced out the window at the first rays of sunlight creeping in. "Do you have class this morning?"

He finished securing the last button and sat down beside me. "No, I have clinic hours first today." He met my eyes. "Is everything okay?" he said after scanning my face for a moment.

I relaxed my forehead. "Yeah, I just still feel bad . . ." *About everything.* "About the other day." It was half-true. I still felt bad about what I'd done to him, but I could get over that. I couldn't get over the other things. The pendant. The rabbit's foot. Sarah. Sam. Holly. That other girl. The lighter.

Iann frowned. "Me too."

"Today's your actual birthday, right?"

He looked surprised. "Yeah."

"I'll take you out tonight to celebrate."

One side of his mouth attempted a smile. "You already gave me my gift and everything. I'm good."

"I know it's not the same, but . . ."

He stood up from the bed. "It's not about my birthday, Harper," he said. "That's not why I was angry. It's fine. Really."

He grabbed his car keys from the nightstand. "I'll see you later," he said without turning around.

If he knew the real reasons I was holding back so much, maybe he could understand. Or maybe he would want out. I was already sacrificing the few pieces of myself that remained intact with this relationship. But I couldn't entirely part with this barrier. It had served me well over the years. And as much as I liked Iann, I couldn't be sure if he was worth giving that up. *One day he'll see you. Truly see you.*

Yes, one day he would. It was inevitable.

And then he'll leave. The more unanswered questions that emerged each day made me less certain if I could really keep this up with Iann. And the more certain I became that I was losing myself. I didn't recognize half the things I was doing anymore.

But I knew I couldn't do nothing.

I pulled out my phone and opened my text chat with Danny. I hadn't reached out to him since our first exchange. I called the number, and the line only rang once.

"This is Danny," he droned, the loud clacking of a keyboard in the background.

"That was fast. I guess it's all hands on deck there, huh?" I said.

The typing stopped. "Harper?" he asked.

"Yeah, sorry to bother you at work."

"No, not at all. I'm glad you called. Did you ditch that imaginary boyfriend of yours?"

"Actually, I was calling to see if you could help me figure out how to research some stuff?"

"Okay . . ." He drew out the word in a long breath. "What kind of stuff?"

I paused. I had no idea how to explain.

"It's fine. Is there coffee?"

"What?" I asked.

"I'll help you," he continued, "but will there be coffee?"

I smiled. "Of course."

He laughed. That sweet music. "Perfect, I'm in."

———

That familiar heat spread throughout my limbs when I saw him. I had raced across town after the studio to meet him tonight. He sat at the table closest to the window, his hair glinting in the fading sunlight. The first couple of buttons of his blue shirt were open, and his sloppily rolled sleeves slid down his arms as he typed on his laptop. He looked up and smiled when he saw me approaching, waving me over.

"There she is," he announced as I sat down. "So, what are we researching, and will it bring the FBI down upon us?" He hadn't changed at all. It was impossible to feel uncomfortable around him.

I put my hand to my chin. "Probably not," I said, mockingly. "Let me get you that coffee I promised first." I motioned to the waitress bringing a cup of water to the table beside us. "Can I get two coffees, please?" She nodded, her eyes lingering on Danny as she walked by. "Thanks for meeting me," I said, glancing out the window at the river across the street.

"Of course. I basically exist in this one-block radius, anyway." He nodded to Tribune Tower at the corner across from us. "So, how can I be of service?"

I pulled a torn piece of paper out of my bag. "Is there a way to find out who lives here?" I slid it across the table toward him.

"Do they own the apartment?" he asked, picking it up.

"I don't know. Probably not."

He furrowed his brow. "Have you considered rummaging through their mailbox?"

I rolled my eyes and laughed. "Are those the kinds of tricks you're learning these days? Whatever happened to journalistic integrity?"

He smiled wryly. "I'm giving you the illegal option, if you choose to use it. I mean, I can find out who owns the property, and then you may be able to find out from them who lives there, if the owner's willing to disclose it or if you're willing to bribe them." He raised his eyebrows, waiting for my reaction.

"Okay, how do I find out who owns the unit?" The waitress was back and set down the two cups with cream and sugar. She had taken her hair out of its sloppy bun.

"Thanks," Danny said as he opened his laptop. "Okay, so we'll look up the Cook County real property records, and then we can verify that with the appraisal district records. That'll give you a name and address. Are you looking for a phone number?"

No, I wanted the name. "Address is fine." I cupped the warm mug in my hands and moved my chair beside his.

His fingers punched the keyboard at lightning speed. "What's this all about?" He glanced down at the paper.

I took a sip. "What do you mean?"

He entered the search, and the next web page loaded. "I mean, come on, what's going on here? Does this person owe you money or something?" He swigged the hot coffee without flinching and set it back down with a clatter.

My cheeks burned. How could I even begin to explain without sounding insane? How could I tell him that I'd followed that strange girl back to her apartment? The lighter? *J. L.* "I think I found a friend of mine who's been missing, but I want to know if that was her."

He clicked on a thumbnail on the screen, and it loaded a scanned document. "Missing, huh? Is it newsworthy?"

I shook my head. "If you're looking for news, you're hanging out with the wrong person."

He looked at me from the corner of his eye. "Okay, so here's the deed from when the current company purchased those condos in the '80s, and that's the latest one on record. It looks like the owner is Humboldt Edge Management LLC, and they have a corporate address listed in the same building."

I sank into my seat. "There's no way to see who lives in that unit?"

"Hmm . . . if I had a name, then I could find an address, but it's hard to do it the other way around if they don't own the property." He glanced at me. "Do you want me to email you this copy of the deed?"

I sighed. "No, that's okay. Thanks for your help."

He shut his laptop and held the coffee to his lips. "I hope everything's okay with your friend."

"It's okay. We're not that close."

He surveyed me through narrowed eyes. "I forgot how guarded you can be."

How could *he* say that? He had seen me through some of the worst moments of my life. "I'm sorry, I—"

He shook his head. "It's fine, Harper. I know what to expect from you by now. And you don't owe me any explanations. Hell, we haven't seen each other in years."

He was right. What was I doing reaching out to him for a favor after all this time? *You're so selfish.*

"But I'm happy I get to see you again." He nodded out the window. "Do you want to take our coffee for a walk?"

I followed his gaze to the Riverwalk. "Yeah, that sounds good."

———

"We didn't get to really catch up last time." He kicked a pebble under the railing and into the water. "So other than making it as a big-city artist, how are you?"

"Don't get too excited." I laughed. "I'm barely making a living."

He shrugged. "Yeah, but you're doing what you've always wanted to. And so am I. That's pretty amazing, isn't it?" He wandered ahead to a bench under the DuSable Bridge and sat down.

I sat next to him, with two hand's lengths between us. "I guess it is." It felt odd to be so close to him without touching. "So, what else is going on in your life now?"

He leaned forward, resting his elbows on his knees. "Nothing much. Work is my life. Tell me about your boyfriend."

My body tensed at the thought of Iann. Danny was right. I kept everyone locked out. Everything I was hiding from Iann was beginning to pile up. "He's great. He's a grad student at DePaul."

He nodded, staring straight ahead. "What's he studying?" he asked half-heartedly.

"Psychology."

This was the first time talking to Danny that his lack of enthusiasm was so obvious. I figured I'd try to redirect to a safer topic. "So, are you still sailing?"

He smiled, meeting my eyes. "Almost every weekend." That explained the tan. "I got my parents to sell my boat in San Francisco, and then I bought one here recently. All the money I make here goes to pay the docking fee. You still won't go near water?"

I hadn't gone near the lake since the accident. Danny didn't know the reason why. "Yeah, give it up. You'll never get me on a boat."

"Have you gone back to Evanston?" His voice grew heavy.

"Never." My fists clenched involuntarily.

He frowned. "Good."

I had no desire to know, but the question hung there.

Danny could feel it too. "I heard he was made dean of the Music Department last year," he said slowly.

"Good for him," I said, coolly, squeezing my coffee cup tighter.

He surveyed my expression. "Sorry, I thought you might want to know."

"Yeah, I do. But I'm not happy about it." It was unfair that he could move on unscathed from everything he'd put me through for years. But I only had myself to blame. I had kept quiet and just run away.

"Yeah," he continued, "I wasn't too thrilled to see that blurb in the alumni newsletter, either, but it is what it is."

"I'm sorry about . . ." *Everything.* "How things ended back then." They hadn't ended, though. Not really. And maybe that was the worst part. To vanish and leave so much uncertainty for years had eaten away at me.

"They didn't end," he said, eerily echoing my thoughts with a sad smile. "They changed. And now that we're both okay, we can be friends."

Friends? I nodded. "Yeah, okay, I like that."

CHAPTER
TWENTY-ONE

Meeting with Danny had been a great distraction, but once we parted, I kept picturing the girl. Issi. The walking ghost from my nightmares. But she wasn't a ghost. Issi or not, she was real.

I hovered around the corner in front of her apartment building until I saw the figure of someone approaching through the glass. I sprang toward the door as a man exited, and he held it open behind him so I could squeeze by. Did he recognize me, or was he too trusting? I jumped into the elevator, but as the doors closed, my thoughts grew troubled.

You saw me die.

Of course. I knew on every level that it couldn't be Issi. I shook my head, and the image appeared of her body floating in the water. But I needed to know her name. It was the last reassurance I needed. And then I could stop obsessing. Wondering.

Or maybe it would only get worse. What did this mean together with what had happened to Holly and Sarah?

The elevator door opened on the ninth floor. I stepped out onto the marbled concrete, my footfalls echoing through the empty hallway.

I could hear the small sounds of a TV playing and a dog growling, and then I reached 906. Silence.

I shook my head again and inhaled slowly.

I twisted the knob, and the door wheezed softly as it opened into the dark apartment. She hadn't locked the door.

Maybe she's planning to come back in a few minutes. Maybe she's still in the building.

My heart raced as I stepped over the threshold. The strong smell of vomit filled my nostrils, and I stifled a gag, raising my sleeve to my nose.

I walked through the dark kitchen, careful to keep my elbows close to my sides to avoid brushing against the stack of dishes lining the sink and counters.

One foot fell in front of the other as if they were leading themselves in a slow shuffle over the tile. I strained my ears but only heard the quickening thud of my pulse as I turned the corner. She was ahead in the next room, collapsed on the sofa, her hoop earrings on the rug beside her drooping arm. I backtracked into the kitchen, light headed. I gripped the edge of the counter, my hand slipping on a stack of paper envelopes. I grabbed the crumpled corner of the envelope on top and tucked it under my arm before swinging the door open wide enough to slip out. It closed behind me, and I gulped for the clean air.

I took the paper out from under my arm. It was addressed to Jenny Langdon.

J. L.

———

I fumbled with the envelope on the train ride home, examining it under the yellow, flickering light. I shoved it into my pocket when I got off at Damen. The return address was from Let's Entertain Chicago LLC.

I folded and unfolded one edge of the paper over and over in my pocket as I walked home. I glanced up at the Robey in passing. Iann was probably going to be getting to his shift soon.

I turned the corner past the park and went through the dirty graffitied alleyway. I stopped when I saw Wilder descending the steps from my apartment. His eyes locked on me, and he started down the asphalt.

Shit.

I waited for him to meet me. He seemed restless, maybe eager.

"I was about to knock down your door," he said.

My heart froze, and I quickly pulled my hand from my pocket. "What's going on?"

"There's been a possible development . . . about Holly."

I unclenched my fists.

He narrowed his eyes. "We have a lead on a potential person of interest," he began, tapping the binder in his hand. "And I'd like for you to identify him."

"I don't understand," I sputtered. "I told you I didn't see anything."

He took a step toward me. He smelled like cigarettes. "I know I've been patient with you so far, but now is the moment for you to step up with what you saw and heard," he said in a low voice.

I shook my head. "I've told you everything. I didn't see the person or Holly. I don't even know where that sound came from."

He exhaled. It wasn't a sigh but more of a growl. "I'll tell you what the sound was." He pulled his phone from his jacket pocket and flipped through it. "Do you know the last thing Holly ever did while she was fighting for her life that night?" He turned the phone screen toward me.

My stomach dropped. It was a close-up photograph of a hand, the skin blue and pale, the fingernails bloodied and broken at the tips. I looked away.

"It takes about ten seconds for someone to pass out from strangulation," he said coolly, continuing to hold up the phone to my face. "And in every one of those seconds, Holly reached for the closest thing she could and clawed at it until she passed out."

I remembered the police huddled around the alleyway, observing the garbage can lid. The metallic sound. That screeching, scraping sound.

He returned the phone into his pocket. "After that, whoever did this to her kept choking her for another four minutes until she died."

My hands and knees trembled.

"You didn't help her then. But now you can."

Asshole. I swallowed. "I want to," I said. "But all I saw was a shadow." I finally met his eyes.

His gaze had softened. "All I'm asking is that you try."

"Okay."

He gestured behind him to his car parked at the curb. "Can you come down to the station now?"

"Okay," I said again. I followed him to his car in a daze. The stench of smoke overwhelmed me as I opened the door and sat in the passenger's seat. When he started the car, I quickly rolled down the window.

He noticed. "Sorry," he said, starting down the road. "I tried quitting, but I couldn't help sneaking one in on my way here. It's been a stressful day."

I stared ahead out the window. It hurt deep inside now that I knew. What if Holly had seen me? What if she'd been trying to get my attention? I saw the police station as we turned into Bucktown, and I gripped the side of the door. My memory suddenly felt blank. How could I possibly remember that night?

"Are you okay?" Wilder asked as he parked in the gated lot behind the building.

"Yeah," I breathed.

"I'm going to have an officer walk the guy in front of you and—"

I froze. "No, I'm not doing that!"

He stared at me for a long moment before digging into his pocket and extracting a stick of gum.

"Don't you think that's a bad idea?" I pressed. "I don't want him to see me."

He flipped the gum into his mouth. "He won't. I'll be standing right by you the whole time, and the other officers will walk him out. To him, you'll just be another person in the station." He opened the car door and got out.

I stayed in my seat, clutching the door handle harder.

He waited in front of my door.

I avoided his gaze, finally stepping out after a minute. The feeling left my body as I followed behind him. He said something to me, but I couldn't hear him. I saw Holly's bloody fingers. I heard the scratching, louder than ever.

Once behind a passcode-protected door, we walked through a busy area with desks and officers, all of them talking with others across the table. Wilder led me to a bench beside an empty desk in the corner of the room. "Okay, sit here for a minute," he said, glancing over his shoulder. "I'll be right back, and I'll stay with you when they bring him out, okay?"

I nodded, pressing my palms against my knees.

He disappeared down the hallway. I counted my heartbeats until he reemerged minutes later.

I took a breath and leaned back against the bench.

"They're going to bring him out now," he said, bending down toward me. "Stand up, and we'll face this direction."

I stood slowly and followed where he motioned me to stand behind him, my knees quaking.

"And Harper." He glanced at me over his shoulder. "We're going to keep investigating whether this is him or not, okay? So, no pressure."

No pressure? What about everything he'd said about how I'd allowed Holly to die alone in the alley? I nodded.

"He's going to come from that hall with two uniformed officers standing at his sides."

I watched the entrance to the bullpen, trying to ignore the people passing by and chattering. I took one step closer to Wilder's back, only half my body visible to the room. I could feel the excitement radiating from his body.

I saw the officers before the man came into view. My shoulders stiffened when my eyes focused on Jeremy, his appearance more haggard than the last time I'd seen him with Erin. He was almost across the room when he suddenly turned and locked his eyes on me. His hazel eyes widened, and he held that gaze until they pulled him into a separate room on the other side.

Wilder turned to me. "So?"

I was starting to feel light headed from the overwhelming pounding in my chest. I gripped his arm.

"What?" He grabbed my hand.

I fell back onto the bench, my thoughts racing. I could barely hear Wilder repeat the question.

"Harper?" He squeezed my hand.

"I know him," I said, meeting his eyes.

His face lit up.

"But not from the alley," I continued. "He was—he came to my work that night. The night that Holly died."

"And you saw him after the murder?"

I shook my head. "No. *Oh god. Erin.* "He came to a class at my studio before I went home and heard Holly," I said, slowly. "Then, I saw him a couple of times after. He's dating my friend." I turned to Wilder. "Why is he here? What does he have to do with Holly?"

He cast a look around the room. "I can't tell you the details," he said. "I'll give you a ride back home."

I stood up beside him. "What? That's it?"

He let out a long breath. "Just to be clear, you did *not* see him in the alley that night?"

"No." I had hoped there was some impression, some face in that shadow that had buried itself deep inside me somewhere. But the shadow was still a shadow in my mind. "I really didn't see who it was."

"Okay, let's go." He gently tapped my shoulder, herding me toward the back door.

"He saw me," I said once we were both sitting in the car.

Wilder turned his key in the ignition.

"You said he wouldn't see me." The panic set in. I had to talk to Erin. "He recognized me."

Wilder's eyes remained focused on the road ahead.

"You have to give me something," I insisted. "Why did you bring him in?"

"Look, I appreciate that you tried, but I don't owe you any information," he grumbled.

"What if my friend's in danger? I have to let her know." What about Iann? Did he know his colleague had been questioned by the police? "What if he comes after me?"

Wilder parked at the curb past my building.

I could make out Bug standing outside the first floor, tinkering with the heating unit.

Wilder patted at his jacket pocket. "He's a person of interest at this point," he said, extracting a new stick of gum. After a moment, he continued. "He's an ex of Holly's, and we recently discovered they had a fight the week she was murdered."

I clenched my jaw. "Will he be arrested?"

"I don't know." His voice was strangely calmer than usual.

Why was he at the studio the night Holly died?

"I'll keep you updated," Wilder said, unlocking the doors.

A tightness knotted in my chest as I walked up to my apartment. Once inside, I turned on the light and let my bag fall to the ground. I closed the door, ignoring the sound of Wilder's engine starting behind me. The sound of his car revved and died as it continued down the street.

It's not him. Part of me had expected to see a different face in the police station. I was relieved. My father wasn't capable of it after all. *Yes, he is. You know what he did.*

But instead, it had been another face I'd recognized. I dialed Erin's number, cursing when it went to voice mail. "Hey Erin, give me a call as soon as you get this." This couldn't wait until tomorrow night's class.

I walked straight to the bathroom and swung open the cabinet door, feeling against the crumpled napkin until my fingers wrapped around two pills. I swallowed them without another thought, then sank onto the floor.

I pulled my jacket off, the envelope from Jenny's apartment peeking out as it fell to the floor. I ripped it open as Woodstock appeared beside me.

It was a pay stub from Let's Entertain. They had paid her $6,558.98 through direct deposit. She got paid that much for one month's worth of work? I set the paper down and unlocked my phone. I typed her name into Google. Her social media popped up immediately. She had all the different kinds of accounts. I clicked on her LinkedIn page first.

Marketing director.

That explained the enormous paycheck. And the downtown one-bedroom apartment. She'd graduated from Northwestern the year before I'd started and had worked at various downtown companies since. She'd been at Let's Entertain, a nightlife company, the longest, at three years.

I clicked back to the results and opened her Facebook page. She wore so much makeup in her pictures that I suddenly didn't feel sure that she resembled me at all. I scrolled down her timeline through the years. Through the pictures of tequila shots. Through the pictures of her kissing guys on the beach, at the pool, and at the club.

I stopped on her high school graduation photo. It may as well have been me standing there but with perfectly straightened hair swapped for my own frizzy teenage tresses. Issi had always had straight hair.

I scrolled farther until I saw the pictures of her family. I was at once relieved and disappointed by the two boys on either side of Jenny and another girl, all with matching smiles shadowed by her beaming mom and dad.

Seeing Jenny and her perfect family filled me with another emotion, one so intense that my fist clenched involuntarily.

Why couldn't that be us?

CHAPTER TWENTY-TWO

His face is distorted through the water before I break the surface. He stands above me on the pier. His eyes are looking through me.

"Dad!" My mouth starts to fill with water once I open it, the waves breaking against my lips.

Without a word, he kneels slowly onto the pier and reaches toward me. I extend my hands, finally able to lift my head above the waves. His eyes finally focus on me, and he grips both sides of my head before submerging it.

The icy water rips through my lungs like knives, my nails meeting the flesh of his hands. A torrent of bubbles explodes in the water in front of me as I scream.

———

A sharp headache shattered the dream. I couldn't remember where I was until my hands curled around my soft blanket. I opened my eyes and jumped, backing up on the bed.

Bug was facing away from me. But I recognized that sweaty back and that smell anywhere.

"What are you doing?" I gasped.

He pulled himself out from the window, knocking his head against the windowsill.

I was still wearing my clothes from the day before, but I pulled the blanket around my shoulders. "What the hell are you doing here?"

He waved his wrench toward me. "The heater's broken," he said, rubbing the top of his balding head. "I knocked, but you didn't answer."

"Get out!" I stood up, steadying myself against the bed. "You can't come in here! Not when I'm sleeping!"

He put his hands up before tossing the wrench into his toolbox. "This is my house—"

"I'm your tenant," I said, my voice growing louder with each word.

He smirked, eyeing me. His gaze lingered on my neck, focusing on the scar. "Oh yeah? Under what lease?" He laughed. "I'm doing you a favor."

"Fuck you! I pay rent." I glanced around the room. Had he seen Woodstock?

"Barely," he grumbled.

"Get out," I said again, this time through bared teeth.

He picked up his toolbox. "I fixed it, anyway." His eyes surveyed my chest before he turned and opened the door with his free hand. "If I see that cat in here again, I'm going to kill it."

My heart thudded in my chest.

"Bitch," he muttered under his breath as he closed the door behind him.

I collapsed back onto the bed, my heart beating hard enough to power a small engine. I leaned my head against the wall. This wasn't the first time he'd seen (or threatened) Woodstock. It happened about every other year, and then he'd forget about it.

A notification buzzed on my phone. I dug my hand under the pillows beside me and extracted it.

Iann (9:07 p.m.): How's everything going?

In all the excitement I had almost forgotten about Jeremy. I ran a hand over my face. I could see that look in his eyes again. Was it recognition or horror?

I turned the phone over in my hands.

Are you still coming over? I texted. His response came immediately.

Iann (9:12 p.m.): On my way.

I gnawed at my fingernail as I recalled the way Jeremy had watched Erin the first time we'd met at the studio. Something about him had always bothered me. If it was Jeremy, there was at least a motive, a relationship to pin it on. But what did that mean about Sarah's death? Did he know her too? Was it a simple case of mistaken identity? And if so, how could his coming to *my* studio be a coincidence?

I heard footsteps on the stairs outside and got to my feet. I swung the door open right as Iann reached the landing.

"Hey," he said. "Did you eat already?" He stepped inside and kissed me.

"No, but I'm not hungry." I closed the door. "I need to talk to you."

"Is everything okay?" he asked, taking off his jacket and setting it on the desk chair.

I shook my head and sat on the bed. "No. It's been a weird day. I don't know how to tell you everything."

He furrowed his brow. "What happened?" He settled on the bed beside me and placed a warm hand on my back.

"Do you remember that murder I told you about? The one in this neighborhood?" It had inevitably come up weeks ago when Wilder had paid me a visit right as Iann drove up.

He nodded.

"That detective—Wilder—asked me to come in and identify someone yesterday."

Iann's eyes widened. "Wow, so they caught the guy?"

My stomach dropped. "I don't know," I said. "I recognized him, but I don't know if that was the person I saw in the alley. But Iann . . ." I turned to face him. "The guy they're investigating is Jeremy."

His expression darkened, and he stood up. "What?" He paced in front of me. "How?"

"He used to date the girl who died. That's all I know."

Iann looked at me. "I can't believe it." He leaned against the drafting table.

"I need to tell Erin."

He shook his head. "Do the police know for sure?"

I fidgeted with my hands. "No, but—"

"Then wait. Telling her now would just freak her out." He looked straight ahead into the kitchen as if he were far away.

"Did you know Holly?" I asked.

He turned back to me, his eyes unreadable.

"Holly Bascom? She's the girl that was murdered—Jeremy's ex."

"No," he said, gripping the back of the chair as he shifted forward on his feet. "I mean I don't really know anything about him outside of school. It's still shocking, though. He seemed like an okay guy."

My phone buzzed nearby. My heart dropped when I saw the screen. Wilder. "I need to take this," I said before answering. "Hello?"

"We had to let him go."

I couldn't speak.

"We couldn't detain him forever, and without any more evidence—" Wilder sighed. "I just wanted to let you know."

"I don't understand," I said once I regained my voice. "I thought—"

"We're going to keep investigating, but for now, he's out."

"What am I supposed to do?" I touched my neck, pressing against the scar. "He knows I'm a witness now." Iann returned to my side.

"He's not going to hurt you," Wilder said in a lowered voice. "I'll make sure of it. He won't try anything now that he knows we're keeping tabs on him."

Maybe.

"Harper?" Wilder's voice broke the silence.

"Yeah, I get it." I hung up.

Iann looked at me. "What's going on?"

I ran a hand through my hair. "They had to let Jeremy go," I said. "He saw me. When I went there to identify him."

"How could this happen? Why is he out?" Iann asked, his voice raised above its usual soothing tone.

"They said there wasn't enough evidence against him right now." I felt like throwing up. I could see Holly's fingers flash through my mind's eye.

You don't care about Holly. You're just scared you're next.

CHAPTER TWENTY-THREE

I paced in front of Erin's apartment, waiting for someone to answer the intercom. As soon as I'd woken at 7:00 a.m. and realized Erin hadn't so much as texted, I headed to her place, calling her over and over again on my way, all the worst scenarios racing through my mind.

"Hello?" Erin's voice was groggy over the speaker.

Thank god. "Hey! You're home?"

Erin didn't answer but buzzed me in.

I was so glad that she answered that it didn't occur to me until the elevator opened on her floor: What if Jeremy was with her?

Erin was standing in the doorway, her red eyes barely open, her silk pajama set and matching robe wrinkled. "What are you doing here? It's *way* too early."

I stepped in beside her and closed the door, looking around for signs of Jeremy or her roommates. "You never called me back."

She leaned against the kitchen counter. "Oh, shit! I totally forgot. But in my defense, we got pretty wasted last night."

"We?" I didn't see any coat or men's shoes near the entrance.

She yawned. "Me and Jeremy. We went out last night."

"Where is he?"

"He left a couple of hours ago. So, what's going on? What's so urgent that you got me out of bed at the crack of dawn?"

"Actually, I wanted to talk to you about Jeremy."

She stared at me. "Okay . . ."

Just spit it out. "Has he mentioned anything about his ex-girlfriend to you?"

"Uh-huh." Her eyes were more alert now. "You mean Holly? Yeah."

That was surprising. "Did he tell you that he's a suspect in her murder?"

"Wait, what?"

"I found out that he used to be involved with the girl who got strangled in front of my apartment a few months ago."

Her expression changed, but she said nothing. Erin would never be so quiet if this was her first time hearing about it.

"Aren't you going to say something?"

She shrugged, then opened the fridge and extracted a carton of orange juice. "I mean it's weird, but he hadn't seen her in months before she died."

"Yeah, but—"

She laughed. "It's ridiculous to me that you'd assume he did something to her just because they used to date."

My mind twisted, trying to come up with an explanation for her cold reaction. "First of all, *I'm* not assuming anything. The police are looking into him. Second, aren't you the one who says, 'It's always the boyfriend'?"

She shook her head. "What's your point, Harper?"

"I was scared for you. I thought Jeremy might do something."

"To me?" she scoffed, pouring orange juice into one of the glasses on the counter. "So what? He had a bad breakup, okay? And he told me that Holly was into some messed-up stuff. We all have rough stuff in our past. And I'm sure you haven't even told Iann about all of your baggage. But Iann's no saint either."

"What's that supposed to mean?"

She took a sip of juice. "Nothing, just . . . I've been out with him and Jeremy's other friends more than you."

All those times I'd brushed off Iann's invites to a happy hour with his colleagues, it hadn't even crossed my mind that Erin would be there with Jeremy.

"And maybe he's not entirely sharing everything with you either."

I was going to resist the bait. I could see from her smirk that she wanted me to ask her more, to demand she tell me what I didn't know about him. "Don't you think it's strange that Jeremy showed up at our studio the night Holly was murdered?" I wanted to point out the resemblance between Holly and me, but I couldn't make sense of that myself.

"He left with his friends that night. You saw him."

I had. And he'd left early enough to get to my street and lie in wait for Holly. "The police asked me to identify him."

"What? Why would they ask *you*?"

"I was on the street when she got murdered. I didn't realize it at the time, but I heard and saw her in the alley that night."

She took a step toward me. "What did you do?"

"I didn't get a good look at anything that night, and that's what I told the police," I said. "But I had to tell them that I know Jeremy and that he was at the studio that night."

Her blue eyes were daggers. "I can't believe you."

"I don't understand. Not long ago you and Jeremy were over and now you're *absolutely* certain he had nothing to do with Holly's death?"

"Yes." She clenched her jaw.

"Okay," I said, defeated. "I'm sorry I woke you up. I just wanted to make sure you were all right." I grabbed my bag and walked to the door.

"He and Holly were still friends," she muttered. "Ask Iann."

Iann? I whipped around, but she was already around the corner, shutting her bedroom door.

CHAPTER TWENTY-FOUR

By the time I met Iann for lunch that afternoon by the campus, I'd replayed Erin's words over and over again in my mind.

Ask Iann.

But I didn't ask him. Instead I listened while he discussed his recent meeting with his faculty advisor. I answered with a terse "It's fine" when he asked how I was feeling about the Jeremy situation.

"I haven't seen him since he got released," he said, furrowing his brow and dipping a fry in ketchup. "I can't stop worrying about what he's doing and if he really saw you that day at the station. Did you talk to Erin?"

I nodded. "Yeah. Apparently she knew all about his ex-girlfriend. She's completely behind Jeremy on this. I'm pretty sure she's not going to talk to me now." I guessed I'd find out tonight at the studio for sure.

He frowned. "You're just looking out for her. She should be careful. I mean, I hate to think that he's capable of doing something like that, but you never know."

Ask Iann.

I studied him. When I'd first told him about Jeremy, he'd said he didn't know Holly. "Erin said something today about—" My phone buzzed. "Hold on, this is her." I quickly answered. Was she in trouble? "Hey, is everything okay?"

"Hey," she said flatly on the other end. "I wanted to let you know Hannah's taking your class tonight. Don't come in."

So she *was* pissed. "What? Why?"

There was a buzz of chatter in the background on her end. If I focused, I could make out Jeremy's low voice among the cacophony on the other end. "It's a private party, and they specifically requested her."

Bullshit. I glanced at Iann as he chewed a bite of his burger. *Don't make a scene. That's what she wants.* "Okay, fine. I guess I'll see you tomorrow night then."

"Yeah, I guess so."

"Is everything okay?" Iann asked after I hung up.

"Erin gave my class away tonight." I imagined Jeremy's smug face from the night when Erin had introduced us. I pushed my plate away, eyeing Iann.

"What were you going to say before she called?"

"Hmm?"

"You were about to tell me something Erin said earlier," he said.

It became apparent in that moment as I looked into his soft brown eyes, the sting of Erin's call still ringing in my ears, that she'd just been trying to make me crazy about this. For whatever reason, she wanted to throw me off Jeremy's scent and onto Iann. I smiled and shook my head. "Nothing. I already forgot."

———

I clutched my jacket tighter around my waist, then cupped my coffee mug between both palms as the wind rattled through my hair. After leaving Iann, I'd realized another reason Erin might have wanted to keep me away from the studio tonight.

It was hard to see inside from the street, but I could make out Jeremy's highlighted hair, never straying far from Erin as she bustled around the studio near the end of class. Hannah had taken off before the customers even began packing, leaving Erin and Jeremy to clean up the place. Although, by the way his head constantly eclipsed hers, his hands around her waist, they weren't accomplishing much.

I took a sip of my coffee, backtracking to behind the streetlamp as they emerged from the studio's front door. I could see them better from this angle as they walked toward the street, pausing to kiss once they reached it. Jeremy extracted something from his coat pocket and folded it into Erin's open palm. I caught the flash of the yellow plastic pill bottle before she dropped it in her purse.

My heart sank. She'd been out of rehab for nearly a year now, and this whole time I'd thought she'd stopped. What was in the bottle? Uppers? Downers? Erin had never been one to discriminate.

Eventually the two untangled from one another, and Jeremy headed in the opposite direction of Erin's apartment. I watched Erin stagger away—she'd had at least three glasses of wine by my count—before I set off after Jeremy.

He never once looked over his shoulder or paused on his way to the train station. I nearly lost my nerve after I boarded the train, suddenly aware that he only had to glance through the crowd of passengers the right way to see me on the other end of the car. I waited a few seconds before exiting after him downtown. To my surprise he transferred to another train heading north.

I tugged my collar up to my ears and faced toward the window, hoping he wouldn't recognize me. My phone buzzed in my hands.

Iann (10:03 p.m.): Just checking in. Are you feeling better? You left so quickly earlier.

I glanced at Jeremy staring down at his phone.

(10:04 p.m.): All good. Just needed to sleep, I think.

Several stops later, Jeremy shot up as the train screeched to a halt. When we got out, I recognized the building across the street. Advocate Medical Center. I stayed back at the crosswalk, watching as he entered the hospital. He had clinic hours at the same place Iann did? It made sense, but I tried to recall if Iann had ever mentioned running into Jeremy there. He was always saying he only saw Jeremy at school.

"What are you doing?"

I jumped, nearly dropping my phone.

Wilder appeared beside me, pinching a cigarette between his thumb and index finger, the light from the changing walk sign flashing against his pale hair. "You shouldn't be here."

My pulse was still racing from the shock of seeing him out here. How long had he been behind me? Was it possible I just hadn't spotted him on the train? "Why are *you* here?"

He nodded toward the hospital. "Willing to bet the same reason you are," he said. "I thought you were afraid of this guy. I'm a little surprised to see you seeking him out."

I shoved my hands in my pockets. "I'm worried about my friend. You said there wasn't enough evidence. Why are you trailing him?"

He glanced at me. "There isn't enough evidence about Holly, but I'm fairly certain he's caught up in something else here. Only a matter of time before I can connect the two."

Here? At the clinic?

Ask Iann.

I shook my head as if that'd somehow dislodge the nagging thought. "I don't understand. What's the medical center have to do with anything?"

"Go home." Wilder crushed the cigarette under his shoe. As the light began to change again, he stepped toward the curb. "I mean it. And leave this alone. Let me do my job."

I watched his back as he walked away, my feet stuck to the spot.

CHAPTER TWENTY-FIVE

The world was quiet on this side of Erin's cold shoulder treatment. Her mood didn't improve the next night, and she said only three words to me at the studio: "Clean up tonight."

As much as Erin's usual chattiness grated on me, I was starving for conversation by the time Iann stopped by my apartment after work. "What are you working on?" He nodded to my drafting table and set his backpack by the bed.

"Book cover." I'd picked up another job online as soon as I'd returned home after class. I wasn't sure how many more of my classes Erin was going to give away on a whim, and rent was due soon.

Iann ran a hand through his hair, tousled by the windy walk from the Robey. "I can't stay long, but I brought you something."

"Oh, where are you going after this?" I hoped it wasn't the clinic. Seeing Wilder homing in on Jeremy had somehow both alleviated and antagonized my creeping doubts about Iann.

"The library. I have a test on Friday, so I need to get at least a couple of hours in before." He fished through his backpack, then produced a small paper box and handed it to me.

I sat beside him on the bed. "What's this?"

He grinned. "I stopped by that new cookie place you mentioned last week."

I'd told him in passing that the late-night bakery was always closed on my way to the studio and then I always forgot to stop by afterward. He'd remembered that?

"Sorry, some of them probably got crushed, but I'm sure they're still good. That place smells amazing."

I opened the box and stared down at the cookies, the warm sugary smell wafting through the room. I felt guilty. As much as I told myself Erin was messing with me, I couldn't get her comments out of my head.

He nudged my arm. "Go ahead and try one." He laughed.

I let the flimsy lid fall shut. The knot in my stomach wouldn't stop twisting. "Did you know Jeremy worked at the same clinic as you?" I blurted out, avoiding his gaze.

His smile faded. "What? Yeah, of course."

"Why didn't you ever tell me that he worked there?"

"I don't know . . . it never really came up. And it doesn't matter. I mean, he and I don't work *together* there. A lot of people in our department go there to volunteer." He seemed surprised but not upset. The lines in his brow deepened as he closed his hand around mine. He was looking at me like I was crazy. "What's this really about?"

"Erin said something the other day. She made it seem like you knew that Holly and Jeremy still hung out after they broke up. But when I mentioned Holly the other day, you acted like you'd never even heard of her." My entire body tensed as I watched his face, but there was nothing. Not even a flicker or a glance to the side.

"I don't know why Erin would say that, but I've never met Holly, or at least I didn't realize it. Not to sound like a jerk, but Jeremy's usually around a lot of different girls at one time. It's hard to keep track."

But he would've remembered Holly. She shared a face with his girlfriend. "I'm sorry. I guess I've just been . . . I don't know, this whole thing with Jeremy and the police has really messed with my head." I slipped my hand from his and stood up, then set the box of cookies on the nightstand. "That detective followed Jeremy to Advocate Medical, and I freaked out. I didn't realize he worked there too."

"I honestly haven't even seen him since the whole police station thing you told me about. And I haven't wanted to. I want him far away from you. I'm glad the police are keeping an eye on him." He stood beside me. "Do you want me to stay tonight? I don't want to leave you upset like this." His arms wrapped behind my back, and I melted into him, resting my head against his shoulder.

Make him stay. "No, I'll be fine. I think I just need to sleep." Maybe now that I'd told him about what Erin had said, I could finally rest.

He brushed a strand of hair from my face and kissed my forehead. "I can come back after the library if you want."

"Are you sure?"

He nodded, smiling down at me. "Of course." He stooped to pick up his backpack. "Please lock the door after I leave, okay?"

"Yeah, I will."

He glanced at me over his shoulder. "Are you really okay?"

"Yeah, I'm good. Really."

He gave me a weak smile and walked out the door, closing it softly behind himself.

I listened to his footsteps retreat before pouncing on the lock. I lay down on the bed, hoping my mind would calm now that I'd resolved everything with Iann, but it still raced with questions. There were little ones, like what did Wilder think Jeremy was up to at the clinic? And was Jeremy's appearance at the studio the night of Holly's murder just a coincidence? But the biggest and most unsettling question weighing on my mind ate away at the very foundation of this case. *Did Jeremy have something to do with Sarah's murder too?*

CHAPTER TWENTY-SIX

I'd called him before 7:00 a.m., but he'd still managed to put himself together in a pressed shirt and khakis before I arrived. Sam stared at me in that same strange way, and I wondered for a moment if he remembered who I was or if he just saw Sarah.

"Hi," I said carefully. "Is now still a good time to talk?"

"Yeah, of course." He nodded, opening the door and beckoning for me to follow him inside. The hallway was a mess of little girl shoes and coats. "I just got Anna on the bus," he said, closing the door. "Do you want something to drink?" He led the way to the kitchen, and in the light streaming from the enormous picture window, I saw the deep shadows etched under his eyes.

"No, I'm good. I don't want to keep you, but . . . I felt like I had to talk to you." After seeing him face to face, I wondered if he could handle it.

He poured coffee into a mug. "You said it's about Sarah's case?" He took a sip and flinched before setting it down on the counter.

I pulled out my phone, unlocked it, and opened the photo I'd saved from Jeremy's Facebook. "Do you recognize this man?" I slid it across the counter so Sam could see.

He looked down at it for several silent seconds. "I don't think so." His tone grew agitated. "Who is this? Is this—"

"There's nothing certain, really," I said quickly, taking my phone back. "It's just someone the police were looking into in Holly's case. They didn't have enough evidence, though. I was hoping maybe he was somehow connected to Sarah too." I glanced up. His expression had darkened, his fist clenching. "I'm so sorry, Sam. I shouldn't have come. I was . . . I wanted to help, that's all. But clearly—"

"No, I'm glad you told me," he said. "I'm thinking . . . I don't know who this is, but Sarah thought someone was following her a couple of times. It was months before her death, but she told me that a guy came up to her and called her by a different name. It really creeped her out."

My chest tightened. "What name?"

He shook his head. "She never told me, or if she did, I forgot. It didn't seem important at the time. It only happened once or twice and only when she was in Wicker Park."

Could Jeremy have been looking for Holly and found Sarah instead? "You're sure it wasn't 'Holly'?"

"No. It could've been, but I honestly don't remember her even telling me that part." His lips were pressed in a thin line.

"Why didn't you mention this to the police?"

"I did. I told Detective Wilder, and he took note of it, but he said it was a pretty weak lead." He pointed to my phone. "You're thinking that guy might've mistaken Sarah for Holly?"

"I don't know." It was my best guess, but there was one other option I could think of. "Did Sarah ever go to Advocate Medical Center for any reason?"

"No. Never." Sam took a step toward me. I suddenly realized how much bigger he was than me. "What's that guy's name?"

I slid my phone into my jacket pocket. It had been a mistake coming here. The look in his eyes was one of desperation—he was willing to latch on to any possible explanation. There was no telling what he'd do with a name. "Sam, I don't think I can tell you. I shouldn't have said anything."

He held my gaze. "I don't think you understand how infuriating it is to have something like this dangled in front of me just to lead nowhere."

"I know, I'm sorry. There's no reason to believe Holly's investigation is even related to Sarah's." At least, according to the police. "I was hoping that if a link existed, I could find it. I can't imagine what you're going through."

"I know what you're trying to do, but Sarah wasn't just a clue or a victim." He hung his head. "She was my whole life. And it's killing me that they haven't found out who did this to her."

I wanted to disappear into the floor. He was right. Maybe I'd become so caught up in my own fear and curiosity that I'd truly stopped caring about Holly and Sarah as individuals whose worlds had just stopped spinning one day. "I'm sorry," I said again, as if it would ever be enough. "I'll go." I turned toward the door.

"And please, leave me out of it," Sam said behind me. "I don't think I can handle any more of this."

———

Iann was parked in front of my building when I arrived home from Sam's house. He opened the driver's side door and stepped out as I approached.

"I'm sorry, did we have plans?" I asked, wiping my eyes with my sleeve so he wouldn't see I'd been crying.

He studied me, his eyes drifting to my red nose. "Yeah, I said I'd pick you up for lunch, remember?"

I honestly couldn't. I'd been half-dead when he'd slipped into bed in the early morning, and I vaguely recalled a comment murmured into my pillow as he left a few hours later. "Oh, yeah. Is it okay if we order in? What time do you have to be back on campus?" I dug my keys out of my pocket, absently rubbing Sarah's pendant before starting up the stairs.

"I'm done for the day," he said, following behind me. "The test was this morning, and I'm skipping my afternoon class. My brain is fried. What do you want to eat? I'll order."

My phone began buzzing before I could respond. I glanced at it on the table. Wilder. I picked it up. "Hello?"

"Harper?"

Iann looked at me.

"Yes, is everything okay?"

Wilder sighed on the other end of the phone. "I have an update on Jeremy Stewart."

My skin chilled.

"Our officers found him deceased in his home this morning," he said.

I couldn't form words, a thousand thoughts racing through my mind. I glanced at Iann. His eyebrows furrowed as he watched me.

"It appears that he committed suicide," Wilder continued. "The good news is he wrote us a note that ties him to Holly's murder, at least."

What about Sarah?

"Are you still there?" he asked.

"Yeah," I said softly.

"Okay, well, what I need from you is a statement about that night that he came to your work for our records," Wilder said. "You can write it, or I can record it. Is that something you can do?"

"Yeah, this is, um . . . a lot to take in right now."

Iann's expression had grown more concerned.

"That's fine, I'll check in with you later. Or give me a call when you're ready, okay?"

"Okay." I hung up. "Jeremy—" I paused, shoving my phone into my pocket. "He, um, they think he killed himself."

Iann's face dropped. "What?"

I took a deep breath. "They found him this morning."

He sat down at the table, letting his backpack slide from his shoulder and hit the ground with a thud.

"I'm sorry," I said. It was strange to say that about a murderer's passing.

He shook his head. "I haven't seen him in weeks. We were all wondering where he was."

I sank into the chair beside him. "Wilder said he left a note. He confessed to killing Holly."

"I don't understand. Wow," he said, putting an arm around me and holding me to his shoulder. "I guess you don't have to be scared anymore, now that he's gone."

But what about Sarah?

CHAPTER
TWENTY-SEVEN

"How are you holding up?" Over the past week since Jeremy's death, I'd grown tired of asking, but I didn't know what else to say.

"I'm so sick of crying," Erin said as she watched me wipe down my easel. It was her first night back in the studio after almost a week. She looked like she might have actually gotten some sleep.

I'd waited to hear from her after I got off the phone with Wilder. I'd known there was no way I could break the news to her, especially not with how we'd left things. It'd taken her a day to find out from one of Jeremy's roommates, and I'd been there for her as soon as she called. I'd sat up with her over long nights at her apartment while she tried to work out how she could have missed the signs. We never discussed our argument, and not once did I even want to say "I told you so." Because I wished I'd been wrong.

"Let's go out tonight!" Erin lowered behind the easel to meet my eyeline.

My stomach twisted. As much as I dreaded the thought, this was the first time she actually looked and sounded like her old self. "Are you sure you're up for it?"

She looked away. "Yeah. I just need to get my mind off of all this. If I spend one more night in, I'll go crazy."

"Okay, let's do something low key," I countered. "What about a bar? Your choice."

She smiled. "Yeah. Come back with me to my place, and we'll get dressed up!"

I shot Iann a quick text as we walked to her apartment.

(8:50 p.m.): Erin's dragging me out tonight.

I'd seen him only in passing while I picked up the pieces of Erin. He'd kept his distance, checking in here and there and never being the first to bring up Jeremy.

Once we were at Erin's apartment, she disappeared into her enormous walk-in closet. "Try these." She pulled three dresses from the back and tossed them to me.

I discarded a tiny blue one with a tear on the waist and a red satin one on the bed. I shimmied on a black nylon one-shouldered dress, then tugged at the hem until it rested at the middle of my thighs. Erin was a little shorter than me, so this was probably the farthest down it would go.

Erin emerged in a skintight red dress that skimmed her narrow thighs, a pair of black strapped heels in her hands. "Your legs are so pasty, Harper." She ran her fingers through my hair. "You look like a doll. You don't curl it like this, do you?"

"No." Outside of the humid summers, I didn't really mind my long, curly hair. It mostly behaved during autumn and winter.

She continued to survey me. "You're so pretty, except for this." She pressed against the scar on my neck.

I turned away from her and pulled my boots back on.

She scrunched her nose. "You're wearing those?"

179

I resisted the urge to glare at her. "Yes." I couldn't fathom how she didn't fall on her face in heels, especially when she was drunk.

Iann (9:32 p.m.): Have fun!

The bar Erin chose overlooked the river, and the cheapest drink was twenty-two dollars.

I shifted in my seat, pulling my skirt down, the backs of my legs ripping from the leather seat.

"What drink are you going to get?" Erin's eyes greedily raced over the menu.

The twenty-two-dollar drink was some weird hipster concoction. Surely a single shot would be cheaper. "I don't know," I muttered. She hadn't outright offered to pay yet, and with the mood she was in, she probably expected me to foot the bill.

"Oh my god," she purred, dropping her menu onto her lap. "Look at that guy."

I followed her eyes across to the entrance, and the air left my lungs.

Danny was shaking hands with an older man who then turned to leave. Danny reached down to the table and shuffled his papers together, glancing around the room, his eyes settling on me. He smiled and waved.

Erin's head whipped around to face me. "Do you know him?" Her voice was accusatory.

I was speechless as Danny grabbed his notebook and walked over to us, holding my gaze the entire time.

"Hey, what are you doing in my part of town?" he asked with a grin before glancing at Erin.

Erin didn't wait for me to respond; she stuck out her hand. "Hi, I'm Erin."

"Danny," he responded, quickly shaking her hand and letting it drop.

"How do you two know each other?" Erin asked, surveying him.

Danny and I exchanged a look. "We were in the same class at Northwestern," he said, simply. "What about you?"

Erin put a hand on my shoulder. "I practically saved her life when she moved here. She works at my shop."

My muscles tensed under her touch. "Her father owns an art studio that I teach at," I corrected, shrugging her hand off.

Danny glanced between the two of us with an awkward grin. "Well, let me get you both a drink. What'll you have?"

"Scotch, neat," Erin chimed.

He looked at me. "Rum and Coke?" he asked.

I smiled and nodded.

Erin's eyes lowered over his body as he walked away. "Is he single?"

Blood rushed to my face. "Erin, no."

She whipped her head around to me. "He's *not* single?"

My heart quickened. "No, well, I don't know. But I don't think it's a good idea."

"Why not?" She stuck out her chin as if she was daring me to say Jeremy's name.

"You've been going through a lot lately. Maybe you should just take it easy."

Her eyes widened. "Oh my god, *you're* interested in him, aren't you?"

"No!"

She smirked. "You can't put Danny on hold. What about Iann?"

I glanced around the room. Thankfully, Danny was out of earshot. "I'm not interested in Danny. He's an old friend, though. I don't want things to get weird between everyone. I'm just worried about you."

She wasn't buying it. "Well, Iann or Danny, whenever you decide which one you don't want, let me know." She rolled her eyes.

Danny was on his way back with the drinks.

He placed our drinks on the table and sat down in front of his.

"We're going dancing later. Do you want to come with us?" Erin asked with a wicked smile. "Harper's boyfriend is coming too." She wasn't merely asking him out—she was twisting the knife.

Danny raised his eyebrows at me. "Ah, yes, the imaginary one. How could I say no?"

Erin glanced at me. "What?"

I pressed my glass between both hands. "I'm not sure if Iann can make it." I didn't relish spending my first outing with him since Jeremy's death at a loud nightclub. Or introducing him to Danny.

Erin held my gaze. "Call him and find out." She turned back to Danny. "There's a new place in the Loop that I've been wanting to try."

I stood up with my phone.

"You can call him here. It's not that loud," Erin said, putting a hand on my arm.

I sat back down and dialed Iann. Maybe he was busy.

"Hey!" Iann answered on the other end.

Dammit. "Hey," I stretched out the word. "I know you're busy, but Erin and I are thinking about going to a club in downtown tonight. Can you come?"

He hesitated. "Yeah, I could use a break."

"Great, I'll text you the address."

———

I trailed behind Danny and Erin on the street, playing through different scenarios in my mind. How would Iann react to Danny? How should I introduce them? *It'll be so loud inside that it won't matter what you say.*

"Hey!" Iann appeared behind me, his arm grazing my back. "I caught you before you got in."

I turned on my heel, and he kissed my lips. "Yeah, you got here really fast."

"I was at home." He looked behind me at Erin and Danny talking as we inched toward the bouncer.

Danny met his eyes and glanced at me before stretching his hand toward Iann. "You must be the boyfriend I've been hearing about. I'm Danny."

Iann shook his hand. "Iann. Nice to meet you."

"They went to college together," Erin interjected over Danny's shoulder.

Iann's smile flickered. "Oh, you're Harper's friend?"

I nodded, swallowing my fluttering heart before it dropped out from my throat. "Yeah, we ran into each other recently, and he met Erin tonight, so she invited him," I said in a rush.

Iann put his hands in his jeans pockets as we made it to the front of the line and filed into the club.

I glanced at him as he followed behind me into the throbbing music. I could see the wheels turning in his mind. All the inevitable questions piling up just behind his lips.

Erin skipped over to one of the only available tables and threw her purse at me. I couldn't hear what she said to Danny, but they both disappeared on the dance floor. I sat at the table, and Iann joined me.

He stared ahead at Erin and Danny dancing. "Do you want a drink?" he yelled over the music.

I nodded.

He took off his jacket and put it beside me on the booth seat before making his way to the bar.

Danny was still wearing his work jacket as he danced with Erin so close to his chest and touching her hips to his. They had both had a couple more drinks before we left the previous bar, but I was entirely too sober. I unzipped my coat, letting it fall behind my dress.

Iann slid into the booth beside me, putting a glass of rum and Coke on the table. He sipped his beer and leaned toward my ear. "I didn't realize you were a nightclub girl."

I downed half the glass. "I'm not," I shouted. At least not when I was sober. I rested my head on his shoulder. He and I had the same idea. People watching was the best in this kind of place. I finished the drink. My hands shook and my face grew hot as Erin's hands crept over Danny's body. "I'll be right back."

I ran to the bathroom and threw Erin's bag onto the sink. I had been clutching it so hard that my fingernails had left impressions in the red fabric. I leaned against the sink and splashed water on my face, the bass outside throbbing behind the mirror. I looked ahead at the vengeful phantom peering back at me. It had been a mistake to come here. To let Erin push me around like this.

I ripped open the clasp on her bag. Inside there were lipstick and a pill bottle. I took the bright-red lipstick and swiped it over my lips, and I shook my hair forward and then let it fall more wildly around my shoulders. I threw the lipstick back in and then extracted the pill bottle. I recalled the night I'd followed Jeremy. This must've been what he'd given her outside the studio.

I rubbed my finger over the label. Xanax. How long ago had she started taking these again? I pushed and twisted the cap. I shook out the usual small pill into my palm, then pressed it deeper into my palm, watching the familiar white color seep into my skin. I threw it into my throat and swallowed, the residue bitter on my tongue.

Before I returned the bottle to her bag, I noticed the date and paused. It had been filled three days after Jeremy was found. That couldn't be right.

When I returned to the table, I caught Iann's arm and kissed him hard, running my hands through his hair. I only had a history with Danny. I wanted to be with Iann. I grabbed his hand and pulled him onto the dance floor, my body fitting into his.

——

Danny was directly in front of me, his hands caressing my skin. I didn't remember finishing my dance with Iann, but I leaned farther into Danny. Our hips met, and I wrapped my arms around his neck.

When I realized how close we were, I recoiled and looked around for Iann, my skin on fire from Danny's touch. I couldn't see past the sea of throbbing bodies. I pushed out of the crowd, sensing Danny behind me.

I collided with someone, hands and drinks flying in the air. The girl dropped her glass, and it shattered. "I'm sorry," I slurred, feeling the wet part of my dress. I met the girl's eyes, and my heart leaped.

Her hair was down tonight, but she was wearing those same giant hoop earrings. I reached a hand out to her. Was she real? My fingers gripped her shoulder. Her warm, smooth shoulder. *Oh my god. She's really here.* "What is your problem?" Jenny yelled, pushing me back.

I staggered, my knees wobbling as Danny caught my elbow. "Are you okay?" he asked.

I searched the crowd wildly, but she was already gone.

Erin was suddenly beside Danny and me, shouting something to him.

I froze, nearly falling again until Danny put an arm around my waist. My legs were paralyzed. I couldn't will them to move forward, to straighten.

"Harper?" Danny leaned in close to my ear.

I rubbed my eyes and stumbled backward, the floor rolling beneath me. My eyes were still closed as I was pulled back up by rough-skinned hands. My legs were limp, and I slouched back down.

"Jesus, Harper," Danny growled, tightening his grip around me.

"I'm fine," I mumbled. My throat constricted, each breath an effort.

He didn't let go and ushered me out onto the sidewalk, the music falling away. "I think it's time to leave," Danny called down the sidewalk.

I leaned against the wall, pressing a hand into the brick to steady myself.

Iann was suddenly by my side, his hand on my arm. "Are you okay?"

I shook my head.

"What happened?" He looked at Erin and Danny.

"I think she drank too much. She fell down inside," Danny said.

My legs started buckling, and I grabbed Iann's shirt.

"I'll get a cab," Danny called over his shoulder.

"Where did you go?" I slurred into Iann's ear.

He placed his arm around me. "I had to take a call. You were fine when I left—what happened?"

Who was he calling this time of night?

Danny opened the taxi door, and I fell down onto the sticky leather seat. Everyone filed in after me. Through my blurry vision, I saw the driver nervously glance back at me before he started down the street.

I closed my eyes, my head leaning back on Iann's chest. He sounded calm talking to me, but I could hear his pulse so quick and loud against my ear.

Erin's legs were pressed against mine. The smell of her floral perfume made me want to vomit. Minutes later the car stopped, and Iann gently helped me out. My legs wobbled when my feet met the sidewalk. I managed to open my eyes for only a moment to see my apartment.

Danny and Erin appeared behind me.

"She'll be fine," Erin muttered as Iann led me up the stairs.

The car doors closed, and it started down the street.

I leaned against the doorframe as Iann looked for my keys, his hand still around my waist. He opened the door and walked me to the bed, setting me down before I immediately slumped onto my side.

He slid my shoes off and put two fingers to my wrist. "How much did you drink?" There was panic in his voice. I could recognize it even then.

It was an effort to even move my lips. "Just one." I had mixed Xanax and alcohol before, and it hadn't knocked me down like this. I gasped a breath, the effort stretching my lungs.

His expression didn't change. Maybe he didn't believe me. "Your pulse is slow, but are you breathing okay?" He bent down toward me.

I fell silent.

He shook my shoulders with a desperate grip. "Harper, listen to me."

"Yeah?" I closed my eyes.

"Did you take anything?"

He knows. "I took one," I whimpered, close to tears. Why did I start taking the pills again? And when had he found out about them?

He pulled me up. "One what?"

I was actually crying now, slouched against his shoulder. "Xanax. It was in Erin's purse."

"Shit," he hissed. He jerked me from the bed and into his arms so abruptly that I almost screamed. "You have to throw it up."

CHAPTER TWENTY-EIGHT

Iann was on the floor beside my drafting table, his laptop resting open on his legs as he furiously typed. Light poured out from the window onto his black hair.

His eyes met mine and widened. "You're awake?"

I flexed my fingers before moving my arms. "Yeah," I croaked. My tongue tasted sour.

He set his laptop down and sat beside me on the bed.

"What happened last night?" I leaned my head against the wall. My stomach twisted as the room slowly rotated. The last thing I remembered was sitting on the bathroom floor.

He brushed his fingers through my hair. "I think you almost—" He shook his head and pulled me to his chest. "Why would you take Erin's pills?"

I didn't respond but melted farther into his arms.

"Why, Harper?"

"How did you know?"

He sighed, then kissed the top of my head. "Someone I cared about had the same problem a long time ago. You weren't acting right last night. You could have overdosed." He hugged me closer.

"No," I said. "I only had one drink at the club."

"It doesn't matter. You can't mix alcohol with that kind of stuff."

I rubbed my eyes. "I'm sorry."

"This isn't the first time you've taken it, is it?" he asked softly.

I leaned against his shoulder. "I've never had a reaction like that."

An unreadable emotion flashed across his face. "You looked upset last night." His eyes watched me. "Is that why you took it?"

I remembered the sound of the car doors closing behind us as we walked up the steps. Danny and Erin had left together. I clutched my throbbing forehead. "No. But I haven't been sleeping well. Not since everything with Jeremy."

He got up and walked to the kitchen. "Coffee or water?"

"Coffee, please." I swung my legs out from under the blanket and dangled them over the edge. I was still in the clothes from last night, the dress wrinkled and sticky from the spilled drink. Jenny's spilled drink.

Iann handed me the warm mug. "Your friend seems like a nice guy."

I took a sip; the coffee was more bitter than usual. "Danny?"

He bent over and closed his laptop. "Yeah. You've never mentioned him before."

I gulped. I couldn't remember the time between dancing with Iann and then ending up in Danny's arms. How much had he seen? "We haven't kept in touch. I hadn't seen him in years until recently."

"How do you know each other again?"

"Northwestern," I said quickly.

"I thought you dropped out of college?" He leaned against the bedpost at the foot of the bed.

I held his gaze. He'd been compiling these questions while I slept. "I did. We were freshmen together." I placed one hand under the cup, letting the heat sear my skin. "Does it bother you that I'm friends with him?"

He laughed and shook his head. "Come on, I'm not *that* guy. Why? Do you want me to be jealous?"

"Of course not." I inched my fingers back to the handle.

"He seemed to be hitting it off with Erin." He left the side of the bed and bent over to put his laptop in his backpack.

I shivered. "Are you leaving?" My voice was finally returning to normal.

"Yeah, I have a meeting with my faculty advisor," he said, slinging his bag over one shoulder. "Are you going to be okay? How are you feeling?"

I took a bigger gulp of coffee, burning my tongue. "I'll be fine."

He stared at me. After a moment he dropped his backpack and returned to my side. "Will you promise me that you'll stop?"

I didn't need to ask what he meant. I nodded, avoiding his eyes.

He kissed my cheek. "I can't lose you."

———

After Iann left, I fell back into a dreamless sleep and woke hours later soaked in sweat. I could feel the judgment in Woodstock's eyes as I finally sat up and dared to look at my phone.

There were no texts or calls from Erin, and the whole day had already passed by. It was 8:42 p.m. Erin was only this silent when she was barricaded in her apartment with a guy.

More sweat broke through my pores as I imagined Danny's hands on her. I twisted my fingers through my hair and shook my head, but the image remained. I replayed all the moments from the night before.

The way Erin had treated me last night. The way she had treated me our entire friendship.

It wasn't just about Danny, I told myself. It was about Jeremy, about all the things she'd said to make me doubt Iann. And yes, it was a little bit about Danny. She hadn't even tried to listen to how I felt about the situation.

I pulled my knees into my chest, the dress riding up to my waist. A quiet thought slipped in.

Why do you care so much?

My anger continued to build on my way to the studio, more memories of Erin's slights and insults replaying with each step.

The class had just ended as I entered the studio. Everyone was tugging their parkas back on and chatting over their final glasses of wine.

I walked past Hannah to the back room. Erin was grabbing her handbag from the break table, already halfway out the door.

"Erin, this isn't working out. I'm quitting." The words spilled out.

She stopped and looked at me, and the lids above her bloodshot eyes twitched almost imperceptibly. "What? Where is this coming from?"

I slid my hood back. "I really appreciate everything you've done for me, but I think I've been using this job as an excuse not to move forward with my own work." Maybe it was true, but it seemed like a lie.

She thought so too. "What's wrong with you? You're really going to abandon me right now?" She threw her bag onto the table.

I'd stumbled all the way here in a rage, but facing her now, a wave of guilt washed over me. "I'm not abandoning you. We're still friends."

She shook her head, pressing her fingers against her eyes as if trying to push away tears. "You know what? No, we're not friends. We never were. I've been playing babysitter for you since you got here, and all you've ever done is made my life harder."

I couldn't speak. It was as though she'd slapped me.

She narrowed her eyes and scoffed. "And good luck finding someone else's pills."

My blood went cold. "What?"

"Yeah," she continued, taking a step toward me. "I'm not blind. I know you've been stealing my pills for a while. And I assume your little show last night was because you snagged another one or two."

"I—"

"Have a nice life, Harper." She swung open the back door and disappeared.

CHAPTER
TWENTY-NINE

For about a week, I convinced myself that walking away from Erin was the best thing to do. For me and for her. Maybe she was right. I had a problem. And being around her didn't help.

Since the club, Iann quietly watched me when we were together, as if he was still trying to work out the events of that night. I wanted to ask for details during my memory lapses, but I was scared. I still remembered Danny's skin under my hands. Every time I closed my eyes, I saw Jenny's angry face in the purple light of the club. Danny must've seen her too.

"How's the book coming along?" Iann dug through his takeout container with his chopsticks, nodding behind me toward the drafting table.

I took the last bite of my eggroll. "I submitted the illustrations a couple of days ago, and I'm working on a different project now."

He nodded, his mouth slightly curved in a stifled yawn.

"Did you sleep at all last night?" I hadn't. But that was normal for me, not for him.

He eyed his backpack by the front door. "I guess I did at some point, but it doesn't feel that way." He pulled it over one shoulder. "If you're not working at the studio tonight, do you want to come over?"

I folded the paper carton closed before pushing away from the table. "Actually, I quit the studio."

He blinked. "Why? I thought you liked it there?"

My mind scanned through the available explanations. All of which would provoke only more questions. "I've been getting a lot of project offers, but I've had to turn them down because of the studio schedule," I lied. I *was* working on a new project, but I was hardly a hot commodity in a city with several art colleges.

He wrapped his arms around my waist and pulled me gently into an embrace. "That's great," he said. "Then, I guess you can definitely come over this weekend?"

"Yes, that sounds good." I sank into my desk chair after he closed the door. The only projects I had lined up were all online orders for last-minute small commissions, barely fifty dollars each for illustrations of the family dog or the new couple about to celebrate their first Christmas together.

As I sketched out a couple onto watercolor paper, I kept glancing at my phone. I couldn't shake the dull ache in my stomach that I had turned my back on Erin.

I set my pencil down and unlocked my phone, then opened my text with Erin. The last message was from the day we'd gone clubbing. I typed out the only three letters that came to mind.

Hey.

I deleted and retyped the same letters over before my index finger finally hovered over the small green button on the screen. I erased it again. I looked at the time at the top of the phone screen. If I left now, I could make it to the studio before the next class started.

I grabbed my coat and ran out through the door, jogged down the stairs, and cut through my neighbors' tiny yards to the street that connected directly to Damen Avenue. The studio was in my sight, but then I noticed the empty parking lot. Saturday afternoons were the busiest days usually. I pulled on the door, but it was locked. There was no sign or note on the window. I cupped my hands against the glass and peered between them inside.

The easels sat at the back of the room, stacked against the wall, imposing figures in the dark. There wasn't any light visible under the employees-only door. I tugged at the door again before backing away and looking around the empty parking lot. This was the class I would normally teach, but they wouldn't cancel it merely because I quit. Hannah would've happily taken my hours as soon as they heard I was gone.

Maybe there was an emergency. I pressed my phone between my palms. Surely Erin would've called me if something bad had happened.

Maybe she's at Danny's.

The image of them dancing flashed through my mind. He was too good for her. She would only hurt him.

I walked to the street behind the studio. Erin's building was on the way back home. There was no harm in checking. I stared up at her fourth-floor window as I passed, ready to bolt if she was standing in front of the wide-open windows. She never used blinds or curtains. She liked the idea that someone would want to watch her.

The window was empty and dark. Her car wasn't parked on the street or in the small gated lot beside the building. It was an electric-blue MINI Cooper. It would've been pretty easy to spot in the cluster of cars. A shoulder sideswiped me as I stood there, spurring me back into motion toward home. I glanced over my shoulder at the window beside Erin's. Her roommate's blinds were slightly open, the broken light of a nearby lamp bouncing against the glass.

I swallowed and crossed the street, backtracking to the apartment doors. My index finger hovered over the intercom button for her unit, before eventually pressing it.

"Yeah?" Ronnie's voice came through clear over the high-tech speaker.

"It's Harper," I said. "Is Erin home?"

She hesitated. She must've heard about our fight. I could only imagine what Erin had told her about me after she'd left the studio fuming that night. "No, she hasn't been home all week."

What? Where did she go? "Can I come up?"

The door buzzed without a response, and I pulled it open. My emotions hovered between anxiety and anger on the ride up on the elevator. The possibility of an extended sleepover with Danny settled like a stone in my stomach. I couldn't put it past her that she was using him to get back at me.

Ronnie was at the door, holding it open when I got off the elevator. She frowned when she saw me. "I haven't seen her since she left for work last Sunday," she said. She blocked the doorway with her lithe body, leaning against the frame. It was the same maneuver I used whenever Wilder came by. "I thought maybe she was with you."

"No, I also haven't seen her since Sunday."

Her frown deepened.

"What?" I asked.

She shook her head. "I just wish I'd paid more attention . . . she said she was seeing some guy, but I don't remember his name."

"Jeremy?"

Her eyes widened. "No, not him. She told me what happened with all that."

Who else could it be? Erin had only met Danny the day before we last saw her. Surely, she wouldn't even bother mentioning him the morning after. Unless he had stayed at the apartment that night with her. The stone shifted and sank deeper into my stomach. "Was it Danny?"

Ronnie rolled her eyes to one side, thinking. "No, that's not it."

I let go of the breath I'd been holding. "Are you sure?"

She pursed her lips. "No, I'm not. I really have no idea. You know how she is. Just nonstop talking," she said. "I can't possibly remember everything she says."

"The studio is locked up. I'm not sure if she's been in all week."

She eyed me. "How are you not sure? Don't *you* work there too?"

I sighed. "No, I quit."

"I'm sure she's fine. I mean, she runs that place. She probably shut it down so she could play around for a while."

But Ronnie had said it herself. Erin was an open book. Why would she leave for a week without giving a long, exhausting explanation first? I thought about the day I'd quit. Erin had been curt and irritable. It wasn't entirely unlike her, but it had seemed worse than usual. "Do you know if she's been using again?" I asked.

"She's not my problem. I don't check her bathroom for coke or anything."

"Yeah, I know. But I thought she was acting a little strange at work."

"Look, I'll tell her to call you when she gets back," she said and closed the door.

"Okay," I sputtered.

The dead bolt clicked into place.

———

The train screeched into Washington Station, and I clutched my bag to keep it from falling off my lap. I stepped onto the platform. As soon as the doors closed behind me, my phone rang. "Hey," I answered.

"Hey," Iann said a little less enthusiastically. "Are you already by my place? I'm going to be a little late today. I have to finish going over my dissertation with my advisor, and she's raking me over the coals."

His timing was perfect. I was just a block away from his apartment. I rolled my eyes. "Okay, no problem." I climbed the stairs to the street.

"This should be over with by dinnertime, but I don't think I'll be able to cook. Can we go out instead tonight?"

I hurriedly pulled my jacket hood over my hair as the first raindrops hit my face. "Yeah, let me know when you're done, and we can meet somewhere for dinner." I couldn't keep the edge of annoyance out of my voice.

"Sorry," he said.

"No, really, it's fine. Good luck." I surveyed the street for shelter as the rain pattered more persistently.

"Thanks."

I hung up and trotted across the street to a small coffee shop on the corner. At least I could wait and get some work done. I followed behind the other people ducking in from the rain and pulled my hood back. They had the heater running full blast, and they were grinding fresh coffee. I edged to the back of the line at the counter, watching the rain pour past the skylight behind the bar. My eyes trained on the curtain of rain to the top of the familiar skinny redbrick building a block away.

Before I could fully understand what I was doing, I had stepped out of line and back out onto the street. No thoughts passed through my mind as I walked down the block, stray droplets hitting my face and eyes. It was as if I were possessed. I couldn't explain it then. I didn't try to.

When I came to my senses, I was already standing in the elevator, water rolling off the hem of my coat. The loud, constant dripping on the wood floor snapped me back into the moment.

What are you doing?

The elevator opened on the ninth floor, and I froze, staring down the long hallway at Jenny's door. My deliberate steps carried me down the hall.

My stomach churned, but my hand was steady as I reached for the doorknob. It was locked. I stepped back, surveying the doorway.

This is the line. If you cross it, it's breaking in.

Was it? Hadn't I already crossed the line by going in the first time? No, this was different. She had been dumb enough not to lock her door before. She was lucky I'd been the only person to wander in.

My eyes focused on the bright-red doormat with the word *hello* printed in cursive. She was the type to hide a key in the most obvious place, wasn't she?

This is too far. The thought weighed down into my stomach, trying to anchor me to reality, but I was already bent over, flipping up the edge of the mat.

There it was.

A single, dirty copper key.

My fingernails scraped against the carpet as I picked it up. I slowly slid it into the lock and braced the doorknob as I twisted it. The door wheezed open gently into the dark entryway, light streaming in from the kitchen. The smell of vomit from my last visit had been replaced by expensive, heavy perfume still lingering in the air and circulating from the radiator against the window.

I glanced behind me into the quiet hallway before stepping over the threshold, straining my ears for any sound. I closed the door softly and tiptoed to the edge of the kitchen. From where I stood, I could see through the living room and into the open bedroom on the other side. Both rooms were empty and still. My jacket dripped over the kitchen rug as I observed the living room. I tiptoed into the bedroom, my heart racing. Yes, it was empty. Of people, at least. Wherever Jenny had gone, she'd left in a hurry. There was a pile of clothes laid out on the bed and a small suitcase discarded on the floor. I looked closer at the clothes and noticed the fine fabrics peeking out.

I turned my head and saw the closet in the corner of the room, door wide open and beckoning. I didn't care much for clothes. I walked in out of curiosity, more for what the clothes said about Jenny rather than the actual clothes. There were beautiful work dresses with colorful geometric shapes on one side, and the dresses grew shorter and shinier by the hanger. There were just as many handbags piled into one corner under the party dresses. I ran my hand over the fabrics, my fingers stopping on a blue silk dress.

I slipped the dress from its hanger. The scooped neck was followed in the back with a plunging deep V.

I glanced back out the closet door. There was no other sound in the apartment other than my breathing and the honking of cars outside the bedroom window.

I unbuttoned my jeans and pulled them off each leg before pulling my sweater and damp jacket off in one motion over my head. Her shoes were the same size. I had to know if this fit too. I shimmied the dress on, past my thighs and stomach, slipping my arms through each of the smooth sleeves. I hadn't worn anything this luxurious before. Even the clothes Erin let me borrow were the cheaper dresses she owned.

I zipped it up in the back too easily. There was about an inch of room in the bust. I looked at the mirror on the closet door and turned around.

"Jenny?" a voice called from the other room.

My blood froze, and I instinctively dove for the wall, clutching the side.

I almost screamed when a head peered into the closet directly beside me.

"I thought you said you were busy tonight?" the man said, stepping in beside me. He looked to be close to Jenny's age, maybe a few years older than me. His brown eyes devoured me standing in the dress, and a wicked grin tugged at his lips. "Where are you going dressed like that?"

There's no way out of this. You can't tell him who you are.

Jail. That's where sick people like you go for this.

I couldn't focus—my heart was pounding, my vision pulsing along with its rhythm. "I was about to leave," I managed weakly.

He walked up to me authoritatively and touched a lock of my hair. I forced myself not to pull away.

"I've never seen your hair like this." He tugged on the large curl draped over my jawline. "It's hot," he said, resting his hand just below my hip and pulling me into him.

My heart thundered.

He went in to kiss me, but I turned, and his lips met my cheek. "Hey, what's wrong?" He gripped me harder, pressing me against the wall.

This. This is wrong.

"I have to go," I breathed.

His hand lifted the hem of my dress, his foreign fingers running up my thigh.

I pushed him away.

He frowned. "Come on," he moaned, pulling my hips into his. "I've missed you."

I braced my arms up against his chest. "Please," I begged quietly.

He maintained his grip. "Who are you trying to impress with this?" He ruffled my dress in the back before trailing his hand up to my chest.

What answer would make him leave? What would Jenny do? "I'm going out with some friends."

He grinned and nuzzled my neck, his beard scratching against my scar. "Then they won't care if you're late." His hands had brought the dress up over my hips, and he had me firmly pinned to the wall.

I was dizzy from the pressure of his body against mine. "I need something to drink first." The words poured out.

"All right!" he said with a wide smile. "You still have that vodka?"

I nodded.

He released me. "Let's do this!" He sauntered out of the closet and into the living room.

I lunged for my bag and slipped on my shoes before dashing from the closet as his footsteps retreated over the tile. "Oh, I left it by the sofa," I called, before he could make it to the kitchen.

He stooped over the sofa, and I brushed by him, quickly turning the corner past the fridge and hurriedly opened the front door. I ran past the elevator and straight for the stairwell, my sneakers flying over the steps until I reached the ground level.

The air ripped through my lungs as I staggered down the side-walk, casting looks over my shoulder in the dark. I crossed at the light with a group of huddled tourists toward the river. They eyed my dress from over the collars of their hooded parkas as they shuffled past. I shivered and opened the first door on the street, the smell and heat of coffee greeting me along with the staring patrons in coats and sweaters.

Your coat! Where's your coat?

"Hey!"

I jumped and turned around. Danny was hovering over my shoulder, a large paper cup of coffee in one hand. "Hi," I panted.

He smiled and motioned to my dress. "Night on the town?"

I tugged the fabric down, but it barely covered the tops of my thighs. "No, laundry day. What are you doing here?"

He held up his cup. "I've got a long night ahead." He set it on the table beside me and slid his gray peacoat from his shoulders, then handed it to me.

"Oh, no, I'm fine," I said, shaking my head.

He laughed. "Come on, you're looking a little blue. And I'm lit-erally going right across the street after this." He pointed to Tribune Tower through the window. "You need it more than I do."

I gratefully accepted it and wrapped it around my shoulders.

"So, I haven't heard from you since the club," he said, picking his cup up. "Are you feeling okay?"

I pulled his coat closed over my chest. My cheeks burned as I remembered that night. "Yeah, I'm sorry. That was a weird night." I thought about Erin touching his body as they danced. My fists clenched.

"Yeah, it was." He rubbed the back of his neck. "Do you want to sit down and talk for a minute?" He pointed behind him.

"Sure." I followed him to a table, and we sat down across from each other.

He ran a hand over his face, his fingers exaggerating the deep creases forming under his eyes. "I'm worried about you," he said. His eyes bored into mine. "You don't seem like yourself."

I looked down at my hands. "What do you mean?" I knew exactly what he meant.

"You seemed upset at the club the other night and then, running into you tonight like . . . this." He motioned to my outfit. "It just seems like you're spiraling out or something. Did something happen?"

Was I that transparent? "We haven't seen each other in so long. How do you know I'm not just like this now?" I said defiantly.

"Fair enough," he conceded. "Maybe I don't know you as well as I used to, but I know something was off that night. You only had one drink at the club, and then you could barely walk."

There was a simple explanation for that, but I couldn't tell him about the Xanax. And I couldn't explain how I lost time to myself. I focused on the dark circles under his eyes. "Well, to be perfectly honest, you don't seem like you're doing so great yourself."

"You don't have to get defensive. I just want to make sure you're okay."

Maybe I was going crazy. "Do you remember right before we left the club?"

He took a sip of coffee. "Yeah, when you fell over?"

I blushed. I saw Jenny's eyes again as if she were standing in front of me. "No, when I ran into that girl. Did you see her?" My heart raced.

"Yeah," he said slowly. "I saw her drop her glass and push you."

I shook my head. "Did you see her face?"

He leaned forward and rested his elbows on the table. "Not really, why?"

I held his gaze, searching for that warmth in his eyes that had made me trust him so many years ago. "Have you heard about those girls murdered near Wicker Park and Bucktown?"

He narrowed his eyes. "Doesn't come to mind."

The words forming in my mind sounded insane. "Never mind." My face grew hot.

He continued to look at me. "Come on. You've hooked me," he said with a laugh. "Now reel me in."

I rested my hands on the table. "When I think about saying it . . . it sounds crazy," I said in a lowered voice. I dared to meet his eyes again. The interest was growing, lighting up his green eyes in a way I hadn't seen before. I took a deep breath. "A girl's body was found a few months ago in Wicker Park," I began. "Right across from my apartment."

Recognition dawned on his face. "Okay, yeah," he affirmed. "I do remember that. Molly?"

"Holly," I corrected.

He frowned slightly. "Wow, that was just across the street from you, huh?"

"Yes, but that part doesn't matter," I said, quickly. He was latching on to the wrong detail. "Did you ever see her picture?"

He hesitated and shrugged. "I really can't say that I did. That was around the tail end of summer, when things were going crazy on the west side." He sipped his coffee. "I was working primarily on covering those shootings. I remember hearing about that murder, though."

There were too many horrible things going on in the denser, more populous parts of the city. To most, Sarah's or Holly's deaths would've been big news, but it was hard to process any one particular horror story in the onslaught of shootings and police-corruption investigations announced every day.

"I saw her," I continued. "On the news when they found her the next morning." I focused hard on his expression before the next part. "She looked like me."

There was no change in his face, only curiosity. "In what way?"

"Every way."

He leaned back in his chair.

I pulled my phone out. I still had the tab open to the story about Holly. "Look for yourself." I slid it across the table to him. My heart raced as he picked it up.

Danny raised his eyebrows and held the phone closer to his face. He glanced back at me. "You're right," he said, handing it back to me. "That's pretty uncanny."

"You don't think that's weird?"

"It's an unsettling coincidence, maybe." He sat back in his seat, relieved or underwhelmed, I couldn't tell.

"What about the added fact that she was murdered right outside my window?" I challenged. "Does that still seem like a coincidence to you?"

He rubbed his chin. "That is pretty strange."

I looked back at my screen and flipped to the next article tab. I held it up this time. "This is Sarah. Her body was found near Logan's Square a couple of weeks before Holly."

Danny furrowed his brow, leaning toward my phone intently. "Okay," he said. "Now we have weird." He opened his hand. "May I?"

I handed the phone to him.

He flipped through the articles, his frown deepening with each flick of his finger on the screen. "The police aren't looking into this?" he asked after a minute.

"They did," I said. "I mentioned Sarah to a detective when he came asking about Holly." I squeezed the edge of the table with my palm until it hurt. "They think they know who killed Holly."

"Okay, then. Have they been arrested?"

I sighed. "He killed himself before they could finish investigating. But they seem pretty certain he did it, though. They say he left a note confessing."

"That's good, isn't it?" Danny asked.

I scratched my fingernail against the table. "Maybe. But I can't stop thinking about Sarah," I said. "I have this feeling it was connected to Holly's murder somehow."

"But the police don't?"

"They don't seem to." I slipped my phone back into my pocket. "They have a pretty clear connection between this dead guy and Holly."

Danny took a sip of his coffee. "So they think her murder was just a one-off? They're not looking into a possible serial killer?"

I nodded. "And maybe it's not. But something feels off about it." I glanced down at my hands. "In the beginning, the detective asked if there's anyone in my past who would want to hurt me."

Danny's face tensed.

"Do you think . . . would he come here looking for me?" My throat tightened. "To hurt me like that?" *Not to hurt. To kill.*

Danny immediately shook his head. "He's your father, Harper. He wouldn't—" He stopped, his eyes drifting to the small scar along my temple. It had long faded. No one else had ever even noticed it. Not even Iann—it was so close to my hairline. But Danny's eyes locked onto it. "Did you tell the detective about him?"

I hung my head. "It's too unbelievable." Maybe he did want to hurt me. Maybe even to kill me. But he wouldn't go around the city murdering random girls. Would he? "Even after everything he did, I can't completely believe he would do that to other girls. Even if he thought they were me."

Danny clenched his fist on the table. "I think you need to say something. What if you *are* in danger?" He raised his eyebrows. "What about the girl at the club?"

I wrapped his coat tighter around my waist. "What?"

"You asked me about her. What does she have to do with this?"

It was comforting to hear Danny affirm my paranoia. Maybe I wasn't crazy. But what I was doing to Jenny was definitely not okay. I tugged on a strand of hair. "Nothing. I remembered that night now, and I was just curious."

His eyes narrowed. He didn't buy it. "Why do you always have to hold something back?" he asked, irritated.

I wasn't the only one holding back. "How are things going with Erin?" I snapped.

He furrowed his brow. "Erin?"

"Yeah. You two went home together, right?"

His eyes changed. "No, we didn't." He shook his head. "And if we had, is it *that* upsetting to you that I could be with someone else? Jesus, you have a boyfriend. What's the matter with you?"

I swallowed, my rage turning into embarrassment. "You're right," I said, putting my head in my hands. "I'm sorry, Danny. I don't know what I'm thinking or doing these days." My skin burned as I thought about Jenny's apartment. What the hell was I thinking?

He waited for more. An explanation. A normal person would have a real explanation for all this.

He tapped the table and stood up. "It's fine," he said. "Look, I have to get back to work. But we're not finished talking about all of this." He squeezed my shoulder. "Hold on to the coat."

"Okay," I said and watched him leave and cross the street into Tribune Tower. He didn't look back. Relief warmed my skin, easing down the goose bumps from the cold. Speaking these dark thoughts out loud made me feel less alone. And now, if something happened to me, at least Danny would know the truth.

CHAPTER THIRTY

I slid the paper and pen across the table.

Wilder lazily picked it up and began reading.

"Was it him?" I asked, my voice echoing off the empty walls of the office. He'd said it was a temporary work space for him while he worked out of the Bucktown Station. He'd seemed excited when he mentioned he'd be heading back to the downtown precinct soon.

He remained silent as he continued scanning the page with his eyes. "Hmm?" he asked, letting the paper drop.

"You said Jeremy left a note. Was it definitely him?"

He stroked his chin before leaning forward, his elbows resting on the table. "His note and the evidence in his apartment helped us piece together a clear picture of what happened and why."

I waited for him to continue, but he returned his gaze to my written statement. "I need to know why," I said after a moment.

He glanced out the small window behind me. "So, you know now that Jeremy and Holly had been together before? Well, based off of what we found, it turns out that they remained very close even after they broke up," he said, leaning back in his chair. "And he had been forging prescriptions for a variety of different opioids and other drugs for Holly. It seems like he may have been selling to college kids all around town. That's how we found him, actually—OD'd on his own fentanyl supply."

"How was he writing prescriptions like that?" I asked.

"Still trying to get all of the details about the how," Wilder continued. "But we caught on to his 'business' relationship with Holly because a neighbor heard a loud fight between the two the week she died. There was some dispute about money, *and* Holly had just started dating someone new."

I remembered the photo of her bloody fingernails. Moving on to someone else? That's all it took for someone to snap and kill another human in such a terrible manner?

"I'll walk you out," Wilder said, pushing his chair back and standing up. "I've gotta have a smoke."

I followed him outside, fidgeting with my hands as he lit his cigarette. "There's something I wanted to talk to you about. I think my friend is missing."

Wilder tapped his cigarette against his finger, ashes falling onto the dirty sidewalk. "Okay, why do you think she's missing?"

"She's not at work, and the studio's been locked up for over a week now," I said. "And she's not answering her phone."

He shrugged. "Does she have family in town?"

"I don't know where they live, exactly." It was some suburb out west. Arlington Heights? Skokie?

"Does she live with anyone?"

"Yeah, but her roommate hasn't seen her in a week either."

"When was the last time you saw her?"

My face burned as I remembered our fight. "I told her I was quitting last week, and I haven't seen her since."

"Okay, what about before that? Did she seem off?"

I recalled her writhing with Danny on the dance floor. "No, she seemed normal. We went to a club the night before."

He raised his eyebrows. "Did she meet someone there?"

"No, we just went with my boyfriend and another friend."

"Did she leave with anyone?"

After Iann and I had gotten out of the taxi, Erin and Danny had remained.

He noticed my hesitation. "Did you two have a falling-out? About a boy?"

I glared at him. "Girls don't always just fight about boys." But this time it *was* about a boy. And pills, I guessed.

He chuckled. "So what, did she steal your boyfriend or something?"

"No." At least not my current one. "Her and my other friend split a cab back home."

He frowned and took a drag. "Okay, what's your friend's name? I'll look into it. And give me the name of the other friend who rode home with her too."

Heat rushed to my face. "The missing one is Erin Braughton, and the friend she split a cab with is Danny Fletcher."

He looked away. "Danny . . . so, the friend she was last seen with was a boy, then?"

I held my breath for a moment. "Yeah, but they just shared a ride."

"Okay, sure." He flicked the cigarette to the ground and stomped on it. "Let me check it out. I'm sure it's nothing. They're probably shacked up together or something."

"No." I shook my head. "I saw him the other day, and he told me they didn't . . . um, *do* anything."

He looked me up and down.

"What?" I asked, pulling my jacket closer around my chest.

"You don't look it," he said, sharply, "but you're still just a kid, aren't you?"

I bit my tongue. Maybe he was entitled to make that statement. He must've been close to forty. To him, I really was just a kid. Or maybe the smoking had taken a toll on him, and he was in his early thirties. But those lines around his eyes and the creases in his brow contained a few decades of stories. "So, what's next in the case?"

He glanced at me sidelong. "Holly's? The evidence we found in Jeremy's apartment is conclusive. We're officially closing it."

"What about Sarah's case? Did Jeremy know her too?"

"It's ongoing. We're investigating it separately." He sighed. "We've been over this."

I focused on the toes of my boots, the water in the puddles displacing into separate streams around them on the sidewalk. "When you asked me before if anyone would want to hurt me, I should've told you about something." I could feel his eyes burning into me. Waiting. "My father used to . . ." How to even describe it? It was complicated. It was painful. "He used to hurt me when I was growing up." Hurt me? Beat me? Hate me? I looked back at Wilder.

He seemed unfazed. "Where is he now?"

"I think he's still in Evanston."

He cocked his head to the side. "Why are you telling me this now? Do you really think he'd want to *kill* you?"

The answer was there, but it was too terrible to speak. "I don't know, but I just can't stop thinking about Sarah."

He waited for more but crossed his arms impatiently in my silence. "When was the last time you slept?"

My cheeks grew warm. "I'm sleeping fine," I insisted.

He surveyed me quietly for a moment. "What's your father's name?"

I couldn't close the lid now. Once Wilder started looking in Evanston, he would know everything. Maybe not everything. I was the only one who would know it all. But maybe he would connect the dots. "Russell. Russell Mallen."

CHAPTER THIRTY-ONE

I didn't voice my fears to Iann. Not about Erin. And not about my father. But the dread lingered in the back of my mind with each day that passed and I didn't hear from her.

"I like this," he said, stopping and leaning over my drafting table on his way to the door.

It wasn't a paid project. I had dreamed about my mom for the first time in years. It hadn't been a sorrowful or frightening nightmare like usual. When I'd woken up from it, I'd tried to capture her portrait as quickly as possible. She was beautiful, but her face was a memory that had steadily faded over the past two decades. "Thanks." I glanced at it.

The longer I stared at it, the more I realized it wasn't her at all.

He continued to the door. "What do you have going on today?" He pulled on his jacket.

I sighed. "I have revisions for that kid's book again."

He leaned forward and kissed me. "Good luck with that," he said with a laugh. "I have the clinic tonight. I'll stay at my place since I'll get out of there so late."

"Okay."

He opened the door and glanced back at me before starting down the stairs.

I closed the door. Standing over the table, I looked at the painting one more time and slid it between the back of the table and the wall to join the portrait of Issi.

A knock sounded on the door. It was harder and longer than Iann's. I looked through the peephole to see Wilder staring at me.

"Good morning," he said when I opened the door. "Do you have time to talk?" His expression seemed stiffer than usual.

"Yeah, of course."

He walked into the apartment behind me and closed the door.

"Is this about Erin?" I asked, my stomach dropping.

"I think you should sit down."

I suddenly felt nauseous. I walked to the kitchen table and sank into a chair.

Wilder followed suit. "After what you said about your father, I decided to look into it." He eyed my balled fists resting on the table. "Harper, he's dead."

The tension left my body. "What?" *How?* "What happened to him?" I ventured when he didn't respond.

"He was in a car accident. I'm sorry."

I wasn't. I felt nothing. *You care more about those dead girls than about your own father. What does that say about you? He was your only family.*

"The funeral is tomorrow. I wanted you to know."

I closed my eyes for a moment. I could feel the sting of my father's palm against my face. I saw the hatred on his face the night of the accident. My heart quickened. Now that he was gone, there was nothing keeping me from going back. "What about Erin?"

He furrowed his brow. "You still haven't seen or heard from her?"

"No."

"That name you gave me of the guy she left with—how well do you know him?"

"Danny? Very well. He's a great guy," I said immediately. "Why?"

"Are you sure? I put in a call to a friend and found out a little more about him." He watched me. "He was under suspicion in a missing person's case in Evanston a while back."

My throat tightened.

"Yeah, I don't know the details, but he got brought in for some minor who went missing," he said, scanning my face. "She's still missing, technically, but they dropped the investigation after she made contact with her father."

I ran a hand through my hair. "Look, Danny has nothing to do with Erin missing, believe me. And"—I took a deep breath—"I was the minor in Evanston."

"What?"

I met his gaze. "I told you before that I ran away from home." I fidgeted with my hands. "I had no idea that they even looked for me when I left . . . or that Danny was investigated for it." My whole body was drained of feeling. It hadn't even been a thought in my mind that everything could come falling down on him when I left.

"Why did you run away?" he asked.

"My father." It was a simple answer.

"That's why you thought he might be caught up in what's going on down here?" His eyes drifted to the scar on my neck.

"Yes." The thought was always at the back of my mind these days. But with him dead, would we ever really know? "I cut ties with everyone and everything when I left. I didn't even bring my phone."

"Well, Daniel was able to find you."

"He didn't *find* me—we ran into each other." It sounded far fetched as I said it. Just another big coincidence I'd accepted without question.

He nodded. "Okay, if that's true and you happened to find each other by chance, how hard would it be for someone to find you if they were really looking?"

I shrugged. "That's why I told you about it. Because I was scared of the same thing." What if my father had come looking for me but instead had found Sarah? Maybe Holly had nothing to do with it.

———

I thumbed at the edge of my jacket, watching him cross the street toward me. I couldn't sit still in the coffee shop.

Danny's eyes lit up when he saw me waiting by the bridgehead. "Hey, I thought we were meeting at the café?" he said, stepping onto the sidewalk beside me.

My heart hurt at the thought of him sitting in jail. "Let's just walk."

"Okay, sure. Is everything all right?" He looked at me from the corner of his eye.

I didn't respond as we started down the steps and onto the Riverwalk, the sound of cars clattering behind us as they rolled over the bridge. "Why didn't you tell me what happened to you after I left?"

He stopped and squared his body toward mine. "What?"

"In Evanston. You were arrested?"

He groaned and sank onto the nearby bench. "Come on, Harper. What good would it have done to bring that up? I mean, I told you he tried to ruin my life."

I paced in front of him. "You made it seem like a joke. I didn't realize—"

He rubbed his face. "Look, nothing came of it, and I'm fine now. He dropped it almost right away when he found out that I knew about"—he glanced at me—"you know. And I had a good lawyer."

Of course. I couldn't forget. And Danny had always seen the after-math. I sank down on the seat beside him, our knees touching. "Tell me what happened."

"Harper—" He shook his head.

"Please."

He sighed and looked at me. "I went to your house when you left, because I thought he had hurt you again or worse. But when you weren't there, I figured, and hoped, you'd run away. He lost it. Then the next day, the police came to my place and started throwing around phrases like 'kidnapping' and 'statutory rape.'" His jaw clenched.

"Oh my god," I breathed, covering my face with my hands. "What happened then?" I managed after a moment.

He glanced down at his hands. "And they checked my apartment and, of course, found out you had been there. But when they found out *why*, they started looking into your father a little more."

"What made them let you go?"

He shrugged. "Right when they were about to start investigating him, he said he'd heard from you and that you were safe in Chicago. And they just believed him, you know? He's a respectable member of the community up there."

I hung my head. "I would've never . . . I should've told you that I was leaving." But if I had talked to Danny, I wouldn't have left. If I had touched him one last time before walking out the door, I would've stayed.

"I don't regret anything," he said. "I mean, sure, it would've been good to know that you were only sixteen and about your insane family, but still no regrets." He grinned, but his eyes were troubled.

I had enough regrets for the both of us. Meeting him had saved my life but almost destroyed his.

"Besides," he continued, "I was so proud of you." He smiled weakly. "For leaving."

I slid my hand into his, my heart racing. "Danny," I breathed. There was nothing I could express. "He's dead."

His hand tensed around mine. "I'm sorry." It was insincere, but I didn't blame him.

I was more than merely indifferent about his death. I was relieved? But that relief still felt hollow. "Don't be," I said.

He responded by putting his arm around my shoulder and drawing me into his chest.

I let my neck relax against his, and we sat there, the river calmly dancing past us. It was like we had never stopped. It felt like, for a moment, he was still mine.

CHAPTER
THIRTY-TWO

I was thankful that Iann had stayed the night at his place. My foul mood had lasted the entire night and carried over to the next morning. I staggered into the shower, my breath reeking of rum. I slumped against the side of the shower, letting the cold water run down my body until it turned hot. I opened my mouth until it was full and gargled, then spit into the drain.

For a moment, the water caught in my throat. I gripped the tiled wall and bent over, gagging. I remembered that night when I was ten, coughing up the icy water, my body convulsing, looking up at the paramedics and sputtering.

I turned off the water and stepped onto the rug, my eyes more alert now.

I considered what I was willingly walking into if I went back to Evanston. He was gone now, but his family wasn't.

I threw on my clothes and brushed through my wet hair. As I caught my reflection in the mirror, I thought about how much my father would disapprove of everything I was right now. He would hate how short my hair was, that it only hit below my shoulders. He would hate that I wasn't wearing a dress and that I was going out with my hair wet. He'd always hated it when I had to wear makeup for performances.

I leaned across the counter and grabbed a bright-red lipstick and swiped it across my lips.

I topped off Woodstock's food in the kitchen, and he came running. On my way to the door, I stretched behind the TV and fished out what cash I had tucked underneath. I would need to buy a new pass to get on the train.

A car rumbled toward my apartment as I locked the front door.

Wilder parked by the curb and jogged up to me as I started down the stairs. "Are you on your way out?" he asked.

"Yes," I said. "What's going on?"

He searched my face. "Nothing, I was in the neighborhood. Thought I'd stop by and check in with you."

I didn't know how to respond to that. It seemed strange that he really cared. Or that he would be that transparent about caring. "I'm surprised you're still up here," I said, coolly. "Aren't you supposed to be back in downtown?"

"I will be soon. Still just wrapping things up." He met my eyes again. "How are you doing with everything?"

I clenched my jaw. "I'm fine." I could still smell the liquor on my breath as I spoke. "I'm heading to Evanston right now."

"You're driving?" he asked, eyeing the dark circles under my eyes.

"No, I'm taking the train. I don't have a car." I walked past him onto the sidewalk.

"That's a two-hour trip one way." He matched my pace.

"An hour and fifteen minutes," I corrected. If I was lucky. The construction at Howard Station might even add a few extra minutes.

"By car it's only thirty," he countered.

"Yes, it is. But I'm not going by car."

He tapped my arm. "Come on," he said. "I'll give you a ride." He turned and walked back to his car.

I stood there for a few seconds before following after him. I was already buckled into the passenger seat by the time I could think better of it. As we started down the road, my stomach filled with a cold, heavy dread.

"Are you allowed to be doing this?" I asked. Traffic was beginning to thin out as we continued north into the suburbs.

"Do what?" he asked, staring straight ahead, one hand on the wheel.

"To give me a ride. Don't you have murders to solve?"

One edge of his lips curled into a smile. "Yes, but I got off the clock a couple of hours ago. This is unofficial." After a moment he continued, "So you're from Evanston originally?"

I nodded and looked out the window. The lake rushed past as we continued faster down the road now that traffic had dissipated entirely. "Yeah." I closed my eyes.

"Do you have any other family there?"

I sighed, opening my eyes and watching the red and orange trees breeze by the window, the gray-blue of the lake gently swaying in the background. "I don't know." It was dismissive but accurate. Surely my father's family still remained, but I couldn't forgive them. "To be completely honest, I'm not too thrilled to be going back."

"Then why are you?"

"I don't know how to explain it." After staying away for so long, there was a part of me that just needed to go home one last time. Without the threat of seeing him again. "But since the funeral's this afternoon, it might be my best shot at avoiding running into relatives, if they're even still around."

"I get it," he said. "I mean, based off of everything you've said, it doesn't sound like you left on good terms."

"Thank you. For giving me a ride. I appreciate it. As much as I hate that place, taking the train would've made it ten times worse."

His cheeks reddened. "It's no problem."

———

Everything had changed in the last nine years in my hometown. More buildings, less green.

"Where to now?" he asked once we'd reached the city limits.

I turned my head to observe the street signs. "Take a right here, and go straight down Church Avenue." The house came into view, sending a chill down my spine. Any good memory there had been wiped out by a thousand bad ones. "It's this one," I said, pointing to the narrow two-story blue house at the corner of the street.

Wilder parked along the road. There was a car in the driveway. Maybe it was a lawyer or a real estate agent already trying to wipe Russell Mallen's existence off the map.

I glanced out the window at the house for a long moment, aware of Wilder's eyes on me.

"Do you want to go in?" he asked finally.

I opened the door and stepped out of the car, my eyes still focused on the house. As if it might disappear if I looked away for a moment. With Wilder behind me, we crossed the street and walked up the steps to the porch. The white trim had peeled everywhere, but it was most apparent on the banisters.

The door opened, and a plump blonde woman gaped at me from the doorway, her eyes wide with horror. She had seen a ghost.

I froze where I stood on the porch.

Her lips quivered, and she bounded toward me with open arms. "Isabella!" With that one word it was as if she had slapped me. I leaned away, but she ensnared me. "My sweet, sweet Issi. I'm so sorry."

My body remained rigid, my arms tethered to my sides.

She pulled away and grabbed my face. "No one knew if—where you were." There was something so cavalier about the way she said it. As if I had just stepped out of the room instead of disappeared for the past nine years.

I opened my mouth to respond, but my voice failed.

She ushered me inside. "It doesn't matter, dear," she said. She suddenly turned around right before we crossed the threshold, noticing Wilder for the first time. "Who's this?"

Again, I opened my mouth but couldn't speak. I couldn't breathe. *Why did you bring us back here?*

Wilder glanced at me before extending his hand. "I'm a friend of Harper's."

Her expression darkened. She frowned at him and blinked. "I'm her Aunt Lydia." She ignored his hand and pushed me inside.

"Come and have a seat—we're still trying to figure everything out." Lydia left me standing outside the front room. "Issi is here!" she called throughout the house and disappeared into the kitchen.

Wilder raised his eyebrows at me. I sidestepped past him and headed down the hallway. When I arrived at the study, I noticed the books strewed all around and objects from my father's desk broken on the floor. I touched my neck. The wooden bookcase still had a slight bow in the side where he had pushed me into it. Tiny white crescent shapes were still etched into the wood where I had dug my nails in.

I passed the remaining shut doors in the hallway until I arrived at the last one. Wilder's footsteps echoed close behind me. My old bedroom was completely dark. Wilder appeared behind me and flicked on the light switch. The blinding pink paint on the walls was chipped, some of the white base paint peeping through.

Wilder walked over to the large oak desk in the corner by the window and held up one of the framed pictures and looked back at me.

"That's not me," I barked.

He set down the frame and narrowed his eyes. "Isn't this your room?"

It's our room. I turned the frame down on the table, but I saw one next to it and froze. Issi smiled from the picture, sitting properly in front of a light-blue backdrop. It must've been from picture day at school. "Yes, it was."

He grabbed the picture before I could put it back on the desk.

The room smelled stale and wet. The bed was still covered with the pink quilt Mom had handmade for Issi. It was too small to reach all the way over the mattress, but we could never entertain the idea of packing it away. My father had thrown out the emerald one she'd hand stitched for me.

I glanced over the bookcase. Many of the books were gone now. I ran my hand over the spines of the remaining ones, my fingers skipping over the gaps. Some strands of dark hair were caught on the splintered wood on the side of the shelf, a memorial to one of my father's particularly violent days. My heart raced, and I put my nails into the matching scratches in the wood.

I knelt down, the floorboards creaking under my weight. I pulled the leather-bound tome of *Anne of Green Gables* off the bottom shelf. Brushing the top layer of dust from the cover, I coughed. I flipped to the center of the book and pulled the photo from within before letting the book fall, more dust kicking up from the floor. "This is me." I handed him the photo over my shoulder.

Wilder took it. "You have a twin?" he asked, glancing back at the photos on the desk.

"Had," I said. *I'm still here.* I stood back up and knocked the dust from my jeans.

When we reentered the living room, Lydia was sitting slumped in a chair, a small man with features like my father's sitting on the couch across from her. He scowled at me, making the resemblance even stronger. A thin dark-haired girl sauntered in from the kitchen. She was wearing my mom's pearl earrings and necklace.

"You remember Lauren, don't you?" Lydia said in a syrupy voice, beaming at the girl.

I did. She was my only cousin and the brattiest child I'd ever met. By the looks of it, she'd never changed.

"She started at Northwestern this year," Lydia continued, eyeing me expectantly. "Why don't you have a seat?"

My feet were itching to run. The air was too thick to breathe. But I obeyed and sat on the chair.

Wilder stood beside me for a moment before gesturing to the back of the house. "I'm going to step out for a moment."

I wanted to beg him to stay but remained silent as he walked through the side door. Turning back to them and looking at their faces, I couldn't believe I had come back.

My uncle was still seething, his dark-brown eyes narrowing as they surveyed me.

Lauren was staring at me down her long, thin Mallen nose.

I wanted to feel anger that she had taken those pearls, but there was nothing. Mom was too distant a scar. There were fresher, more painful wounds.

"You missed the funeral," Lydia said suddenly with feigned glumness. "We wanted to let you know, but . . ." She glanced at my uncle. "He's buried at the plot in St. Boniface with the rest of your family."

The rest. That was the first time I truly understood I was the last of us. "Next to Isabella and Mom?" I had found my voice, but it still came out strangled.

They stared at me with wide eyes.

"This is because of you," my uncle spit back, getting to his feet. "*You* destroyed him with your deranged little games!"

I stood up as well. Despite the resemblance, he was shorter and frailer than my father had been. "It's not on me." *They* had allowed him to turn into a monster. They'd allowed him to raise Issi and me. They'd allowed him to live in a fantasy world until he'd snapped. If they hadn't turned a blind eye, Issi would still be alive. And so would I. "I'm glad he's gone." I trembled as soon as the words ripped from my mouth. I had wanted him gone since that day.

My uncle lunged toward me and slapped me so hard it turned my head until it popped. I fell backward, my shoulders and neck slamming into the brick fireplace.

Wilder clattered in through the door, cigarette in hand, waving smoke out of his face. When he saw me on the floor, he threw the butt down and stepped between us. "Get back," Wilder roared.

My uncle took a step back, and Wilder bent down to help me to my feet. "What the fuck?" he muttered, his arm around my shoulders.

I pushed him away and went for the door.

"Don't come back here!" my uncle bellowed behind me, storming into the kitchen, a violent clatter of metal echoing through the hallway.

Still shaking, I grabbed the doorknob, Lydia frantically waddling behind me. "I'm sorry," she huffed. Her face crumpled as she turned and scurried after her husband.

I pushed through the front door, then doubled over, my hands pressing into my knees. I picked up my head and stared into the darkening street. The sun had set, and the air felt lighter.

Wilder gripped my shoulders from behind. "Are you okay?"

I nodded, still filling my lungs with fresh air. I straightened back up. "Let's go."

Without looking back, I stumbled to the car. I fell into the passenger seat and leaned my head back, closing my eyes, my cheek and jaw still burning. I didn't open my eyes again until the car jerked into motion.

"Why did she call you Isabella?" Wilder asked.

I fished the picture from my back pocket and squinted at it into the dark. This was the only photo of me as a child that had survived after the accident. It was also the only truly happy photo I had from when Mom was still alive. Issi and I were both leaning on our elbows and smiling at the camera from under a blanket, our hands pushing our cheeks up toward our eyes. "After Issi died, my father pretended I was her." I spoke the words cautiously. They had never been uttered before beyond my desperate pleas as a child. "He did everything short of having my name legally changed." I dog-eared one corner of the picture. "He told everyone that Harper died."

He was silent for a moment. "That's fucked up," he said quietly.

I rolled down the window. The smell of smoke emanating from his side was stifling. "I'm an idiot for coming back here." The air hit my face as he continued down the road, winding to the highway. "I'm sorry," I said, rolling up the window again.

He smiled wryly, eyeing my stinging cheek. "Believe me, I've seen much worse."

CHAPTER THIRTY-THREE

As we turned onto my street, I saw a light in my apartment through the blinds. Iann. I could've almost cried with relief. I couldn't imagine being alone tonight. "Let me out right here," I said, pulling on the door handle.

"Jesus, hold on!" Wilder said, slamming to a stop a block away as I swung the door open.

"Thanks for the ride," I called over my shoulder and shut the door behind me.

He shook his head and drove past me back onto the main road.

I glanced at my phone. It was only 8:00 p.m. Iann's shift must've been shorter than usual. As I climbed the steps, my back still ached from having been thrown against the fireplace. I pulled my keys from the bag and turned them in the lock. It was silent as I opened the door. Iann's jacket and shoes weren't in a heap by the door like they usually were. "Iann?" I called.

Two yellow paws swatted at me from under the bed, and I leaped back as Woodstock emerged from underneath. But no Iann.

I surveyed the room. My pajamas were still strewed across the floor, my empty coffee mug still by the bedside table. I'd left in such a hurry this morning that it was possible I'd forgotten to turn off the light. I pulled out my phone.

Are you still coming over later?

I sent the message before thinking about the questions that would come with his presence.

I walked to the bathroom, biting my lip and forcing myself to look in the mirror. My right cheek was still red from the blow. I splashed my face with cold water, saying a silent prayer that it wouldn't bruise.

I glanced down at my phone. No response from Iann yet.

I wound my fingers into my hair, sinking to the floor. I opened the cabinet and pulled out my bundle of pills. I thought about Iann. About my muttered promise from the other night.

No, he's wrong. You're in control of this. You need to sleep.

I dry swallowed one of the pills. I could feel it settle into the base of my throat before sliding down. I stumbled to the bed, lying there until the voices in my head fell silent and my vision blackened.

The bed creaked when Iann slid under the covers next to me. I kept my eyes closed. I didn't want to talk about where I'd been.

His body wrapped around mine, hotter than usual, as if steam were emanating from him. With heavy fingers, he pulled my hair away from my neck. He slid closer to me, his breath sour and his hands resting on the skin on my stomach as I lay on my side.

In that warmth, I fell back into a deep sleep.

I walk barefoot through tall green grass in the dark cemetery. I pass among the worn gravestones and mausoleums, my hand touching each cold one as I walk by.

The next one is completely covered by tall grass, vines strangling the granite. I kneel on the ground and violently pull away at the vines and rip the grass from its roots until my fingers are bloodied and covered in dirt. I look up at the stone and touch the engraved letters, blood staining the stone.

Harper Anne Mallen.

I knock on the stone.

———

The sound rattled me awake.

It was still dark. I jumped from the covers and looked through the peephole. Iann stood there, illuminated by the glow of his phone screen.

I turned the lock and opened the door.

"Oh, I was just about to call you," he said when he saw me. "You didn't answer when I knocked the first time."

I blinked and opened the door for him to come in.

"Were you asleep already?" he asked, pulling the lamp cord, light flooding the apartment again.

I closed the door, my head swimming from the dream. "You didn't let yourself in earlier?" I asked, hoarsely. A chill ran down my spine.

Who had been in bed beside me?

Maybe it was just the pill. Maybe I'd been dreaming.

He took his jacket off. He smelled like gin. "No, the dead bolt was locked. I didn't think you would be asleep already. You must be really tired."

I sank back into the bed, narrowing my eyes against the light. "You smell like liquor."

"Oh, yeah. One of the waiters spilled a drink on me," he said. He turned off the light and lay on the bed next to me, his bare chest warm against my back. No, the smell was on his breath. We were both liars.

I turned around to face him and put my arm around his waist. "Do you think I'm too messed up?" It was a question that had been lingering unspoken between us, but sleep had removed my filter and laid all my issues bare.

With his eyes still closed, he pulled me into his chest. "Yes, but that's why I love you." Apparently, he'd lost his filter too.

My body tensed under his hands. I didn't know if I loved him. I didn't know if I could love anyone. Those words sat on a shelf in the dark somewhere deep inside me, covered in cobwebs and tethered together with rust.

CHAPTER THIRTY-FOUR

I hadn't been able to fall asleep again. I lay awake until dawn, thinking about what Iann had said. How could he love me if there was so much he didn't know?

When he woke up, I pretended like I was waking too. "Good morning," I said, stretching.

He rubbed his bloodshot eyes. "Hey." He leaned in and kissed me. "Sorry I woke you up last night."

As the night had worn on, I'd grown more convinced I'd dreamed of Iann—or someone—beside me before he'd actually arrived. "No, it's fine. I didn't realize I locked the dead bolt."

He rolled to the other side of the bed and got up. "What time is it? I have a class at ten."

I sat up and reached for my phone. "9:23," I said.

He felt around for his shirt from the night before. "Okay, I've got to get ready," he mumbled, before disappearing into the bathroom.

I put my phone back on the nightstand. That was when I noticed the note lying beside it. I picked it up. It was a notice from Bug about rent for the month.

Iann came out minutes later, quickly rubbing a towel through his hair. "Did you bring this in last night?" I held the note up.

He looked at it from across the room. "I don't think so," he said. "But I don't remember. I had a couple of pretty strong drinks last night. Mike wanted to come up with a new signature drink, and I was his guinea pig."

I scanned the paper again.

"What does it say?" He started buttoning his shirt all the way to the collar.

"It's about rent. I need to pay Bug." I set it down. Luckily, I had enough cash lying around.

Iann grabbed his keys from the nightstand. "Okay, I've got to head out. I'll call you."

———

As usual, I waited until the last minute to drop off the money for Bug. I had carried the envelope full of crumpled dollar bills with me all afternoon while hopping coffee shops, trying to finish a commission. I pulled it from my bag as I rounded the corner of the street and my building came into view.

I crept to his unlit door. As I slid the envelope with cash through the crack of the door above the handle, it creaked open, the envelope falling to the ground. I stooped to pick it up, and the door opened wider from a gust of wind behind me. I straightened and observed the cracks above the doorframe, probably the reason why it wouldn't stay shut.

I softly pushed the door. "Hello?" I called in. The stench of stagnant water and garbage overwhelmed me. Everything in my body screamed for me to leave. But something outside of myself prodded me over the threshold into the dank unit, the only light coming from a computer in the far corner of the room. I set the envelope on the cluttered kitchen counter, careful not to touch anything on it. It smelled of rotting food.

My eyes lingered on the computer screen on the other side of the room, where a black-and-white video was pulled up. Immediately, my stomach dropped, but my feet crawled forward. My hands shook as I drew closer. Those were my bedsheets and bed on the screen, Woodstock curled on top of my pillow. There was a time stamp in the bottom corner, rolling forward every second. I staggered back, but my hand gripped the greasy mouse. On the side were thumbnail images from each day in November.

I scrolled up.

October.

September.

My heart drummed in my ears, knocking against my chest furiously. I swallowed the bile pooling in my throat and clicked on a random video in October. My moans and Iann's roared through the speakers as our bare bodies intertwined, the sheets slipping off the bed and exposing my body as I dug my fingernails into his back.

My hand slipped on glossy paper on the table. I picked it up and dropped it, my fingers trembling. It was a photograph of Holly on the pavement, her eyes open and glassy—deep, dark impressions around her neck.

I tripped over myself as I ran through the dark and collapsed, vomiting onto the bushes in front of the door. I could still hear my own moans through the speakers growing louder behind me as I wiped my lips with my sleeve. I staggered to my feet, my head swimming, and stumbled down the sidewalk. I jogged to the edge of the street, feeling in my pocket for my phone. The screen lit up, and I searched frantically through my call log for Wilder before dialing.

"Wilder," he answered, flatly.

The video on the computer replayed in my mind. "It's Harper . . . I don't know what to do."

"What happened? Are you okay?" His tone grew more urgent.

"My landlord." My voice trembled. "I found photos and video . . ." Another wave of vomit filled my throat, and I gagged.

"What kind of photos and video?" he demanded.

"He's been filming me," I stammered. "And he has pictures of Holly." I saw the red-and-purple lines around her neck. That glassy look in her eyes.

"Where are you now? Is he with you?"

I steadied my free hand against my knee, rocking gently forward. "No, I don't know where he is. I'm outside my apartment."

"Okay, is there somewhere safe nearby you can wait for me?" I heard the rattling of keys and his chair squeaking over the phone.

My mind raced. "I'll wait at the park," I breathed. I could be there around the corner in three minutes.

"Call me when you get there." The sound of his engine revved.

"Okay." I hung up and turned the corner toward the park. *No.* My footsteps halted on the pavement. I couldn't leave Woodstock in the building with that creep. What if he came back before Wilder and I got there? He would know I had been in his room. What if he came looking for me? *It'll only take a minute.* My stomach twisted in knots as I ran back toward the apartment.

I grasped the stair rail to steady myself, splinters from the unfinished wood piercing my skin. When I flung the door open, a sick smell overwhelmed me.

The light from outside poured in behind me and illuminated the red stains on my bed. Blood was rubbed all over the white fabric. It had been too quiet when I came in. No purring, no meowing as I entered. Holding my breath, I walked to the foot of the bed and screamed. The sound ripped from me and scratched my throat as I fell to my knees.

Woodstock's bloodstained collar was limp on the floor by my bed. My drawings were ripped in shreds on the floor, red flecks dotting the paper.

A clatter sounded behind me, but before I could turn around, my head suddenly jerked back, and my phone crashed to the floor. I gasped and fell, my head hitting the bed frame with a thud.

My body pressed harder into the floor as someone sat on my stomach. I couldn't see a face in the dim streetlight filtering in through the window, but it smelled like Bug.

"What did you do?" he demanded, grabbing a fistful of my hair.

I pushed him away, but he tightened his knees around my waist. I gasped as he sank more of his weight onto my body and put both his hands on either side of my head.

"I didn't hurt anyone," he yelled, sinking his fingernails into my scalp. "Why did you go in there?" The pressure became greater with each word he spat at me.

Both my legs were pinned under his, but I managed to lift one into what I hoped was his groin. He made a guttural sound and loosened his grip, giving me the chance to pry his fingers back.

He recoiled and staggered to his feet, stooping over me. I kicked him in the chest so hard he landed on his back. I grabbed my phone and sprang toward the door. I reached for the handle, but he yanked my hair again from behind.

A scream erupted from my lips as he slammed my head into the nightstand, the lamp rolling off and shattering beside me on the floor.

My scalp was wet and hot, my vision clouded by black dots.

His footsteps approached slowly.

He lowered himself back onto my chest and ripped my hair away from my neck. I raised a hand and pushed his arm, but he grabbed my wrist and slammed it to the floor, then pinned down my other hand with his right leg.

I had regretted surviving for so long. But now, all I wanted was to live.

He gripped my hair. "I didn't do anything wrong!" he yelled, slamming my skull back to the floor. The black dots reappeared. Both my arms were free again, and I used them to pull at his hands, now wrapped around my throat. "You stupid bitch!"

My head popped as it hit the floor. I choked on my own blood, trying to breathe.

Issi's back was to me in the water.

If you give up, you will die.

My lungs burned. I could hear my own gasps, growing more stifled and panicked. My arms collapsed back to the floor, my injured wrist landing on something sharp. I wrapped my hand around the piece of ceramic from the lamp, the shard burrowing into my palm. I tried to pick my hand up, but it dropped down on the wood floor with a thud.

"I'm not going away for this," Bug's voice quavered as he relaxed his grip. "You don't even know—"

I remembered what Wilder had told me about Holly's death.

Ten seconds.

We only have ten seconds.

My throat spasmed as I gripped the shard again and swung my arm off the floor to plunge the piece into the side of his neck as deep as I could manage. His body slumped over mine.

I gasped and rolled to my side as he stumbled to his feet, a fountain gurgling from his mouth out onto the floor. Blood dripped from my palm and from my forehead, streaking the wood floor as I dragged myself toward the door, only making it as far as the nightstand before the door flung open. Wilder appeared and fell to his knees beside me. "Harper?"

The back of my head felt cold.

He gently turned my face to the side. "Shit," he exhaled loudly. There was sudden pressure against my head and neck. "Harper?"

My eyes focused on him, but I couldn't speak. I opened my mouth, but only a terrible and haunting rattle escaped.

"Hang in there," Wilder said.

The chill spread from my head and into my limbs. I closed my eyes.

"Stay awake! Look at me!"

I succumbed to the darkness.

———

I heard the beeping first. Then I felt the pain.

I was awake, but my eyelids were so heavy. I swallowed. I could taste iron.

My fingers twitched, rubbing over the rough fabric. I slowly opened my eyes to the white blankets and white walls ahead of me. The steady beeping of the vitals monitors beside me continued. I looked at the IV needle pinching the vein in my hand. I was alone; the only other sounds were the people rushing past the open door in the hallway. I turned my hand over and saw the gauze secured over my palm.

Iann walked in, and his eyes grew big when they met mine. "Thank god! You're awake!" He pulled a chair away from the wall and set it closer to the bed. "How do you feel?"

I swallowed. It was a little easier now. "What happened?" My voice was hoarse and foreign. I remembered Bug sitting on top of me, crushing my throat as he slammed my skull. I remembered the blood pouring from him. My entire body stiffened. "Where is he?"

Iann frowned and ran a hand across his face. "You don't have to worry about him."

"What does that mean?" I croaked. "What happened to him?"

He opened his mouth to speak but closed it quickly.

"Where is he?" I asked again, my heart beating faster.

"He's dead."

I touched my neck. I still felt that cold ceramic shard in my hand. "I don't—how did I get here?" The back of my skull throbbed.

He fiddled with his hands and leaned forward, his elbows propped on his knees. "The cops found you."

Yes, that's right. Wilder. Oh god. Woodstock. My eyes burned. I remembered the little blue collar caked with blood, and a sob escaped. "Is Woodstock . . ." My voice cracked.

Iann looked down. "I haven't found him yet."

I pressed my palms to my eyes as the tears came. If they couldn't find him, then he couldn't be dead. But all that blood . . .

Iann stood, resting his hand on my shoulder. "He's still out there somewhere," he whispered. "He's okay. We'll find him."

"She's awake?"

I opened my eyes again and rubbed the tears away from my cheeks.

Wilder was leaning into the room, against the doorway, his eyes narrowed as he glanced from me to Iann.

Iann kept his hand on my shoulder but stepped back a bit. "Yeah, she just woke up."

Wilder stepped farther into the room. "Are you up for talking right now?" he asked, looking at me.

"She *just* woke up," Iann hissed.

"It's okay," I said.

Iann glanced at me. I nodded, and he pulled his hand away. "Okay, I'll be outside," he said and walked out into the hallway.

Wilder watched him go and then sat in the chair. "How are you feeling?"

Terrible. "Fine." I swallowed a sob. *You have been through worse. You have been through worse.*

He nodded. "Okay, good. I thought I told you to go somewhere safe and wait for me." It was more of an accusation than a statement.

I held a hand to my aching temple. There was a bandage wrapped around my forehead. "What happened?"

He scratched the back of his neck, irritably. "You were attacked. You remember that, right?"

"Yes." I saw Bug's outline as he sat on top of me, his legs digging into my sides. "I was just going to get my cat and leave when it happened." My lips trembled. "How did I get here?"

He sighed and settled into the seat next to me. "You never called me from the park, so I drove straight to your apartment." He rubbed his hands together. "Your landlord didn't make it to the hospital."

"Did he kill Holly? What about Jeremy? You said—"

"It's too early to know for sure. We got all the photos and videos you told us about." He avoided my eyes. He had already seen what was on them. "We should know more after reviewing everything."

I thought about the videos. "I can't believe all of this. How long was he watching me?"

He shrugged and leaned back in the chair. "That's the part we have yet to figure out. From what I saw, there were videos dating years before you moved in. Looked like he might have had a thing for a previous tenant's girlfriend too."

My stomach turned. "Does Iann know about everything?"

He pointed his thumb over his shoulder. "Your boyfriend? No, it's up to you to tell him what you want." He surveyed me. "I'm glad you're okay. You put up one hell of a fight. When I got there, it didn't look too good for you. You lost a lot of blood."

I raised a hand to my head. Stiff gauze ran from the front and wrapped around my skull. It was tender to the touch. I remembered the way my head rammed against the nightstand. The way Bug had bashed my skull against the floor over and over again.

"You're going to be all right," he repeated. His expression had softened. "I'll be in touch as we learn more. Focus on getting better for now."

CHAPTER THIRTY-FIVE

"I'm sorry you're missing work again. I can do this alone."

Iann set my bag on the floor, and my hand rested on his arm as I sat on the bed. "No," he said. "I'm not leaving you alone like this."

I observed the room. My broken lamp was gone, and all the blood from the floor had been scrubbed out.

"So what do you want to bring with you?"

I rested forward on my knees and cradled my head in my hands.

He kneeled on the floor in front of me. "I can bring you to my place and come back here on my own if you want."

My head throbbed. "No, it's fine." I let my hands fall into his. "I'm going to grab some more clothes." I stood up and walked into the closet. My eyes drifted over to Woodstock's food bowl, and I swallowed the lump forming in my throat. Leaving felt like I was giving up on finding him, but we'd searched everywhere.

I sank onto the closet floor and began grabbing whatever clothes were nearby and draping them over my arm.

Iann appeared in the doorway. "Do you have a suitcase?"

I motioned to a duffel bag in the closet corner.

He grabbed it and brought it over to me, and I poured my bundle into it.

My skin itched and crawled as I thought about the cameras. There was no evidence of them now, but Wilder had pointed out where they'd been planted around my apartment. I could feel Bug over my shoulder in the dark of that night. In the hospital, I'd thought about that night before the attack happened. The night I'd thought Iann had slipped beside me in bed. The moment I'd convinced myself was a dream.

"Are you okay?" Iann rested his hand on my shoulder.

I looked down, my hands blurring with my tears. "I can't come back here."

He sank down beside me and pulled me into his chest. "You don't have to," he said, softly. "Move in with me."

———

I stood on the sidewalk outside the station, my hands shaking. I regretted telling Iann not to come with me to give my statement. Recounting that night had torn through me like knives ripping their way out. I saw Bug's eyes glowing in the darkness as he went limp on top of me. I saw the blood every time I blinked.

Wilder came out through the front door beside me. "Hey, are you okay?" He pinched an unlit cigarette between his index finger and thumb.

I clutched at my stomach. "Yeah," I managed through a choked voice.

He lit the cigarette and leaned back against the wall beside me. "You did a good job in there."

I gulped air, trying to keep from vomiting. "So." I struggled. "What happens now?"

He took a drag, glancing at me. "Now?" He puffed the smoke out in a long line. "You move on from this."

———

I doubled up on the anxiety meds from the hospital and slept on and off for days. Giving my statement had made it worse. Iann had theorized that I'd feel better after talking about it, but it only cemented everything in the forefront of my mind.

I passed out in a dreamless sleep only to wake in a sweat, paralyzed in the middle of the night. Once I could move again, I'd shakily pop another two pills in my mouth, lying beside Iann until I fell into another stupor.

When he left in the mornings for school or work, I'd crawl right back under the covers, reliving the sensations of that night.

Pressure. My throat still didn't feel the same when I swallowed, even a week after.

Slice. The shreds of skin breaking from under the ceramic shard.

Crack. My skull against the wood.

Drip. The gush of blood pouring from Bug onto the floor.

I jumped as my phone rang. I rolled over under the blankets to grab it from the nightstand. "Danny?"

"Hey, where have you been? I tried texting and calling you earlier this week."

I looked at the half-unpacked boxes in the corner of the bedroom. This wasn't an update to be shared over the phone. "I'm sorry," I answered simply. "I—"

"Do you want to grab some coffee today?" he asked without pause.

I glanced at the clock above the closet. 3:09 p.m. Iann wouldn't be back for another couple of hours. "Sure."

"Can you come to downtown, or is Wicker Park better?"

"I'm downtown, so I can come to you."

"Okay, great. Let's meet at that café by the river, from last time," he said, shuffling papers near the phone. "In twenty minutes?"

"Sure."

———

I hadn't thought about telling Danny anything yet. But the stitches were still prominent, and the dark bruises where Bug had throttled me still stained my neck.

I caught a glimpse of him through the glass door as I swung it open and stepped inside the café, tugging at the scarf around my neck. It was too tight.

Danny smiled when he saw me and stood up, but as his eyes studied me, his expression darkened. He looked at my forehead and my hand.

I avoided his eyes and sat across from him.

He sank back into his seat. "What happened? Are you okay?"

I had pulled at the scarf a little too much, because his eyes settled on my neck and widened.

"Did Iann do this?" he demanded.

My mind tried to wrap around his questions. "No, of course not!" The response really answered the last two.

He didn't believe me.

"I wanted to tell you in person because I didn't think there was any way to explain over the phone," I began. My throat still convulsed when I spoke more than a few words.

He waited, his eyes flickering to my neck.

"My, um, landlord attacked me." My voice wavered as I imagined his hands on my skin again.

"What?"

I rubbed my hands to keep them from shaking. "He had been filming me in my apartment, and I found out, and . . . he attacked me." I pressed my good hand against the table edge to steady myself as I recounted the incident. Danny's hands immediately closed around it.

"God, I had no idea."

"I think he killed Holly." I saw Holly's glassy, piercing eyes. I dared to look at Danny.

His eyes were on me but actually somewhere else. "I'm so sorry," he said after a moment. "I'm glad you're going to be okay . . . You're going to be okay, right?" His hand was a little tighter around mine.

I nodded. "Yeah, I mean, I've been through worse." I actually didn't feel like that was true anymore.

He furrowed his brow. "You were attacked," he argued.

"Yes, but I'm alive."

"Yes, you are." He squeezed my hand and settled back into his chair.

I inhaled and pulled away from him. "But I killed someone, Danny," I breathed. It had all happened so quickly that night, but I saw his face as I stabbed him. I felt his blood on my skin every time I closed my eyes.

Danny leaned forward again. "No, not *someone*. A monster who was trying to kill you, Harper."

But he wasn't really a monster, was he? He'd bled like a human. His heart had stopped like a human's.

"So, that was you," he said quietly. "One of the reporters mentioned an attempted murder on a woman around Wicker Park in her home, but it didn't even cross my mind that it could be you. When did this happen?"

"A few days ago."

"I don't think anyone knows about the possible connection to those murders yet."

I stiffened. "Everything I've told you has been as a friend. I don't think the police have entirely tied the two together. You're not going to say anything, right?"

He shook his head. "Not my story, and you're not my source."

I relaxed again.

"You're not going to stay in that place, right? Do you need help finding an apartment?" From his eyes, I knew what he was really asking.

"No, I can't go back there," I began. "I, uh, moved in with Iann."

He immediately looked away from me. "You're going through a lot right now. You probably shouldn't be making any big decisions."

"Why don't you like Iann?" I studied his expression.

"I don't feel any way about him. I don't even know him."

I ran my finger along the stitches on my palm. "Why did you assume he did this to me?"

He avoided my eyes. "I know what you've been through. I wanted to make sure you weren't in that type of situation again."

This time I put my hand on his. "I'm not. Iann's a great guy. Maybe a little too great, for me."

He frowned. "Don't say that. No one is great enough for you." He ran his hand through his hair. "I don't know. To me, something feels off about him."

"Like what? He's perfect."

He grimaced at that. "Nothing, forget I said anything," he said with a shrug. "I'm just glad you're getting out of that place. I'm sorry I wasn't there for you when it happened." He stared at me.

"What?"

"No, it's just . . . I don't get it." He furrowed his brow. "I thought they already knew who killed Holly."

My stomach sank. Every time that same thought had entered my mind, I'd popped another anxiety pill. I couldn't do that here with Danny. "It must've been a mistake." I thought about what Wilder had said about Jeremy's suicide note. Did it leave that much room for interpretation?

"But if it was this guy, why? Why would he kill Holly? It just doesn't make sense to me."

It was the same question that played over and over again in my mind at night while Iann slept.

But why?

WINTER

CHAPTER THIRTY-SIX

I stared at the boxes in the corner. It was hopeless.

Moving into Iann's had been slow and painful. I had survived on one bag of essentials for weeks before the inevitable happened. I had turned down all his offers to take a few days off to help me.

When I came back to my old apartment alone, I wasn't strong enough to pack. I sat for hours, trembling as I folded my things into boxes until, exhausted, I left only to try again the next day.

After a month, this had to stop. I told myself I had to finish in one week. I couldn't continue coming back and sacrificing a piece of my sanity each time. The smell of fear and death still overwhelmed me when I opened the door and replayed the night in my mind.

I got to my feet and slumped to the bathroom, then dug through the cabinets and emptied most of my small bottles into the trash. I opened the cupboard under the sink and pulled out a bottle of bleach. My hands froze when I saw the small, crumpled napkin at the back. I grabbed it and unfolded it, hungrily eyeing the tiny pills. My prescription for anxiety meds had already run out. I ran my fingers lightly over them before plucking each one and dropping them into the toilet.

That took the last of my strength for the day. I flushed them down, watching the small white dots circle the bowl before disappearing with a gurgle. I stalked back to the boxes piled onto my stripped bed and grabbed the smallest one, which had been hastily duct taped diagonally across the top. It was just clothes, so it would be easy enough to carry onto the L train and maneuver through the street without bumping into too many people.

I locked the door behind me and carefully gripped the stair rail with my gloved hand as I took each step down. I really had to meet my own deadline to make this move happen before the latest blizzard was due to shut down the city.

I crossed to the next block past the park, shifting the box to my other arm as Erin's building came into sight. I peered past the fence into the parking lot. My heart sank. Still no blue MINI Cooper. I continued past, staring up at her window as my feet crunched over the snow. Ronnie had quit answering the buzzer after I'd stopped by the fifth time. The last I'd heard, she'd claimed Erin's stuff was gone when she returned from work. This had provided some comfort. Surely if her roommate wasn't worried, I shouldn't be either.

But still, I felt uneasy.

I quickened my steps, looping by the studio before turning onto Damen Avenue. Still locked. My arms started to sag under the weight of the box as I climbed up to the platform. I set it down beside the bench, then leaned against the railing and surveyed the neighborhood as I pulled my phone from my pocket. Damen Station had the best view of Wicker Park. It wasn't as high up as the Robey, which was why it provided a truer sense of the neighborhood. It was raised above the alleys and the smaller buildings. I could hear people coughing from their patio and met their eyes as they came to the window to open the blinds. I could see underneath the L rail for a good mile each way, at the abandoned backpacks and garbage and now the piles of dirty snow clawing their way up the graffiti of neighboring walls.

I dialed Wilder's number. He'd been hard to get in touch with since I'd given my statement about Bug. It felt like he'd forgotten about me and, more importantly, about Erin.

"Yup?" His voice hummed through the phone.

I hadn't expected him to actually answer. "Hey, it's Harper," I said, looking over my shoulder at the small herd of people forming along the platform.

"Yeah?" he said lightly, as if he was distracted. "What's going on?"

"I wanted to know if you were able to find anything about my friend Erin?"

"Oh," he said. "You don't have to worry about her anymore." His tone made my stomach turn.

"What do you mean? Did you find her?"

He sighed. "Yeah, she's fine." He lowered his voice. "She's in rehab in Waukegan. Been there since Thanksgiving."

My heart resumed beating. "What facility?"

"I don't know, Shady Oaks or Shitty Creek, something like that. Look," he scoffed, "I'm not a goddamn PI . . . It's not my job to track down your druggie friend."

My cheeks burned. "But it *is* your job to find missing people, isn't it?" I shot back.

I could hear the background noise die out on his end and the wheeze of a door closing. "Turns out she's not missing. She's just a burnout. So, not my problem."

I hung up, the hair raising along my skin, and my hands gripped and wrung the handrail. My phone buzzed in my pocket. I took a deep breath and pulled it out. He was calling back. "What?" I snapped.

"It's Shady Oaks Rehab," he said, his voice softer.

I said nothing.

"You there?"

I sighed. "Yeah. Thanks."

I heard the hiss of his lighter. "How are you doing?" he asked.

"Why do you care? I'm not your problem either."

He exhaled. "Well, I saved your life, so you are kind of my problem."

"I'm fine," I muttered.

He could sense my anger. "I'm sorry about earlier. Just leave your friend alone for now for both our sakes."

My fingers were freezing around the cold plastic of my phone. "What do you mean?"

"I wanted to help you out, but I'm not supposed to be using department resources for hunting down people's friends." He puffed beside the microphone. I almost instinctively coughed from the smoke. "When I talked to Erin's parents, they weren't thrilled that I found out she was in rehab. They threatened to talk to my supervising officer."

"Why didn't you just tell them she was reported missing?" What kind of parents could be angry that someone cared?

"Yeah, they didn't care. And there is no official report or statement, so if they do complain, it's not going to look great for me." He laughed dryly. "Leave it for now. They're rich assholes. They don't like common people like you and me realizing they're human."

I shoved my free hand deeper into my coat pocket. "I'm sorry. I didn't think . . ."

"I'm glad you asked me for help, but I had to take a step back."

"I get it." I turned around as the train growled down the rail. "Thank you for finding her."

"You got it," he said. "And you heard from the DA's office about your case, right?"

I turned toward the platform. "Yeah, they called a couple of weeks ago and said I'm not a murderer."

He chuckled. "I guess that's the gist of it. They're not going to press any charges against you for that bastard's death, of course. The video evidence made it pretty open and shut, but they took their sweet time confirming it." His voice faded at the last word as the train roared in front of me. "Jesus, that's loud!" he hissed.

"Sorry," I said, once the train settled and the doors swung open. "I got to go. Thank you."

"Bye."

I shoved my phone back into my pocket and quickly scooped up the box before sliding onto the train. I sank down onto a seat right as the train kicked back into motion. I set the box under my feet and pulled out my phone. I typed *Shady Oaks Rehab* into Google.

I couldn't remember the name of her previous rehab facility. She didn't talk about that time in her life as much as the other parts. I flipped through the pictures of the tranquil white building set in bumfuck nowhere outside Waukegan, an idyllic vision of the summer lake as the backdrop. I slid the phone into my messenger bag.

How had I missed that Erin was struggling? Maybe I'd been too caught up in my own problems to recognize hers. For all that I resented the way she treated me, I was the worst friend.

I rested my head back, lifting away and falling back softly to the metal wall as the train halted at the next station. She had been aggressive and irritable the night we'd gone clubbing, but I hadn't seen anything in her purse that night other than the Xanax. Maybe that's how it had started. She wasn't supposed to be on any addictive anxiety medicine. The stuff they put her on after her first stint at rehab was much weaker but kept her from wanting more. How long had Jeremy been giving her Xanax? And where did she get it from after he died?

I scrolled through the sad string of unanswered texts I'd sent her over the last few weeks. I hadn't even tried to help her. That night when she got plastered at the Up Room, I should've said something. Maybe it wouldn't have helped. But maybe it would've.

At least she's not dead.

The thought bit to my core, again triggering the unspoken dread that I had feared over the past month. After I got off the train, I carried my box up the stairs and started down Washington Avenue. My worries about Erin had grown darker each day that went by. Even if I hadn't been there for her, someone had, and she was getting what she needed. Maybe she never wanted to see me again. Maybe she shouldn't. I was as toxic as the other friends she'd cut off long ago. She'd tormented me, and I had stolen from her to feed my own darkness.

I punched in the code to Iann's building, leaning the box against the wall before opening the door and climbing more stairs. I hadn't entirely thought through the idea of carrying the box up all the flights of stairs in existence. I let the box fall in front of the door as I dug through my bag for keys.

When I opened the door, Leo raced from Iann's room, panting and wagging his tail. I lifted one aching arm to pat him on the head before continuing to kick the box all the way to the bedroom. He thought it was a game and barked each time the cardboard slid across the wood tile. I liked having Leo around. He had a different energy than Woodstock but a similar playfulness. Only louder.

Once I reached the bedroom carpet, I hoisted the box up again and brought it into the closet. Iann had cleared out half his closet for me, and I only had a dismal collection of six items hanging. I ripped the tape from the box and searched for hangers when I noticed the bulge of clothing busting through the drawers of the dresser backed against the inside of the closet. I pulled open a drawer, and shirts spilled out onto the floor in relief right before the drawer itself collapsed to the ground. Iann didn't have anywhere to put his stuff, so he'd just crammed it in to make room for me.

I smiled to myself and grabbed the wire hangers from the top of the drawer and started hanging his things up. I didn't need an entire half of the closet for my wardrobe. I picked up the drawer but paused right before setting it back into its place. In the empty void where it had sat in the dresser was a small stack of pictures. I placed the drawer down on the floor and reached for them, my heart suddenly racing.

It was Iann in high school regalia, the graduation cap pushing his dark, straight hair against his forehead. I sighed in relief. It wasn't an embarrassing picture. If that was him at his most awkward, he had lived a more blessed life than I'd realized. I shuffled to the next picture. It was his whole family smiling at the camera with a scenic mountain view behind them, his arms around the shoulders of his laughing sisters. It was identical to the photo he had hanging on the bulletin board in his office at school. I flipped to the next one and froze.

I was staring into my eyes. But it wasn't a picture of me.

Jenny?

No, the hair color was darker, and her hair was curly like mine, pulled back into a messy ponytail, loose curls escaping past her ears. She was looking over her shoulder at the camera, one hand reaching for something in her backpack, a thick background of green forest behind her.

I sank to the floor, letting the pictures drop and fan out. I flipped to the next one. High school Iann and the girl standing and posing at the beach, their feet hidden in the sand, his arm wrapped around the bare, tan skin between her two-piece swimsuit. I tossed the photo to the side. They were smiling, their hands laced together, the same mountain view as the family picture in the background. As I traced the familiar shape of her eyes and the length of her nose, I couldn't deny it.

Something deep within me erupted. The worst years of my life were an echo of this moment, doomed to repeat.

You are *just a copy.*

I rattled the thought from my head and dropped the picture, my hands shaking.

The front door closed, and Leo's paws scraped along the floor. "Hey, boy," Iann said in a high tone, muffled by the walls between us.

I waited, the girl's eyes mocking me from the photo.

The bedroom door swung open. "Hey, you finally brought another box!" he rejoiced, poking his head into the closet. His eyes flickered and widened as they drifted from me to the pictures strewed across the floor.

"Who is this?" I couldn't feel my mouth move, but somehow the question came out.

His expression darkened. "Were you going through my stuff?" he asked, stepping into the closet, towering over me.

I searched for the reason why. Why was I there again? How had I found these? "The drawer broke because all of your shit was piled into it," I snapped.

He glanced at the drawer beside me.

"Who is this?" I repeated.

His eyes lingered on the photo. "Alayna," he said in a quiet voice. He bent down and picked it up.

I waited for more, my skin lighting on fire.

"We were—she was my high school girlfriend," he continued, looking at the photos. "She died the summer before we were supposed to leave for Chicago together."

I stood, my pulse picking up and drumming in my ears. This was the secret he'd been clinging to. Condolences didn't come to mind, only accusations. "Why were you hiding these?" My voice was loud but cold.

He set the photos on top of the dresser. "I wasn't hiding them—I . . . I don't know. I didn't want you thinking I was hanging on to all of that." He'd misunderstood. He thought I was just acting like a typical jealous bitch. I didn't care if he was over Alayna.

"She looks exactly like me, Iann," I said through clenched teeth.

He held my gaze. "What does *that* matter?"

"If it doesn't matter, then why wouldn't you mention it?"

"Everyone dates people that look like their exes," he fired back. "I didn't think it was a big deal."

"Maybe in the sense that they're all brunettes or blondes or whatever, but not to the extent they look *exactly* like your dead girlfriend," I yelled. "That's not normal."

He looked away from me. I was cutting open an old scar with a dagger. But I had scars too.

I went deeper. "Is that the reason you came up and talked to me?" I demanded.

He met my eyes. "What?" His brow was furrowed, and his arms tensed by his sides.

"The day we met, is this the only reason you approached me? Because I look like Alayna?" I swallowed the hard lump forming in my throat. The backs of my eyes were stinging.

He didn't look at me. "Harper," he said, slowly. "This doesn't mean anything. What will it take for you to move past this?"

His pause already gave me the answer I'd dreaded. "You're the psych professor." I scowled. "You figure it out." I turned on my heel and grabbed my coat and bag from the bed before stalking past Leo. My ears were ringing and my vision blurring at the edges with tears as I reached the front door.

I couldn't look back.

CHAPTER THIRTY-SEVEN

I turned my phone over in my hand. I had sat in that same seat at the bar across from the police station for over two hours, my muscles easing with each sip from my glass. I couldn't even be sure if Wilder had returned to his downtown office or if he was still working out of Bucktown.

I dialed his number one more time. It went to voice mail, but I hung up.

I drained the last of my rum and Coke. The bartender said nothing but slid a glass of water in front of me. "Can I get another?" I asked, pushing the water away from me down the counter.

He nodded and walked to the other side of the bar.

Embers flickered in the dark across the street. I squinted through the window. "Never mind," I called down to the bartender. "Just give me the check."

He rolled his eyes but quickly started punching into the computer, ignoring a drunk woman waving her glass at him from the other end.

I glanced at the check as he set it down and dropped my last twenty-dollar bill before staggering to my feet and out the door. As I turned the corner, I searched for cigarette smoke as the station came into sight.

I spotted him leaning against the brick wall, talking with a uniformed police officer in between taking drags from his cigarette, only the dim light of a streetlamp illuminating them. I cautiously hung back at the edge of the parking lot. He nodded and shook the officer's hand before they parted ways.

He threw down his cigarette and strode toward the parking lot, halting his steps when he saw me. He quickened his pace. "What are you doing here? Is everything okay?" He had reached me by now, standing a little too closely, the smoke on his breath making me gag.

I averted my gaze to the asphalt.

He cast a look around the lot and put a hand on my back, turning me around to guide me toward his car. I got in, and he closed the door before he climbed into the driver's seat. "What's going on?" he asked again.

I tried to focus on the layer of dust on the dashboard, but my vision rolled in small circles. "I need to see Erin."

He hit the top of the steering wheel with his palm. "I thought I told you to cool it with that, okay? She doesn't want to see you right now."

I laid my head against the seat. "I need to see her." My voice cracked. "I have to talk to her." I should've drunk the water.

He sighed. "Are you drunk?"

I closed my eyes. "I'm sorry, I—I don't know why I came here."

"Do you want to talk inside?" He gestured back at the station.

"I thought you said I would get you in trouble," I slurred.

"Where do you want me to drop you off?" he asked.

"Where were you about to go?" I opened my eyes and stared straight ahead. The streetlamp above the parking lot was flickering.

"I was about to go home. I just got off a long shift."

"Okay. Let's talk there."

He said nothing and started the car.

———

His apartment was in worse shape than mine. It was buried in the less trendy side of River North and reeked of smoke. "Sorry." He kicked a stack of old magazines away from the door so I could pass. "I wasn't planning on having company."

I waded behind him through the mess of cardboard boxes to his kitchen. "Did you just move in?"

He dragged a chair across the floor and put it by the table, then motioned for me to have a seat. "Yeah, eight months ago."

I sat in the chair cautiously. "Why haven't you unpacked yet?" I pushed a stack of mail and papers to the other side of the table.

He set a bottle of water next to me and sat in another chair across the table. "I thought you said you needed to talk. What does that matter?"

I peeled the label away from the bottle, ignoring his gaze.

"Did something happen?" He rested both his elbows on the table and leaned toward me.

I thought about Iann, about Alayna's face in the photo. I tore the label in half, then into fourths. "I saw another girl," I said.

He blinked. "What girl?"

I shredded the fourths. Alayna was too much. I couldn't even begin to piece that together. "I saw another girl who looks like me and Holly and Sarah."

He straightened in his seat. "What are you talking about?"

"I saw her walking around downtown." I waited for more questions, but they didn't come. "If Bug—Todd, I mean—if he killed Holly, did he kill Sarah too?"

He rubbed at his eyes. "I can't talk about that with you." He surveyed my face. "But that idea has been thrown around."

My chest constricted. "Then what about Jeremy? What about the letter he wrote?"

He scratched the back of his neck. "I don't know."

"How can you not know by now?" I snapped.

"Well, in Todd's case . . . I mean, being a pervert isn't the same as being a serial murderer. And right now we only have absolute proof that he was a pervert."

"What?" My blood felt like ice, carrying a chill through my veins.

He looked away from me. "There's a lot going on in the case, but so far none of the physical evidence on Holly or Sarah points to Todd."

"He tried to kill me," I blurted out. "And he had pictures of Holly's dead body. How can you try to tell me it wasn't him?"

He leaned back in his chair. "Look, I'm leveling with you. At this point, we're looking into Holly's case again. The, uh . . . recent events have complicated matters a bit."

The inevitability of what was coming started to dawn on me. The radius around me was closing in. *You're next. Or Jenny.* Shit. What if Jenny was already gone? Everything had become so chaotic that she'd become a more and more distant thought in the back of my mind.

Wilder's hand reached for mine. "You're going to be fine."

I glared at him. "How do you know that? You've seen the resemblance yourself, and now you're telling me the murderer is probably still out there?"

He retracted his hand. "Nothing is definitive at this point."

I pushed away from the table and stood. "I can't believe this! What have you been doing all this time? Sarah was found back in July!"

"I've been doing my job," he yelled, shaking his head and taking a step toward me. "And I don't have to justify any of this to you. I told you all this as a courtesy!"

I stepped backward toward the door, but my stomach sank. I was so alone now. I had been alone before, but having and then losing Iann cut deeper. *You never even really had him.*

Wilder was fuming, his hand gripping the edge of the table. He was standing so close.

I wanted to be closer. I wanted to punch him, to scream in his face. Instead, I leaned forward and kissed him.

He jerked away, and I stepped back, a knot twisting in my stomach. Then, without a word, he pushed me against the wall. He dug his fingers into my sides and enveloped my lips with his.

Cigarettes and mint gum.

My eyes watered as he wound his fingers around my hair and tugged my head back. I didn't ask him to stop.

I had made so many mistakes. The worst one was surviving my father, and then surviving Bug. Then believing Iann really wanted to be with me. I must've known on some level the whole time. Why else would I have hidden so many things from him?

I had been afraid of being exposed for what I was. A hollow duplicate.

But Iann had known all along.

Wilder pushed me to his dark room and shoved me onto the unmade bed. My heart pounded against my chest as I pulled him into me, his hands fumbling over the buttons of my jeans. I unbuttoned his shirt, revealing beads of sweat on his fevered skin.

This is wrong.

His hands hiked up my top, but I tugged the edges down around my stomach. He didn't stop, his fingers grazing over my ribs and breasts until I was covered in goose bumps.

I grabbed his hand as he reached for the button of my jeans. Something resembling frustration flashed across his face, and he lightly pressed against my neck with his fingers as he leaned in to kiss me again. It was hard to breathe, the force of his hand plunging me deeper into the covers.

I began to panic, pushing my fists against his chest, but he continued, tugging my hair harder this time. "Stop," I managed between tight breaths.

He pulled away, staring down at me.

"I can't do this. We shouldn't," I said, my voice louder this time.

His gaze was piercing even in the dark. "Okay." He lingered a moment before sinking on the bed beside me.

I gratefully gulped the air as the pressure released from my throat.

Panting, Wilder slid his arm under my neck and began absently playing with my hair. The gentle action was in sharp contrast to only moments before. My scalp still tingled from his grip. I'd sobered up from the pain. "You're not like them," he said.

"What?"

He pulled my chin toward him and studied my face. "You keep saying those girls are just like you, but they're not." His expression had changed, his gaze too intense to meet. I looked away, but he drew me closer to him. "They never had to struggle through anything like you did."

"How would you know that?" I hated that he felt he knew anything about me.

He lowered his hands to my waist. "I've learned a lot about them through the investigation," he said, his breath warm in my ear. "You're one of a kind, Harper."

I sat up on the bed, glancing at the door. "I should go," I said, my stomach flipping.

The bed rustled as he sat up beside me, his hand heavy on my shoulder. "What?"

I swung my feet over the side of the bed. "I'm sorry. I made a mistake coming here."

"I'm sorry you feel that way." His words were deliberate. I could hear the unfilled blanks trailing behind that sentence.

I couldn't bear to look through the darkness to see his face.

"Let me give you a ride," he said, getting to his feet as well.

The thought of the awkward car ride back to that damn empty apartment made me woozy. "No," I said quickly. Too quickly. "I'm going back alone."

He turned the light on. "Are you sure that's a good idea?"

No, I wasn't. I couldn't feel safe here, though. "I'll take a taxi. I'm not walking that whole way, so don't worry about it." I forced a slight smile. "Let's go back to the status quo. I don't know what got into me tonight." *You're starving for pain.*

He inspected my face with slightly narrowed eyes, the dark circles underneath more pronounced. After a moment, he shrugged. "Whatever you want."

I wanted Iann. I wanted to go back a few hours and never see that photo.

"I'll see you around," I said and opened the door to the living room. I looked back as I let myself out through the front door and saw him sitting on the bed, his back to me.

CHAPTER THIRTY-EIGHT

The phone rang once. Then twice.

"Hello?" Danny answered, his voice thick.

Hearing his voice filled me with shame. About what exactly was a mystery. There were too many reasons to choose from. "Hey, it's Harper," I said.

"Huh? Is everything okay?" His voice was thick.

No. I swallowed. "Can I come over?"

He was silent.

"I know it's late—"

"Yeah, of course," he interrupted. "I'll text you the address. Let me know when you get here, and I'll buzz you in."

———

I paced in front of the elevator in Danny's building before finally riding up to the fourth floor, my heart pounding loudly against my ribs.

When I made it to his door, I sent him a text. Within seconds, he opened the door, his eyes narrowed against the light in the hallway.

"Come in," he said in a lowered voice. "My roommates are asleep."

I stepped in behind him into the dark apartment and followed him into the farthest room. He flicked on the light and softly closed the door behind me. The items in his apartment were exactly the same as his room in Evanston, but the order had changed. And there was even more paper littering his desk.

"Danny, I'm sorry about this. I woke you up, didn't I?"

He looked me up and down. "No, it's fine. What's going on? Are you all right?"

I leaned against the bookcase facing toward him. "Iann and I broke up," I said, my stomach dropping. "I couldn't go back to my old apartment alone right now, but this was stupid. I'm sorry."

He shook his head. "No, I'm glad you called. But . . . well, sorry about Iann." His face didn't betray anything. "What happened?"

I sat on the edge of the bed and clasped my hands together. "I found . . . something."

"What?" He sat backward on his desk chair, facing me.

It would sound ridiculous to him. I'd never spoken about Issi with him either. "He was only interested in me because I look like his dead girlfriend."

He blinked. "Okay . . . wait, what?"

The heat flooded to my cheeks again. "You think it's insane to break up over that, right? It isn't that big of a problem?"

He rubbed his eyes. "*I* think it is. But I want to know why it matters to you. I mean, even if he was interested in you because of that, you two were together for a while, right?"

I clasped my hands together, still remembering earlier with Wilder. I wanted to throw up. "It's a big deal to me because . . ." I hadn't said her name aloud in such a long time. It sat at the back of my throat. "I could never really tell you why my father did what he did to me."

He leaned forward. "What do you mean?"

I rubbed my index finger over my thumb. "I told you that I was in a bad car accident when I was ten, right?"

His eyes flickered over to the scar on my neck as he nodded.

"It wasn't just me and my father in the car that night." I swallowed. "My twin sister died in that accident."

He said nothing, but his gaze grew more intense.

"I survived, but she didn't. He wanted her, but instead he was stuck with me." For the longest time, I'd wished the same. Tonight I felt that more than ever.

"That's not—"

I raised my hand. "I *know* that he didn't want me to survive," I said firmly. "After that, he started calling me by *her* name and making me dress like her and act like her. He told everyone that Harper died. They all thought I was grieving and crazy, and they believed him."

Danny's eyes widened.

"That's why . . . he did all that to me." Danny was the only one who really knew what my father had been capable of back then. He saw the evidence of the fights—the bruises, the gash on my forehead the night I'd finally left. "He couldn't ever completely control me, but he tried." I swallowed. "I can't live in someone's shadow like that again. I won't."

"Why didn't you ever tell me?" he asked quietly.

I shrugged. "Because it's messed up. And I wanted to forget too. When I met you, that was the first time I felt like I could be myself again."

He stared down at his hands.

"You said before there was something off about Iann," I started. "What did you mean?"

He shook his head. "It's nothing. I was only saying that."

I held his gaze. "Really, Danny. What did I miss?"

He looked down again. "I don't know. When we were at the club, there was something off about the way he was watching you." He caught my steady gaze and continued. "It's not how normal people look at their girlfriends. It was like he was studying you or something. I don't know how to describe it. It was some feeling I had."

I tried to remember, to conjure any memory of how he had looked at me that night or any other night.

"Come on," Danny said, standing up from the chair. "You should get some sleep. Take the bed. I'll take the couch." He grabbed a pillow from behind me and straightened the sheets.

"No, I feel bad enough. *I'll* take the couch," I protested, gripping the pillow under his arm.

"Absolutely not." He laughed. "I'm not leaving you to deal with my crazy roommates and their questions alone out there."

I released the pillow. "Well, I can't take the bed. I don't want it."

He rolled his eyes. "Here's a compromise. You take the bed. I'll take the floor."

"That's worse than the couch, isn't it?"

"No, it's good for my back. And you're taking the bed no matter what," he emphasized. He grabbed a couple of smaller blankets folded on the edge of the bed and let them fall to the floor. "But try not to step on my head when you get up to pee in the middle of the night." He glanced at my clothes. "Do you want to change?"

I could still feel the taste of Wilder's lips. "Yeah, actually, can I take a shower?"

"Of course." He started for the closet. "I'll get you something to wear." He handed me a faded red Sacramento T-shirt and flannel PJ bottoms. "Please keep in mind that it's a shared bathroom for three guys . . . so proceed with caution," he said with a smile. "Take a right outside my door."

Contrary to Danny's warning, the bathroom was remarkably clean, especially compared to mine. I wanted more than anything to empty my mind, but the events of the day kept flooding my thoughts, switching from one betrayal to another until my head ached. I scrubbed every inch of skin until it was rubbed raw, shaking my head as the images flashed through my mind. I felt like my lungs were closing. I leaned against the tile with my hand, holding my head away from the stream of water until the breathlessness passed.

When I crept back into Danny's room, he was already asleep, sprawled on the floor with his mouth open. He looked exactly like he did in Evanston, only with a couple more pounds and a few more lines around his eyes, marking all the laughs and fun he'd had since college. He was still that beautiful boy with the whole world waiting to open for him.

What did he think when he looked at me? Did he still see that small, shaking girl with bruises and cuts under her huge sweaters and long pants? *Was* I still that same girl?

I opened my bag and shoved my dirty clothes inside before zipping it closed. I turned off the light and tiptoed over Danny into the bed.

What had really changed since then? I was still scared. Still being used and bruised by the men I let into my life. That wasn't fair, maybe. Iann had never raised a hand against me or even really raised his voice. But then again, maybe not all cuts and bruises were physical. Even though I couldn't articulate what the Alayna revelation truly meant, it gnawed at me. It wasn't only sadness. There was a pang of fear now.

I rolled onto my side and peered down at Danny, his chest quietly rising and falling. My body relaxed merely from being beside him. But I knew I had messed up running to him again. I was the most destructive force in his life. I needed him, but I was the thing tying him to a terrible part of his past. Maybe Iann would soon think of me in the same way.

I closed my eyes and recalled those pictures of Alayna. Maybe he already thought of me that way.

I didn't remember falling asleep, but I heard movement near the foot of the bed and opened my eyes to a room warmed with sunlight coming in through the closed blinds. Danny's back was turned to me as he stooped over the floor. "Danny?"

He whipped around. "Sorry, I was trying not to wake you up. You looked like you could use some sleep."

I sat up and glanced at the clock. 7:04 a.m. "What are you doing?"

He stood up straight and kicked something to the side. "I was trying to roll up the blankets I used last night, but screw it. It's staying a pile."

My eyes focused on his blue sweater and khakis. "Are you getting ready for work?" I shook my head. "I'm so sorry, you must be exhausted."

He pulled a jacket from his desk chair and slipped it onto one arm and then the other. "Believe it or not, that's actually the most I've slept all week. Are you going to be okay today?"

I thought about the overwhelming mess of everything. The taped boxes piled at my apartment and the unpacked ones at Iann's. "I think I have to go back to my place."

He looked at me for a silent moment. "How does that work, you renting that place since the landlord is, uh . . . gone?"

"At least for now it's okay, until they settle his estate. That's what the police told me." Besides, I didn't have a real lease, nothing on paper. My stomach twisted at the thought of going back.

Danny sat down beside me on the bed. "You do whatever you need to, but you're welcome to stay here for as long as you want."

I didn't have even the slightest clue of what I *needed* to do. I forced a grateful smile. "Thanks, I really appreciate it."

"Do you want me to go back with you to your old place?"

I had the answer to my question from the night before. "No, I'm fine. It's not a big deal." My face grew hotter with embarrassment. I hadn't changed at all. I *was* still that helpless little girl to Danny and everyone.

"God, Harper, it *is* a big deal." He shook his head and stood up. "You almost . . ." He held my gaze and trailed off. "It's fine if you want to stay here. In fact, I insist. At least until you find a new place." I recognized the same frustration from years before in his narrowed eyes.

I swung my legs over the side of the bed so my toes hovered above the blue rug. "Thanks. Sorry again about all of this."

He opened the door. "Don't be. Oh, and my roommates will both be out of here before nine, if you want to wait it out. I mean, I filled them in, so they know you're here, but if you don't want to answer a thousand questions . . ." He glanced out the door into the living room. "You can eat anything in the kitchen, but don't touch Carlos's gluten-free snacks, or he'll have both our heads," he added with a wry grin.

I smiled weakly. "Sure thing."

He looked back at me one more time before closing the door.

I waited on the bed and listened for the front door to close. I looked around the room at all the familiar things—the trophies and medals. But my eyes focused on what had changed. The suit jackets outnumbered the Northwestern hoodies and T-shirts in his open closet. Above his desk were photos of him sailing with women I didn't recognize, and it hit me how strange this all was. Danny today was a stranger to me. Maybe he hadn't really changed, but he had years of experiences I would never know about, years of moving on from Evanston while I had spent those same years steeped in my past.

I took off Danny's borrowed clothes and pulled on my jeans and sweater from the night before. I cracked his bedroom door open and listened. I could hear stirring across the living room behind the other closed doors. I tiptoed out, my bag in one hand, and slipped my shoes on before leaving through the front door.

CHAPTER
THIRTY-NINE

As the train pulled into Damen, a pit formed in my stomach. Not just because of Bug or my near death, not even because of Woodstock. I realized maybe nowhere would truly feel like home. Maybe I had never really had a home anywhere.

I descended the steps onto the street and winced when I saw the steeple of the Robey looming above. I instinctively walked past Erin's apartment building. I stopped and peered up at her window. How long did people stay in rehab?

I resumed my trudge down the pavement, my heart beating faster the farther I got away from the station, until it was pounding nearly out of my chest as I turned onto my street.

Each time I came back, I expected the house to have changed somehow, but it still stood quietly between the two adjoining better-kept houses, only completely dark within. I avoided looking at the ground-level floor and instead stared straight ahead at my door as I dragged up the stairs, my hand aching as I gripped the damp, unfinished wood railing. I took a deep breath and held it as the door swung open, squeaking on its hinges. My heart jumped at the silhouette of my remaining boxes towering beside the empty bed.

I stepped in and turned on the light. The smell of the house was fouler somehow. I left the door ajar, the cold air rattling through the room.

I pushed the boxes away from the bed toward the wall and ripped open the one on top, then pulled out my comforter and down blankets. I wrapped all four blankets around my shoulders and shut the door before sinking onto the bed. My eyes flitted to the fire alarm in the corner of the room. It seemed smaller now that the police had removed the tiny camera from it. I reached across the bed and cranked on the radiator under the windowsill before settling back into the blankets.

I lay there, my teeth chattering, as I relived that night and replayed the videos in my mind. Then suddenly I swung myself off the bed, letting the blankets fall behind me, and charged into the dark bathroom. I kneeled on the peeling laminate tile and pulled open the cupboard under the sink and reached as far back as I could, my hand bumping against the pile. Maybe there was one more. Somewhere. My fingers scraped along the dusty, waterlogged wood paneling. Nothing.

I sat back on my heels, my eyes stinging. I gripped the edge of the sink and heaved to my feet. There were other drugs. The heat from the radiator punched through the room as I stepped into the kitchen and opened the cabinet above the sink.

Thank god. There was a bottle of crappy red wine and an old bottle of Captain Morgan still half-full.

I pulled the rum out and drained it into a mug. I sank onto the kitchen floor. I had left my ramshackle kitchen table and chairs at the curb during the move, and they had been promptly picked up by a bohemian couple living down the street.

I had to plot out my next move. *You can't stay here. You can't stay with Iann.*

And I wouldn't stay with Danny again.

I couldn't afford another apartment, at least not a legitimate one with a real lease and real background check.

I took two big gulps from the cup, the rum burning the lump in my throat as I swallowed. I surveyed the dark room, grateful to have most of my boxes still here. I'd have to figure out how to get my art supplies from Iann's. Maybe I could slip in later when he was at work. After all, I still had a key.

My eyes drifted from the stack of boxes to the unmade bed and then were caught by a dark outline under the bed, the light from the window hugging a cylinder. I got to my feet, pushing against the cabinet doors behind me for support, the rum already warming my limbs. I set the cup on the counter and lunged toward the bed, crouching down onto my knees and reaching for the object, laying my shoulder against the wood floor and straining until my fingers closed around the familiar sensation of cool plastic.

I pulled the bottle out, and my eyes focused on the letters on the label in the dark. *Braughton, Erin Marie. Xanax.*

My heart raced. How long had it been here? *How* did it get here?

The bottle was nearly completely full. I put my hand to my temple. Maybe it had fallen out of her bag when she'd spent the night after her outing at the Up Room? I scanned the label for the date. 12/07. That was months after she had spent the night.

I closed my eyes, recalling the last time I'd seen her. It was that day at the studio, when I'd quit. That was absolutely the last time. She was holding her bag, and she left. Then I left and went home. I hadn't had the opportunity to snag the bottle from her bag. And I would never take the entire bottle. I wasn't that bold.

A knock sounded on the door, and I jumped. I hadn't heard footsteps on the creaky stairs. I looked at the unlocked door and dropped the bottle, letting it roll back under the bed.

I crept to the peephole and swallowed. Iann was standing outside the door, glancing down into the street behind him. My feelings of relief instantly gave way to profound guilt. Guilt and fear. My hand rested on the dead bolt lock for a second before I twisted the doorknob.

"What are you doing here?" I asked, steeling myself. I wanted more than anything to be standing on the same side of the door as him. Hell, I wanted to be far away from here with him.

"We need to talk," he said, his brow furrowed.

I put up a hand to stop him, but he pushed past easily. "Iann, there's nothing to talk about." I closed the door and turned to face him.

"Of course there is, I don't like the way we left things before. I think there's been a big misunderstanding." His body was so close to mine that I could smell his skin.

"Were you only interested in me because I look like your dead girlfriend?" I demanded. It was a cruel question.

He winced and looked down. That was the only answer I needed. "No," he said firmly. "And even if that is the real reason I approached you initially, it doesn't matter. I love *you*, Harper."

I turned to walk to the kitchen. He grabbed my arm but let me pull away. I reached for my mug on the counter and took a swig. Maybe to him this wasn't a big deal. Maybe to a normal person it wouldn't be a big deal. Maybe it would be merely unsettling. But to me, it was unforgivable. He had unknowingly forced me to live out my worst fear. Again.

He walked over to me. "Harper?" His fingers grazed my arm, goose bumps rising along my skin.

"I need this to be over," I said, forcing the words from my lips. *Please stay.*

"I don't understand why," he breathed into my hair. I let him wind his arms around me.

You love him. Maybe.

You can't do it again. And I couldn't forgive anyone asking me to.

I put my hands on his chest and pushed away. "Please." It was all I could muster. He didn't relent and instead braced his hand behind my head and kissed me.

If he'd known I'd had someone else's hands on me the night before, he wouldn't want me. I finally broke away. "I can't do this anymore, not after knowing," I said.

"You have to help me understand."

I took a step back. "I have my own problems. I can't deal with you dumping all your issues on me too."

His eyes changed. Now he was angry. Good. Then it would be easier. "I can't believe you're going to throw this away."

"I can't trust you." *And he can't trust you.*

"What was I supposed to do? Go out of my way to tell you about my ex?"

"The whole thing is messed up." I leaned farther away from him. "All of your bullshit about fate. How did you find out where I worked?"

He shook his head, his eyes narrowed. "I didn't. All of that was real. Why would I lie about that?"

I didn't know the answer, but I couldn't believe in that big of a coincidence. Not now. Not after knowing about Alayna. I looked down at my feet. "It's already done."

He was silent for a moment. "You leaving in the middle of an argument doesn't qualify as a breakup, Harper."

"Then, fine, consider it over as of now."

He glanced around the apartment. "You really hate me that much now? That you would rather come back to this place alone instead of hearing me out?"

"I did hear you out," I said through quaking lips. *Hold it together.* I wanted to go home with him. "And I'm not staying here much longer."

His eyes pleaded with me. "What can I do to fix this?"

I pressed my feet deeper into the floor, wishing I could fall through it and disappear.

"You can trust me."

I shut my eyes for a moment, assessing that. It wasn't only my past trauma. There was doubt now. Suspicion. I opened my eyes again, meeting his. I thought about the other girls. If they looked like me, they looked like Alayna. "I . . ." I ran my hand over my face. "There's nothing. I'm done."

He shifted his weight.

"I don't think we should be together anymore." My voice broke on the last word.

He opened his mouth and closed it, running a hand through his dark hair, his brow furrowed. He turned on his heel and left through the front door without another word.

I sank to the floor, my hands shaking. I crawled toward the bed and grabbed the bottle. I stared at it again before twisting it open and shaking out two pills. I closed my palm over them and rested my head back against the bed.

Yes. You need to sleep.

I opened my hand and popped the pills into my mouth.

CHAPTER FORTY

My eyes whipped open, sending a jolt of pain through my temple. I raised a hand to my forehead and gasped as I tried to massage the headache. It was completely dark outside. I rolled onto my side and picked up my phone from the floor, ignoring the missed-call and text notifications.

It was 9:08 p.m. Had I slept for ten hours?

The phone buzzed in my hands. My eyes struggled to focus again on the screen, but I managed to accept the call. "Hello?" My mouth was chalky and rough. That chemical, plastic taste was still on my tongue.

"Thank god," Danny exclaimed on the other end. "Where are you? I've called you, like, fifteen times."

I pushed the hair back from my face and sat up. "I'm sorry. I fell asleep."

He took a deep breath. "I was freaking out when you didn't answer. I don't even know where you live. Are you okay staying there?"

I glanced around the room and immediately wished I were back in my dreamless sleep.

"I think you should come back and stay with me, only until you can figure out your next move," he said in my silence. "What happened there is . . . well, it can't be good for you to stay there alone."

"Yeah," I answered.

He sighed. "Is Iann there with you?"

"No," I answered, quickly. "Sorry, I'm still kind of out of it."

"Okay." He sounded relieved. "So, are you coming over?"

I looked down at the floor, hoping to see a couple of orange paws emerge or a tail twitching. "Are you sure?" A sob lodged in my throat, and I swallowed it back down. My eyes drifted to the upper corner of the ceiling, where the fire alarm dangled.

"More than I've ever been sure of anything . . . except that the Cubs will never win the World Series again."

I rubbed my swollen eyes. "Wow, you're that sure, huh?"

"Yep, it was a fluke," he said, dryly. "It'll never happen again."

I stood up off the bed and grabbed the pill bottle, then shoved it into my bag. "Those are fighting words around here."

He laughed. "Are they, though? I feel like everyone secretly knows."

"You're not on the street, are you?" I straightened up and surveyed the apartment. Everything else I needed right away was at Iann's place.

"No, why?"

"Good, just keep those opinions to yourself when you're in public, or move to Wisconsin." I peeled the clear tape off a cardboard box and rummaged through the clothing inside.

He snickered. "That's good advice. Wait, so you're coming over, right?"

"Only if I sleep on the floor tonight and you take the bed."

He scoffed. "Absolutely not. What are your other demands?"

"Danny, I'm serious." I set a clean hoodie out on the bed before digging through the remainder for another top. "I don't feel comfortable upsetting your routine like this. I already feel bad enough about last night."

"Why?"

"I insist you take the bed."

He hesitated. "Okay, fine. Text me your address—I'll give you a ride."

"No, I'll take the train."

"It's already late, and I enjoy driving. Just humor me, okay?"

I sighed. "Okay. I'll text it to you now."

"Great, see you in a bit."

I ended the call and quickly texted the address before setting my phone on the bed and replacing my two-day-old sweater with the gray hoodie. I folded a clean sweater and jeans and put them into my bag, my fingers grazing over the pill bottle before freezing. I stared down at the label again. I dropped my bag to the floor and picked up my phone. I pulled up my texts with Erin. There were new messages but sent from my phone to her.

(4:05 p.m.): I'm sorry.

(4:06 p.m.): About the pills.

My heart sped up. I didn't remember sending these. I called her phone, pacing along the floor. It didn't ring.

"This is Erin! Leave a message or text me."

I hung up. Her phone was dead now. Maybe just turned off.

I started at the knock on my door. I strode to the peephole and unlocked it. "That was fast," I said.

Danny's eyes widened as he took in the hellscape of my apartment. "Oh, Harper," he said, stepping in beside me after I opened the door. "This is where you've been living all these years?" He stared at the mismatched, warped laminate where the blood from the body had seeped through. I suspected the crime scene cleaning crew had replaced it but hadn't tacked it down properly.

My face reddened. "Believe it or not, it was more livable *before* the murder." That look of disdain on his face cut me. Had he always secretly looked down on me like that?

He stiffened before turning to me. He opened his mouth and then quickly closed it again. It was rare for him not to have a witty response on the tip of his tongue, unless he intentionally held back. "Are you ready to go?" he asked after a moment.

I grabbed my bag. "Yeah."

I followed him out the door, and he waited behind me as I locked it. Our eyes met briefly before we started down the stairs, and I could tell he was working something out in his mind. We silently got into his SUV. He hesitated behind the wheel before starting the engine.

"Hey, I'm sorry about, uh . . ." He looked straight ahead as he started down the road. "I shouldn't have said anything about your place. I didn't mean anything by it."

I sighed, anxiously watching us escape Wicker Park. "Look, I know it's not great," I said. "But it's not like there are a lot of places you can get into as a sixteen-year-old runaway."

He glanced at me. "You act like that's still who you are."

"That *is* who I am."

He shook his head. "I mean, you're twenty-five. You're not some kid anymore. You're an adult."

I gazed out the window, quietly watching the cars weaving more erratically as we drew closer to downtown. He was right. But people got stuck in either the hardest or the peak period of their lives. Normal people like Iann and Danny grew and progressed without that kind of weight. I nervously scratched at my hand. *Iann.* That didn't apply to him, I guessed. He was stuck in his own cycle. "You've seen where I live now," I began, turning back to him. "What exactly about my life seems 'adult' to you?"

He sighed, tapping his steering wheel as we waited at a red light. "Okay, fine, you're Peter fuckin' Pan. I'm sorry I called you an adult. Is that what you want?"

"No, but stop pretending like you know what I've been through or what I should be doing," I snapped before resting my head against the seat.

We remained silent as he pulled into the parking garage and into his reserved spot. I got out of the car first, waiting with my back turned to him and clutching my bag until he started past me toward the elevator. I followed after him at a distance.

I couldn't pinpoint why I was lashing out at Danny, which only made me angrier. He unlocked his front door and held it open for me as I passed by him, his eyes slightly narrowed as he watched me. I could imagine all the biting remarks that he was holding back building up in his head.

The lights were on in the apartment, but it was quiet inside, both of his roommates' doors closed with light pouring from underneath onto the wood floor. I strode through Danny's open door and set my bag on the floor. He closed the door behind us. "Did you already eat dinner?" he asked finally, kicking his shoes off.

Had I really only had rum the whole day? "No, but I'm not hungry," I evaded, my tone colder than I intended.

He raised both of his hands in mock surrender. "Okay, fine. You can use the bathroom first if you want." He reopened the door and took a step back. "There are extra towels under the sink if you need them."

I pulled my bag over my shoulder once again and tiptoed across the hall to the bathroom. Thankfully, it was empty. It was much less orderly than the previous night. There was a small pile of used towels in the corner beside the toilet, and the mirror was completely fogged up.

I ran my fingers through my hair, tangled from my restless tossing on the bed throughout my daytime slumber. I scooped the hair from my neck and wrapped it into a low ponytail before stooping down over the sink, carefully keeping my eyes on the granite counter as I washed my face. The mist started to disappear from the mirror as I dug through my bag and rearranged my clothes before grabbing the bag and turning off the light.

Danny had already changed into the same pants and shirt as the night before and was sitting on his pallet on the floor, rubbing the dark half circles under his eyes.

I set my bag down and closed the door. "You promised," I said, pointing to the bed. "I'm taking the floor."

He smiled and shrugged. "No. I'm a filthy liar, and you're taking the bed."

I shook my head and sat on the edge of the bed, looking down at him. "I'm sorry for . . . well, a lot of things at this point. I feel like I'm constantly apologizing."

He waved his hand as if he were brushing my bad mood from the bed. "Whatever you're sorry about, let's forget about it and move on."

I clasped my hands together in my lap. "I feel like I break everything . . ." I swallowed the lump forming in my throat. "And I have no way to fix it."

His hand covered mine.

I dared to meet his eyes. He was staring into mine, his brow furrowed with concern. "What's wrong with me?"

"Nothing's wrong with you," he said softly. "You've been through things that no one should have to deal with. And survived." He squeezed my hands once before sliding his own back to his lap. "You have to keep . . . well, surviving. And if someone wants to help you, accept it." He finished with a grin. "I know you don't *need* my help, but you don't have to suffer alone."

I nodded, biting my tongue to keep from protesting. I was too tired to fight it anymore. I actually did need his help. Or someone's.

He ran a hand through his hair and stood up. "I'll be right back." He walked through the door and down the hallway to the bathroom.

I slid my boots off my feet and pushed them under the edge of the bed. I debated whether to take over the floor before he came back, but the door swung open, and Danny gazed at me from the doorway, white faced.

He closed the door behind him. "What is this?"

I focused on the small yellow bottle in his hands as he held it out toward me, and my heart raced.

"This was in the bathroom. I guess it fell out of your bag?" he said, watching me.

I leaped from the bed and grabbed it from him. "It's nothing. Erin left it at my apartment."

"I don't understand why you would be carrying that around, then."

My sweaty hand squeaked against the plastic as it closed around it.

"Have you been taking her pills?" he asked, his frown deepening.

I felt the heat pulsing through my limbs, that same hot shame from the day I'd last seen Erin.

"Harper?" He was standing right in front of me now, but my lips were locked.

I inhaled, breaking the seal. "No," I lied.

He eyed the bottle. "Then why the hell do you have that?"

I shook my head and looked down.

"How long has this been going on?"

I still didn't meet his eyes. "I don't know. Occasionally. It helps me sleep, and I can't afford it." I glanced up at him. "I don't have a problem with it. I can go without it."

He sighed. "What you're doing is dangerous."

"I know. That's why I only take it when I haven't slept in days." I thought about the night in the club and covered my face with one hand. "And the night we went to the club."

His eyes widened. "You said you were drunk."

"I only had one drink that night, but I guess the Xanax really knocked me out."

"Jesus," he said and sank back onto the floor. "Do you take it with alcohol all the time?"

I swallowed. "Yeah, usually two with a drink."

"You have to stop," he said after a moment.

I looked at him. His blond hair was disheveled now, and he was staring ahead, avoiding my gaze. "I know. I did. But I couldn't handle everything today. It was too hard."

He suddenly looked up at me. "Didn't you say Erin's missing?"

I nodded.

"You've been acting all torn up about her, but then you're carrying around her pills and popping them any chance you get?" The disgust in his voice cut me.

"I was wrong. She's not missing," I said quickly. "She's in rehab."

He shook his head. "Wow, that's irony, right?"

I sighed.

"I'm sorry," he said after a minute. "I'm just worried about you."

"Why are you doing all of this for me?" Although it was painful, I met his eyes. "Why are you even bothering?"

He sat beside me on the bed. "Come on," he said softly. "You must know why."

"No. I don't. I'm nothing but mean to you. And knowing me has caused you so much trouble."

He covered my hand with his. "You are a little difficult sometimes." He smiled. "But I'm always going to care about you."

I laced my fingers around his palm.

"I love you, Harper."

I looked away. *You're only going to hurt him again.*

"You don't have to say anything. I don't want you to feel weird about it. I just want you to know." His arms wrapped around me, and I clung to him. "I didn't mean to make you upset. But I didn't realize you were in this kind of trouble." His hands were warm on the small of my back.

I pulled away from him, and he released me from his embrace. "This is what I was talking about. I'm . . . broken. And I don't want to drag you into all this again." I turned my back to him, but his fingers rested on my arm.

"I'm going to help you through this," he said. "I want you here. And if you insist on leaving now because of this, I'm going to have to drive you back, and I'll probably fall asleep at the wheel on the way back, and I'll die in a fiery car crash. Is that what you want?"

"Danny—"

"Come on," he interrupted. "Stay. But promise me you'll stop with the pills." He held out his hand and glanced at my bag.

I'd already made the same promise to Iann before and broken it. It was meaningless. I reached in and pulled out the bottle, then set it gently into his palm.

"I'm going to go get rid of this real quick," he said, walking around me back out into the hall.

I sank back onto the bed and threw my bag to the ground. I remembered the disgust in Erin's eyes when she'd confronted me. She had her own addictions, and even she thought I was repulsive. I could hear the water running and the soft clattering sound of the pills hitting the base of the sink.

Danny reemerged and leaned back against the door as he shut it. "It's been taken care of," he said with a sly smile, as if we were accomplices in something.

I grinned weakly back at him. "Thanks. For everything."

"Are you ready to sleep?" His hand hovered above the light switch.

I glanced down at my leggings and sweatshirt. "Yeah."

He turned off the light and itched at the collar of his shirt before lying back on his pile of blankets. He wasn't used to wearing a shirt to sleep in. I recalled his bare chest against my skin those nights in the dead of winter. My breath caught in my throat as I leaned back on the bed, pulling the blankets over my legs and up to my waist. I turned on my side and squinted through the dark, watching as Danny settled onto his side facing me, two pillows piled under his head. His shirt clung to his biceps.

"I'm glad you're here," he said after a moment.

My eyes had adjusted, and I could make out his face clearly now. My stomach knotted both from the pain of thinking of Iann alone and from yearning for Danny. "I'm glad to be here," I echoed quietly.

"Good night," he said before rolling to the other side.

I was wide awake. My heart raced as I tossed away the blankets and swung my legs over the side of the bed before lowering down beside Danny.

"What are you doing?" he asked, stiffening and turning back toward me as I slid under his blankets.

I rested my head on the other side of the pillows. "I . . . I don't want to be alone. Can I sleep down here?"

"Okay," he said. "You know, it would make more sense for us both to just sleep on the actual bed, right?"

"I hear sleeping on the floor is better for your back."

He laughed. "Suit yourself."

I turned on my side, watching as his chest rose and fell, slowing with each breath. This was better than sleeping alone, but I couldn't stop wishing it were Iann beside me instead. That's why I couldn't love Danny back—at least not the way he wanted.

CHAPTER FORTY-ONE

The next day, instead of coming back and working on the projects I was getting paid to do, I'd only been able to mindlessly doodle a sketch in cheap pen. I had drawn out the photo of Danny and his sailboat, minus the two random girls.

He noticed. "Wait, where are the girls?" he laughed, looking over my shoulder.

"This way is better."

He shook his head, still smiling. "They're just friends." He disappeared into the closet.

I stared down at my drawing. I hadn't got the smile in his eyes quite right. "Well, maybe you're too friendly. I mean, I'm a friend, and I'm basically living with you now," I teased.

His laugh echoed in the closet. "You're not *just* a friend." He reemerged in the same shirt but now was wearing jeans instead of trousers. "You're an old friend." He sank onto the edge of the bed. "Harper?" His tone had deepened.

I looked up from the desk at him.

"I need to tell you something."

I swallowed. I wasn't sure I could handle whatever he wanted to say.
He sat on the bed across from me. "It's about Iann."

My heart sank, and I turned to completely face him.

"There's something that's been bothering me since the other night."
He ran his hand down the back of his neck. "You've been using pills
for a while, right?"

My muscles relaxed slightly at the redirect. "Yeah, on and off. But
I told you I don't have a problem stopping—"

He shook his head. "Yeah, it's not about that," he interrupted
quickly. "It's . . . well, that night at the club . . . have you ever reacted
to Xanax like that before?"

I could feel the pulsing of the music and Danny's skin against mine
as I'd come to in the middle of the dance floor. "Not exactly like that,
but when I first used it with alcohol, I fell asleep really quickly." I had
never lost time like that night before or had trouble breathing.

"And usually you take the pills with alcohol, right? How much?"

I blushed. "I don't know," I said quietly. "Sometimes four or five
drinks with two pills."

His eyes widened, but he slammed his mouth shut. "That's why I'm
bothered by that night. You said you collapsed and blacked out because
of the pill. But it was only one and then one drink, right?"

I rubbed my hands against the edge of the chair. I recalled the
blaring music again, the half-finished rum and Coke when I'd left for
the bathroom. "I think so."

"I don't think it was the Xanax," he said slowly, watching me. "Or
not *just* the Xanax. I think what you took was laced with something else
or that maybe someone slipped you something."

I turned my head back to the desk, trying to wrap my mind around
what he was really saying. That night was such a blur. "Are you sug-
gesting that someone drugged me?" There was no emotion behind the
question, only confusion.

"Not intentionally, maybe," he said. "But I've been working on a piece about how these pills get passed around through college students, and it's very common that—"

"You think Iann did something to it, don't you?"

He was silent.

I looked at him again. "Why would he do that?"

"I don't know."

"It doesn't make any sense, Danny," I said after a moment. "You're looking for something that's not there. When I saw you after I got out of the hospital, you thought Iann had hurt me."

He glanced down at his hands. "Okay, maybe. But there's something else."

I waited.

He leaned forward, resting his elbows on his knees. "Today I looked into that ex-girlfriend of his that you mentioned."

I frowned. "Alayna?"

He nodded. "Yeah, Alayna Vasilikas. I read about her death in Washington." He raised his head and met my eyes. "Iann was interrogated by the police for it."

My head swam. I was right. I couldn't handle anymore. "Then, how is he here right now?"

Danny straightened up. "They ended up letting him go, and they determined it was an accident."

I exhaled. "Then what the hell, Danny! For god's sake, *you* were arrested when I went missing."

He pursed his lips. "That was different."

"How do you know he wasn't falsely accused? They always look at the boyfriend or spouse or whatever, right? And they let him go!"

"I read the autopsy report. That wasn't an accident," he said, clenching his jaw. "She had fentanyl in her system and lacerations on the back of her head."

"And you think that's Iann's fault somehow? How would a high schooler even get his hands on fentanyl?" My face grew hot with frustration and wasted breath.

He shrugged. "I don't know. But he was the only person there when she died."

I scratched my nails against the edge of the desk. "What was the accident?"

"The paper reported that she slipped while hiking. Apparently, a storm blew in that day, and she fell off a cliff. And that's what the police ended up concluding too," Danny said.

"Then, as a journalist, what does that tell you?" I was losing patience.

He frowned. "I'm not talking as a journalist right now. I'm telling you this as a friend."

I shook my head. "I think you never liked Iann, and your mind is playing tricks on you."

"Did he ever tell you that he was under suspicion for Alayna's death?"

"Do you tell everyone you date that you were arrested in college?" I countered.

He turned his head down toward the floor. He looked back up after a minute and stood, then paused by the door with his hand on the knob. "I'm not trying to tell you that I know exactly what happened, but . . . I think you should trust yourself. You left Iann for a reason." He walked out and closed the door behind himself.

I picked at a splinter that had formed on the top of the desk.

Trust yourself.

That was hard to do when I was fractured beyond recognition.

———

Stopping the pills made it harder to sleep.

Thankfully, Danny was a heavy sleeper. It made it easier for me to sneak out of the bed and creep into the closet with my laptop and sketchbook. Those quiet moments at night with the bare bulb shining overhead were the only times I actually worked on paying projects, it seemed.

Brushstroke of rose for the sash on the flower girl's dress.

Flick of the pen for the bride's corkscrew curls.

The tip of the pen broke through the paper. I let the wedding party portrait fall onto my legs, and I leaned my head back against the wall, the sleeves of Danny's dangling coats grazing my cheek.

I saw Alayna's smiling face every time I blinked. I pulled my laptop onto my crossed legs and clicked onto Google.

Alayna. What had Danny said? *Vasilikas.*

The results immediately began with pictures of Alayna from news articles. I clicked the first headline.

Local Girl Dies in Hiking Accident in Thurston County.

I searched for the dates in the body of the article. March 14, 2009.

Ten years ago. Of course Iann hadn't wanted to mention what had happened all that time ago. I had kept so much more from him about my past. Things that he couldn't even search for.

Then why can't you forgive him?

I picked up my phone from the carpet and opened my pictures. The first one saved was of him, his black hair in stark contrast to the pale winter sky behind him.

"What are you doing in here?"

I dropped my phone. It fell screen-side down with a clatter.

Danny squinted against the light in the closet, scratching the top of his head.

I grabbed my phone and shoved it under my laptop. "Did I wake you up?"

He blinked through narrowed eyes. "No, my alarm went off."

I glanced at my laptop. "It's already six?"

He stepped in and sank onto the floor beside me, then leaned his head against the wall opposite me. He closed his eyes. "What are we doing again?"

I laughed. "I *think* you were trying to get ready for work?"

He shook his head. "That can't be right." He opened his eyes again suddenly. "You couldn't sleep?"

I shut my laptop. "Yeah."

He frowned. "I'm sorry if I stressed you out with everything last night. I guess it doesn't matter anyway, right? Now that you guys are over."

My eyes drifted to my phone screen. Things were so complicated with Iann, but I couldn't help but feel an urge to see him. To be with him. "Danny . . ."

His forehead wrinkled, and he leaned forward. "No. You can't," he said firmly. He was wide awake now.

"What you said last night made me think about . . . I mean, how can I blame Iann for Alayna when I haven't told him a single thing about my past?" I rubbed my dry eyes.

He shook his head. "It's completely different."

"I don't think it is," I said, quietly. "I didn't even tell him when my father died." *How can any relationship survive like that?*

Danny surveyed me. "You're exhausted right now. Promise me you won't do anything."

I tugged at the hem of my borrowed plaid pajama pants. I nodded.

CHAPTER FORTY-TWO

Once Danny left, I stumbled back under the covers, propping my phone up on the pillow beside me and scrolling through my messages with Iann. The last one was from three days ago.

Iann (10:21 a.m.): Can we talk?

Maybe Iann wasn't the one who'd messed up. But I had. With Wilder. Why? I squeezed my eyes shut.

Because you hate yourself.

The thought of seeing Iann's face now was both exciting and nerve wracking. When he'd come to my apartment before, I had still been in the cloud of delusion that he was the one who'd screwed up. But it was me, and I felt it in my core, deep behind my belly button.

It's always you.

I glanced out the window at the snow as it picked up again. It was soft this time, nothing like the slanted downpour of a few days before.

My phone buzzed, and I rolled my head across the pillow. Wilder was calling.

My finger hovered over the screen before I accepted the call. I was still so embarrassed from the last time we'd spoken. "Hello?"

"Harper . . ." His voice was solemn.

I sat up. Something was off.

He sighed. "Where are you?"

I said nothing.

"A call went out this morning about a possible overdose," he said.

My body tensed before I could really understand where he was going.

"It's your friend."

Something sharp burrowed in my stomach.

"They're still trying to notify her family, but you need to know."

"Where is she?" I jumped to my feet, my eyes wildly searching around the room for my coat.

"She's deceased."

Words froze on my tongue, unformed. "What?" I finally managed.

"Your friend Erin . . . her body was found this morning."

The room twisted around me. "I don't understand. Are you sure?" I placed my hand on the bed to steady myself.

"Yes."

I swallowed but couldn't feel my throat. "How could this happen? I thought you said she was in rehab?" My voice was growing louder, shakier.

"She was . . ." He paused. "I don't know the details."

"Where *was* she?"

"Harper—"

"Where?" I demanded.

"They found her outside of a club downtown."

My lips started quaking. *Downtown.* "You said she was in Waukegan," my voice trembled.

"I know. I don't have any answers right now." His tone was so much gentler than usual.

But it only made me angry. "I have to see her."

"You can't," he said quickly. "Her parents don't even know yet. I'm not supposed to be telling you any of this."

My vision completely blurred with tears. They spilled over and fell when I blinked.

"Are you still there?" he asked.

I sniffed. More tears came, seeping into the blanket and making the blue deeper with each drop. I let the phone fall and pushed to end the call.

I couldn't recall how the rest of the day passed. The next thing I remembered was Danny's voice. I couldn't understand what he said. Or asked.

I couldn't make out his face in the dark, but the warmth of his arms enveloped me.

There were no words for the longest time. He slid the empty bottle of gin away from me across the floor and brought his body closer to mine.

I could barely keep my eyes open—they were so heavy. I had so much to say, but my lips were anchored together.

"Did you take anything?"

I could understand him now even though his voice was quiet. I shook my head, barely able to control the movement before my head fell back to his shoulder.

He held me closer.

"Danny . . ." I choked, and my voice died.

"I know," he said after I fell silent.

CHAPTER FORTY-THREE

The heat on my skin woke me. I blinked into the daylight streaming through the window. Danny's arm was draped across my torso, his wrist bent against the blanket. I rolled over on the bed, and he stirred awake.

He was still wearing his starched white button-up shirt from work, the sleeves rolled up to his elbows. He blinked and removed his arm, pushing the hair from his eyes.

My head pounded in time with my pulse. I stared at him through my swollen eyes.

He noticed and angled his body to face me. "Are you okay?"

No. "You said you know," I said, my dry mouth smacking. "Does that mean it's true?"

He frowned. There was something dark in his eyes.

"How?" I sat up. "How can you be sure?"

He leaned forward on his forearm. "Harper," he said softly.

"Tell me."

"I was sent there when the news broke," he said slowly. "I saw her."

I looked down at my hands. So that was it. She was gone. I thought about all the petty arguments. All the stealing from her. The times I'd hated her for how she treated me. There was nothing I could ever do to take back the last time I saw her. If I hadn't quit that day, maybe she could've held on a little longer. If I hadn't been so angry about the thought of her and Danny together.

———

The next few days only brought more questions. The biggest one was, How did Erin get from Waukegan to downtown? And why?

These questions tormented me. I followed the news stories about her death, but they offered no answers. They were short blurbs in the Breaking News sections on websites, lost among the other headlines of shootings and tragic deaths. Her hometown paper in Skokie didn't even mention how she'd been found, but went into great detail about how her entrepreneur father had amassed his wealth. They mentioned Erin's name only twice in the five-hundred-word article.

I closed out of the article and pulled up a new tab. I rocked back onto my knees, the blankets from Danny's bed scratching my skin. Wilder had mentioned the name of the facility before. Shadow? Sandy? Shady.

I typed in *Shady Rehab Waukegan*. The first result was Shady Oaks Rehabilitation and Addiction Crisis Center.

The door creaked as Danny slipped back into the room. He hadn't mentioned it, and I had been scared to ask him about it. But the question had kept me awake the previous night. It was harder to focus on reality. He sank into his desk chair and turned on his desktop. He was researching something of his own, although he didn't tell me what.

"Danny?"

He swiveled and looked down at me. "Yeah?" He hadn't slept well either. He'd been hovering and fussing over me, too scared to talk most of the time. We had barely said five words to each other in the four hours since he'd returned from work.

"Why haven't you asked me about the pill bottle?"

He blinked. "What?"

"Erin's pill bottle that you found," I said.

"What about it?"

"The date on the bottle was from around the time she went missing."

He narrowed his eyes thoughtfully. "She didn't go missing. She went to rehab."

I crossed my legs on the blankets. *Did she? Did she really go to rehab?* I turned away from Danny and back to my laptop.

I heard his chair squeak as he faced the computer again.

I couldn't explain how the pill bottle had ended up under my bed. I couldn't explain the nightmare of me hurting Erin.

My phone lit up beside me. It was Iann. I glanced at Danny's back and quickly left the room, phone in hand. I stalked to the bathroom and closed the door behind me. It was an impulse. Not a decision. "Hello?" I craved his voice.

"Hi," he said. His voice sounded new now, as if I'd answered the phone to the studio again and he was calling about a class. "I know it's late, but I wanted to ask if you'd like me to bring your stuff over?"

I puzzled over the words.

"I mean, I didn't hear from you, and I didn't want you to think you had to feel weird about taking your stuff back," he continued.

"No, I . . ." I swallowed. "I can come get it."

"Okay. If you let me know when, I can bring it with my car if that's easier," he said. "I really don't mind."

I fell silent again.

"How's tomorrow afternoon?"

My heart raced. With guilt. Excitement maybe too. "Yeah, okay. Thank you."

"So, how are you?" he asked after a pause.

I could imagine the feeling of his lips on mine again. The comfort of staying at home with him and Leo on the bed, watching TV. But in my vision, I saw the looming shadow of Alayna behind us. I shuddered. "Iann . . ." I swallowed. "Erin passed away."

"What?" he asked quietly.

I inhaled. "She died. They found her a couple of days ago." I slid down the wall onto the floor. I grounded my toes into the soft blue rug by the sink, my hand quivering.

"Oh my god," he said. "I'm so sorry. Are you okay?"

"I feel like it's my fault." My voice caught on the last word. "She OD'd."

"Harper," he murmured, "you can't blame yourself. She had her own demons way before she met you."

I closed my eyes. "The last time I saw her, we had a big fight. She hated me." And maybe I had truly hated her in that moment too.

"I know that's not true. She cared about you."

"It was so bad," I said, raising my hand to my temple. "I said so many things to her that I didn't mean." And what was the point? I had wanted to protect Danny. But no one was looking out for her.

"There's no way you could have known."

I chewed my lip. "I'm glad you called."

"Yeah, me too. I had no idea. I'm sorry." He fell silent for a moment. "Let me know if you need anything. And I can bring your stuff some other time. It doesn't have to be tomorrow."

I opened my eyes again; they were close to overflowing. "No," I said. "You should come over."

CHAPTER
FORTY-FOUR

You didn't think this through.

At no point during the train ride did I think through what I would do once I arrived at Shady Oaks.

I rubbed my hands together as I sat on the bench, shivering against the wind. It had been completely still in front of the facility for nearly an hour. As I had walked closer, a car had approached and parked. A wealthy older couple got out and hesitantly entered the building.

Otherwise, silence.

The small line of trees across from me took the brunt of the wind from the lake, but with each crash of the waves, a new chill breezed past.

The couple came out now, flanking a thin, dark-haired girl.

I sprang from my seat, my knees popping as I jogged across the street. I slowed to a walk as I neared their car. Their backs were to me as they loaded a TUMI suitcase into the back.

"Excuse me!" I called before the girl could get into the open back seat door.

They all turned toward me, the couple instinctively closing around the girl.

"I have a quick question." I locked my eyes on the girl.

She backed away.

"Who are you? What do you want?" the woman demanded. She looked me up and down. She took in my rough hands with bitten-down nails and leered at the dark circles under my eyes.

I focused on the girl. "Did you meet someone named Erin in there?"

The couple turned to the girl and tried to usher her inside the car, but she held her ground. "Why?" she asked hesitantly.

My heart started beating normally again, the feeling returning to my limbs. She *was* in rehab. "I'm a friend of hers and . . ." I surveyed the fragility of the girl. She could be no more than sixteen. She couldn't handle this news. "I'm trying to track her down. I think she was here for a while, but I don't know if she's still there. They won't let me visit her."

The girl stepped up beside her parents. "She was here," she said. She glanced back toward the front door of the building. "A man came to pick her up."

"Her dad?" I asked.

"I don't know. She didn't say that. She just left." The couple had allowed a little space for the girl to lean closer toward me. "I saw her go out to the common area and walk out with him."

I swallowed. "What did he look like?"

She rocked back on her heels. "Um, he was tall. I didn't really see him very well from the front."

The mom glared at me. "Are you done now?" she asked through clenched teeth, waving her daughter into the car behind her.

"Thank you," I said absently before they closed the door on the girl.

The woman eyed me even once she was sitting inside the car and as they pulled out of the parking lot.

I glanced at the building. It was worth a shot. I strode in through the door, the smell of disinfectant and lavender assaulting my nose and stinging my eyes. The attendant at the front desk didn't acknowledge me until I was upon her. "Yes?" she asked.

"A friend of mine was staying here, but I heard that someone checked her out?"

She waited for more. An actionable reason to help me.

"Her name is Erin Braughton."

She frowned and looked back at the desk. "Unless you are on a list of approved guests or one of her doctors, I can't even discuss the status of any patient here. What is your name?" She shuffled through a small stack of papers in front of her.

Damn. "So, no one could have checked her out unless they were on that list, right?"

She glanced back up at me. "That's right. Your name, please?"

I shoved my freezing hands into the pockets of my coat. "Never mind." I backed away and turned from the counter, the frigid wind blasting against my face and body as I stepped out the door.

CHAPTER
FORTY-FIVE

I pulled up the article. My face crumpled at the picture of her. She was beautiful. I remembered that picture from one of the frames in her apartment. My eyes stung.

It wasn't really what I was expecting of an article in the Crime section. Danny had written a memorial of sorts. He glossed over the details of where and how she'd been found. He wrote about her work, her schooling, and her family.

Her Wicker Park community mourns the loss of a kind and dedicated friend. "She was the only person who took care of me when I first moved here," a close friend of Ms. Braughton said. "She saw something special in everyone."

It wasn't sensational. It wasn't interesting. It was kind. It was almost unbelievable that it had gotten published.

I closed my computer and slid it across the bed, leaning my head against the wall. Danny was right. I should've gone to the funeral. He'd tried to tell me I'd regret not going, but my stomach had turned at the thought of seeing Erin stiff in the casket.

Eventually, that would be me. A lump hardened in my chest. But no one would be there. What did it say about me to think of my own death at this moment?

I heard the front door close gently. Footsteps across the wood floor.

The bedroom door creaked softly, and Danny's sandy hair appeared first through the doorway. He looked at me on the bed and smiled weakly.

"Hi," I said, sitting up from the wall.

He closed the door and leaned against it, unzipping his coat. "Hey." His face was pale. He threw his coat in the general direction of the closet and grabbed at his necktie.

From his expression when he returned, I knew I had been right not to go. "I read your article," I said.

He finished unwinding the tie from his neck and tossed it on top of the coat.

"You quoted me."

He walked into the closet. "I didn't think you'd mind since I didn't name you."

"Yeah, I don't mind. It was nice." I couldn't ask the questions I wanted to. How did she look? How were her parents? What kind of sick questions were those?

He came out in a black sweatshirt and jeans. "You should've been there," he said, sitting beside me on the bed.

I shook my head. "I couldn't." I shivered and pulled my legs into my chest.

"Are you going to be okay?"

I nodded. "Yeah." If I kept saying it, eventually it would be true. "I went to Waukegan."

"What?"

"That's where she was in rehab."

Danny's eyes were intent upon me. "Why did you go there?"

Because of my nightmares. "I needed to be sure."

His brow furrowed. "Sure of what?"

Sure that I hadn't hurt her. "I needed . . . closure." Closure. What a stupid word.

"Funerals and memorials are for closure," he said. "But you didn't want to go to either of those. What aren't you telling me?"

"Nothing. I wasn't thinking." I sighed. "I need to go back to my place."

He frowned. "Come on, Harper."

"I need to get my life back together," I said. The crappy little existence I had somehow managed to build had been slowly unraveling for so long that I hadn't realized exactly how lost I was. But losing Erin was a reminder of how close I was to falling off the edge. "I'm going to find a new apartment." I held his gaze. "This week."

He sighed and tapped my knee with his finger. "Where is this coming from all of a sudden? Do I snore?"

I smiled. "No, I really appreciate everything you've done for me. But this isn't fair for you. You're paying god knows how much for rent, and you're sleeping on the floor and dealing with all of my baggage."

He opened his mouth to say something, but the buzz of my phone stopped him. We both glanced at it between us on the bed.

I quickly grabbed it and flipped it over, but he had already seen the name.

His body tensed. "Why is *he* calling?"

I scratched my fingernails against the fabric of my jeans. "We've been talking. I called him."

Danny stood up. "Are you getting back together with him?"

I uncrossed my legs on the bed. "I don't know." We'd parted that afternoon with nothing resolved. He hadn't asked, and I hadn't offered anything.

He shook his head. "Jesus Christ, Harper! What about what you said? About living in someone else's shadow? That suddenly doesn't matter anymore? What about what *I* told you? That doesn't matter?"

"It does," I said, quietly. "But he didn't do anything wrong. He kept this one thing to himself when I've kept so much from him."

"Don't you think it means something that you haven't told him about all your shit?" he shot back.

It had been nice to pretend. To imagine I could exist without everything bad in my life coming to the surface. "I don't think it does."

"How many times are you going to let other people use you like this?"

The words stung.

His cheeks were red. "He's using you. You know it, and you're willingly going to walk back into that?"

"He's not using me. What could he possibly gain?" I had nothing to offer him. Maybe I looked like Alayna. But I believed him when he'd said he loved me. He wouldn't have stuck around if he didn't.

"What can *you* possibly gain from that relationship?" he countered. "You don't know what you thought you knew about him, and he clearly has no idea who you really are. So why? Why bother going back to that?"

"I love him." The words fell out with such force that they made my lips quiver.

Danny clenched his jaw and turned away from me, then grabbed his coat and slammed the door behind him.

CHAPTER
FORTY-SIX

"Okay, so I'll need pay stubs from the last two weeks."

I stopped writing. I knew it had been too easy. "I'm a freelancer."

The man's smile was unflinching. "That's fine. You can bring a printout of last month's bank statement."

I dropped the pen completely. "I don't have a bank account."

The smile disappeared. "How do you get paid?"

"Cash and check," I said reluctantly.

He glanced over his shoulder into the glass office at the older woman typing away at her computer. "I'll tell you what," he started, wriggling his graying mustache. "If you can pay the first six months' rent up front, then we won't need income verification."

"And that would be?"

"Six thousand, six hundred and fifty dollars," he said cheerily. "That includes the security deposit as well."

I sighed. *Right.* This was how I had ended up at Bug's upstairs apartment. I slid the application back over the table toward him. "Okay, thank you."

He looked down at the paper. "You can take this with you and fill it out. That way once you come back, we can get you in that unit right away!"

I pushed back from the table and grabbed my bag. "No, it's fine. I'll fill it out later." I tuned out his parting words and left through the office door. I stood on the curb, staring at the traffic passing by. I was looking in the wrong neighborhood. I couldn't afford Wicker Park. Not safe, new Wicker Park.

My phone chimed, and I pulled it out of my pocket. Danny had sent me a link. I clicked on it. It brought me to the Classifieds page of the *Chicago Sun-Times*.

Month-to-month studio near Logan Square.

Even though we had barely spoken since our fight, Danny had been incredibly active in my new apartment search. I figured it was because he feared I might try to move back in with Iann out of desperation. I had already begun regretting asserting my independence and leaving Danny's place that night.

I had been awake for the past three nights straight because I couldn't fall asleep in my apartment. I had lain across the empty bed with all the lights on, keeping my eyes focused on TV reruns to avoid the imagined shadows creeping in across the room.

I called him.

"Hey," he answered flatly.

"Thanks for the lead," I said, ignoring his tone. "I struck out again in Wicker Park."

"Um-hmm."

I rolled my eyes. "I'm going to call about that listing."

"Okay." A car horn honked in the background on his end.

My patience was thinning. "I wanted to say thanks. That's it," I said. "Bye."

"Wait!" he said, his tone livening back up. "Are you free tonight?"

I hesitated. "Yes."

"We need to talk. Let's get dinner." The words sounded serious, but his tone was light.

I smiled. "Okay. I'll come over at six?"

"Perfect. See you then."

———

I had raised my hand to knock on the door when it suddenly opened. It was Carlos. We had only had quick exchanges during awkward run-ins going to and from the bathroom in previous weeks.

He grinned. "Hi?"

"Hi, is Danny in?"

He shook his head. "I don't think so."

"I'm supposed to meet him for dinner."

He opened the door wider. "I'm heading out, but you can wait for him inside."

I slid in behind him. "Thanks."

He closed the door and locked it from the hallway.

I walked past the kitchen and sank onto the sofa, still wearing my coat. I dug my phone out from my pocket. I was actually twenty minutes late, so I wouldn't have enough time to make myself cozy.

———

"Harper?"

My eyes blinked open. The room was dark, only the one lamp in the corner switched on, the light blocked by Carlos crouching over me on the couch. I leaned away from Carlos, but his hands were still resting on both my shoulders. "What's going on?" I picked my head up from the cushion. My body was heavy from my coat, still zipped up to my neck.

His face was pale. He stepped back.

"I'm sorry," I said weakly. I cleared my throat. "Did I fall asleep?" I looked around the room for Danny.

"Harper," he said again. "Danny was in an accident."

My muscles tensed.

"Harper?" Carlos sat beside me. "They took him to the hospital, but . . ." He swallowed. "He's critical right now. They don't think he'll wake up."

I focused on my hands. I couldn't feel them. They blurred in the dark in front of me. "Where is he?"

"He's at UC Medical," he said softly.

I stood although I couldn't feel my legs.

"I'm heading there now. Let's go together."

I didn't remember walking outside the apartment or the car ride. I saw the blindingly white halls of the hospital. I smelled the musk reeking from each room as I followed Carlos. He spoke to me, but I could only hear a murmur beyond the ringing in my ears. I trailed behind him into a room.

Danny was lying on the hospital bed. His head was wrapped in white gauze; only his forehead and down were visible. His mouth gaped open, tubes trailing out and down his chest, like electrical cords.

I blinked, and my cheeks were wet. I touched a hand to my face.

Carlos put his hand on my shoulder, but I couldn't feel it.

CHAPTER
FORTY-SEVEN

I lay on my bed, staring up at the ceiling, the room rotating. I pushed the bottle of rum away from my chest, and it fell to the floor with a thud, the last drops swishing.

There was a large blank spot from the early morning from when I'd seen Danny lying in the hospital to when I'd watched Carlos's car drive away from the curb in front of my apartment.

Car accident. Coma.

Those were the only words that had stuck. The "how" was lost somewhere in my blackout hours.

Everyone you care about is hurt.

I sat up, leaning my head back against the wall until my nausea subsided.

You are toxic.

There had been no sounds from the street for hours now.

You are a disease.

My eyes clouded with tears.

I rolled over to the side and dangled my feet for a moment before standing. I grabbed a used blue sweater hanging out from under the bed and tugged it over my head, inhaling old cat fur as I did. I scrambled through a pile on the floor and found a pair of crumpled jeans and pulled them over my hips before I realized I was still wearing my pajama shorts. I sighed and buttoned them anyway. I wasn't sure I had the motor function to redo that whole movement.

I stumbled out the door, fumbling with my keys for several minutes before finally locking it behind me.

I surveyed the street before I descended the stairs. It was quiet, but I saw some dark figures in the corner of my eye, walking and laughing together. I blinked, and I was at the train station, swiping my card and rolling through the turnstile, my bag getting stuck before I violently yanked it out.

I closed my eyes on the train. The sharp ding of an elevator woke me. I stepped out onto the ninth floor, staring ahead at 906. I hovered in front of her door, leaning against it and digging in my bag.

What are you doing?

My bag fell to the ground, the keys inside clanging. I picked it up and fished around for my sketchbook. I ripped out a page and grabbed my red colored pencil. I held the paper up to the wall and scrawled, *Be careful. Call me. (312) 567-8834.*

The message looked so menacing in red. I folded the paper and slid it under the door, almost losing my balance as I straightened. My face grew hot. There was no way she would call me. She would think I was some crazy maniac. And now she had my number. I got to my knees and peered at the door. It was almost airtight, and I couldn't see the paper through the slight gap underneath. I tried the doorknob.

Locked.

I turned around and surveyed the hallway. There were no security cameras. Once I reached the bottom floor in the elevator, I saw her through the glass door, punching in the building code outside. I stumbled to the mailboxes and turned my back to the elevator. I caught a glimpse of her in the elevator, her heels off like before, but this time her hair was down and curled. The doors shut, and I ran out onto the sidewalk.

My feet had carried me down another unexpected path.

I was suddenly outside the police station, the rain seeping through the hood of my coat and sending a chill down my back. Wilder's car was parked outside. I looked at my phone.

It was 1:46 a.m.

The lot was mostly empty. I suspected most of the patrol cars were in the gated parking lot behind the station.

I stood there, my eyelids growing heavier with each blink. I wanted to tell him something, but I couldn't remember what. I spun around and started walking down the road, the sound of a door clanging shut behind me. I made it to the nearest alleyway running under the L before I doubled over and retched onto the pavement, one hand on the side of the building to keep steady.

A hand grabbed my shoulder, and I almost fell, but Wilder pulled me up by my elbow. "What are you doing?" he demanded, holding me up against the wall until I could straighten my legs. His hair was soaking wet, and he was squinting against the rain.

I opened my mouth to answer, but he waved his hand in front of his face. "Never mind, I can guess." He rolled his eyes and let go of my arms.

I peeled my hood away from my hair. "How did you know I was here?"

He rubbed the water from his face. "There are windows in there—you know that, right?"

I gaped at him.

"Why are you here?" he asked.

I couldn't focus on his face. "Danny is . . ." The words came out garbled. I rested my head against the wall.

"Go home," Wilder said and walked away. I felt heavier with each step he took away from me until I sank to the ground with a splash.

CHAPTER FORTY-EIGHT

"Okay, get out."

I started awake in a dark car. I looked directly in front of me out the windshield. I was in front of my apartment. Wilder was in the driver's seat looking through the opposite window, facing away from me. "How did I get here?" I asked, my voice cracking.

Without a word, he got out of the car and walked around to my door and yanked it open. I grabbed onto his shoulder to keep from falling out, but he leaned away. Raindrops hit my face as he pulled me out of the car by my arm. My knees hit the sidewalk, and I gasped as he guided me, stumbling, up the steps to my door. I reached for my bag, but he already had my keys in his hand. He opened the door and pushed me in over the threshold. I collapsed onto the bed, my clothes dripping.

He came in and closed the door, then turned on the overhead light. "You have a massive self-destructive streak," he said.

I rolled onto my back and slipped my coat off from only one arm before I gave up.

"What set you off *today*?" He leaned against the closed door with his arms crossed.

I raised my head to glare at him before letting it fall back onto the bed. "Never mind."

"What were you doing at the station?" He was standing over me now.

I groaned, remembering the folded note at Jenny's. "I did something stupid." *Again.*

"Why is that *my* problem?" he asked, echoing my thoughts.

"It's not." I tried again to remove the jacket from my other arm by shaking it off.

He scoffed and leaned forward, tugging my arm out of the sleeve. He lingered there, his wet hair grazing my forehead. He slid his hand behind my ear, his fingers digging into my hair. I froze. I couldn't remember how I'd arrived in front of Jenny's door. I couldn't remember getting into Wilder's car. Or the ride to my street.

"What are you doing?" I asked, letting out the breath I'd been holding.

He wound his fingers tighter around my hair and slowly pulled my head back, exposing my neck.

My chest tightened as he roughly kissed me, the stubble around his mouth burning my lips. I clenched my fist around the blanket underneath me until my knuckles numbed. Fear seeped deep into my gut as he continued, pinning one of my arms down. He bit my lip in his frenzy, the taste of copper tainting my mouth. I pushed my free hand against his chest, but the liquor had made me weak. His fingers fumbled with the button on my jeans.

"This isn't a good idea," I wheezed when our lips separated.

He threw his jacket to the floor before straddling me on the bed. In one swift movement, he ensnared both of my wrists in his hands. "Why? This is why you came to my office, isn't it? You wanted to play with me again?" It was impossible to discern if it was anger or desire in his eyes. I wasn't sure which one I'd rather see.

"No, I'm sorry."

With his free hand, he used a finger to wipe the blood from my lip. "Why won't you leave me alone?"

"I-I will."

He released my wrists and left the bed. "Fine," he said coldly. He turned and walked out the door without another word, then slammed it behind him.

I scrambled to the door and locked it before turning off the light. I crouched at the window, peering through the blinds. He was sitting in his car, his lighter flashing as he lit a cigarette. I crawled back to my bed and collapsed onto the wet blankets, kicking my boots off. My breathing calmed back to normal as I heard his car start and the sound of the engine faded down the road.

I lay down on the dry side of the bed and unlocked my phone. The top message thread was from an unsaved number, but it wasn't marked unread. I clicked the thread.

Unknown (2:35 a.m.): Who's this?

It had been sent from an out-of-town area code. I was sure it was *her*. My heart raced. I searched for the saved news links in my phone. Once I found the articles about Holly and Sarah, I sent them in a text.

Can we meet somewhere? Today? I responded, my hands shaking as I rested the phone on my knee.

Unknown (2:38 a.m.): Nero's Coffee Bar at 8:30.

CHAPTER FORTY-NINE

My entire body was quaking when I opened my eyes hours later, standing in front of the bathroom mirror. It was cracked all the way down the middle, shards underneath in a red pool.

Blood streamed down my hand and into the water running from the faucet and into the sink.

I fell against the wall with a gasp, blood dripping from my fingers onto the white tile floor. I couldn't tell where it was coming from. A gash on my knuckles stung as I clawed at the blood with my nails, but it was everywhere.

I tugged my shirt off. It was soaked in blood that had smeared onto my face and hair as I'd pulled it over my head. My jeans were plastered to my thighs, red stains on my pale skin as I wriggled out of them and staggered into the shower. The water hit my body and burned into the aches and scrapes from last night. The cuts on my knees stung where they had cracked on the sidewalk when Wilder had pulled me from the car. My swollen lip throbbed. The thin slices on my hands burned.

As I closed my eyes, an image flashed through my mind. My hands cutting and slicing into Jenny, the glint of glass as I reared my fist back and plunged into flesh.

Flesh ripping.

Blood gurgling.

It couldn't be real. It was just another dream.

But there was so much blood. Far more than I'd ever seen before when I'd hurt myself during night terrors. Red swirls gathered around my feet, circling into the drain. Finally the water ran clear. I stepped out, my hands latching on to my used clothes and piling them into the tub. I closed the shower curtain and quickly pulled on a fresh shirt and leggings.

I didn't have time to deal with this right now. I had to meet Jenny.

———

Although the rain was gone, the chill in the wind bit through my thin clothing all the way to the train to downtown. When I arrived in front of the coffee shop, I lowered my hood and smoothed down my hair the best I could.

"What can I get for you?" The barista's eyes drifted to the scratches on my hands.

"A red-eye, please." The only solution for this type of headache was coffee with a shot of espresso. I paid and brought my mug to the table by the window, facing out to the street and river.

I took a gulp of the coffee and checked my phone.

8:26 a.m.

I leaned my head against the column beside me and took another sip.

8:45 a.m.

I nervously peered out the window. The sun was lightly glimmering in the river ahead.

9:34 a.m.

I scooped up my bag and pushed out onto the street, bumping into a few early bird joggers speeding past as I started down the sidewalk toward her building. I looked at each face passing by, hoping to catch her on the way to the café.

As I neared the building, I caught the door as a woman pushed a stroller into the lobby. I bypassed the elevator and instead jogged up the stairwell. My knees throbbed and ached as I reached the ninth floor. It wasn't until I was standing on her mat that I realized the door wasn't completely closed.

I swallowed. With sweaty palms, I opened the door. Music played quietly nearby. It was "Clair de lune" by Debussy on piano. I stepped into the kitchen and looked around the corner into the dark living room. In the bedroom beyond, a light was on. With a deep breath and clenched fists, I stepped slowly toward the light. Before I turned the corner, I glanced around the living room once more. No one in sight. As I entered the bedroom, I immediately saw her on the floor. Her arms and legs were twisted in unnatural positions, and she lay staring at the ceiling, her eyes cold and unblinking, blood caked around her chest and pooled all around her in a gruesome halo.

I cried out and fell to the floor beside her, my hands trembling as I reached toward her. Dried blood was crusted along the skin of her forehead. A fly landed on her mouth, which gaped open as if she were screaming. I laid a finger to her neck and pulled away. She was like ice. And so still. She was wearing the same blue dress from the last night I'd seen her, but it was now covered in blood, and her heels were beside the bed.

I put both hands to either side of my head and focused on breathing. As I stood, I swallowed a mouthful of bile and choked. I grabbed my phone from my bag and pressed 911 but didn't dial. There was something tangled in the hair under the nape of her neck. I bent down and pulled the piece of paper out from under her head and then dropped it immediately. It was my note in red from the night before.

The sound of my heart pounding drowned out all thought. My breathing quickened until I couldn't see the rest of the room, only her and the note. I folded the note into my palm and surveyed the room. Her phone wasn't anywhere. *Don't touch anything.* I glanced under the bed and on top of her twisted bedsheets.

I backed away and then ran out of the unit, gasping in the empty hallway. I covered my hand with my sleeve and closed the door, tugging my hoodie tighter around my face as I ran back into the elevator. I reached the first floor and pushed the door and ran half a mile before I doubled over and fell to the pavement.

CHAPTER FIFTY

Shadows flashed past on the floor of the train as it crawled over the river. I held the note in one hand and my phone in the other. The note had become damp from the sweat on my palms, the red letters bleeding onto my skin. I saw her body when I blinked.

"Evanston Main coming up." The conductor's voice shattered through the bloody vision.

As the train pulled up to the platform, I grabbed my bag and stood directly in front of the doors. My stomach dropped as I left the station. The thought of going back filled me with dread. But where else could I go? Where else was safe?

Once I was on my old street, I could see the for sale sign posted in the dying grass on the lawn. They weren't wasting any time getting what money they could from my father's estate.

My hands hadn't stopped shaking since I'd left Jenny's apartment. When I stood on the porch of the house, I tried to steady them as I cupped my hands around my eyes and peered in through the glass inlay on the front door. I glanced to the empty driveway before walking down the steps and jumping the rickety wire fence to the backyard and landing in the tall grass. I took a ballpoint pen from my bag and shoved it under my bedroom window, prying it up until I could force it the rest of the way up with my fingers. The window had always jammed on the way down, and it could never be properly locked from the inside.

Once the window was open wide enough, I slung my bag to the hardwood floor and paused for any sound before grabbing the window-sill and hoisting myself inside. My shoulder clipped the bookcase on the way in, and I gasped as I rammed into the floor. My chest immediately tightened upon entering the house.

I sat up, clutching my shoulder and leaning against the bed frame. This was about how far I had made it when my father had grabbed my neck that day and rammed me against the bookshelf the night I left for good. My pulse quickened, and my throat burned with the memory.

I stood and turned the light switch, but nothing happened. They had probably cut the utilities. I peered out into the hallway, which stretched farther into the darkness of the house. It was still midday, but it was so dark inside. The house had absorbed this gloom long ago. It was hard to remember what the house had looked like when Mom had been alive. With heavy feet, I walked down to the study; the double doors were wide open. Now there were books in boxes stacked along the floor, only a few remaining on the shelves. His imposing oak desk was still perfectly intact from my last visit.

I sank into the leather armchair, goose bumps rising along my skin as if he were watching. His favorite photo of Mom was framed on his desk and then a picture of me at sixteen, in the clothing he had picked out, exact replicas of what Issi had worn years before. Each growth spurt after her death had resulted in a violent tantrum. The other framed photos were all of Issi and me when we were little. I leaned forward in the chair and opened each drawer. They were full of loose papers with his scribbles all over them.

I pulled out the very bottom drawer. There was the old scotch bottle. I reached for it, but something shook beneath it. I set the bottle on the desk and touched the bottom of the drawer, and it immediately flipped up to expose additional space underneath. I removed the false bottom and froze. There was a small manila envelope with *Harper Mallen* scrawled on top in red.

I stared at it, my heart racing faster until my fingers wrapped around the envelope. I abandoned the scotch and staggered back to the bedroom, then closed the door behind me. I wasn't ready to see what was inside. Not now.

I crammed the envelope into the bottom of my bag before slumping down onto the floor. I brought my knees into my chest and faced underneath the bed. Her eyes were wide open, looking into mine from the dark. I shuddered and refocused my gaze.

There was a lump underneath the bed, against the wall. A blanket, maybe. I reached across the floor, my hand scraping the dust from the surface, and grabbed the lump and dragged it out. I recognized the coat immediately.

I rubbed my hand over the small parka, the fabric stiff with age, the top layer of dust coming off on my fingers. It was the coat I hadn't taken the night of the accident. I clenched my fists around the fabric and squeezed it close to my chest.

Hot tears burned my eyes. No one had seen that night for what it was. They'd all seen what they wanted to believe. A terrible accident befalling the professor and his daughters after his wife's untimely demise. They'd forgotten my real name. They'd pretended I was as talented as Issi while I was constantly beaten in darkness for my inadequacies. They'd forgotten who I was. And I'd forgotten too. I thought running away would save my life, but I'd never truly regained myself.

I squeezed the coat, balling it into my fists, my shoulders shaking with fury. Those years of torment at his hands were not far enough away. I couldn't forgive him for leaving me to continue suffering alone. A true orphan. A faceless, blank human standing on my own.

I thought about Jenny, lying alone like that.

It should've been you.

———

I awoke, cold on the floor, in complete darkness. My eyelids clung together from tears that had dried in my sleep. I slowly sat up, glancing over the shadows in the room. It was dark outside. How many hours had I slept?

I glanced at my phone. The battery was low. I had a missed call from Iann and eight from Wilder. No voice mails from either. The number of calls from Wilder sent my heart racing again. I picked up the red note from Jenny's apartment that I had discarded on the floor. My first mistake was taking anything from her. My second and worst mistake was not calling Wilder. Would he have believed me? I considered how bad it all looked—my obsession with Jenny, the breaking in, the note.

A strange clatter sounded outside the bedroom window. I looked outside, but it was black. I slowly lay flat on the floor and pushed myself underneath the bed, my phone still in tow.

I stayed there in crushing silence for a long time. I started to relax, staring at the hexagon pattern on the box spring above, and began drifting off again.

A bang jolted me alert. A shuffle as two booted feet appeared under the window and inside the room. My body froze.

You're dreaming. This isn't happening.

The boots were still by the window. After a few more moments of stillness, they lumbered across the room toward the closet. The doors swung open with a squeak of the hinge. Next, the bedroom door opened.

I carefully tilted my head to the side and peered underneath the bed frame into the room. The shadow of the man stood at the door, staring into the hallway before disappearing behind the door. I couldn't make out any features other than wide-set shoulders.

My mind raced.

Who is that?

Who would even know you were here?

Stay or run?

The thud of footsteps sounded distant, maybe in the kitchen.

My pulse quickened when I spotted my bag on the other side of the bookcase. Maybe I had enough time to grab it and drop from the window before the man returned. I listened for the sound of boots, but it was silent. Was the person on the other side doing the same thing? Were they listening for me?

The steps jogged back into the bedroom and paused in the doorway. The feet were angled toward the bookcase. I silently cursed myself and closed my eyes again, trying to keep my breathing quiet. With my eyes still closed, I heard the footsteps rapidly approach, and a creak of the floorboards sounded nearby.

A hand pulled my arm. I cried out as I was dragged from under the bed. I was staring up at the figure suddenly, my eyes focusing on the familiar wide gray eyes. "Hey, it's me," Wilder barked. "Calm down, okay?" He released his grip on my shoulders.

"What are you doing here?" My body was still trembling.

"That other girl you told me about." He ran a hand through his hair. "I think we found her body today." He stared at me through the dark. "Did you know?"

I shook my head and wiped the sweat from my forehead. There was pressure on my shoulders as he pushed me forward into his chest and wrapped his arms around me.

"Then why are you here? When I couldn't find you at your apartment, I figured you found out and got spooked and came here." He glanced around. "God knows why. Surely this place is worse than anything waiting for you in the city." His hand traced down my back. "I promised you you'd be fine," he said quietly.

He had promised that. But yet another girl was dead now.

"Come on, let's get out of here." He got to his feet and extended a hand toward me. He handed my bag to me and started back toward the window. While his back was turned, I grabbed the note from the floor and put it in the bottom of my bag.

"I guess this is the only way out without leaving the front door unlocked when we leave, right?" he asked, peering out the window.

I shrugged.

"Come here. I'll help you out." He took my waist and lifted me onto the windowsill. He kept his face close beside mine until I turned away to look down and out the window. His hands twisted around mine as he lowered me to the other side of the window onto the grass.

I stared ahead at the chain-link fence.

He appeared beside me. "Okay, let's go."

I passed through the gate first, the pit of my stomach somersaulting. The image of Jenny staring up at me burned into my eyelids as I blinked.

"Are you okay?" he asked, closing the gate behind him.

I nodded and started toward his Charger. He held the door open for me and softly closed it.

He started the car. "Harper, tell me what really happened." His tone was deep but firm.

He knows what you did.

I rolled down the window. It was hard to breathe. "Can you take me back to the train station?" I asked as we exited the neighborhood.

"No, I'll drop you at home."

I scratched at my hands as if I could remove Jenny's blood.

We passed the train station. "You have to tell me what happened," he said. "I'm trying to help you."

My heart pounded, the artery under my scar throbbing. "I was going to meet her," I said, my voice breaking. "But when I got there, she was . . ." I couldn't say it out loud.

He didn't look at me, staring straight ahead through the windshield. "How did you know where she lived?"

"I'd met her before," I lied. "What happened to her?"

He glanced at me, a strange look in his eyes that I didn't quite recognize. "I don't know for sure yet. She was stabbed, but that's about all I know for now."

I remembered the first night watching her in the hallway. She hadn't locked her door. But it had been locked last night. I was sure of it. "How did you find the body?"

He gripped the steering wheel with both hands. "Her neighbor found her." We were silent for several minutes, the view dark out the windows, but I could see city lights at the edge of the horizon.

"I'm scared." Of ending up like Jenny. Of what might happen to Danny.

Wilder didn't say anything the rest of the drive, but his hand closed around mine.

CHAPTER
FIFTY-ONE

I sat for a long time by the river. Everything was so still. Only a siren sounded nearby.

Wilder had dropped me off in front of my building. He'd waited at the bottom of the steps until I was inside. But my eyes drifted to a spot of blood in the corner of the room, and I ran back outside, hearing Wilder's car engine in the distance. I hadn't even bothered to lock the door; I just wandered. Down the street and onto the train until I'd ended up in downtown.

I stood up from the Riverwalk steps and surveyed the road. There weren't any cars parked along the road, but I continued glancing over my shoulder as I walked down Wacker Drive, scared that I'd see someone behind me.

Thunder sounded as I reached the stoop of Iann's apartment building. I stared up at the door. It was late. I couldn't buzz up. His roommate would be pissed. I sat on the steps and pulled out my phone.

Are you awake? I texted. I was about to put my phone back into my bag and wait when a response appeared.

Iann (12:24 a.m.): Yes, everything okay?

I quickly typed. Can you come downstairs?

He immediately called me. "Hey, what's going on?" His voice was still hoarse from sleep.

"I'm downstairs. Can you let me in?" My voice cracked. I couldn't remember my last drink of water.

"Yeah, hold on. I'll buzz you in."

I stood up as the buzzer sounded, and I pulled the door open. "Thanks, I'm coming up." I ended the call and walked onto the elevator. I didn't know what I'd say to Iann. Any of it. How could I tell him about Jenny? How could I explain this dread and panic building in my chest with each moment?

The doors opened, and Iann was waiting there, a wrinkled white T-shirt on and his hair tousled. I fell into his arms, intertwining my hands behind his back. I could feel his surprise, but then he pulled me closer against him, his face in my hair. "I'm sorry," I whispered.

He looked at me and wrapped my hands in his. "Come inside."

I leaned against him.

"Are you okay?" he asked, leading me into the kitchen.

"Won't we wake up your roommate?" I asked, patting Leo on the head when he bounded up to me.

Iann set me down in a chair at the kitchen island. "No, he's out of town this weekend. What are you doing out here so late?"

"It's such a long story," I said.

He sank down in the seat beside me. "Okay, you have to give me something," he said. "What's going on?"

I swallowed. "I couldn't sleep." I saw Jenny's eyes, the blood everywhere and shuddered. I rested my face in my hands.

"And you figured you'd go for a walk in the rain?" His lips formed into a grin.

"No," I said quietly. "I wanted to see you." *You're scared to be alone.*

He held my gaze. "Me too. I've missed you."

I looked away. "Iann . . . a lot's happened since—"

"Harper, whatever happened while we weren't together, it doesn't matter now." He grabbed both of my hands. "You're exhausted." His fingers laced with mine, and we walked to his room. Leo followed behind, panting, and then curled up at my feet as I sat on the edge of the bed.

Iann grabbed a pillow from the other side of the bed and turned.

"Where are you going?" I asked.

He glanced over his shoulder. "I—uh." He pointed behind me toward the living room. "I'll take the couch."

Given the events of the last couple of days, all my fears and doubts about him melted away.

Say it. "No, you should stay here. With me."

He lingered in the doorway for a second before walking to the bed and sitting down beside me. We both lay down on our backs. "I wasn't exactly sure where we stood right now."

I turned on my side and put my hand and head on his chest. "I'm sorry."

He ran a hand through my hair. "For what? It was my fault. I should've been honest with you from the beginning." His words slowed as he started to drift off. "But, I love *you*. You know that, right?"

"Yeah, I do." I didn't know what was going to happen to me, but I did know that and one more thing. "I love you too."

CHAPTER
FIFTY-TWO

I woke with clarity. In all the excitement, I'd almost forgotten about it entirely.

The sound of water trickled nearby. The sunlight had spilled through the blinds and made stripes on the white blankets. The bed was empty beside me, the imprint of Iann's head still in the pillow. I looked at the clock on the bedside table.

7:45 a.m.

I couldn't go back to my place. The events of the previous day made me shiver. If I went back home, I'd just be waiting. Waiting for someone to find me like they'd found Jenny.

I combed through my bag beside the bed.

"What are you doing?"

I jumped.

Iann was standing in the doorway with a towel wrapped around his waist. He shook his head and sat on the edge of the bed, facing away from me. "You're so jumpy. What's going on with you?"

A lump caught in my throat. "I'm sorry."

He glanced over his shoulder at me. "You're saying that a lot these days. What exactly are you sorry for?"

So much. "Nothing."

He walked into the closet. "I have to get ready for class." The sound of the hangers clanging together stopped. He walked over to me. He was now wearing his typical school clothes—sweater and jeans. He touched the cuts on my hands and frowned. "Let me take you to dinner tonight when I get back."

You might not make it to tonight. I nodded. "Okay."

I waited for the sound of the front door latching before I lunged across the bed and grabbed my bag. I dug through it, my fingers closing around paper. I pulled out the envelope.

In the light I could see that my name was scrawled in red, block-shaped capital letters. It wasn't my father's handwriting. It was harsher and foreign. I flipped it over. The manila flap on the back was worn and wrinkled. It had been revisited many times since it had first been unsealed.

My pulse echoed in my ears as I shook the contents out onto the bed. There were photos. Erin and me talking on the sidewalk, her arm outstretched toward me with a coffee cup. We were sitting at the little café by the studio where we'd first met. From the roundness of my face and neatly braided hair, I knew it was that day. I turned to the next picture. It was a photo taken from the other side of the street from my apartment, the silhouette of my face in the window. The last page was a handwritten list.

My apartment address.

My cell phone number.

Erin's full name.

I picked up the page, and something dropped from between the folds. My hand trembled as I reached for the business card.

Evanston Police Department. Sgt. Elliot Wilder.

I stared at the letters on the card. *How?* What did this mean? Wilder had known about me and where I lived for nine years.

I flipped the card over.

Case number: 3409872-M was scrawled in red across the back in those same block letters.

I fumbled behind me for my phone. My fingers shook as I searched for the number and dialed.

"Evanston Police Department," a woman's voice answered flatly.

My heart raced. "I need to look up a case number," I breathed, my voice stifled.

"I'll transfer you to Records." The line buzzed.

With each ring, my breath became more labored.

"Records," a man's voice boomed suddenly.

I took a breath. "I need to request a case record."

"Do you have a case number?"

"3-4-0-9-8-7-2-M." My voice quivered with each syllable.

"Okay," the man said quickly. "I can't give you the info over the phone, but you can submit a request by email. Be sure to include that number."

I hung up and let the phone slide to the bed.

———

As much as I hated the hospital, it was the first place I thought to go after leaving Iann's place later that day.

The remote control was sticky. I glanced at Danny's closed eyes. They said he might be able to hear.

I continued flipping through the channels. The previous channel had turned into prime-time sitcoms. There was probably no worse torture for him. I stopped at CNN.

I turned back to him. Had Danny found out about Wilder? If so, *what* had he found out? Why would Wilder pretend he didn't know me? Why would he follow me and give this information to my father?

What if this wasn't an accident? Wilder knew that Danny was around because I'd told him. Would he really do something to Danny to keep this buried so I wouldn't find out about his role in the past?

I reached for Danny's hand. His skin was warm. Even the remote possibility that I was responsible for him being like this was too much to bear.

I squeezed his hand harder in mine, until my knuckles popped. *Wake up.* I glanced into the empty hallway before leaning closer to his ear. "Danny?"

Nothing.

"I was hoping you'd stop by."

I jumped in my seat.

Cindy, Danny's mom, was smiling weakly at me from the doorframe. "I'm about to head out for the night, but I wanted your help with something," she said, grabbing a notebook from the sink counter, then sitting in the chair beside me. She flipped the notebook open and pulled a piece of paper out of it. "There's a lot in here, but I thought you'd like to see this." She handed the photo to me.

It was a picture of Danny and me from way back then. I remembered exactly when it was taken. We were posing proudly with a massive rock that we'd drawn our initials on with chalk by the bonfire pit. It was as close to the water as he could get me. The beach and the outline of the Chicago shore in the distance were behind us.

"Would you like to keep it?" she asked.

I ventured a glance at Danny in the bed. I couldn't speak, so I nodded.

Cindy handed me the notebook. "There's a lot in here," she continued. "It's mostly pictures and news clippings for stories he was working on. I was wondering if you could help me figure it all out."

I accepted the worn spiral notebook. "Of course," I said. "Thank you." I wasn't sure how much help I would be, but she didn't really want my help. She was doing me a favor. I'd been haunting her son's hospital room frequently since our awkward introduction.

She squeezed my hand. "I really appreciate it." She stood again and grabbed her purse from the floor. "Don't stay too late. You need to get some rest too." It was hard to take the instructions seriously when it looked like she'd barely slept at all. Her blonde hair was in a heap on top of her head, and her heavy eyelids were punctuated by the lines under each eye.

"I will. Good night," I said, trying to smile. I couldn't understand how she did it. My lips spasmed and gave out halfway. Everything about this situation was terrible.

I watched her go before flipping through the pages of the notebook. Near the middle, a few pages had been ripped out. Past that, there were more pictures and newsprint pages folded up. On the last page, a folded stack of papers.

I pulled out the papers and froze when I saw the letterhead at the top. *Evanston Police Department. Case 3409872-M*

It was my case. I flipped through, my eyes devouring each word. *Mallen, Harper Anne*

Potentially missing minor.

Last seen the night of 02/16/2010.

I skimmed past more pages until I saw it. *Interview Record: Fletcher, Daniel Evan*

Claims he was a friend of Mallen (minor). Does not know her whereabouts. When asked why her personal items were found in his apartment, he offered no explanation.

I skipped past the remaining notes. *Interviewing Officer: Sgt. Elliot Wilder.*

The pages blurred, but I continued scanning to the very end. *Case closed: Father claims minor made contact and is located in Chicago.*

Then why the pictures? Why would Wilder do this? Why had my father lied to the police?

Did Danny find out all this? Did he find out Wilder was the detective in Holly's and Sarah's murder cases?

I shoved the notebook into my bag, beside the envelope. I pulled my phone out, my fingers hesitating over the keypad. I wanted to call Wilder, to demand an explanation of some kind, but I stopped.

Danny's eyelids twitched. They did that occasionally. It was as if he were only napping and were about to wake up any second. Those little movements made it more painful.

What had he wanted to talk to me about the night of the accident? We hadn't seen each other in almost a week by that point. He could've done anything on his own in that time. I replayed our last conversation in my mind.

"We need to talk."

I slung my bag over my shoulder and stood up. I had to tell someone about Wilder. I had to try.

I paused in the doorway, like I always did before leaving, waiting to see if he was awake and peering back at me. I sighed and walked down the hallway. My thoughts were lost in the new questions that emerged with each step.

What now? There were so many police precincts nearby. Surely one of them was safe.

I stepped out of the hospital, breathing the clean air gratefully. I could never get used to that smell inside. It was dark outside already. Iann would be getting back home soon.

I glanced toward Michigan Avenue, the glow of the stores flickering as tourists passed. I cut through the smaller side street, passing by the ambulances along the curb and turning down the dark stretch of pavement.

There was a loud crack and then, black.

CHAPTER FIFTY-THREE

Movement shuffled me around. Cigarette smoke. Tires on asphalt.

I opened my eyes, blinking into the dark car. The back of my head was cold, as if something was trickling down toward my neck. I turned my head to the side, seeing only the top of a dark figure in the driver's seat, the windshield in front of them. It was dark through the windshield. No streetlights. No car horns sounding nearby.

I tried to sit up, but my wrists burned and hit against each other. I squinted at my hands and saw the rope becoming taut with each tug. My pulse quickened as my head slowly stopped spinning.

My eyes darted around the back seat for something. Anything.

A hand reached for the rearview mirror and angled it toward where I lay. "I didn't think you'd wake up," Wilder said, his eyes meeting mine in the mirror. He sounded disappointed.

"What are you doing?" I asked. My head felt heavy again. I rested it back against the seat.

"I have my own questions," he said, each word laced with ice. He looked back at the road but held up something. It was the envelope from my purse. "Why do you have this?"

I struggled to swallow; my mouth was so dry. "Where are we?"

He slammed the envelope down on the seat beside him. The car veered to the right and then stopped after a few bumps. The car door beeped as he opened the driver's side and got out.

He opened my door, and I kicked at him. He grabbed my foot and slid me down the seat toward him. I screamed, but then he was on top of me in the back seat, pinning my legs down before striking me across the face.

My jaw went numb. He grabbed my hair, the intense pain beside the cold part of my head making me cry out. I dug my heels into the snow outside the car, but he pulled me away. We were by the lake. But it was darker and colder outside the warmth of the city. He had taken off my coat, and I was shivering.

"I gave you a chance to walk away from this, but you just kept digging." His fingers wrapped around the gun at his waist. "I didn't ever think it would come to this. I didn't think you would ever do something like this to me."

My legs weakened, and I fell to my knees. "I-I swear," I stammered. "I don't know anything." The words were hard to press through my lips; my lungs were tensing inside my chest.

He glared at me. "From all the shit in your bag, it seems like you're caught up."

I shook my head. "No, I don't understand," I said. "Why? Why are you doing all of this?"

He seized my shoulders and lifted me to my feet.

My legs trembled and buckled again.

The cold metal of his gun grazed the skin under my shirt. "Get up."

I wanted to obey, but I sat frozen in the snow.

He sighed and holstered the gun, reaching down and gripping my hair with his fist before he dragged me down the beach.

I screamed as we drew closer to the water, bringing my bound hands to my hair and clawing at him. "Please!" My knees almost touched the waves lapping at the shore. I realized it then. He was going to drown me. "I didn't say anything to anyone," I pleaded, my fingers digging into his.

"Do you know how much I've done for you? I've tried to protect you," he said after a moment.

Protect me?

His gaze softened as he looked down at me. "You were so broken when I found you. I never wanted it to come to this. Not again."

Again? Oh, god. "Sarah? Did you . . ."

He gripped my hair again, searing pain at the base of my skull. "Sarah was an unfortunate accident," he said. I flinched as his fingers trailed down my cheek, the gentleness of the gesture in such contrast with the cruelty of a few seconds ago. "I thought you'd rejected me, but it was that bitch."

It became clear then. She'd just had the misfortune of looking like me and telling Wilder off for what he was—a creep.

"If you'd seen the way she looked at me . . . you've never looked at me like that." He stared down at me as if he saw that same look now, and he didn't like it. He bent down. "After all I've done, you're ready to turn on me like this? You were going to report me, weren't you?"

"No." My mouth was so dry I could barely speak. "I would never do that to you." Maybe a part of him wanted to believe me. I saw a flicker of doubt in his eyes. "I care about you. You saved my life."

He studied me. "I wish I could trust you. But I'm all out of chances, Harper." He kneeled down, cupping my face into his hands.

I resisted the urge to pull away. I forced myself to meet his gaze.

He leaned forward and kissed me, the heat from his lips clearing my mind.

I pressed deeper into him, sliding my bound hands to the side of his coat, willing them steady as they closed around the car keys in his pocket.

His kisses became more frantic, his hands tightening around my waist. For a moment he loosened his grip, and I took my chance.

I reared back, then struck his face with my forehead, a small snap sounding upon impact.

He roared, clutching at his nose as he staggered backward onto the snow.

I struggled to my feet, only taking one step before I was pulled back onto the ground, the keys flying from my grasp as I collapsed onto my arms.

Wilder flipped me over, looming above, his face covered in blood. He raised a hand and struck me across the face. "Dammit, Harper!" He grabbed the collar of my jacket and pulled me along the ground, closer to the water.

He said something else as he continued to haul me toward the water, but I could only hear the sounds of the waves. Taunting me. They would reclaim what they'd been robbed of all those years ago. He paused as we reached the lake's edge. "You know something? Who's going to even notice if you disappear? You're not on a single person's radar. You've made sure of that." It was true. The only person who would care was Iann. And if he started asking questions, Wilder would just need to remind him that I had been a teen runaway. That was it. Harper Mallen: once a runner, always a runner. Case closed.

"All I did was help your father out," he said, lifting me to my knees. The calm in his voice unnerved me. He'd accepted what he was about to do to me. I hadn't given him any other choice. "I did that kid Danny a favor too. If I hadn't found you back then, they probably would've locked him up for good." He sighed. "The saddest thing is that you and I are actually alike."

The thought that I had anything in common with him was too much.

"After what you did to Jenny, I didn't even think twice about taking care of that mess you left behind," he continued. "I had to protect you in any way I could."

"Jenny?" I remembered my shattered, bloody reflection that early morning. No, it was a dream. It had only been a nightmare.

"Yes, it doesn't matter to me what you did. I took care of everything for you. But to you, that means nothing."

What you did.

Jenny. The blood.

The nightmare came rushing to the front of my mind. My hands on the knife, the handle scratching the skin of my palms as I plunged it into her again and again.

There could only be one of us.

A heat rose in my chest. "No, I didn't do that. I didn't hurt Jenny."

There was something like pity in his eyes. "I'm sorry, Harper."

I stared at the water below. I removed my hands from his, and his grip loosened, but the pressure behind my neck remained. After a moment, his fingers relaxed, and he kneeled beside me, reaching both hands toward my face.

I thrust my bound wrists toward him, knocking him in the chest and setting him off balance. I stumbled to my feet and kicked him as he reached for his gun.

He grabbed my ankle and twisted it before I could pull away. As he attempted to stand, I brought my foot down on his head. I dug the keys out of the powdery snow with my frigid fingers and turned to run to the car.

I continued to run, even as my ankle rolled with each step until I fell beside the car, my head hitting the closed door. The pain nearly knocked me out, but I braced against the door and gripped the mirror to pull myself up.

The sound of Wilder's footsteps grew louder than the waves. I fumbled for the door handle and jumped into the driver's seat. Without closing the door, I turned the key and gripped the wheel with my bound hands. I hit the gas, and the engine started grinding, but the car stayed in place. I looked at the gearshift and switched it into drive with both hands, my foot lingering on the brake pedal. I couldn't move, my eyes trained on the rearview mirror, only the darkness reflecting back at me.

I wasn't sure what I was waiting for until it appeared.

CHAPTER

FIFTY-FOUR

He had taken my phone. He'd typed out a message to Iann saying it was over and I needed time alone. I knew he had no intentions of leaving me alive that night. They found concrete blocks in the trunk of his car. I could only assume he planned on dumping me in the icy lake after drowning me. Or worse, maybe he planned to sink me to the bottom of the lake while I was still alive.

I had tried three different gas stations at the outer limits of Kenosha that night until I found one manned. My pleas to the teenage night clerk were barely out of my mouth before I collapsed on the floor. I didn't remember much more between that and waking up in a hospital room, monitors beeping and police officers waiting outside the door. The story came out to them the same fragmented way it played through my mind.

Iann drove up to visit me at the hospital in Kenosha every night until I was released.

"What do you think about leaving?" he asked on the drive back to Chicago.

I rested my head against the window. The painkillers made me slightly dizzy. Or it might've been the head injury. "I'm fine," I said. It seemed like a weird question. I'd be happy to never be in another hospital for the rest of my life, especially not as a patient. "It'll be nice to sleep in a real bed again."

He shook his head. "No, I mean, what do you think about getting out of Chicago? Out of Illinois?"

I glanced at him. His face had been tense and in pain each day since the incident. Whenever he knew I was looking, he'd attempt a weak smile.

"I think you could use a fresh start," he continued.

I looked out the window, the lights growing denser as we approached Chicago. "I think so too."

SPRING

CHAPTER
FIFTY-FIVE

"How are you feeling about the move?"

I glanced out the window at the small patch of gray sky between buildings. The days were still cold and drizzly but a welcome relief from the bone-deep chill of earlier months. "Good," I said.

Her pen glided silently over the notepad in her lap. "You're moving to Washington, right? With your boyfriend?" Dr. Linda's smile warmed as she surveyed me.

I couldn't help but smile a little too. "Yes, to Seattle."

"When do you leave?"

"In a week. We've already mailed the bigger stuff to his parents' place," I said. "He finished his dissertation, so we'll come back in a few months for his graduation."

"I bet you'll be happy to get a little space from here."

My smile faded. "Yes." The months following Wilder's death had provided few answers. Yes, he'd taken under the table investigation jobs and bribes while at Evanston PD. Yes, he'd been obsessed and following me since my father had paid him to find me when I was sixteen. This was what we knew from what had been found in Wilder's apartment.

Based on the information I gave the police, they were able to tie him to Sarah's murder. And despite my hunch about Holly, the police insisted Wilder had no connection to her murder. Even though Wilder had been in charge of that investigation, they felt the evidence (half-baked as it was) pointed most satisfactorily to Jeremy as the culprit.

As for Jenny, the police concluded she might have been another unfortunate victim of Wilder. But perhaps we'd never know for sure since surveillance footage outside her apartment had disappeared shortly after her death. I had come to accept my own version of the truth, despite what Wilder claimed I'd done to her.

Wilder's hand in all these cases had made such a mess of those issues, and now that he was dead, we'd likely never know the whole truth.

Dr. Linda tapped her pen against the notebook in her lap. "How are you feeling about the attack now that you've had some time to reflect on it?"

Reflect?

I remembered staring, unblinking, into that rearview mirror until my eyes hurt. I remembered the shape I'd been waiting for appearing, frantically running toward the taillights of the car, gun drawn.

He'd thought I would run, drive away while I had the chance. And I could have.

I stared at her. "I think I've made peace with it."

She leaned forward. "What do you mean by that?"

Wilder's eyes had glowed red in the lights as I switched into reverse. There had been an instant when I saw a flash of fear as he realized what was happening before his body disappeared with a thud of the bumper. The heavy sound of grinding tires, the pulling of the undercarriage over flesh.

"I don't know," I said. "It's hard to explain."

"So," she continued, pressing the bridge of her glasses. "From what you're telling me, you seem to be moving forward. How are you feeling overall? How are you sleeping?"

When I could get to sleep, my dreams were where the darkness still enveloped my life. I'd tried everything, but Iann put up with my erratic screaming and even when it came to blows in my sleep. "Still not great." Instead of just Issi, there was now a full cast in my nightmares.

She frowned. "Are the dreams still violent?"

"Yes." Sometimes it started with violence against me. Sometimes I was the aggressor. But it always ended the same way. "This morning I woke up kicking and screaming at Iann in bed." In my dreams, I woke up covered in blood, standing over Erin. Jenny. Wilder. Bug. Danny.

"But you're not sleepwalking anymore?"

"Not that I know of."

"That's good," she said. "Whenever you wake in a panic like that, don't forget to do your counting exercises. That should help."

It did help usually. For some reason, counting my heartbeats seemed to focus enough of my nervous energy until I calmed down.

"How is your friend doing?"

My heart sank at the thought of Danny.

"You seem upset by that question," Dr. Linda said when I didn't answer. "Can you tell me why?"

I leaned forward in the chair, the leather squeaking from the fabric on my jeans. "I feel guilty."

"Why?" she asked soothingly.

I was glad for the help, but it was annoying sometimes how she insisted that I walk her through everything. She knew why. It was in her stupid little notes somewhere. "He's in there because of Wilder. Because of me."

"We've been over this," she started slowly. "I know it's hard to accept, but it was just an unfortunate accident."

The police had looked into Danny's accident after I'd connected the dots for them about Wilder. They couldn't find any proof that Danny and Wilder had ever interacted since Evanston. They couldn't even establish that Danny knew Wilder was in town. Danny had kept the case file in his notebook for a long time. They figured he'd had it with him all these years, hung up on my disappearance. That thought broke my heart.

Moreover, they couldn't find any tampering with Danny's car. I had briefly doubted the connection myself. But I was certain.

I nodded. There was no use arguing with her over it. Even after my story, she still implicitly trusted the police.

"Is everything still going okay with the detective on your case?"

"Yeah." Detective Dowdy was definitely an improvement over Wilder. She was smart, and more importantly, she was angry. She had been on to Wilder for misconduct for years, but finding out that he'd been stalking me since I was a teenager sent her over the edge. To say nothing of the bribe from my father and uncouth moonlighting as a private investigator in a missing person's case all those years ago. I didn't blame her for not tying Wilder to the other cases. There was a lot of information I'd never shared with her. And I never would. I would never tell her about my strange nighttime habits. I would never tell her about my obsession with Jenny. Jenny. The nightmares about her were the most vivid, the look in her eyes replacing the ghost of Issi.

"You're thinking about Danny, aren't you?" Dr. Linda leaned toward me slightly.

"They said there's still a chance he'll wake up. I feel like I'm giving up on him by leaving." I looked down at my hands folded in my lap.

"You're not. You're doing the best you can. In this case, you need to get out for your own sake."

I still had hope that she and Iann were right. Maybe the nightmares would go away once we'd left Chicago. Maybe I could really start over this time. Maybe I could forget about that night at Jenny's and the grip of my hand on the knife. Maybe I could forget about Wilder too.

———

I paused in the doorway of the hospital room. Danny's mom looked exhausted. She was keeping up the rent at Danny's apartment but barely slept five hours there each day. "Hi," I said, stepping inside.

She looked up from the book she was holding and removed her glasses. "Oh," she said with a smile. It was Danny's smile. It didn't hold anything back. "I thought you'd already left us." The words pricked me, but I knew she didn't mean anything by them.

"Not for another week." I glanced at Danny. "I'll be back in a few months. I'm going to visit regularly."

She followed my eyes. "Well, we're glad to hear it." She did that. Acted like Danny was in on the conversation. Maybe he was. Maybe he could tell I was abandoning him again.

"How are you doing?" I asked her, walking around the bed and sitting in the chair beside her.

The smile cracked for a moment. "I'm making it." The days when the police had looked into Danny's accident had been especially hard on her. And for nothing. She believed them too. But I knew they were missing something. "Danny's dad and sister are coming up again this weekend for a visit."

I leaned toward the bed. "I'm going to be here for a while. Why don't you take some time off?" It was already late in the day. She had a habit of skipping most meals on her full days at the hospital.

She wrapped her hand around mine. "I'm going to miss having you here, Harper."

Another stab in the heart.

She released my hand and stood from the chair. "Carlos and Will said they were going to stop by after work today."

"Okay," I said. "I'll keep an eye out for them." Danny had been in good company. He was well known and well liked by everyone he'd ever come in contact with. I'd met more people spending a few hours in the hospital room with him than I'd met in all my time in the city.

Cindy pulled her coat over her arms. "I'm going to run a couple of errands, and I'll be right back."

I smiled at her. "There's no rush. Get some dinner, and maybe take a nap . . . please."

She laughed. "I must be looking a little rough today. You're the third person to tell me that."

I gestured to Danny. "He's in good hands."

She patted my shoulder gingerly before leaning in for a hug.

I froze but settled my hands on her back in a limp return. It was easy to see where Danny got his openness from. His mom just went for it.

She straightened. "Okay, I'll leave you two to talk." She looked over her shoulder at Danny as she left the room.

I rested forward in my seat and grabbed his hand in both of mine. "This doesn't let you off the hook, you know," I said quietly. "You still have to wake up."

CHAPTER
FIFTY-SIX

I turned on the TV and sat next to Leo on the sofa. "An inquisition into the death of a thirty-eight-year-old Chicago homicide detective suspected of stalking and attempted murder of a witness is still underway." My body tensed. I switched the channel. In addition to Danny's, Erin's case was one more that had no conclusion. Not for me, at least. The rehab facility had confirmed that she'd been checked out of rehab by a man. Detective Dowdy could share no further information with me, and I suspected Erin's father had something to do with that.

Everyone, police included, suggested Erin had sneaked out to party the night she died. But to me, it was just one more bad deed Wilder would get away with, although I couldn't understand why. Erin had never even met him. Why would he want her dead? But he was the only one who would have had the means to get into the facility without raising suspicion.

I walked into the closet and grabbed a clean DePaul sweatshirt from one of the hangers before pulling it over my thin T-shirt. I bent down and looked for my jeans. I tugged them on, one of the legs catching under Iann's shoe rack. The jeans dislodged but sent several pairs of shoes tumbling onto the floor. As I picked up one of the stray sneakers, something rattled. I dropped the jeans from my other hand and dug inside the shoe. My fingers closed around the familiar feel of plastic and paper. I stared blankly at the pill bottle in my hand.

Alprazolam. Martin, Christopher. Advocate Illinois Masonic Medical Center.

I trained my eyes on the small black letters. I picked up the matching shoe and dug inside, pulling out another bottle.

Lorazepam. Wendt, Margaret Ann.

I swallowed the lump forming in my throat and dropped both bottles, then knelt and grabbed at the next pair of cast-aside shoes.

Clonazepam. Marshall, Samantha.

Clonazepam. Pham, Nancy.

Alprazolam. Bascom, Holly.

Alprazolam. Braughton, Erin Marie.

Each bottle was completely full except one, with only two pills rattling in the orange plastic. I left the bottles in a heap beside me and dove through the shoes remaining on the rack. They were empty.

I sat back on my heels, my pulse only growing more rapid. Was Iann taking all these pills? I took a deep breath.

You're a hypocrite. Look what you've done.

There was a difference between snagging a few pills from a friend to sleep and stealing complete prescriptions from patients. Wasn't there?

I thought about Erin's pill bottle under my bed. About the night I'd seen Jeremy handing her a bottle. I remembered the night I'd followed Jeremy back to Advocate. When Wilder had told me about Jeremy forging prescriptions for Holly, it had made sense due to his grad work at the medical center.

I examined the label in my hands. It made a certain sense that Iann might have these, too, didn't it?

You're overreacting.

I picked up each bottle and carefully slipped them back into random shoes before reorganizing the rack. My hand brushed against something underneath the shoe rack.

My pulse quickened as I dug my fingers under the wood, grasping at the hard, flat object. The tips of my fingernails closed around the edge of stiff cardboard. I pulled out the shoebox. I hesitated before opening the lid. Rolls of cash were stacked to the brim, held together with rubber bands. Folded paper was jammed on one side. I tugged out the paper and unfolded it, my stomach twisting.

I could recognize Danny's handwriting anywhere. These were the torn pages from his notebook. My eyes darted across the paper. It was mostly a list strung together with a note or two.

Iann—Advocate Med.

Jeremy—Advocate Med.—dead

Holly—dead

Erin?—dead

Alayna—dead (Washington)

My hands shook. How did Iann have this? I thought back to what Dowdy had said. I'd assumed she'd missed something when she said there was no indication that Danny and Wilder had ever crossed paths here in the city.

But Iann? Danny had been directly in his path all along, hadn't he?

I looked down at the list. Iann's name was underlined and traced over again and again.

Another memory emerged at the back of my mind. Something Erin had said.

"Ask Iann."

Although he'd denied a friendship, he and Jeremy had always been tied together by at least one thing. Their work at the clinic.

Iann must've known Holly. Or at least Erin had thought he did. Iann probably knew about Jeremy's enterprise too. And the bottles at my feet and Danny's list suggested Iann was more than merely a passive partner in that business.

The rattle of keys sounded in the other room. The front door closed.

I straightened, staring at the paper, my heartbeat counting out the seconds. One. Two. Three.

"Hey, are you home?" Iann called from the kitchen.

I slid the shoebox back under the rack and got to my feet. "Yeah, I'm back here," I called out.

My feet carried me out of the bedroom.

Iann was leaning against the counter in the kitchen, drinking from a glass of water. "Are you okay?" He raised his free hand to my cheek. "You seem really flushed."

My lips twitched into a smile. "I'm tired." I leaned in to kiss him.

"How's packing going?" he asked, after we parted lips.

My heart was still drumming the same rhythm. One. Two. Three. I stared up at him.

What have we done?

ACKNOWLEDGMENTS

From the time I was five years old, one thing has remained the same—my desire to be a writer. It really is a dream come true to have *One of Those Faces* in the hands of readers.

I want to start by thanking my amazing husband, who has ceaselessly encouraged me to write this book and all the others. I'm eternally grateful that we found each other at a bookstore over a decade ago. From brainstorming story ideas to cooking and making cocktails for me so I can carve out time to write, your support means everything.

My parents have been there since the very beginning of my writing journey when I'd constantly demand to know the meaning of words and log them in a handmade notebook. Special thanks to my dad, who brought storytelling into our home and who is always available to answer my questions or recount his experiences to help my writing.

Abeonim, Ummanim, thank you for your constant support of my dreams and for welcoming me into your family. I'm so thankful for the encouragement of my brother-in-law and sister-in-law as well.

My agent, Abby Saul at the Lark Group, has been a fantastic partner in this process, and I'm so thankful she took a chance on Harper and me. Along with Abby came a community of her incredibly talented authors, and I'm endlessly thankful for their support and time.

Thank you to Liz Pearsons, my editor, and everyone at Thomas & Mercer, who have all been wonderful to work with during this process.

Finally, I'm grateful to the people who inspired this story—all my doppelgängers out there in the world and the random strangers over the years who adamantly believed I was someone else.

ABOUT THE AUTHOR

Elle Grawl is a lawyer and thriller writer. After obtaining her BA in English Literature, she took a detour into law before returning to her love of writing. Her lifelong interest in true crime and experience as an attorney have provided her with plenty of writing material. Grawl enjoys traveling and spending time with her husband and their two dogs. *One of Those Faces* is her first novel.